DAUGHTERS OF MEMORY

Janis Arnold

DAUGHTERS

OF

MEMORY

A Novel

ALGONQUIN BOOKS OF CHAPEL HILL

1991

Published by
Algonquin Books of Chapel Hill
Post Office Box 2225
Chapel Hill, North Carolina 27515-2225
a division of
Workman Publishing Company, Inc.
708 Broadway
New York, New York 10003

JUL 3 0 1992   © 1991 by Janis Arnold.

This is a work of fiction. All names, characters, places,
and incidents are either the products of the author's
imagination or are used fictitiously. No reference to any
real person is intended or should be inferred.

Library of Congress Cataloging-in-Publication Data
Arnold, Janis, 1951–
Daughters of memory : a novel / by Janis Arnold.
p.   cm.
ISBN 0-945575-68-8 : $16.95
I. Title.
PS3551.R4847D38   1991
813'.54—dc20   91-14582 CIP

2 4 6 8 10 9 7 5 3 1

FIRST PRINTING

For Steve and Will,
with love.

DAUGHTERS OF MEMORY

Prologue

FAMILY PICTURES have, over time, been a big thing in the Richards family. My grandmother had an oil painting done of her with her two children back when my father and my Aunt Claire were young. And the man who painted the picture wasn't some fly-by-night either; he was a sure-enough established artist. I've been told some of his paintings hang in museums to this day. One thing our family has going for it is, it is well documented, photographically speaking, that is.

Unfortunately, Mother never had portraits of my sister and me painted although, heaven knows, she had plenty of photographs made. Probably we would have been painted if it hadn't been for the fact that all her life Mother was hellbent not to do things the way her mother-in-law did them. Since I have the painting of Grandmother and Daddy and Aunt Claire hanging in my living room now, it occurs to me it would be nice if there were one of Mother and Macy Rose and me. As a sort of companion picture, I mean. But of course it is far and away past time for portraits at this late date. Fortunately, we do have, as Grandma would have said, a gracious plenty of photographs.

We, my mother and father and sister and I, had our family picture taken every year when the photographer came to town and set up shop in the Town and Country Motel for a week. Mother always saw the announcement in the Molly's Point weekly about the photographer from Chadwick studios coming, but long before the advertisement came out in the paper she'd have had the date marked on the calendar that hung on the inside of the pantry door. Since we Richardses were such regular customers, we always got a postcard announcing the dates the photographer was going to be in town. He came some time in October; however, invariably, we had our appointment scheduled by the first of September. As soon as the card came in the mail, Mother would call long distance down to Houston and make an appointment for Tuesday morning at nine o'clock. Tuesdays were the best days, Mother decided, because if anything was going to go wrong with the cameras, it would have already happened and been taken care of on Monday. By taking the first appointment on Tuesday we hit the photographers when they were fresh, and after the picture taking she could get us over to the school by about nine-thirty at the latest, which meant that my sister and I didn't miss too much of our schoolwork.

We'd have one group family picture taken, with us all wearing Christmas colors, and the one she liked best Mother had printed up and sent out as our Christmas card that year. Mother also had a big print of our family Christmas picture made, which she framed and hung in the dining room, where we had, by the time I left home, nearly wall-to-wall pictures. Every year Mother would stand in the dining room with her hands on her hips and say, "Our dining room walls are covered. I don't for the life of me know where on earth this year's picture is going to go."

And my father would answer her, "Well, Corabeth, why don't we just skip the photo session this year and send out last year's cards? Not a one of us looks so different folks wouldn't recognize us. Save us a little money too."

Mother always gave Daddy her drop-dead look then and told him he wasn't the least bit funny. And every year, for sixteen years, she found a spot for the new picture. I suppose it's a blessing we had a nice-sized dining room, long on walls, short on windows. That helped.

It wasn't enough for Mother that we have a family picture taken once a year. She wanted individual ones made of my little sister Macy Rose and me, as well. Lots of folks make do with school pictures, she was fond of saying. Nothing wrong with them, she'd add, but she herself preferred professional portraits of her children. Our professional portraits were made every June. We drove into the Houston studio for those since the Chadwick studio folks didn't come out to the motel but once a year. The week after we got out of school we'd go have our pictures taken. Up until our pictures were made, Macy Rose and I were under strict orders to stay out of the sun. Mother didn't want any peeling noses on her living room wall, thank you very much. The individual pictures she hung in fancy gold-leaf frames in the living room; every summer the frames came down and the new pictures went in. The old ones were placed in cheap frames she bought at the dime store, and hung in different spots around the house, wherever she could find a space for them. They were nice pictures, some of them at least. When I redid the house, I had them all taken down and reframed in something decent. Mine line one wall of the upstairs hallway. My sister Macy's I sent to her after having them all reframed. I know good and well she got them, although for all that I ever heard a word of thanks from her, she might not have seen them to this good day.

Of course, those weren't the only photographs taken of us. There were others, boxes and boxes of faded little black and white old-timey-looking snapshots. I still have them. I keep them in the old wardrobe in Mother's room. One of these days I'm going to arrange them into albums.

3

What got me to thinking of pictures was when I ran across one that was stuck in an old cookbook. Funniest thing, I was looking for Mother's recipe for caramel pie, the one that used to be Daddy's favorite. I had a dim memory of sticking the card the recipe was written on in one of the cookbooks. So I was holding the books up and shaking them out. One by one, I'd carefully hold each cookbook by its spine and shake back and forth while I sort of fluffed the pages. I never did find that recipe, but out of the blue *Joy of Cooking* that Mother used all her life fell a picture of what I am sure must have been my fourth birthday party.

There I stood, my hair combed in long blond curls that fell down my back. I remember the dress; it was blue, to match the ribbon in my hair, and it had lace trim on the petticoat that went with it, and lace on the collar and cuffs of the sleeves as well. The front of the dress was smocked. Grandma did that. She used to smock our dresses all the time. When she first started smocking she could only smock checkered fabrics, but after a while she got to where she could smock anything you might want. You can't see it in the picture, but I remember I had black patent shoes and my socks were white and had lace on the tops.

There I stood, smiling, party hat listing to one side, my cake in front of me with its candles all lighted. I remember how I felt when the flash went off. I felt scared. Back then I was afraid of sudden flashes of light as well as loud noises.

I looked at that picture a long time, and I swear I remembered that day as well as if I had gone back in time and were reliving the moment. My father took the picture. My mother stood behind me, looking proud, like she'd made the dress, she'd made the cake, she'd done my hair. My mother looked like she thought she had done a good job. She was pregnant with my sister that year, although you can't really tell it from the picture.

Probably that was why she stood behind me instead of beside me. And then there stood my grandparents and my aunt and my two cousins, and there were two other kids in the picture. Their mother was friends with my mother and we played together, which is how they got to be invited, I guess. Back then it wasn't usual for anyone but our relatives to come to our parties. I guess that's because we had so many relatives, we couldn't fit all of them into our house, much less any outsiders, so to speak. That's not the case anymore. Of course we still have relatives, but the Richards family togetherness isn't at all what it used to be.

There I stood, smiling for the camera, a big cake in front of me. A doll cake it was, the kind Mother made with the doll stuck inside with just her head and shoulders showing, and the cake was five layers, all of them in graduated sizes, the layers dressed up with icing to look like they were the doll's prom dress, all stiff and fluffy with rows and rows of ruffles. The doll's dress was blue that year, just like mine.

After I blew out the candles, my mother took the cake into the kitchen to cut it, and my father slid the presents, which had been mounded behind the cake, toward me.

"Party time, Claire Louise, here's your loot." He grinned at me, and I guess it was the flash I had just had in my eyes made him look so funny to me. It was like my father was caught in one of those fun-house mirrors. His mouth was huge and his teeth looked longer than yardsticks, and then his face backed off and got little, like it was a pinhead on the top of his body. Just before it looked like it was going to disappear completely, his head got normal looking and then it was his hands that ballooned up until they were as big as kites, the biggest kites I had ever seen.

I shut my eyes to close him out. I could feel bile welling up inside me and I knew if I kept looking at him, I would throw up.

5

"What's wrong?" he asked, and I have this image of everyone else gathered around the table clasping hands and chorusing together, "What's wrong, Claire Louise, what's wrong with you?" And the "with you's" echoed in my head and the mouths were all I could see. Every mouth was moving and getting bigger with each "with you" that came out of it.

"Which are you going to open first?" my father asked, but before I could reach out for one of the brightly wrapped packages, the choruses of "with you's" started at me and the force from their words felt like the winds of a hurricane. I staggered back until I reached the wall and could go no farther. It felt as if their words were going to blow me through the wall. And there my father was in front of me, a package in each hand. "Choose," he said, and I could see his teeth, which looked like animal teeth, longer and longer they were. I've seen pictures of barracuda who had fewer teeth than he did that day.

"Choose," he said.

"I can't," I said, only I screamed the words so he could hear me over the chorus. "I can't choose, I can't." And I couldn't, I was paralyzed at the thought of opening one of those boxes. I had absolutely no idea what was inside a single one of those packages. It might be something I wanted and then I would worry I would hurt it. Suppose it was a puppy and it got run over, the way my puppy did last week. It wasn't my father's fault his car tire ran over my dog; it was a little dog and he didn't see it. But I was afraid to get another dog. And if the packages contained something I didn't want, what would I do? I would have to clap my hands and say thank you, I like it, and they would know I didn't really like it at all and someone would get their feelings hurt. You have to be ready for opening packages; you have to practice in front of the mirror, smiling and saying, oh, how wonderful, I like it.

6

"No, I can't," I said, and now I was whispering because the faces with the voices were getting closer and closer to me. They huddled around me, anxious to see what I looked like when I was afraid. And that was all of the party that day. I ran out of the room. I never did like to let people see what I looked like when I was afraid. I never did like that, don't to this very day. Funny thing, no matter how much I thought back the other day, standing in the kitchen and hearing the voices from the past, no matter how much I thought about it, I couldn't remember if I ever opened those presents. Surely I did, although I have to say I have no recollection of doing so. It bothers me to forget things. I wish I could remember.

I

I REMEMBER the day Claire Louise started first grade. Everyone claims I'd have been too young to remember that, that at two years old I couldn't possibly remember Claire Louise starting school. But I do remember. She had on a red dress. Red was always my favorite color, still is for that matter. The dress was red checks and had a starched white collar and puffy white sleeves with white cuffs on them. And the belt that went with the dress my mother bought from the store to go with it, the dress she made herself. Mother made all our clothes. Mostly she made Claire Louise's clothes and I wore them four years later. And Claire Louise even had red socks to go with her dress and she wore her black and white saddle oxfords that my mother bought to be her school shoes. She had a book satchel my grandmother bought for her, and all the school supplies the drugstore had printed on the first-grade list on the lowest shelf. She had those in the book bag. She had carefully printed her name on everything that went in her bag. We watched her do it, my mother and me. I sat in my mother's lap and watched Claire Louise get ready for her first day at school. That was a Saturday, I'm sure, because I can remember the sound of the lawn mower as Claire Louise carefully wrote her name, and my father only mowed on Saturday morning.

We waited for the school bus Tuesday morning, and when it pulled up at the gate of the white picket fence in front of our house, Claire Louise opened the screen door and walked down the sidewalk and boarded the bus. I'll be back at four, she said as she left, and no one is to set foot in my room while I am gone, she said. We didn't. Neither my mother nor I went in Claire Louise's room while she was gone. Memories are funny things. Whenever I try to call up the first day of school, what I get is Claire Louise's first day at school. Not mine, hers. My first day of school was just the day that I got on the bus with Claire Louise for the first time. I don't remember what I had to wear. I remember, though, that she told me where to sit on the bus and I sat. Then she walked me down the hall to the first-grade room and told Mrs. Hayes I was her sister, and she expected Mrs. Hayes would want me to sit in her old seat. Glory me, Mrs. Hayes said, I don't remember which was your seat, Claire Louise.

Claire Louise walked around the room once, looking with cool calculation at every desk and chair in it. The one that was the first one in the row over by the windows already had someone in it. Misty Wade, the undertaker's daughter, sat there, holding her book satchel clutched in her lap. This is it, Claire Louise said, I remember these marks here and under the desk. Yeah, there they are, you'll have to move Misty, she said. My sister has to have my old desk. You move back to the one behind her. Misty moved without a word and I sat down. Mind Mrs. Hayes, Claire Louise said, and left the room. That's all I remember about my first day. I'm sure that I minded Mrs. Hayes, though, because I think I was the only child in the whole first grade who never once had to stand outside the door. Sometimes I might have made some mistakes on my schoolwork when I was in school, but you may rest assured I minded the teacher. Just like I minded my mother at home.

My mother wasn't always fat. I've seen pictures of her before she and my father married, and back when she was a child. She wasn't fat a bit then. She was tall and stood up straight with very good posture. Her hair was always long and she wore it braided and then coiled around her head. She was a pretty lady. Then come the pictures of her with Claire Louise. After Claire Louise came, the pictures are all of Claire Louise doing something and my mother helping. Later I'm in the pictures too, standing by Claire Louise or watching her. There are very few pictures of me by myself. When I was little it was always me and Claire Louise. By the time she left home for those ten years she was gone, I guess my father had more or less retired from the picture-taking business.

Back to my mother, though. She was tall and had good posture and even after she got fat and gained more than a hundred extra pounds she still took a certain amount of pride in her appearance. My mother wore these heavy rubber corsets she had to powder herself to get into. When she was set in her corset she was just as solid as a piece of furniture. She once mentioned, after coming home from the dressmaker's, that her measurements were perfect, her bust and hips were exactly ten inches larger than her waist and although she realized she needed to lose a few pounds, it was a relief to know that she was still

9

in proportion. I doubt she ever measured herself without that corset. I remember from hugging her, though, that she felt real different without it. When she had on one of her housecoats, one of the model's coats she wore around the house daytimes before she dressed, she was loose and soft and squishy. Her breasts were huge soft things, hanging loosely almost to her waist. Her stomach sort of billowed out to meet them. She felt pillowlike. A person could get lost in all that softness. Most of the time, though, my mother wore her corsets, and then she had her perfect proportions securely anchored around her.

I think, from studying the pictures I rescued from my grandmother's attic, that my mother got fat a little after she had Claire Louise and a little more after she had me, and then very very fat before she got old. And then she got trim again and then thin and then skinny and then she died. I think she wasted away, her body as well as her eyesight, and now that it's too late I wish I had talked to her, asked her why she was letting go like that. But at the time of my mother's death she hadn't been speaking to me for some time, a fact that pains me to remember, because even though I can still feel angry at her, I regret not knowing her better. Make sense of that one if you can.

The first time Claire Louise married I wasn't even there. Neither were my parents, for that matter. Claire Louise ran off with a boy from an undesirable family. Not only was he not in college, he had never finished high school, and as far as anyone knew he wasn't exactly working either. I never really saw what she did that for, running off with Ralph the way she did. He was awfully handsome, in a chiseled-out-of-stone sort of way, but he wasn't particularly nice to her. I saw him hit her right across the face once. I was watching out the window and they were sitting on the side porch about ten one Friday night. My mother had already been out once to tell Claire Louise it was time to tell Ralph good night and they were still sitting and swinging, because Ralph never left before my dad went out and yelled at him, and Daddy never went out before Claire Louise ignored my mother at least twice. My mother and father were in the den having an argument themselves about Claire Louise and Ralph. "You tell her she is not to see him again," my father said.

"Now, Stu," my mother said, "you know good and well if we forbid Claire Louise to do something she just goes ahead and does it anyway. The thing to do is to just ignore it and not let on we don't like him, and she'll get tired of him soon enough."

"There is no way I can not let on I don't like that sleazy creature who has been parked on our porch for over a month now. I'm telling you, you're her mother, and I want you to talk to her and tell her she is not under any circumstances to see him again."

It was like listening to two radio stations at once, the nights when I sat in the kitchen and listened under the barely open window to Claire Louise and Ralph courting on the porch while my mother and father argued in the den behind me. My dad fairly hated Ralph, who was Claire Louise's first boyfriend, and he was always ranting and raving about him to my mother. It wasn't like he kept his feelings a secret from Claire Louise, either, for all my mother told him that he ought to. As it was, we never sat down for a meal that spring that my dad didn't light into Claire Louise about that creature she was sheltering on our side porch. My dad said awful things about him, about how he didn't work and his poor widowed mother supported him, and how he had no use for anyone who didn't have enough gumption to finish high school. By this time, though, Claire Louise was sixteen years old and had finished her junior year at Garfield High where she was extremely popular, and she had pretty much gotten to where she could ignore my father. Which she did, sitting eating as daintily and carefully as if he weren't right across the table from her sputtering food as he talked, he was so angry.

But the time I started talking about, the time I saw Ralph hit her, she was just walking back to the porch after coming in the house to talk on the phone. "Who was that called you?" he asked.

She kind of smiled up under her eyes at him, in the way she has of making herself look all twinkly and coy, and said, "I'd better not tell you, you'll just get mad."

Claire Louise was so busy looking cute at him she didn't notice he was already mad.

"Who was it?" he repeated, the words all growled out at her.

"I couldn't possibly say," she simpered, which is when he hit her. He just hauled off and hit her with the back of his hand across her face. Her head swiveled around and then snapped up as she realized what had happened. There was a red mark on her cheek almost immediately, and her eyes got big with tears and her mouth was sort of hanging open where he'd hit it.

"Who was it?" he repeated as if nothing out of the ordinary had happened, but he didn't growl his words this time. This time they were smug sounding.

"Pattie," Claire Louise said in a subdued whisper. "She wanted to know what I was wearing tomorrow."

He nodded, satisfied. Claire Louise continued to hold her face and her eyes never left him. She looked downright spellbound. It was only a month or so after that night Ralph and Claire Louise ran off and got married.

I remember the night she called home, it was a Sunday night. She'd been supposed to be at Pattie's for the weekend, Friday night and Saturday night, because they had all these cheerleading clinics and practices and it was easier for her just to stay in town with Pattie than run back and forth. That's what she told my parents. And lucky for her they never called Pattie and asked her anything, because Pattie could not lie at all and would have spilled the beans for sure. But instead the first they heard was from Claire Louise herself. She called about eight, just when they were getting worried. This was the Sunday night before Labor Day, and of course school was due to start in earnest the day after, and this was to be Claire Louise's senior year, and here she called and said she was in Mississippi with Ralph and they were married and had been since Saturday.

Typical Claire Louise. She told my mother, who is the one happened to answer the phone, and then my mother gasped and dropped the phone right there on the kitchen linoleum, where it dangled until my father picked it up and asked, "Who is this?"

And then she told him, Claire Louise did, and he about dropped the phone his own self, he was so shocked. And after that we didn't see hide nor hair of Claire Louise for ten years.

2

IT WAS DEFINITELY a mistake to run off with Ralph, but at the time all I wanted was to get away from my parents and he had a car and asked me to go. Basically, that's why I went. I didn't expect to stay with him very long, just long enough to get to New York, and I certainly never expected to go back to Molly's Point. I'd had enough of that nasty little town to last me forever.

Also, in spite of what I told my parents, I never married Ralph. I had a lot of ambition back then, and I certainly never expected to tie myself to someone with no more gumption than he had. But I stayed with him for some little bit, though I never could say why that was. At first it was exciting, driving around in the truck he traded his car for soon after we left Texas. We got a cute little apartment and he worked on engines down at Jonestown Marine in Lake Charles and I spent most of my time at the library reading about life in other places I was planning to see. But then it started to occur to me that my daddy had been right; it is hard to respect someone without even the gumption to finish high school. Of course I hadn't finished, either, but I went down to the public education office and got myself enrolled the first September after I turned seventeen. I figured they'd send for records and my parents would hear I was in Louisiana, not Mississippi like I'd told them, and they might come looking for me. So I waited a year before I registered. It wasn't till lots later I found out they never looked for me in the first place. That did make me angry, because I could have been in school that first year we were in Louisiana, instead of just hanging out at the library like I did. And that's why my graduation record is in his last name, too. I figured they'd make something of it if I used my right name. And since I was using Anderson as my last name, I went ahead and called myself Lana Louise Anderson. I'd always liked the name Lana.

Going to high school in Lake Charles was not at all the same thing as it would have been had I stayed home and finished. In the first place, I didn't exactly go to the high school. I only needed four courses to graduate, so they enrolled me in this class that met at the church rather than the school. There were only six of us in that class, and I was the only one who wasn't pregnant. By December I had my four credits and they gave me a diploma with no more ceremony than the teacher coming in

14

and saying, "Lana, here's your diploma and good luck to you." Whereupon I left and took the bus back to our apartment and began to think about the next part of my life.

He was awful handsome, Ralph was, at least until he started drinking and got all puffy looking. Then he started doing drugs, and that was when I left him. Lucky for me I never had married him, so all I had to do was take up and leave. Never had to mess with getting a divorce or anything like that. Last I saw of him, he was in some little town in Florida where we'd gone because he thought he could find work on a boat. Only work he ever did was on boats; he did like to be near the water, that man did. As it was, I left in September, right after I found a bag of white powder in the glove compartment of his truck. I wasn't going to have anything to do with drugs. Lucky I found that powder too, because I was pregnant with Britt then, although I certainly didn't know it. Ralph's just the kind might have kicked up a fuss if he'd known I was leaving with a kid of his. So this is what I did. I got on a bus and rode for what seemed like forever, and arrived in New York City. There I was, not quite twenty years old, and the only money I had, that I had managed to salt away over the year I'd been planning this break, was not quite five hundred dollars. And to top it off, I also had what I thought was the flu, although that of course turned out to be Britt.

In all honesty, I have to admit New York was not what I had expected it to be. First thing is, it was so big. I got off that bus and had absolutely no idea where I was to go from there. I just stood and looked around, and as soon as I had my bag I went into the rest room and washed every part of me I could reach. Then I combed my hair and brushed my teeth after I scoured out that sink with a bit of soap and some paper towels I found in the bathroom. Then I brushed my clothes off and straightened myself up as much as I could and sat down to think. I had my diploma, which was fortunate because I felt I would need it to get a job to get me started. But what I needed first was a place to stay, and I felt reasonably sure a hotel would eat up my savings too quickly. I'd read in books about staying at the YWCA but I had absolutely no idea how to go about finding one. And, to tell the truth, I didn't want to ask anyone, because I felt as if asking a question such as where is a safe inexpensive place for a girl to stay while she looks for work would make me look like some hick just off the bus and in to see the big city. The best I could think of was to get a cab and ask the driver. I was sure cab drivers were used to directing girls to the Y. But I'd never been in a cab before and I had no idea what one should cost, and I didn't want to be taken advantage of. Just do it, get on with it, I told myself, and then I made myself stand up and pick up my suitcase. As I left the rest room a tall fellow with shifty eyes and elevator shoes and slicked-back hair touched my arm. "Need some help, little lady?"

You may rest assured that I had read enough about New York to know that no one but pimps met the buses, and I had no intention of falling into the hands of such as that. "No, I most assuredly do not," I answered him with my most superior look. And I walked straight over to the ticket counter and bought myself a ticket for Houston, Texas. Now it is not generally known that I actually spent less than five hours in New York City in my whole life, and the reason for that is I told every-one when I finally came home to Molly's Point that I had been in New York. It was no one's business but mine that I had not stayed for longer than it took to get a bus coming back in the opposite direction. To be honest, it has always bothered me that I more or less chickened out on New York. After planning all my life to go there and be discovered as either a famous writer

16

or a television journalist, I was heading back home before I even so much as gave it a try. But I imagine that my lack of courage at that juncture in my life had more to do with hormones than a true lack of courage. I was, after all, pregnant, although it was a while before I realized that fact.

Houston, Texas, while it is not far in distance from Molly's Point, is in actual fact quite a ways. People on Molly's Point do not, as a general rule, go to Houston. The only time anyone does, it is for some serious medical problem that our doctors out here are totally unequipped to handle. Like the time Jimmy Perez was in his trailer and the oil truck out on the highway went out of control and barreled into it. No one ever could believe Jimmy was alive when they got him out of that trailer. He had burns over just about every part of his body and the doctor right off called up an ambulance and ran him straight to Ben Taub Hospital in Houston. And that doctor, Dr. Blynn, the young one, rode all the way to Houston on the ambulance with Jimmy making sure he didn't die on the way. Jimmy stayed in Houston over a year, getting treatment and therapy and whatever he needed and then he came home. And he still goes back every so often for more surgery. I myself have not seen Jimmy. He doesn't leave his house often. He used to go to the drive-in movie with his brother but since that closed down they just rent movies and watch them at home. Jimmy doesn't feel like getting stared at, I hear, and from what they say he looks as bad as some of those aliens in science fiction shows. Some folks say Dr. Blynn made a mistake rushing Jimmy off for medical treatment the way he did. They say that he would have been better off dead, rather than a freak to look at and in pain all the time and such a burden to his family. But in my opinion, where there is life there is hope, and I fully support what young Dr. Blynn did.

. . .

I never expected to lay eyes on my parents again either. Life's funny, though, because here I am back in the very town I thought I'd seen the last of and I'm living back in the same house in the same room, even sleeping in the same bed. There are some changes, though. Daddy's dead and Mother passed on as blind as she always pretended to be, and the closet has been ripped out of the wall. That's the first thing I did, the morning after Daddy's funeral. I called up old Jonas Starling who has done construction work around Molly's Point for as long as I can remember and told him to come right out, because I had some remodeling to do.

He came, Jonas did, because he could tell from the tone in my voice I meant business. "But, Claire Louise," he whined, while he sat sipping coffee and eating a piece of one of the dozen cakes sitting over on the counter going stale, "Mr. Stuart's funeral was just yesterday afternoon and your poor mama, Miss Corabeth, is still prostrate with grief. I don't think this is the appropriate time to start knocking out walls and hammering around upstairs in the hall right outside her bedroom. Why don't we just wait and start this little project next week?"

Which is when I looked Jonas right in the eye and said, "Jonas, I plan to have this part of my project completed by next week. I certainly have no intention of waiting until then to start. So if you can't do it, then I think I will just say good day to you and get on the phone and call someone who can start today."

"Well, if you're determined, then it might as well be me as the next man," he said, "but are you sure you have your mama's agreement on this? As far as I know, this is still her house."

"What my mama thinks is no concern of yours, Mr. Starling," I told him, "and I will thank you to attend to my remodeling, which is all I have asked you to do around here." I gave him my frostiest glance, and his eyes dropped as I had expected them to do. The nerve of that man.

So Jonas Starling came in and, first thing he did, he tore the entire cedar closet out of the wall. "But, Claire Louise," Mama wailed, "where will I put my linens and woolens?"

"I have plans for them," I told her, "but for now we can just set them in there in Daddy's room because I don't expect we will be needing it in the near future." Mama didn't ask me why I was ripping that closet out of the wall, because she knew if she asked I would tell her.

Once the closet was gone that hallway was a good-sized room, exactly eight feet square. There were doors to all four of the bedrooms opening off it, and of course the opening at the top of the stairs, so there wasn't right much wall space. Which is why my plan included built-ins. I had Jonas build bookcases and a desk and some cabinets with drawers, and when he was through I had me an office that was well planned and efficient. Of course at the moment all the bedrooms opened on to it, but I had some more plans for that.

3

THE FIRST THING my mother did after she took note of the fact that Claire Louise was gone was call the preacher. "Brother Rhine," she said, "you had best come over here because we have trouble." She did not say a word more than that on the phone, because of the fact that on a party line you can never be sure that all the neighbors aren't hanging on your every word. Soon as she got off the phone, my daddy started in on her.

"What'd you call that nosy preacher over here for? You might as well take out an ad in the *Houston Chronicle* that our daughter Claire Louise has run off with a no-account."

"But, Stu . . ."

"Don't 'But Stu' me, we don't need to wash our dirty linen in public. You call him up and tell him he is not wanted out here."

When Mama just sat there, he added "*now*" the way he did, and she picked the phone up and told Brother Rhine it was not such a good time to come calling after all. Turned out Ralph had called his widowed mother who had also called Brother Rhine, so there wasn't any keeping it a secret anyway. It was all over town the next day that Claire Louise and Ralph had run off to Mississippi. It wasn't till Claire Louise came home ten years later that we knew they had only gone as far as Louisiana. Not that it would have made that much difference, in my opinion. I don't believe that my father would have gone after her if he'd thought she was only right down the road in Houston. And Ralph has not come home to this good day. Claire Louise says, with the drugs and all, he's probably dead by now, leastways his widowed mother is long dead, and with them not having any relatives in Molly's Point to speak of, it's doubtful we'd hear of him anyway. Seems strange, but then Claire Louise is not known for her long-term relationships.

I was twelve when Claire Louise left, just fixing to start junior high. First day of school, that's all anybody could talk about, about how the head cheerleader had run off with Ralph Anderson, who was never going to amount to much. My best friend, Corrie, said she thought it was romantic and she was sure Claire Louise had run off for love, not because she was pregnant, which you may be sure everyone was saying.

I said Claire Louise was not pregnant to my certain knowledge, because just the day before she took off she made my mother get in the car and make a special trip to town because she was out of Kotex and needed some in the worst way. So I did my part to squelch that particular rumor. I heard Corrie repeat my story at least four times, one of which was to her mother, Ruby Smith, who was the phone switchboard operator and could be counted on to pass it on whenever anyone called up.

When the kids asked me what my father was going to do to Claire Louise, I just shrugged and said he was real mad and I was afraid of what he was going to do. Which was the actual truth. He *was* mad and I *was* afraid of what he was going to do. Which turned out to be exactly nothing. He said she had made her bed, now she could lie in it as far as he was concerned, and she better not come home whining to him with a brat to raise when that no-account Ralph left her high and dry. My mother said if it'd been her that had run off, her father would have been after her with a shotgun, and she thought my father should go after Claire Louise and bring her home. Claire Louise being a minor and all, they could have the sheriff throw Ralph Anderson in jail, which would be none too good for the lowlife who had run off with her daughter, the one who had such potential. My mother cried and carried on for a week when Claire Louise left, then she had her a migraine and didn't get out of her bed except to run to the toilet to throw up for about another two days. Turns out my mother liked Claire Louise a lot better after she was gone.

Once she was gone we all started calling her Claire Louise again, at least I did and my mother did, although come to think of it my mother had always called her Claire Louise except when she was talking right straight to her. Back before she had left she'd had us all, even my father, calling her Lana because she hated the name Claire Louise. I can't say that I have ever been overly fond of my own name, Macy Rose, but at least I never changed it. The way I feel about it is this, if you have a name you are born with, then you are stuck with it. You just get used to it, and if you really don't care for it then after a while you don't hear it anymore. You know what I mean? You hear it but you don't exactly, it's like you put the bothersome part of it right out of your mind. For good. That's what I had to do, because like I say I myself was never overly fond of my name. Unlike my sister, who finding she disliked her name bullied each and every one of us into calling her something else. That's something, isn't it?

First thing I did after school on the day after Labor Day, I went out to the barn to check on my horse. Then I went inside the house by the back door and went to the stairs and listened, and sure enough there was my mother upstairs crying in her bed. "I've lost her," she moaned, and I could hear my grandmother saying back to her, "Now, now, Corabeth, you have got to pull yourself together. Likely as not she'll be back, and you have still got Macy here to think about."

From the way my mother kept crying and moaning it was obvious that the fact that I was still at home was not much consolation to her. My grandmother on my father's side had never been all that fond of my mother, but the year after Claire Louise left she was real nice to her. First thing she did is she started cooking dinner at our house every night. I'd come home from school and there would be Grandma at the stove cooking, and my mother sitting there at the metal table in the middle of the kitchen drinking a cup of coffee and talking to her. Then my father and my grandfather would come in, all sweaty from working out in the pasture or the barn, and they'd wash up and we'd eat. After dinner I'd do my homework at the table while my grandmother washed up the dishes and cleaned out a cabinet or something and my mother watched television. My father always went in his office after dinner and didn't come out till bedtime, and my grandfather would go on over to his house and watch television until my grandmother walked home. I have never thought about this before, but the best year of my life was the year after Claire Louise left, the year my mother let my grandmother take over.

She took to baking cookies in the afternoon, so when I'd come in there would be a snack for me all hot from the oven. Then she'd help me with my homework if I needed it, which to tell the truth I did not. My schoolwork was a point of pride with me and I always took pains to do it well, but I let my grandmother start looking over it, particularly the English and history papers, which had been her major when she was at college. My grandmother had gone off to Baylor in Waco, which is where my mother had graduated from, and they were both hoping I would go to Baylor also when the time came. That is what my grandmother told me just about every afternoon when we sat down to do my homework and then my mother would tune up and say in a mournful voice, dripping tears, "If only Claire Louise were here, I thought we'd be getting her ready to go off to college and here it is almost Thanksgiving of what was supposed to be her senior year and we don't even know where she is."

I always reached over and patted my mother's plump hand and Grandma said, "Now, now, we'll hear from her soon. Just you wait and see. Claire Louise will turn up."

Later I heard my grandmother say to my grandfather, "Oh, she'll turn up, that one will. She's a bad penny if ever there was one, and they always turn up."

One of the things I liked best about my grandmother was that she liked me better than Claire Louise, even if I didn't have naturally curly blond hair and big blue pools for eyes. I did have right nice eyes, big and kind of hazel colored. The color of my eyes varied according to what I wore, and several people who had no reason to wish to flatter me had told me that my eyes were far and away the most expressive they had ever seen. Still are, I would suppose. My hair, however, has changed right much in the past years. When I was a child, it was brown with red highlights that came out in the summer. Up until I was in high school I wore it long and pulled back in a ponytail or braided most of the time. I had thick bangs, which I went to the beauty shop every so often and let Miss Minnie trim up for me, along with the rest of my hair, which hung halfway down my back. When I was younger, my grandmother liked to braid my hair in two pigtails and then wrap the tails in loops hanging on the sides of my head. My mother didn't care for those loops, so until I was old enough to say no, the two of them were always looping and unlooping my hair. Claire Louise, to give her credit, put an end to that nonsense before it ever got good and started with her. When she was in first grade she went to sleep with a big wad of gum in her mouth and woke up with that mess stuck all in her hair. My mother tried ice to get it out and then peanut butter, and by then Claire Louise was howling so loud she just cut her hair off in a real short Dutch-boy cut, which took care of any loops for her. But I had my hair in loops up till the seventh grade, which is the year my grandmother took care of us. Finally, I just had to tell her that I looked out of it with that hairstyle. "No offense, Grandma," I told her, "but I can't keep wearing my hair the way you wore yours when you were a girl. All the kids are calling me a baby."

"Oh," she said, "is this like the time when you told me I don't know from nothing?"

When I was little more than a child I had apparently said that to my grandmother, and for some reason she thought it was the funniest thing and she must have repeated it to me at least every other day for the rest of her life. "No, it is not," I said, because I didn't want to hurt her feelings, but then I took out my yearbook from the last year and had her look at all the hairstyles and she had to admit I looked more like old Mrs. Jones, who had taught Latin since before it died just about, than I did any of the other kids. So that afternoon my grandmother said to my mother, "Corabeth, I think you need to call Miss Minnie and get an appointment for Macy. We are going to have to get her hair cut in a nice bob. I have noticed she looks out of it." My grandmother always was one to pick up on any slang expression that I taught her.

I held my breath when my grandmother told my mother what to do, because in the past that had been enough to set my mother off on a screaming fit. But all she said was, "Why don't you call for me, Mom. I'm just too upset to talk on the phone today."

"Macy," my grandmother said that year, "you are going to have a fine time when you go off to Baylor University. You will meet lots of new people. I can tell by the quality of your work that you have a great future." My grandmother said that just as we all, my mother and father and both my grandparents and me, sat down to dinner. I knew what she was leading up to. I had brought home the paper from the school about the summer enrichment program that I wanted to go to, and was worried my mother and father would say it was a waste of money. So I just nodded and said thank you very much and waited to see what would come next.

"'Bout like you did?" my father asked her, mumbling around the biscuit that was in his mouth.

"I did have a wonderful time at college," my grandmother answered with dignity. "My only regret is that I didn't stay to graduate."

Whereupon my father whopped a laugh that was more sarcastic than amused, and even my mother perked up from the depths of her depression. "Graduate?" he said. "You didn't even go back after Thanksgiving of your freshman year! You cried and cried for two months and when they let you come home early for Thanksgiving that was the last Baylor University ever saw of you!"

This was the first I had heard of my grandmother coming home from college before she graduated, and I have to admit I was interested.

"Why were you crying, Grandma?" I asked her.

"Well, I had never been away from my family before and I did miss them," she said. "And, in retrospect, I was so busy feeling sorry for myself that I never did get around to getting out and making any friends. So when I got home again, I just couldn't bear to leave right off. And then, if the truth be known, when I was ready to go back they all thought it was such a joke I'd come home because I was so homesick that I was embarrassed to ask to go back. Which is not to say you can't learn from my experience," she admonished me. "You go on to school and I'll be the first to tell you homesickness never killed anyone." She glared around the table, and both my grandfather and father just kept on eating and didn't talk about my grandmother's college career anymore after that. "Which," she added, "brings me to the topic I wished to talk about in the first place. Macy has been invited to that special summer program they have at the high school for advanced students and I think she should take advantage of the opportunity."

When my grandmother stopped talking, everyone at the table

more or less sat and chewed and thought over what she said. It was not often that my grandmother got on her high horse, but when she did so they all knew they had best pay attention to her.

"School buses don't run in the summer," my father said.

"I can certainly drive her to and from school for six weeks," my grandmother replied.

"And I don't suppose it is free," my father said, looking at me instead of my grandmother.

"No, it isn't, but the cost won't break you," she told him, "and Fred and I can certainly help with the tuition."

"What do you think about it, Corabeth?" my father asked my mother. I held my breath. This was already March and my mother had been showing signs of recovering to her former self, and I felt extremely nervous when my father asked her what she thought. In the past, just knowing my grandmother was for something was enough to set my mother dead straight against it. But that wasn't one of her good days, so she just sighed and said, "You will have to do what you think best, Stuart, because I have been so worried about Claire Louise today that I cannot think straight."

So my father signed the paper and wrote a check, and that is how I got to go to the summer enrichment program at the high school the summer after my seventh-grade year.

4

IT WAS ON the bus ride to Houston that I began to suspect that perhaps it was not exactly the flu that had been troubling me. The more I thought about it, the more my suspicions grew, so I decided to make a little test. I got me some saltine crackers and a 7UP and when that made me feel better I knew for sure that I was going to have to start planning for two, me and the little girl I was sure I was having.

When the bus stopped in Houston, it was just ahead of a hurricane that was pounding its way up the gulf. The air was completely still and so heavy and ominous that I would have known a storm was on the way even if the man next to me hadn't had his radio tuned to the weather station for the last three days straight. He seemed like a right nice person for a man. He was about thirty and had sandy brown hair, which he wore in a flat-top. He had sort of nondescript blue eyes and was real tall and lanky looking. His ears stuck out a bit but not so much you couldn't overlook it and his Adam's apple was particularly pro-tuberant, which has never appealed to me, but all in all James Wilcox was a presentable sort of person.

What attracted me to him the most was he had just been furloughed from the air force, and he had some real interesting stories to tell about places he had seen while he was overseas. And now he was in such a hurry to get home to his mother and his sister, who lived all by themselves in an old two-story house in West University, his father having died before he went in the air force about eight years ago. He was even a college graduate, having finished at University of Houston just before he enlisted. It was a wonder to me he hadn't married, being such a nice person and so eligible and all.

He was right proud of his family, too, pulling out pictures of his parents and his sister and their house to show me. The pictures were all creased from carrying around in his wallet, and I could tell they'd had a lot of looking at over the past few years. At this particular time, James had not seen his mother and sister in at least a year, due to the fact that he had been stationed too far away to get home on leave. And he was worried about his sister Cheryl, he told me, as we rode through state after state, heading down to meet that hurricane. She had been going out with a man and was looking to marry him, and James's mother just didn't feel right giving her blessing until James got home to meet him and form his own opinion, being the man of the family now. It did occur to me that a grown woman like that, twenty-six years old she was, shouldn't have been waiting around for anyone's blessing to do what she wanted to do, but I didn't feel I knew James well enough at that point to tell him what I thought.

When the bus stopped somewhere in Kansas we got off to stretch our legs and get a bite to eat. James walked behind me into the coffee shop and more or less assumed we would sit down in a booth together, it seemed to me. When the waitress came over he asked me what I would like to order just as if we were traveling together. "Nothing but coffee," I said.

"Now, Lana," he said, "that is not nearly enough for you to have. We still have a ways to go and you can't tell when the bus will stop long enough for you to get something hot to eat." By now the waitress was tapping her long nails against her order pad impatiently so he turned to her and said, "Just bring us some coffee right now and we'll decide what we want to eat before you get back."

"James," I said, "I can't tell you how much it means to me, you being so sweet to me and all." I was blinking hard to keep the tears from falling out of my eyes, I was so moved at his kindness. "But I really cannot afford to spend money on restaurant food. I have just a bit of savings and I am going to hang on to it to get my feet under me once I get to Houston."

His eyes warmed up when I said that and he reached over and put his hands on top of mine, which I was more or less wringing on the tabletop, and then he said, real softlike, "Lana, I feel as if you are as close to me as my own sister who I have not seen in over a year, and I will not permit you to do without food. Now I am going to order you a real breakfast, which I fully intend to pay for, and we will sit here until you eat it even if that bus leaves us."

"Oh, James," I said, losing the battle to the tears, which were running down my face by this time. "It feels so good to be taken care of, even for a little while, that I can't say no. But I would like to go to the rest room and clean up before that waitress comes back and sees that I've been crying." I had by this time gotten control of myself again.

The rest room was exceptionally clean. I have always thought well of Kansas, although the only memory of it I have is that bus station and the nice little coffee shop with the squeaky-clean rest room. I washed all over and brushed my hair and my teeth. Then I got out my makeup and repaired the damage the tears and a night on the bus had done. I would have liked better than anything to put on a clean blouse and clean underwear but I had nothing like that with me, so I had to content myself with brushing myself down and a splash of perfume. Just a little, though, because I doubted James was the type who liked much perfume, and for the same reason I was very sparing on the makeup, putting on lipstick and wiping most of it off and then just using powder and a bit of blush and next to no eye shadow. My mascara I went ahead and used because it was water-resistant and so could be counted on not to smudge.

The rains started almost before we got into Texas good, and it was coming down so heavy it was a miracle to me that the bus driver could see to drive. By the time we were in Beaumont we were wondering aloud if we shouldn't just lay over there and wait out the storm rather than push on in to Houston, which is where the thing looked to be heading. But then the weather report said it seemed stalled out in the gulf, and the news was saying there was no telling what direction it would head in when it picked back up speed, so the bus driver announced we would go on as planned and barring the unforeseen, should be in Houston in an hour or two.

"Lana," James said, "I notice you are wringing your hands again. Is that a sign you're worried about this weather?"

I sighed. "It is scary, isn't it? I know you'll be glad to get home and look after your family, won't you?" He had called them from Beaumont and they were probably already headed for the bus station to pick him up.

"What about you?" he asked. "Did you call your family and tell them you were on your way?"

I looked away. I had told James all about my parents over the last hours, how they had been so vile to me and had kicked me out of the house when I was sixteen. I'd also told him about my younger sister, Macy, who was on the face of it nothing like his sister Cheryl. I'd told him how Macy was always jealous of me and made up stories about me that my mother never failed to believe. As I'd said to James earlier, I was resolved to go home and square things with them because I firmly believe family is important but I was nervous about seeing them after so long a time. "Did you call them?" he repeated when I didn't answer him.

I just nodded at him and when he asked his question a third time, I said, "James, I'm sure you don't want to know what they said." When he insisted, I finally admitted that Macy had said, "Oh, it's you, we'd hoped you were dead," and my mother had told me I'd burned my bridges and not to expect to come home at this late date. This was not exactly true. I had phoned them

31

but had hung up before anyone answered, because I did not want to go home and listen to my father say I told you so unless there was absolutely no alternative.

James was frankly appalled. "What are you going to do?" he asked.

"What I always planned," I told him. "I will get myself an apartment and a job and they will not hear from me again. I have my pride." I was fighting tears again, and some time during this conversation James and I had begun to hold hands, although I could not tell you exactly how that happened.

We didn't talk for a while, just sat there holding hands and looking out at the rain, which was starting to pick up again. "Lana," James said, "you cannot simply disappear off into a hurricane when we get to Houston. You are going to go home with me until this storm has passed and you have had an opportunity to find you a job. There's plenty of room at our house, and my mother and sister will be happy to have you stay with us."

"Oh, James, how can you say that? They don't even know me."

"They know me. The fact that you're a friend of mine will be enough for them."

I looked out at the rain again and back at James. "Are you sure?" I asked.

"Of course," he answered, which is when he leaned over and hugged me and before I knew it, he had kissed me on the top of my head and then on my cheek. "Don't you worry about a thing," he said. "I am going to look after you."

5

I T WAS AFTER Claire Louise had been gone for over a year that my father decided he was going to sell her horse. "Not much use in feeding and grooming an animal nobody but Claire Louise can ride, is it?" I had been feeding Showstopper every morning when I fed my own horse and brushing her down too, but I hadn't been riding her much because I was used to my own horse, and besides, Claire Louise had never wanted anyone to ride Showstopper but her.

"But, Daddy, what will Claire Louise say when she comes home if her horse is gone? You can't sell her, Claire Louise loves that horse!" I was appalled.

"She should have thought of that before she took off," he said. This was at breakfast, which my mother had been fixing for the past month ever since she came back from the hospital where they shocked the depression right out of her. I preferred my grandmother's cooking, but my mother's doctors had told us it was important my mother take over her own house again so my grandmother had given up coming over and cooking the meals. Mother cooked exactly the same thing every morning. Eggs and bacon and toast and jelly, and I had milk and they had coffee. We also had the little bittiest glasses of orange juice you could imagine. And only two pieces of bacon. But at least she was up and around again. "So you get out there and brush that horse down good, you hear, and be sure you clean around her feet. And you better give her a good long ride this morning, because the man coming to look at her wants her for his little boy, so we don't want her too spirited looking."

I could tell my father was watching to see if I was going to mind him straight off, so I just picked up my dishes and set them over by the sink and went to my room to change from my shorts to some jeans and my riding boots. It was probably already ninety degrees outside and not yet eight in the morning, and if I'd known he wanted me to ride that horse for a couple of hours I would have been out there by five-thirty, before it got as hot as it was, but I knew that it would not do a bit of good to tell my father that so I didn't bother.

After I patted my mare, Emily, and gave her the apple I'd brought her I explained that it was not my idea to ride anyone in this heat, but I was going to have to take Showstopper out for a while so not to get her feelings hurt. I also whispered to her that Showstopper might be getting sold, which I regretted but it did no good at all to try to argue with my father. I did think to myself that I would make sure to remember the name of the people who bought Showstopper, so when Claire Louise came back she would know where to go to find her. And I found myself hoping that the little boy coming to get her was not an obnoxious little brat. It wasn't Showstopper's fault Claire Louise had run off.

I decided not to use a saddle at all, hot as it was. Of course it gets your jeans all sweaty and messy when you ride bareback in the summer, but I wasn't going to add a saddle to Showstopper's miseries so I just threw her bridle on and led her out of the stables. Then I grabbed hold of her mane and hoisted myself up on her back and headed off toward my grandmother's house. I could see my father's pickup back behind Grandma's parked at the big barn where they kept the feed and hay for the cows, so I knew better than to stop for so much as a hello. I took a long look at the sparkling blue swimming pool in the backyard of my grandparents' house and promised myself a refreshing swim just as soon as I had been gone long enough to satisfy my father. Showstopper was plodding along, no more interested in this outing than I was, and it did occur to me then that another family might be better for her, one that was more interested in her than anyone in our family seemed to be. "If they're not nice, we won't sell you," I whispered in her ear, although I doubted my father would pay much attention to that. "We'll go to Claire Louise's favorite place," I told her, and I think she knew exactly what I said because as soon as I turned her south and headed back to the pasture way out of sight of the houses she perked right up and trotted happily along.

I hadn't been back here in a long time, years in fact. The grove of trees must have been over an underground spring or something because it was all green and lush inside the trees, and had ferns and mosses growing like it was in the middle of a rain forest instead of a hot south Texas pasture.

When we were little we used to go there a lot, me and Claire Louise and our cousins, who used to be over to visit about every day in the summer. Our cousins Amanda and Kara were both older than me and younger than Claire Louise. The four of us would ride our horses or walk back here and play for hours in the summer. Our favorite game was boxcar children, which we learned about from a book checked out of the school library. The story was about four kids whose parents died and, rather than split up and get sent to an orphanage or worse, they moved into this old boxcar and lived together. The story was in chapters and told how they earned the money for the things they had to buy but mostly just took care of themselves, gathering food and hauling water and all. The four of us played that book over and over, with Claire Louise being the oldest—Henry—who took charge of things and told everyone what to do and no one ever argued with Henry because he was always right. My cousin Amanda, who was nearest in age to me, played Jessie, the next oldest in the boxcar family, who was kind of motherly and comforted people when they got scared and did most of the cooking, which they did over an open fire in front of the boxcar. Then I was Violet, the third from the oldest, who was kind of outdoorsy but didn't talk much. Even though I was the youngest of the four of us, I never played Benny, the baby whom everyone petted and spoiled and looked after. The reason was my cousin Kara, who was almost as old as Claire Louise and a head taller, threw a fit if she could not be the baby. So even though she was the biggest of us all, Kara had to be the baby or she wouldn't play.

I hadn't seen my cousins even one time that past summer. They were the only two children of my father's sister, his only sister for that matter. Her name was Claire, she also being named after my great-aunt like my sister Claire Louise is. But my mother and Claire had had a falling out over what my aunt said about Claire Louise after she ran off, and my mother told her that as long as she was willing to talk like that about her own niece she was no kin to us. I never did hear what my aunt said about Claire Louise, but it must have been awful to make my mother so mad.

So now my Aunt Claire and my cousins would go right next door to me almost every day to visit my grandmother but they did not so much as look in our direction. And I was under strict orders if they came in while I was at Grandma's I was to get up and leave immediately, even if I had only just gotten there. My Aunt Claire was also very angry at my father, her own brother, for siding with my mother, but my grandmother told her it was as much as his life was worth to try to reason with my mother when she got in an uproar over something. Even that sanitarium did not shock this notion out of my mother's head, although that may have been because she did not go back for the additional therapy that her doctors highly recommended. Both my father and my grandmother offered to drive her down to her doctor's appointments, but my mother had had more than enough of those doctors by the time she got home, and no amount of talking would convince her otherwise.

Of course once school had taken up again I saw my cousin Amanda every day. We had almost all the same classes. And we sat together in algebra, but we agreed that when we ran into each other and our families were around, at least all our families except for Grandma, we would act like we were still mad at each other. There was no point in getting them started.

But even before my mother and Claire had their falling out, we hadn't been coming to the grove. I guess we had more or less outgrown the boxcar family about the time my grandmother and grandfather put the pool in their backyard. After they had a pool, we just gathered over there and swam and drank the Cokes my grandmother kept in the refrigerator in the little house out by the pool. She called that little building the pump house, back from the time the house had a pump in it. Now the pump was underground and you couldn't even see it, so she put in the refrigerator, which she kept full of Cokes and several cases of spares beside it. My grandmother had lived through the Depression and did not like to run out of things. Back when I was little I used to call her and ask her to bring me notebook paper at school, because she always tucked a package of M & M's in the bag along with the paper. She'd come up to the door of my room and say to Mrs. Gray, my fourth-grade teacher, "Mrs. Gray, I have brought Macy some paper. I think she is about out."

And I would go to the door and take the paper bag and whisper thank you, and walk back to my desk and open up the top and slip the bag in without looking, like I didn't want to disturb anyone more than we already had with my interruption. But later, when everyone had more or less gone on about their business, I would slip my hand in and quietly open up that candy and eat it real slow all day long. The problem was my grandmother always bought the five-hundred-sheet packages, because she didn't want me to run out, so I was always having to give paper away to keep ahead of her. But after the day I slipped my hand in and ripped the bag wide open instead of just a little and M & M's rained down out of the little hole in the middle of the bottom of my desk, I had to ask my grandmother not to bring me any more paper. Mrs. Gray just wasn't up to it.

When I got to the grove and Showstopper and I stepped inside, it was as if we had stepped into another world. It felt twenty degrees cooler in there and so moist that little water drops hung in the air. I tied Showstopper to a tree near some thick green grass and gathered up some ferns to make myself a nice soft nesting spot and settled down to relax. I wished I had thought to bring me a book, but I hadn't been to the grove in so long that I had forgotten about it. It was nice, though, even without a book. I kind of leaned back against an oak tree and sat daydreaming and watching Claire Louise's horse munch out. I missed her sometimes, Claire Louise, that is. Funny thing, now that she was gone I was starting to like her better, just like my mother did.

It was while I was in there, and the grove was so still and cool it might have been a dream, that I remembered the time I'd found Claire Louise in the grove all alone. I had forgotten all about it but the memory came back to me as clear as when it was just happening, and I have never to this good day forgotten it. She must have been about twelve years old then, which would have made me eight. Or maybe she was only eleven and I was seven. One or the other. But she had gone off on a nature walk, which is what we used to do then, and had told me not to follow her. I didn't follow her, but I knew almost for sure she was going to the grove, so I waited thirty minutes and when she didn't come back, I headed for the grove myself. When I got there, I heard her before I saw her. She was crying and sobbing like something terrible had happened.

I forgot all about I wasn't supposed to be there and ran inside the trees, shouting, "Claire Louise, where are you? Are you hurt?"

She quit crying as soon as she heard me and sat up, and then I saw her, sitting beside the tree where I now sat and wiping her eyes with the tail of her shirt. "Go away, Macy," she said, but she didn't sound like Claire Louise at all when she said it.

"But what's the matter? Are you hurt?" I demanded.

"No, I'm not hurt."

"Then why were you crying?"

"Just because. You don't want to know."

"Yes, I do!" Back then I really loved my sister, and I wasn't nearly as scared of her as I became later.

She looked at me then and said, "Macy, did it ever occur to you that I get tired of getting sent to that closet to wait until my father comes home?"

The temperature in the grove got even colder when Claire Louise said what she said, and I sensed danger around me. I always went outside to play or turned on the television in the den when Claire Louise was getting punished, because I hated it when she got sent upstairs to wait on my father, who always walked up the stairs taking his belt off and slapping it against his hand as he climbed those stairs with his heavy clump, clumping steps.

"Then why do you keep sassing Mama?" I asked her, because she always got punished for talking back to my mother, and it had occurred to me time after time to wish she would quit talking back so she wouldn't keep getting punished.

"I don't know. I think about it every time I get punished. I think over exactly what happened and what she said and what I said and I promise myself I am not going to say those things ever again. And then in another day or two, something happens and I'm right back there waiting on my father to get home. Macy, I don't think it matters what I do. I'm always going to get in trouble with them. No matter what, Mama will get mad at me and send me to the closet for Daddy to punish." She started crying again, but softly now.

I reached over and patted her on the shoulder. I couldn't think of what to say to her, but I wanted her to stop crying. "Next time she gets mad at you, I'll tell Mother to tell him to spank me, too." I said.

She sat straight up then and looked at me and said, "You don't understand a bit, do you? You can't even imagine what it's like in there! I wish the only thing he did was spank me!"

As she said that, she sort of shuddered all over her whole body and sat there looking straight through me like I wasn't there. For a minute, she looked like she wasn't even alive anymore. This sounds so weird, but Claire Louise looked like a dead person, stiff and cold, and there were her big blue eyes staring straight out into nothing whatsoever.

"Claire Louise! Claire Louise! Don't!" I shrieked at her. I grabbed her arms and shook her to make her come back from where she'd been. As I shook her, she focused her eyes on me, and she sort of shuddered one more time and then shook her head like she was getting whatever was in there out of her sight.

"Macy, you're such a kid," she said, sounding like a little kid herself. "I hope he never does spank you," she told me in a voice that sounded all raspy. "Hang on to that asthma, kid, I think that's what saves you!" She laughed then and sounded like Claire Louise again, but before she stood up she gave me a hug and whispered thank you in my ear, which was not at all like Claire Louise. As we walked home, she said in her authoritarian way, "Macy, I want you to forget this afternoon ever happened. Do you understand me? Just wipe it out of your mind. A few spankings don't worry me at all and you never saw me crying. Got that?" I must have gotten it because I didn't think of it again for years, not until Claire Louise was long gone.

6

WHEN THE Trailways bus stopped in Houston, we were sure enough in the middle of a storm that promised to get much worse before it got better. James's mother and sister, Mrs. Wilcox and Cheryl, didn't do much more than say hello to me and "Of course you are to come home with us" when James had us all in their car and headed home. I sat in the back with Cheryl while his mother sat up front with James, who was driving like it was his car, which I found out later it was. They were all talking like crazy, telling about what all had gone on since they last talked to him, which couldn't have been more than a week, since he had told me he had not missed a Sunday of calling and checking on them the entire time he was away in the service. Even when he was overseas he called every single Sunday. I did wonder some what their phone bill must have been like.

As James drove, his sister Cheryl, who was sitting right behind him, leaned up and over the back of the front seat and kept patting on him like she couldn't believe he was really there. Every now and again one of them would remember I was there and turn to me and make a little polite conversation, but the truth is they as good as ignored me, when I had just gotten off that bus and was bone tired and as nervous as could be about the hurricane, which seemed to have settled all around us.

The pictures James carried of his family in front of his house did not do justice to the house. In the first place there was no way that you could tell from the picture that his house was situated on one of those streets that has a little tree-filled park all the way down the middle of it. Or that the driveway that led up to the house also swooped around the side of the house and ended up at a garage located back behind the house that had spaces for four cars, and then a section with rows and rows of shelves for storage.

James pulled up in front of the house, which was situated behind a circular driveway, and stopped the car at the front door. "Everyone out in the front," he said. "I don't want you ladies getting soaked!"

I was sitting there in a sort of befuddled state thinking to myself, my word, I had no idea, when the front door swung open and there stood a black lady in a gray and white maid's uniform. She didn't appear to notice the rain in the slightest as she ran out and gave James what appeared to me to be an entirely too familiar hug. While he was hugging her back and laughing at something she said, he turned to Cheryl and me and said, "Hurry up! It's wet out here!" He was by that time opening the car door for his mother and ushering her out of the car like she was spun glass. The weather had gotten so bad that the wind was driving the rain in sheets and we were getting soaked even under the wide awning that covered the front porch all the way out to the driveway.

Cheryl started toward the house with a fast hitching kind of step and I walked briskly along behind her, followed by James and his mother. As soon as we got inside, he turned right back around and ran out in the weather to get our suitcases, which were in the trunk of the car. When he came in the house this time, he was soaked clear through. All of us were just standing around watching him like he was a movie or something. "Go on inside," he said. "I'm going to put the car away." He shut the door with a slam that caused us all to look around for what came next.

I stood there dripping all over an Oriental carpet, with my suitcase at my feet. Beside it was a duffel bag that belonged to James. Mrs. Wilcox looked at me and said, "Lana, let's find you a room and a place to settle down in. I'll bet you're exhausted after your bus trip." A room with a nice bed and a clean bathroom next to it did sound good to me, although I wondered if she wanted to get me out of the way before James came back from parking the car.

"That would be nice," I told her. "It is wonderful of you to take me in and I don't want to be a bother."

"No bother at all," she said, turning to the maid who was standing over in the corner talking quietly to Cheryl. "Lana, this is Annie, who has been part of our family since before James and Cheryl were born. Annie, this is a young lady James met on the bus from New York. She is going to weather out this storm with us." I nodded to Annie, who said, "Pleased to meet you" to me, and then we just stood there for another awkward minute. "Annie, I'm going to take Lana upstairs to the guest room so she can get out of those wet clothes. Cheryl and I both need to change as well. Then I'll bet we can all sit down to something to eat."

The upstairs of the Wilcox house was just as elegant as the downstairs appeared to be. The stairs leading up were wide and lined with a heavy walnut rail, which was as smooth and polished as if hands had been sliding over it for years and years. I'll bet James and Cheryl used to slide down the rail, I told myself. I had never been in a house that had a stair rail wide and smooth enough to slide down.

There were five bedrooms up there, all arranged in a row with the two end ones being twice as large as the three in the middle. All of them opened onto a wide hall that overlooked the downstairs living room, and they also had French doors opening onto a balcony that overlooked the backyard. The balcony at one time had been a large screened-in sleeping porch, but it was just an outdoors kind of room now, since the house was air-conditioned. They called it the sun room, probably because of all the plants that grew there. The white wicker furniture and the bright cushions made it a pretty place, although with the storm coming everything had been moved inside or tied down.

James had one end bedroom, the one closest to the stairs. At the other end of the hall was his mother's room. Her room was done in turquoise and green and had its own bathroom, as did James's room, which had been redecorated while he was gone and was done in masculine red and brown plaids and had one wall filled with bookcases overflowing with his books and model airplanes.

The room closest to Mrs. Wilcox was Cheryl's, which had

a bathroom connecting it to the middle bedroom, which was connected to another bathroom that connected to the third bedroom. That was the bedroom that they gave me, the third one, so I could have my own bathroom. It also meant I was sleeping in the room closest to James's room, which I was glad to learn, as I was feeling more and more uncomfortable with his mother and sister. Or perhaps it was the storm that was causing my uneasy feelings. The wind had begun to howl louder and the sky was as dark as night, even though it was not yet five o'clock in the afternoon.

As Mrs. Wilcox showed me my room and bathroom, she said, "I don't want to alarm you, Lana, but I think we had better all hurry with our baths and dressing. Sometimes in this kind of weather we lose our power, so we may soon be navigating around with candlelight." She gave an excited little laugh when she said that, and I realized she was not a bit scared about the hurricane coming to town. Her eyes, the same blue as her son's, twinkled and her wrinkles crinkled as she smiled at me. She had on a sort of faded dress that was damp looking and her hair was gray with that blue cast that ladies get when they go in for those beauty-parlor rinses. It had been arranged in waves, which you get from sitting under a dryer with those metal clamps arranged on your head, and her hairdo had been sprayed with a thick coat of Spray Net. The rain hadn't done much to it, other than make it a little more solid looking. Mrs. Wilcox was a stout, short lady. I guessed her husband must have been tall and lanky like James had turned out to be, because Cheryl was short like her mom and dumpy, and was sure to be stout herself in a few years.

There was a suitcase stand at the foot of my bed where I placed my old leather case. It was one that had been my mother's when she went off to college, so you can imagine how old it was, but it was large and in good shape and held everything I owned. It bothered me, thinking a single suitcase held everything I owned. I felt poor, destitute, dependent on these people to take me in. I hated that feeling, the poor-little-me one that came over me as I looked at my pitiful suitcase inside their big fancy house, with the maid in a uniform opening the front door and showing people to their rooms. It won't always be this way, I told myself. Like the hurricane, this will blow over and I'll be on top again. I may have given up on New York, but that didn't mean I had lost my ambition. I still planned to make something of my life.

Besides the French doors, which had already been covered with wooden shutters on the outside, there were two doors to my room. One led to the hall that we had just come from. The other opened onto a gray and maroon tiled bathroom. The bathroom also had another door that opened onto the bedroom between my room and Cheryl's bathroom. I stood there a moment thinking. I do not like unlocked doors, particularly bathroom doors, but I was not sure what the etiquette involved would say in this situation. If I locked the other bathroom door, then no one from that bedroom could get to the bathroom. But no one was staying in that bedroom and Cheryl had her own bathroom, so there was no reason for her to come into mine. Or anyone else for that matter. So I locked the door and then I walked back through the bathroom and locked the hall door as well. With the doors locked and the French doors covered over I felt as if I were in a cave, a very safe, secure one. Even the wind noises seemed less threatening in here. But I realized that I would not be able to see a thing if the lights did go out, which led me to open every drawer in that room to look for candles or a flashlight. There in the drawer of the mahogany bedside table was a flashlight, which worked: I tested it. The candles on the dresser were in heavy glass candle holders, and I saw a book of matches in one of the top dresser drawers. The other drawers were empty except for paper linings.

It occurred to me that perhaps Mrs. Wilcox had been expecting me, what with the suitcase stand having been out and a flashlight with batteries already by the bed. Besides which there were sheets on the bed and towels sitting out in the bathroom. I unlocked the other bathroom door and looked again at that middle bedroom. It was not at all like mine, which was furnished with mahogany pineapple-post furniture, twin beds with a night table between them, and opposite the beds a solid-looking triple dresser.

The middle bedroom had a couch that pulled out to make a bed and a desk and wall unit that was filled with books and a collection of Hummel figurines. The floor in the middle room had a rag rug covering it and behind one of the cabinet's doors was a television and stereo. Sure enough, in the drawer of the lamp table beside the couch was a flashlight identical to mine, and there were candles and matches on the desk. I don't believe they knew I was coming at all. It looked to me like Mrs. Wilcox or Cheryl or perhaps Annie had gone around and put out candles and flashlights in all the rooms just in case.

The knock on my bedroom door startled me. When I opened the door there stood James, soaked to the skin. His eyes looked just like his mother's, excited and happy. I could see that he was having the time of his life. "Finding everything okay?" he asked, giving me a quick hug like he had known me for years, which it was beginning to seem like he had. Something about coming to this house and meeting his family and having them seem like such strangers was making James and me feel more and more like old friends.

"Yes," I said, but my voice sounded unsure and he noticed

that right off. I was beginning to realize that James was a very observant person.

"What's the matter?" he asked.

"James, this is going to sound very silly to you, but there is nothing I would like so much as a nice tub soak, only I am afraid to be in that bathtub if the lights go out."

"Take the flashlight in with you," he said, as if that were the only thing I was worried about. I was holding it in my hand as if that is what I meant to do. "And then after your bath, come on downstairs and we'll eat. Mother and Cheryl are already down there and I'm just going to take a quick shower before I join them."

"Well, I will, but . . . I don't know this house, James. Could you maybe wait while I bathe and then go downstairs with me?"

"Sure, I'll wait on you," he said, his eyes all warm as he smiled at me. "Just knock on the door by the stairs when you're ready. Actually, you can bang on the wall if you need anything. I'm right next door."

"James, you're so nice to me. I don't feel a bit scared about that storm anymore. I'll hurry, I promise."

"Take your time."

After he left, I opened my suitcase and thought about unpacking. It would be nice to shake out my clothes and put them on the padded hangers in the closet and put all my folded-up things in those drawers with the scented lining. But I had told James I would hurry, so I just shook out a clean skirt and a blouse with ruffles on it and got out my nicest set of underwear, pink with lace on the bra and the panties, and headed into the bathroom. There was a jar of bath salts on the counter in there. The bath salts were in a heavy glazed pottery bowl that was the prettiest colors of pinks and purples. The silver scoop in the jar looked like an antique. I helped myself to several large spoonfuls of those bath salts as I sunk into the tub, which I had filled as high as it would go with steamy hot water. Getting in that water, I relaxed and felt better than I had since I bought my first bus ticket back in Florida over a week ago.

My first bath in over a week. My first bath ever in a tub that had a marble rim big enough to hold a tray of food. I could get to like this, I told myself, wondering how long our hurricane would last.

I didn't stay in the tub but for about fifteen minutes or so, since I knew James was next door waiting on me. Even then when I had only known him for about two days, I knew that James was a person who did what he said he was going to do. If he said he would wait on me, he would wait. Even if I had stayed in there an hour, I am sure James would have sat next door waiting on me. I have always admired that in a person. It is a quality I try to emulate myself. Once I say I am going to do something, then I fully expect to do it. Or know the reason why.

Since I did not have time to do much with my hair, it was, I must admit, a frizzy mess. I have hair that curls in humidity, and between the rain and the steamy bathroom, my hair was nothing but curls. I would have liked to have had time to plug in my curlers and straighten it out a bit because at that time I liked to wear it in a smooth page-boy style, but because of James I just tied a ribbon around it and did a little quick makeup and hurried to knock on his door, which was open when I got there after all. "I like you in ruffles and ribbons," he said when he saw me, which told me something else about him.

When we got downstairs there was food spread out all over this large square coffee table in the middle of their family room. That coffee table was about four feet on each side and was heavy old pinewood, scarred from years of use. Cheryl told me once her mother had had the legs of the table cut down. It used to be a game table in her grandfather's house. Of all the furniture they had in that house, that is the one piece I remember that I would truly have liked to have.

"There you are," said Mrs. Wilcox, sitting up straighter on one of the three couches that were in the room. In addition to three couches and four wing chairs and the big coffee table and lots of little tables and stool-type things, the room had a game table and chairs and an entertainment center on one wall and a bar next to it. There was a huge fireplace in the middle of one long wall with a moose head bigger than a Volkswagen above it. One wall was all glass, but it was covered with drapes that night so I couldn't see the pool outside at all. This was the room the hall upstairs looked down on, and it was so cozy it might have been a movie setting.

I fixed myself a plate and curled up in one of the chairs and ate as slowly as I could make myself, enjoying the warm thick clam chowder and the grilled-cheese sandwiches I washed down with Tab, which was all I drank back then. It seemed the ideal meal to sit out a hurricane with. After a while they got to talking about people and events I had no knowledge of, and I more or less just drifted off thinking my own thoughts and not listening with more than half an ear to what they were saying. Cheryl was telling James all about her boyfriend, Mr. Wonderful I started calling him in my head for how perfect he sounded. She couldn't wait for James to meet him; he was an engineer worked for Sun Oil and he wasn't even in town but had gone out to help them evacuate some of the rigs in the gulf and then was going to go home to Galveston. I did perk up when she mentioned where he lived, because that town was not twenty miles from Molly's

Point and our family knew right many of the people lived over there. But when she said his whole name, Chet Brooks, I knew we never met any Brooks from Galveston or anywhere else for that matter, so I relaxed again. But I was glad that I had not yet mentioned the town I was from to James.

Cheryl looked over at me and smiled in a friendly sort of way. "Lana, I apologize. We must be boring you to death. Why don't you tell us about yourself?"

Maybe she meant to be friendly, maybe not. I thought about what I wanted to say. Feeling kind of shy, I stared down at the Indian-looking rug on the floor and ran my foot back and forth on the stripes in it. "There isn't much to tell. Unfortunately, I did not have as secure a childhood as you and James seem to have had, and I was thrown out of the house by my parents when I was sixteen. So for the past seven years, I have been on my own." I added three years to my age, thinking twenty-three sounded more compatible to thirty than twenty did.

"Oh, how terrible for you," Cheryl said, looking genuinely sorry.

"Well, I'm pretty self-reliant and I can do a good job of managing," I told her. "I had planned to come home and try to see my family, more or less square things with them, because I am not one to hold a grudge, but my efforts were rudely rebuffed."

"Oh," she said, staring at me as if I were a snake. I could see she was thinking my family was not as good as hers was and that made me angry, so I resolved to quit talking for the time being. I yawned and stretched a little and then tried to hide a second yawn behind my hand. My eyes fluttered so wide they made tears.

"Look at her, she's dead on her feet," Mrs. Wilcox said. "I'll bet you're tired as well, James. Let's all go up and get some sleep."

I stood up fast when she mentioned going to bed. I had had enough of this cozy movie setting for now. Resolving to make myself useful, I began to gather up dishes. "Lana, you're our guest, and tired at that. Put those dishes down. Cheryl and I will carry them out to the kitchen and we can wash them tomorrow."

Just as I was wondering what had happened to Annie, the maid, Cheryl said to James, "Annie went home to stay till after the storm." As she said the word storm, a clap of thunder sounded so loud I thought the house had been hit. We all jumped, no one higher than me, who nearly knocked James over, I was that startled. He laughed and steadied me with both his arms. "Now, don't get all scared again, Lana. I heard a report on the weather radio out in the kitchen not ten minutes ago. The storm has turned toward the east and they expect it to hit land somewhere near Lake Charles. All we're likely to get is more heavy rain."

I was in my bed wearing my frilliest nightie when the wind started up again. I had been asleep for a while, maybe as much as two hours. I reached over to switch on the light to check the time and it clicked and clicked again but wouldn't come on. I knew immediately the storm must have knocked the power off, and as I was thinking that the wind seemed to grow louder and louder. When I heard a loud crash somewhere outside, I thought to myself, storms that turn one time can turn again and it sounds like this one is headed in my direction once more. I went to the hall door and listened but there didn't seem to be anyone up and about. Shining my flashlight up and down the hall I saw that all the bedroom doors were closed except, of course, mine. Even the middle room, which had no one sleeping in it, had its door shut. Carefully I tiptoed next door to James's room. I felt sure he was awake in there listening to the weather station on his battery-powered radio, and I just could not put myself back to sleep before I heard where that storm was heading. I knocked softly so as not to wake up the rest of the house. No answer. I knocked again, a little louder the second time, being careful not to wake up anyone. Still no response. Even so I felt sure James would be awake, probably he had his attention glued to that radio and could not hear my soft knock over the noise of the storm. Carefully I tried the door. The handle turned smoothly under my hand and the door slid open. James's room had the French doors shuttered just as mine were, and the two windows on the side wall had also been covered up with storm shutters. His room was totally dark, I could see the mound that was James in his bed but that was more or less all I could see. Apparently I had been wrong. James did not seem to be up listening to the weather station. Cautiously I crept partway into the room keeping my flashlight focused on the floor so as not to disturb him if he was sleeping. A second loud crash took me by surprise and I jumped, knocking into a chair and causing it to scrape across the floor and into the table that was beside it. James sat up in bed, saying sleepily, "Who is it?" just as I gave a quickly muffled shriek.

"Me," I answered. "I'm sorry I woke you, James, but I got worried that the hurricane might have turned around again and headed back our way. I do think the wind sounds worse out there than when we went to bed." I heard a clicking sound that told me James was discovering that we had no electricity. "Here's my flashlight," I said, walking over to hand it to him. He took the light I offered and shone it around the room.

"I think we're just fine, Lana, but it's impossible to tell anything all boarded up in here. Let's go downstairs and see." He gave a laugh like we were about to have an adventure. I felt better just being with him. James threw back the covers and hopped out of bed. He was sleeping in his underwear, the baggy boxer kind, and he grabbed a pair of khaki trousers that were thrown on the chair and pulled them on. He sat down in the chair and began to lace tennis shoes onto his feet, and as he did he looked over at me and said, "You'd better go back to your room and get a robe. Not that your nightgown isn't awfully fetching," he added, grinning at me.

"Oh!" I had forgotten I wasn't dressed. I was that glad the lights weren't working, otherwise he would have been able to see clear through the sheer gown, which was all I had on. I hurried back to my room and grabbed the robe that had come with the gown I was wearing. It wasn't any heavier fabric but now I had on two layers, which made me presentable enough. I decided to go barefoot, since I had no house slippers that went with the gown and robe.

James and I crept downstairs to the kitchen. He reached over to turn on the overhead light, forgetting we were without power even though he was holding the flashlight we had used to see our way downstairs. "Come on," he said, "let's go outside." He opened the kitchen door and the moist warm night air rushed in to mingle with the cooler dry air of the house. We stepped out onto the porch and had to tug hard to get the door shut behind us. The wind had definitely picked up and was howling all around us. The porch sheltered us from the worst of the rain, but it was an eerie night and there was no convincing me that the storm had not come back to find us.

"James, I think it has turned around. Look at the trees." I am sure I sounded as scared as I felt. The heavy oak trees back behind the garage appeared to be bending farther than it was possible for them to go without breaking clean off. As we stood there, a sheet of lightning illuminated the sky and we could see clearly that there was at least one tree that had already been splintered and knocked over by the winds.

"Oh, no, not the oaks. My father planted those trees before I was born. Let's go see."

James had a note of real dismay in his voice, and although I thought it the height of foolishness to go out in the storm, I hesitated to dissuade him, because he would not have been up and outside at all if it had not been for me. So I walked out into that driving rain wearing only a flimsy robe over an even flimsier gown and without shoe one on my feet. We followed a flagstone path from the porch to back behind the garage, and between the lightning and our flashlight we could see clearer than we wanted to the damage the storm was doing. One tree, the one farthest from the house, was down and covering almost half of the stone fence that separated the back of their property from their neighbors behind them. The other trees all seemed to be standing, although from the way they were moving there didn't seem to be much keeping them from joining their brother there on the fence. The yard was covered with limbs and debris, and as we stood there gaping at nature's magnitude a leaf-covered branch blew into us, knocking me off my feet and against a concrete birdbath that was on its side beside the path.

"I'm okay," I told James as he pulled me to my feet. The truth is I was not hurt, but I was soaked to the skin and beginning to shiver from the driving rain. It wasn't cold at all, humid and warm actually, but the wind must have been blowing over fifty miles an hour and I was feeling the storm's force and it made me all shaky. James hugged me to him, warming me with his body heat. He was soaked clear through himself.

"Nothing we can do here, let's get back inside." As we turned to retrace our steps, a branch at least six feet across sailed in front of us, throwing us both off balance. It blocked the path we were following and as I began picking my way around the limb James noticed for the first time that I was barefoot. "You'll cut your feet," he said, picking me up as if I were a leaf myself and carrying me into the house. He didn't stop in the kitchen but went straight up the stairs to my room not caring a bit that we were dripping water all over his mother's expensive carpets as we went. "Let's get you dried off," he said, pulling one of the thick gray Turkish towels from the bar and beginning to rub it briskly over my hair. He grabbed another towel and dabbed at my shoulders a minute, but when I continued to shiver he said, "This isn't very smart. Get those clothes off and change into something dry. Hurry up. Then come in my room and we'll listen to the weather report." He left the bathroom, shutting the door behind him.

I was glad to get out of my soaked nightclothes. Quickly I toweled off, combed and fluffed my hair, wrapped a towel around me and prepared to make a mad dash to my suitcase. James had left my room but my bedroom door was ajar and I assumed that meant he was waiting on me. I pulled on jeans and a shirt and tiptoed down the hall. Lucky for us the storm hadn't awakened his mother and sister. Morning would be soon enough for them to learn the extent of the storm damage.

James had apparently made another quick dash downstairs, because beside his bed sat a bottle of wine, two glasses, and a long loaf of French bread. "A bottle of wine, a loaf of bread, and thou," he said with a smile when I tiptoed over toward the bed. "We're having a picnic."

I could see he was not worried about the damage we had seen, which was a relief to me. "Let's hear what the weatherman says," I reminded him, nodding toward the radio, which was over on the dresser next to two candles that were glittering against the mirror.

"Right," he said, bounding off the bed and bringing the radio and candles over to where he had put the food. He handed me a quilt and said, "Wrap up in this if you're still cold and we'll pretend we're gathered around a campfire." He was as excited as a kid and I must confess I enjoyed the playacting myself. We both settled down on the rug beside the bed with that quilt around our shoulders and stared at the lighted candles and listened to the weatherman tell us that most of Houston was without power and that the storm was just then going ashore near Port Arthur and we should be getting rain and wind like we were getting for the next twelve hours or so. They were warning of flooding in low-lying areas and saying how everyone should have long since evacuated along the coast, and I thought of the people I knew in Molly's Point and was sure that they had left to move inland hours ago. But where I was we didn't have to worry about flooding unless something completely unexpected happened.

"So now you have heard the weatherman," James said, grinning at me, "and you know we have nothing to worry about. Let's have some wine and celebrate." So we did. We drank the wine slowly and pulled off pieces of bread and ate those, and as we sat on that floor together and talked of the most inconsequential things, it felt as if we had been together like this for years rather than simply hours. I grew sleepy while James told me about the squadron he had commanded overseas and when my head fell on his shoulder he leaned over and kissed me on the lips and that kiss felt like we were sealing our souls together forever. I don't know whether it was the storm or the difficulties we had each of us been through the past few years in our lives, but coming together with James was the most wonderful thing that had ever happened to me. "I don't want to leave you tonight," he whispered.

"I know," I whispered back. "Somehow we belong together."

Then we slowly stood up and crawled into James's big double bed and he held me and covered my face with the softest sweetest kisses imaginable. When his hand moved to my breast, I felt my body arching forward to meet him and I knew that as long as I lived, I would never have another moment as right as this one felt.

After we made love we lay quietly together, James's arms around me. I liked the feel of his warm breath on my hair. We drifted off to sleep and slept for an hour or two until we both woke at more or less the same moment, stiff from the unaccustomed postions we had fallen into. "I've got to leave," I whispered. "I don't want your mother and sister to think bad of me." For the moment the storm was the least of my worries.

"Don't go," James said, pulling me back toward him. "I want you with me."

"I want to stay with you, too," I told him, "but I know I'll be awfully embarrassed in the morning if your mother knows we spent the night together. I'm not sorry for what we did, you understand. It felt perfectly right to me . . ." My voice trailed off as I wondered what James truly thought of me. "I hope you don't think I'm cheap or anything," I said, fighting tears. "I've never done anything like this before."

"Hush, Lana," James said. "I love you."

My eyes flew open at that and I felt the warmest rush in my heart. "You don't know me," I whispered. "How can you say that?"

He chuckled softly. "Beats me, but I can. I love you, Lana. You're what I've spent all my life looking for. Stay. Please."

"But . . . we're not married or anything. Only married people can sleep together."

James laughed. "Lana, you are innocent, aren't you. We just made love. We're lovers. I don't intend to give this up. If we get married, we'll still sleep together, but we have just proven that unmarried people can and do sleep together."

I started crying then, not caring who heard me.

"What did I say?" he asked, acting as if he truly did not understand how he had just hurt me.

"You do think I'm cheap, I know you do. Otherwise you would never have said we are lovers."

"Lana, there isn't anything wrong with being lovers," he whispered.

"Only cheap girls are lovers," I sobbed. "Good girls wait until they get married. I should never have come here with you, storm or no storm."

"I don't believe this conversation," James said. "What can I say to get you to quit crying?" he asked me, holding me by both shoulders and looking right straight into my eyes.

I was still wiping back tears and I frankly at that moment did not care how I looked. "I believe I have just made a big mistake, James. I'm afraid that the wine and the storm completely befuddled me. I never should have let you know how I felt about you."

"Lana, what we just shared was wonderful. I have never felt closer to another human being in my life. Can't you please quit crying and let's enjoy being together?"

"No," I wailed. "I want to forget it ever happened. Oh, no . . ." I sat upright in a panic. "What if I get pregnant? I'll never be able to pretend this didn't happen. I had a friend in high school who made one mistake and ended up pregnant and it about ruined her life." My sobs were real now as I imagined myself alone out in the storm with a child to raise. "What will I do?" I moaned.

"Are you saying this was your first time?" he asked me, wonder in his voice.

Not trusting myself to speak, I just looked at him. "And now I can never go home again, for sure."

"You poor kid. You are home. This is where you live. We'll get married as soon as the storm lets up." He hugged me to him and I could hear his heart pounding in my ear.

We stayed that way for the longest time and then I pulled away. "No, James, you don't have to marry me because you feel sorry for me. I couldn't live with that. As soon as this storm is over, I'll be on my way."

"Lana, haven't you heard what I said? I love you. I want to marry you."

"Do you mean it?" I asked him, my heart full of fear.

"I mean it. The question is, do you love me?"

"Oh, James, I loved you from the time you made me eat breakfast yesterday. I just resolved never to let you know."

I looked down then, feeling shy again, and he took his hand and gentle as you please raised my chin up and kissed me on the lips. Before I went back to my room that morning we made love another time and I was surprised. The second time was wonderful also. I never expected two such occasions in my life.

When I stood up and put on my jeans and shirt, James held out a hand to me and said, "Don't go."

"I have to," I told him, "before someone else gets up."

"But I thought we settled that," he muttered, still sleepy and holding out his arms to me.

"Well, we did settle that we are in love and are getting married," I said, "but I still want your family to respect me so we mustn't sleep together again until after the wedding. I have my future with them to think about, you know." And as we were married within two weeks I was able to stick firmly to my plan and not enter James's room again until he carried me over the threshold as his wife.

7

I EXPECTED Claire Louise and Ralph to drive in for the first family reunion after she left. She knew as well as I did that on the Fourth of July all our family, on both my mother's and my father's sides, gathered on Galveston Island, some of them coming from as far away as Lubbock. Some of the cousins usually stayed at our house, others stayed at my grandmother's, and some of them camped at the KOA campground out on the island or stayed at the Days Inn. We had as many as fifty or sixty people every year. One year over eighty showed up. I thought it would be just like her to drive up and hop out of Ralph's car right in the middle of the afternoon, when everyone would be sitting around my grandmother's pool talking ninety to nothing with four or five barbecue grills sending clouds of smoke into the air.

It never occurred to me she would stay gone for as long as she did. Claire Louise liked to run things, and I'd have thought she'd have been worried to death what we were doing without her around to tell us how it should be done. I looked for her off and on all day, but we never saw a sign of her. Everyone was talking about her to beat the band, though, because my mother was still in the sanitarium at that time and my dad was out back with the barrels of beer and the cookers so my aunts and cousins were free to speculate about where she was and what on earth had gotten into her to run off like she did. I had to tell them over again how I was sure she wasn't pregnant, and my Aunt Thelma allowed as how she might have come to some foul play and she for sure thought my mother and father ought to put the law after her. And my grandmother said they'd tried to tell my mother that very thing, but she was so irrational it just wasn't possible to get any sense into her. Hopefully, now that she was away getting some therapy that would change, my grandmother added. When my grandmother said therapy it rhymed with syrupy. I had given up on trying to tell her the correct way to pronounce it. Just letting someone in my family go in for therapy was a big step for my father and his parents. They did not at all agree with the use of head doctors, thinking people should solve their own problems. But my mother being so depressed and all, they had decided to try it, although it was considered an embarrassment as no one we knew had ever had to go to the nuthouse before. My grandmother got angry when my grandfather talked about Corabeth off in the nuthouse, but I had heard her at her own bridge-club party saying if ever anyone was a candidate for the nuthouse it had to be my mother.

By dark that Saturday night I knew Claire Louise wasn't coming. She would never have come somewhere late as it was, after the main event was over so to speak. That just was not her style. I wondered if Aunt Thelma was right, if something bad had happened to Claire Louise. But I thought I would have known if something had happened to her. Somehow I always knew Claire Louise was still alive and not in any big trouble even though we never heard from her for those ten years. And for what trouble she caused this family when she came back, it would have been better by far in my opinion if she had stayed Lana Anderson and never showed her face in Molly's Point again.

The second year after Claire Louise left was the year my mother took back over the running of her own house, and when summer came again and it was time for the family reunion in July my mother said one morning toward the end of June, "We are going to have to do something about Claire Louise's room." Both my father and I put down our forks and looked at her. Because of my mother's nervous nature, the doors to Claire Louise's room had been shut and not opened for the past two years. Well, that is not strictly true. Once a week our cleaning lady, Belle, would open up Claire Louise's room and dust and sweep it, and twice each year Belle had taken down the curtains and washed and dried and pressed them and hung them back in the windows. But we had not messed with Claire Louise's clothes or books or records or anything. Everything in Claire Louise's room was right where she left it, as far as I knew.

"There is no point in letting that room sit there waiting for her to show up. We need to clean it out and put fresh sheets on the bed. The family reunion is coming up week after next and someone can sleep in there."

"What about Claire Louise's stuff?" I asked Mother.

"Get rid of it," she told me. "If there are things in there you want, fine. Otherwise send it all home with Belle. I'm sure she has outgrown her clothes, and as far as I am concerned Claire Louise has been gone entirely too long to waltz in here at this late date and expect her things to be right where she left them."

My mother had certainly changed. She was as down on Claire Louise as I had ever heard her, and in my opinion she would have done well to remember her assessment of Claire Louise's selfish ways when Claire Louise finally did come home. But then you never could convince my mother of something once her mind was made up. Claire Louise must take after her that way.

As soon as Belle walked in that Friday, my mother said to

her, "Belle, you and Macy are going to clean out Claire Louise's room today. I am turning it into another guest room. What Macy doesn't want, you take home with you. I want that room empty by tonight."

Belle's eyes rolled back in her head like they do when she is surprised. Of all the people close to me during my childhood, Belle was the only one still speaking to me by the time my grandmother died. Belle, like my grandmother, always saw right through Claire Louise. Pity my mother was not as perceptive.

"Belle, you can clean out all Claire Louise's clothes and take them home with you. I have spent all my life wearing her hand-me-downs and I do not intend to do it any longer." Before we started we had opened up all the windows to get some breeze in that room. We shut the door that led to the bathroom connecting Claire Louise's room to my father's room, and we also shut the door that led to the big square hall all four of the bedrooms opened onto, but we left the door that connected my room to Claire Louise's room open. When I went in and opened the windows in my room it made a nice cool draft and I resolved to open up that door and her windows more often in the summer. When Claire Louise had been home, the door between our rooms had always been closed because she liked her privacy.

While Belle was shaking out Claire Louise's clothes and tsk-tsking at the waste, I was going through her desk and dressing table. All the makeup looked dried-up, and I put it straight in the trash. Her books I shook out carefully, because Claire Louise had a habit of leaving notes folded in them and I didn't want to miss things. The books I left on her bookshelves. It occurred to me since she was gone I could use her room as my study, so there was no reason to move her shelves and books to my room. Claire Louise had a nice window seat overlooking the front of the house and I felt it would be a good place to sit and read or think. It was beginning to sink into me that Claire Louise just might not be coming back and I might as well enjoy some of the things about her room as have them sit there going to waste.

Funny thing though. I never actually used Claire Louise's room all that much. It occurs to me that the reason I didn't was because of the way her room connected to my father's through an adjoining bathroom. Once you were in Claire Louise's room, you always knew there was the chance someone could open that bathroom door and walk right in on you. And all my life I was funny that way. About privacy, I mean. I liked to know the doors to any room I was in were locked and I wasn't going to be taken unaware, so to speak.

So, although Claire Louise clearly had the nicer room, once she was gone I mainly used it to store things. For all I called it my study, I never ever went in there and relaxed.

Aside from her makeup, Claire Louise's desk contained a stack of letters and notes about six inches high tied together with a red ribbon, which I knew came from the valentine box Ralph gave her the year they ran off. Those I put in a carton with Claire Louise's high school yearbooks and her diaries.

Every year for Christmas my grandmother was in the habit of giving me and Claire Louise nice leather-bound diaries in our stockings. And we both wrote in them pretty regular and kept them locked away in our rooms. My grandmother always gave herself a diary every Christmas as well, and she wrote in hers every day without fail. Unfortunate thing about it was, my grandmother kept her diary on the table by the toilet in the bathroom off the kitchen where she went every morning right after breakfast to sit a spell. My grandmother all her life drank hot lemon water first thing she got up every morning, and it always worked like a charm for her. But since her diary was right there and out in the open and all, we all read it for entertainment while we sat in that bathroom. I used to feel guilty about reading Grandma's private thoughts, but Claire Louise said there wasn't ever much in it but the weather and how many new calves been born and who had been to visit her and what she fed them and all. Still, it should have been private, and if my grandmother were still alive today and writing in her diary I would not read it no matter how out in the open she left it and how long I sat in there waiting for nature to take its course.

I must confess I was surprised that Claire Louise had run off without her diaries. There were five of them in the table by her bed, and I knew since I was on my sixth one, she must have taken the one for the year she was working on when she left. I was sorry not to find that one as well because it might have told me why she ran off, although as I said, if I had it to do over again I would not under any circumstances read other people's private thoughts. I have discovered that what my grandmother always said about eavesdroppers never learning anything good about themselves to be perfectly true. And reading something that is private to someone else is worse than eavesdropping.

It did not take more than an hour to clean out Claire Louise's room. We had her clothes packed into cardboard boxes and loaded in the back of Belle's black Buick with leather seats before my mother had finished watching her morning shows and my father had come in for lunch. The things we were throwing away we put out in the barrel to burn, and the only thing I took was the box of papers and diaries I was saving for Claire Louise should she come back and her jewelry box, which had only the things in it she hadn't wanted to take anyway. Claire Louise also left five framed pictures on her desk, family pictures they were, one of my mother and father holding her when she was six weeks old and wearing the heirloom christening gown my father and his mother had both worn. Those pictures I wrapped in tissue paper and put with her papers. The only thing I was not sure about were the pictures on the wall. Most of them were posters Claire Louise had tacked up against my mother's express instructions, but if we took them down they would leave holes, which my mother would notice. On the other hand, if we left them up they looked like Claire Louise. So we took them down and rolled them up and Belle took them home to give to her grandchildren, who probably didn't like them any better than I did.

As soon as I got in my room, I moved the shoeboxes aside and pushed the box with Claire Louise's things back in the corner of my closet that held my winter things. Then I arranged the shoes in front of the box so looking into the closet you would never know it was there. And there it stayed for another year before I got curious enough to read Claire Louise's diaries.

Claire Louise's first diary started when she was eleven years old. She wrote in it from the first page to the last clear through, not leaving any blank spaces. She ignored the printed dates, scratching them out when she needed more than a single page for one entry and not writing every day. Seems like she wrote more like twice a week, just when she had something to say. I could never decide whether the things in Claire Louise's diary were true or not. Some of them I more or less remembered and thought were the way things had happened. Others I had no memories of at all and it seemed as if some of them at least I would have noticed when they were more or less happening all around me. Once I started reading the diaries I read them all straight through staying up late into the night to finish the fifth book. Then I read them straight through again. Lots of the stories in those books have got to be lies but even so I could never ever look at my parents in the same light after I read the tales Claire Louise told about them.

Then I had a dilemma. I didn't want to leave those books around for anyone else to find and read, but I felt that diaries are almost sacred and it seemed sacrilegious to destroy someone else's diaries even if I did suspect them to be full of lies. In the end I just pushed them back in the carton in the back of my closet where they stayed. Last I looked they were still there, although doubtless Claire Louise has been through everything now and done away with them.

Funny thing about diaries, it now occurs to me they're not all that interesting for the most part. Take my grandmother's for instance. I never read a single thing in Grandma's diaries that I didn't already know. Either I had myself observed what she wrote about or she had told me all about it with her very own mouth. So, although I have reason to know that Grandma's diaries are to this very day stacked in a carton and stored up in her attic, I have to admit they probably wouldn't make very good reading for anyone at all, even me, at this late date.

Claire Louise's diaries, on the other hand, are, as Grandma would have said, a horse of a different color. Now I am not about to assert that her diaries are out-and-out lies. Not at all. Many of the things Claire Louise wrote I am reasonably sure were the truth. But there's truth and then there's truth, if you know what I mean. For instance, take the matter of my father and his drinking. It is true enough that my father liked to have a drink or two evenings. Not every evening you understand but, to be honest, most evenings my father would not have said no to a beer or a glass or two of bourbon on the rocks. And, as my grandmother said to my mother on more than one occasion, if my mother had unbent the least little bit and allowed beer in her icebox and bourbon in her cupboard, my father wouldn't have been forced to frequent the beer joints, which he was wont to do.

As it was, many was the night we ate dinner without him, my mother and Claire Louise and me. Later, on up in the night, we'd be upstairs in our beds and we'd hear him come in. You could always tell if my father came home drunk because, no matter how drunk he was, he was never too drunk not to remember the time he'd come home all walleyed, as the saying goes, and thought to put his truck up and ended up with it halfway through the back wall of the garage. So after that particular experience, he'd drive into the backyard and slam on the brakes and set his emergency brake and come on in the house. We knew better than to lock the door when my father was still out. Because if we did, sure enough he wouldn't be able to get his key in the lock and he'd sit on the doorbell until someone gave up and went downstairs and let him in. Not me. I knew all my life that nothing triggered an asthma attack worse than stepping out in the night air with nothing on more than my nightclothes. Besides which, for my entire life, I had the well-deserved reputation of being far and away our family's soundest sleeper. So it wasn't me that would have to wake up. My mother would. Or she'd yell at Claire Louise to get up and get down there and let her father in the house before he woke the dead. So the parts in Claire Louise's diaries about my father drinking and coming home smelling like a brewery and staggering around downstairs knocking stuff over until he managed to get his boots off and get up the stairs are, sad to say, true. But you wouldn't read anything like that in my diary nor my grandmother's. We were much too genteel to write about such as that, my grandmother and I were.

Sad to say, Claire Louise didn't care the least little bit what she wrote in her book. And they were nice books, too. Keepsakes if you will. Leather-bound.

Now, like I said, diaries aren't for the most part all that wonderful. I suppose if Claire Louise had grown up to be someone interesting, say the first woman president or some such, then her girlhood scribblings, penned in her own hand, would have been of interest to historians and others such as that. But she didn't. Grow up to be important, that is. And her diaries didn't in the long run matter a hill of beans to anyone at all.

But, back when I read them that time, those diaries worried me, the things she talked about. I mean, I remember thinking, suppose someone else saw them. So I got mine out and tried to compare hers to mine, to find out for myself if for no one else just how many lies my sister had written. It wasn't easy, comparing my diaries to Claire Louise's. Mine were like my grandmother's, neat and the day I wrote about was the one that was printed on the top of the page. Claire Louise's, on the other hand, were scribbled and messy. Sometimes she'd use red ink, sometimes peacock blue. Sometimes she'd even write in pencil for heaven's sake. And she didn't pay the least bit of attention to dates. She'd write and write, scratching out the printed dates as she went. She didn't write every day, she didn't seem to follow a regular pattern at all. She'd write until she stopped and then the next time she happened to feel like writing she'd start where she left off. So comparing hers to mine was no picnic, let me tell you.

My grandmother and I, we'd tell what happened every day. That's how we wrote. We'd write what we did or who we saw or even in my grandmother's case what food she ate. Like you can tell looking back, if you were interested to do so, that near about every single Sunday my grandmother cooked a roast. Which meant hot roast-beef sandwiches on Monday and hash on Tues-day. Winter, summer, it didn't matter, she'd thaw out the roast overnight on Saturday night, and it'd cook Sunday mornings while she was sitting in church. And if I ate over at my grand-mother's house, there it was written down in black ballpoint pen.

Claire Louise, to look at what she wrote, you'd know good and well she didn't give the least little bit of concern to what food she ate. Looking back, it seems to me, she was just a little old country girl trying to make herself sound exciting. Dramatic, if you will. Like she'd write about boys, who liked her and what he said to her and what she said back and so forth and so on. Sometimes she'd get to going and you would think to yourself, all this can't be true because if Claire Louise and that boy did all that talking during history class the teacher would have for sure sent them both straight down to the office. But of course I had no way of verifying what Claire Louise said about what happened while she was at school. I wasn't there after all.

Other things, for instance, what all she wrote about how she hated my mother, those things I could have an opinion on. She talked an awful lot about my mother and her, about how no matter what she did Mother was always on her case. It was true, back before she ran off, Claire Louise and Mother were at each other's throats most of the time. But it wasn't just Mother, it was Claire Louise too. She just could not let things lie, Claire Louise couldn't. Claire Louise would sass Mother at the drop of a hat. And Mother would say to her you'd better watch your tongue, young lady, I'm not going to tell you again. And then sure enough just about every single time they got into it, Claire Louise would back talk her again. I hate you, she'd yell at Mother. If I had a nickel for every time I heard Claire Louise yell I hate you, you fat old woman, no wonder my daddy doesn't like you anymore,

71

I could retire rich for sure. After she'd yell the part about hating my mother Claire Louise would run upstairs and slam the door to her room so loud it would echo on and on for what seemed like forever. And my mother would storm up the stairs after her and slam that door back open and they'd be at it again. Mother always had the last word though, because she was the one said that's it, I'm telling your father the minute he gets home. You stay right here in your room and when your father gets home you are going to get it, let me tell you. Who cares what he does, not me, Claire Louise would yell at my mother's back, but then she'd cry and cry so I know good and well she did too care.

At first, when I was younger, I'd try to talk to my sister. For all I was so much younger I had more sense than she did when it came to my mother. Just shut your mouth, I'd tell Claire Louise, shut your mouth as tight as your lips will clamp shut, and don't say a single word back to her other than yes ma'am you're right I'm sorry. That's what I do when she flies off the handle. And then she'll get over it and go up to her room and lie down and forget all about what she was so wrought up about. I'd tiptoe into Claire Louise's room where she was lying on the bed sobbing and crying and pat her back and whisper to her don't keep back-talking her, Claire Louise, you hear me, it doesn't do you the least little bit of good. I know good and well if I gave my sister that piece of advice one time I gave it to her a hundred. Not that she ever, to my knowledge, took my advice. But I did try to tell her. Over and over, I tried to tell her.

I never was able to actually compare our diaries. To put it simply, they were too different. It was like we grew up in different families. Maybe it was because as a child I was sickly, I had allergies. I had asthma attacks. They couldn't even let me take the polio shots because the vaccine grew in eggs, and eggs made me break out in a rash and wheeze for hours. Claire Louise wasn't sickly, all she had was a temper. Which she was never afraid to use, sad to say.

Looking back, I'd say maybe her diaries were true, even the parts about my father making her go in the linen closet and beating the living daylights out of her. To be honest, the closet part was true. Claire Louise did in fact get sent to the linen closet time after time for punishment. I hated reading about it in her diaries after she left every bit as much as I hated knowing she was in trouble back when we were kids. But I won't say it wasn't so.

Back then it bothered me having those kind of parents, the kind that yell at their kids and go so far as to hit them. I wanted my parents to be the nicey-nice kind of parents you saw on television. I used to pretend they were. Not anymore. Pretending isn't all that good for a person. I can see that now.

Therefore, to give the devil her due, Claire Louise wasn't a complete liar. They did treat her bad. Only another thing she wrote, the thing that I to this day cannot forgive her for writing down, was that my daddy took his belt off and then he took his pants off and then he let her have it. Claire Louise never could tell a story straight, she always had to embellish it.

Maybe it was true. One thing I remember, when they all got to screaming and screeching at each other, I'd take my book and go outside and I'd sit and read to myself. Sometimes I'd read out loud. Or I'd read silent in my head but I'd hum real loud. Because even when I got far enough away from the house not to hear them, I'd have to work some to get the sounds of their voices out of my head.

Say Claire Louise's diaries were true. Even so, she never should have written all that down, especially the parts about hating them and my mother being fat and crazy and my daddy punishing her for not doing a thing other than talking out loud like any human being has the right to do. And she said more than once how disgusting it was, watching my father drink himself into a stupor. Now that isn't true. My mother never, to my certain knowledge, allowed liquor in her house. So how could Claire Louise have watched him? I ask you that. And now you can see the problem. Because once you catch a person in a lie, even a little one, every single other thing they have said becomes suspect.

I guess it's fortunate Claire Louise didn't grow up to be important. At least no historians are poring over her diaries desperately trying to ascertain their accuracy.

8

JAMES AND I forewent a proper wedding and honeymoon, out of consideration for his mother and sister, a fact that I explained to them so they would realize the sacrifice we were making. It would not have been kind of us to marry and go off on a trip with James just back from the air force and them having been waiting for over two years for him to get home to take charge of things. And then there was all that damage the storm had done, damage we had to attend to, and there was Cheryl's marriage proposal to sort out. She and her mother had been planning this big church wedding for years. She had a scrapbook full of pictures they had clipped out of *Bride's* magazine, and naturally it was up to James and me to figure out how to pay for it all, because as I soon discovered, Mrs. Wilcox, sweet and well-intentioned as she was, had absolutely no sense when it came to money, or people either for that matter.

So James and I, we just stood up before a minister of the church who had known the Wilcoxes for years. We married in the little chapel off to the side of the main sanctuary and went out for a wedding lunch with his mother and sister and his best friend who did not turn out to be such a good friend in the long run. And of course Cheryl's fiancé, Chet Brooks, was there with us and I believe I can say with some accuracy that that meal we ate with him was the first time James and I realized just what a pompous ass he was. I do hate to speak ill of a person but the truth is, he was so full of himself and his oil rigs and his geological samples I thought I would have liked to say to him, I wish you would shut up and let some other people talk about something interesting. I felt we were right lucky Cheryl would be marrying him and moving out come summer. Probably with them living off to the other side of Houston, we would see them not much more than Sunday dinners and such.

It came as some surprise to me that a family that lived in as nice a section of town and in such a fancy house and with a maid and all could be so short of money. Turns out Annie the maid had worked for the Wilcox family since forever and the only reason she was still there was first, she and Mrs. Wilcox, or Mother, as I started to call her, were more friends than anything else. To sit and hear them talk about their kids and recipes and all while they polished silver or gardened, you could not have told one owned the house and the other worked for her. Second, it was James had been sending the money to pay Annie every month, just as it was James had been sending money to keep that house running. Turns out Mrs. Wilcox owned that house and nothing more. James was right surprised I hadn't realized that, but I say you live like rich folks, don't be surprised when people take you for rich. I never did believe she didn't have accounts and stocks and things hidden around like my daddy did, but if she had stuff squirreled away she must have planned to take it to the grave with her, because nothing ever turned up anywhere as long as I was around.

Cheryl and Chet married in June, she naturally having planned on being a June bride all her life. By then we had the garden back to order. Turns out Mother Wilcox and Annie had natural green thumbs, and I must admit it did look pretty when they got all their flowers to blooming. Between all those plants and that big house, I had to admit to James that Annie was not a luxury but a necessity, but it seemed to me if we were paying the bills she should look to us for her orders. Not to mention the house being in his mother's name instead of ours. James said to leave it alone, and being pregnant at the time, I turned my attention to other matters.

I had my redecorating to attend to. All my life I have been interested in interior decorating, and I am quite good at seeing the potential in a room, which is often quite lost on anyone else. And with a baby on the way and Cheryl moving out it was time for us to redo our living quarters so I began to look at every room in the upstairs with an appraising eye. As I explained to James and his mother, creative thinking requires the ability to visualize, to look at what is in a place and see what is not there except in your mind. I can block out completely the furnishings of a room and see what I would rather put there. This is a talent not shared by many people. Certainly James and his mother and sister were not able to share my visions.

Mother Wilcox being quite attached to her room, that left me four rooms to consider. It turned out Cheryl felt a sentimental attachment to her room also, and James's room, which was now our room, having had a bundle spent on it in anticipation of his homecoming, that left me with the options of the two guest rooms for the nursery. The middle room was already an upstairs TV room, so I decided to redo the room I had slept in the two weeks before my wedding for our baby, which was due around the time of Cheryl's wedding as near as we could figure.

Still, I have never been one to put off to tomorrow what can be done today, so by March I had that room turned into the cutest yellow and pink rainbow room you have ever seen. As I knew all along I was having a girl, I had no compunctions whatsoever about using pink. The yellow was just to keep the peace with James and his mother and sister. As it turned out, I was wise to be so foresighted because Britt came over two months early. We were extremely fortunate that she was not as small as many preemies, however, and in point of fact she weighed several ounces over seven pounds. However, in my family large babies are the norm. I believe, if I recall correctly, my own sister weighed almost ten pounds when she was born.

Both James and his mother spent some little time talking to me about didn't I want to call my family, now that I was married, and when Britt was born they took it hard that somewhere in Texas not all that far from them, some grandparents didn't even know of the existence of the sweetest little baby that ever was. I finally had to cry and let them see how distressed I was at them continuing to yammer at me to call some people who had thrown me out and wished me dead. As I told Mother Wilcox, I was beginning to think that she and her son and her daughter didn't consider me family, as much as they were after me to call those folks who had been so cruel to me all my life.

Fortunately they all thought Anderson was my family name since the only papers they had ever seen, my high school gradua-tion papers and my driver's license, plainly named me Lana

Anderson. And I had held firm in my resolve never to tell them the name of the little town on the coast I was from, so there was no way they could get nosy and find out any more than I wanted to tell them. And turns out that was a wise move on my part, because Cheryl Wilcox, now Brooks, was just sneaky enough to snoop around. Reminds me of my own sister Macy that way.

If ever a man was besotted with a child, James was with our daughter. He was working over on the far west side of town, flying planes for Mr. Sanerford when he needed to go somewhere and taking care of the aviation side of the company when he wasn't in the air. He left the house before seven the mornings he was in town, but sometimes when he was flying his schedule was stay home all day and leave for an overnight in the afternoon. You couldn't plan meals around him, much less a baby's schedule, but try and explain that to a man as besotted as he was. He wanted Britt sleeping when he was gone and up and playing with her daddy when he was home. And if she was asleep when he came home he would contrive to make enough noise so that he had her up within ten minutes of his arrival. I began to wish I had put the nursery on the other side of the house.

And he didn't outgrow that silliness, either. Up until the day we left him, Britt was Daddy's little darling. For a man who wanted a son, he sure forgot all about that fast enough. Of course when I left she was five and I was pregnant with Maryanne and he might have switched over to her, but I couldn't take a chance on what was going to happen. I thought I had to leave when I did and I still believe I made the right decision. A person cannot stay somewhere and be lied about indefinitely. Eventually, it wears away at the soul.

The first I began to realize we had problems was when James had to go to Europe for six weeks for his boss, Mr. Sanerford.

By then Sanerford Aviation had grown to be a large corporation, and James was an officer in the company and an important person. Six weeks is a long time to be away from your family, your wife, and your baby not yet two years old, and James begged me to bring Britt and stay in a hotel in London while he was over there taking care of business. Actually, his first idea had been that he, his mother, the baby, and I all go to Europe. At that time Cheryl and Chet were still in an apartment, and he thought it would be just dandy for them to stay at our house while we were gone. I explained to James that not only could I not rest easy for six weeks knowing my house was empty except for a maid who might or might not show up when I was not there to supervise her, I could also not rest easy when someone who did not regularly inhabit my house was living there and me off across the Atlantic Ocean. But this is Cheryl's house, too, Mother Wilcox chimed in, which was a real bone of contention, because it did not sit well with me that James and I were pouring all our hard-earned money into a place that someone else held the title to. Like as not I told him, she could leave it to Goodwill and we would be out in the cold. Don't be silly, James would say, but I would remind him I had been out in the world and seen more of its nastiness than he had any knowledge of. Maybe so, he would say, but my mother has no part of any nastiness you have observed. It just is not in her. Maybe not, I would tell him, but I have been surprised before.

So, as it turned out, to keep the peace in the family, James and Britt and I flew over to England in February, where Britt and I spent days after days sightseeing while James traveled from one place to another, sometimes not getting back to London for three or four days at a time. Traveling with a small child is not easy and I was ready to get home long before we actually left

London. The next time James brought up that we should go with him, I said no right off and did not get into any discussion about the whys and wherefores. It is easier to say what you plan to do right up front when you know good and well you are not going to be talked into a trip you have no wish to make. And besides, that summer I started working at the Westview Methodist Church and had responsibilities of my own to attend to. James had absolutely no desire for me to go to work, but when I began volunteering as the part-time person to answer the phones while Britt went to the playschool run by the church, he had no problem with that. And as events would have it, after I had been there a year Mrs. Lacy Landview, who had worked there for twenty years, decided to retire. She told me she had been there so long she thought she had seen everything, but as things were going she believed she should leave while she still had some sensibilities intact. I had to agree with her and could only encourage her to retire at her first opportunity. In my opinion, it is a mistake to stay in a position too long, and Mrs. Landview was showing unmistakable signs of burnout. At the time of Mrs. Landview's retirement I had been as good as running the church office, and so it was natural for them to ask me to take over her position. Especially as the only other person who worked in the office itself was in the process of looking for another job and plainly had no real calling for church work.

It was difficult going from being a full-time housewife and mommy to holding such a responsible position, and I have never been a person to do things halfway. Many were the nights I was after dark getting home but with Mother Wilcox and Annie and James himself so besotted with Britt and her being three now and in Montessori school all morning, I knew for my own peace of mind she was well cared for and knew that her mommy loved her more than anything. But the two years I worked at West-view Church were difficult ones, no doubt about it, and put a strain on my marriage to James. With an eye toward dealing with the problem, I approached Reverend Smythe about counseling. I had expected him to recommend me to one of his colleagues, but when he offered to counsel with me himself I realized it would be inconsiderate of me not to take him up on his gener-ous offer. Particularly as I was at the church with him all the time and it would have been taking away from my job if I had started leaving in the middle of the day to go across town to see someone else.

James and I had begun to argue more and more about my career, which he saw as completely unnecessary. I tried and tried to explain to him that my career was every bit as important to me as his was to him, but it was like talking to a board fence trying to tell him anything. It did not help at all that we lived with his mother and she sided with him every discussion we had. Why can't you be satisfied to stay home and raise your daughter? he would ask me, and I had to be honest and tell him I could not in all fairness call a home someone else held the title to mine. And Mother Wilcox, thinking to be helpful, offered to see a lawyer and put the house in James's and Cheryl's names. I pointed out to her my name was neither James nor Cheryl, and as far as I was concerned she could keep her own title to herself.

And then to add to my troubles, Reverend Smythe was trans-ferred to a church in Oklahoma. Methodist churches are known to move their ministers around and he had been in this one for almost ten years so it was time he moved up the ladder, but it came as a shock to me. I was so distressed, my marriage falling apart and my mother-in-law on my back all the time and my sister-in-law telling lies about me at every opportunity and now it looked as if I was going to have to move to Oklahoma. While it is not always true that a person who is transferred moves his office staff with him, Reverend Smythe asked would I consider it, and as my career happened to be the only thing in my life that was working for me, I felt as if I had no choice. As it turned out, I was in Oklahoma for less than three months.

After I flew to Reno to get a divorce, I went out to Enid to find myself an apartment and to enroll Britt in kindergarten. I planned to start work immediately, but it turned out that the church-secretary position was filled by the wife of the mayor of the town and Reverend Smythe, as much as he wished to, could not give me the job. I was able, however, to get an excellent position running a doctor's office, and I soon began to feel as if I had made the best decision possible. Divorce is never easy, particularly on children, but I could see that it was in Britt's best interests to get her away from James and his mother, who had been dangerously overindulgent, and from Cheryl, who had a vicious tongue on her. Reverend Smythe, who by now insisted that I call him Tom, was well liked in Enid and I think it would have been only a matter of time before we were married if he and his wife had not been killed in an airplane accident not two weeks before Christmas. The irony of the situation was not lost on me. My own husband, James, who flew all over the world in small planes, was just fine, and Reverend Smythe, who I had begun to look on as my salvation, was killed when he went up in one with the wife he was fixing to leave soon as she overcame her fears of the unknown. Life is not, and never has been, fair.

Britt and I stayed in Enid until three months before Maryanne was born. I would have liked to have stayed forever, but raising a child on a meager office-manager's salary is not easy and, because my condition was preexisting, my insurance was not covering my maternity expenses. I thought long and hard about what to do, but realized in the end I had been gone too long. Pregnant or not, it was time to go to Molly's Point and make my peace with my family. Had it been just me, I would have died rather than return, but I had my children and their inheritances to consider.

9

I T WAS exactly one week before spring break of my senior year at Texas Tech that I discovered Claire Louise was back. I called home to tell my parents when I was leaving and who I was bringing with me, and some child who turned out to be Britt answered the phone. "Hello," squeaked this little voice.

"Oops, I've got the wrong number. Sorry."

"Hello," she said again. "Hello, hello, hello, my mother says I can answer the phone."

I had a sinking feeling right about then. Somehow I knew. "Who are you?" I asked.

"Britt Nicole Wilcox," she said, "and I'm home to live with my grandparents. Who are you?"

"Probably your Aunt Macy," I muttered. "Could you get one of your grandparents to come to the phone?"

"My grandma is outside talking to the milkman and my grandfather isn't here either."

"Well, get me your mother then," I snarled at her. It irritates me no end when people let their kids talk on the phone. Any time I call somewhere expecting to speak to a grown-up and get some inane kid on the line, I'd just as soon hang up as talk to them.

There was a clunk when Britt Nicole, who I was already picturing as a prissy miniature of her mother, dropped the phone. "Telephone, Mama," I could hear her shrieking.

I waited a good minute before I heard Claire Louise's sweet little voice say, "Hello. This is Claire Louise. Whom am I speaking to?"

"This is your sister Macy," I told her, wondering how you talked to someone who had been gone ten years and not once said she was sorry for leaving you all alone there with your parents.

"Macy," she gasped. "I can't believe it's you. When are you coming home?"

When was I coming home, she asked, when was *I* coming home! I'd been home all along. It was she who had run off for ten years without so much as a postcard to anyone, and now she was there answering the phone and asking when I was coming home like she owned the place. I had not known she was back five minutes and already I didn't like her again.

I laughed, but not because I was amused. "More to the point, when did *you* roll in?" I sounded like my father, sarcastic and superior, and I always hated it when I heard myself sounding like him, but I couldn't help it. What right did she have to run away for ten years and leave me there to manage everything and then turn up overnight and act like she was in charge?

"We've been here since Saturday," she said in that oh-what-a-big-girl-I-am little voice of hers.

"Who's we?"

"Why me and Britt, my little girl, and"—here she gave a nervous giggle—"the new baby who is due to arrive in about two months."

"Oh, my God, what happened to Ralph?"

"Why, Macy," she said, "that did not work out at all. We

84

were divorced some time ago." She managed to imply that I had missed out on all her news simply because I had not been paying attention.

"So you have one, almost two children, and no father for them?" I asked bluntly.

She gasped as if shocked. "Oh, dear, it is the saddest story. I can't bear to dwell on it, but I'll tell you as much as I can stand when you get here. Just exactly when will that be?"

"Why don't I speak to Mother?" I asked.

"Mother's outside and I don't like to disturb her, not to mention running up this phone bill. I can certainly give her a message."

"Well, tell her I'll be in Thursday night late, maybe after twelve, and I'm bringing Leigh Anne and Karin with me."

"Oh, Macy, do you think that is a good idea? I'm here now, and I had so counted on us having time together. We do need to catch up, you know."

"I've been planning this for months, Claire Louise. I had no earthly idea you were due to arrive from wherever you have been for the past ten years. We've got parties to go to and most of our friends are going to be out on the island. This is my senior year, for Christ's sake!" I was squeaking and bleating at her like I was eight years old again. She made me so damn mad.

"Now, Macy," she said like she was placating an old sow, "I don't want to upset your plans, but this house isn't all that large, you know. I was just trying to be practical." That last remark was accompanied by a little sniff.

"Oh, shit," I said, as I heard her sob and say to the room behind her, "Mother, it's Macy. You better talk to her."

"What did you say to Claire Louise?" Mother demanded. "You made her cry."

85

"I didn't say anything," I said, still bleating. "I wanted to talk to you and tell you Leigh Anne and Karin and I are getting in late Thursday night. That's all."

"Well, you'd think you'd have more to say to your own sister than just talk about your own plans. Now I know when you'll be here, what else did you want?"

"Mother, I called to talk to you and see how you were and what's going on, and now that I find out she is home, it seems as if I've done something wrong. Would you please tell me exactly what I have done that is so wrong?"

"Macy, there is no call to be dramatic. You be careful driving home and we'll see you when you get here."

"Claire Louise said I shouldn't bring my friends, the house was too small."

"Well, Britt can move out of your room and sleep in the room with her mother. And you can have the rollaway in your room for your company. We'll manage."

"Britt's in my room! What's wrong with her mother's room?" Now they had me doing it too, arguing over the pettiest crap!

"For heaven's sake, Macy, how selfish! Begrudging a little child your room when you're five hundred miles away and have no need for it at all."

"You're right," I said, too tired to argue with her. "I'll see you this week. Bye now."

I started to call my grandmother right then and there but I didn't want to sound like a whiny little kid to her, so I put on my running shoes and went out and did five miles in under thirty-five minutes. If it hadn't been time for my chemistry lab I would have done another five. When I'm upset about the only way I can calm down is exercise, running or a good game of tennis or a fast exercise class. But right then I wanted to be alone, to sort out my feelings and figure out how the sister I thought I had been missing for the past ten years had made me madder than hell just by showing up. My mother had called me selfish and that's how I felt, selfish and hateful. I didn't want her back home in her room, which had been my study since I'd cleaned it out and rearranged it to suit myself. I didn't want her eating at our table, and the idea of her fat and pregnant and waddling around drawing attention to herself was more than I could bear. If we hadn't been planning this trip to the beach since the one last year, I would have cancelled out on my friends and stayed at school. As it was I was locked into going, although I certainly was not looking forward to getting reacquainted with Claire Louise. She's twenty-six years old now, I told myself, and she's probably had a hard ten years. Would it kill you to be nice to her?

Then I began to speculate about where she had been and what she had been doing. That's when it occurred to me she wasn't calling herself Lana anymore. I doubted if I could believe much she said. I'd long since decided most of her stories were lies, but I began to get a little curious about how she was going to explain away ten years and two babies and not a husband in sight. Even my mother ought to be able to see through her now, I thought. I was wrong. My mother did not to the day she died see through Claire Louise and her lies.

Lucky for me I had not planned on moving back home after graduation, because by summer Claire Louise had Britt and the new baby installed in my room. All my clothes had been moved into the linen closet to make room for their stuff, and the yard was running over with tricycles and playpens.

And there was Claire Louise, who may have left home a sinner but had for sure come back a saint. Nothing was too much trouble for her to do for her mother and father. She was always fixing caramel pies, which were my father's favorite, and you may be sure she fixed them just the way he liked them. And then she'd be telling Mother to go out onto the porch and rest and let her take care of dinner, and apologizing for the baby crying and disturbing them all. Next thing you knew she was driving around in Mother's car like it was hers, and before he knew what hit him my father had bought her a station wagon, because it was so much trouble with the kids in a two-door car.

I stayed at home exactly two nights before I moved into my grandmother's guest room, which is where I stayed until I left in September to go to graduate school. After that, when I was home on vacations I just automatically went to Grandma's. It wasn't so much that I minded sleeping on the sofa bed in my own house, but I got to where I could not stomach all that cloying sweet talk she was spouting. Now, Britt Nicole, go give your grandpa some sugar, she'd simper, and I'd like to gag while that poor kid went over and hugged on his sunburned, sweaty old neck. Hand your grandma her afghan, she'd say, and cute little Britt would be off and running. She must have raised that kid on Shirley Temple movies. It was unnatural the way Britt hung around her mama, yes ma'aming and no siring folks. But why should that surprise me? If ever there was an unnatural mother, Claire Louise was it.

"Don't you ever miss your daddy?" I asked Britt once while she and I were the only two sitting out by my grandparents' pool. I would never have had the nerve to ask such a question had my sister been there. She looked at me and shut her lips in a tight straight line. "My daddy doesn't want to see us," she said.

Poor kid, that was the first time I ever felt sorry for Britt. It's not her fault she's here, I told myself, and she can't help it she looks like her mother. After that I tried to be a lot nicer to her and her little sister, Maryanne, who was turning out to be a fat replica of my mother with eyes sunk so far in her face you couldn't tell what color they were.

After I finished my master's in social work, I took a job at the Harris County Department of Social Services and got an apartment over in the Galleria area. My college roommate Leigh Anne and I lived together until she got married and moved to Waco, and then I lived by myself until I married Carlton. Claire Louise wasn't living with my parents herself by that time. My grandmother had been right: wait her out, she had said, she'll lose interest before long and be off and after something else. It didn't matter, the die was cast, and there wasn't any call for me to ever expect to go back out there to live anyway.

She hadn't run off this time. She had worried my father until he built her her own house in town. It was a little red brick ranch-style with three bedrooms and two baths and a living room, dining room, and combination kitchen/family room. And a poured concrete slab off the kitchen she called her patio. She got the plans out of a magazine. The house was nothing fancy, and situated where it was catty-corner to the elementary school she had to look out for the kids and traffic. She had a three-car garage built about a year after she moved in. Likely as not my father paid for that as well, although I never did hear for sure, and then she started her up a little preschool in her garage so she could be self-supporting and not have my father having to take care of her and her kids, if you can believe that story, which I did not for one minute.

She ran that school until Maryanne started kindergarten and then she gave it up, decided it wasn't for her after all. Which meant that she was no longer able to dispense wisdom to all the ladies every afternoon when they came to pick up their kids.

It also meant she was free all day to get into mischief, and if I had not been so busy at that time with my own new baby, who had turned out to be babies, twin boys, I might have been more curious about what she was up to.

My grandmother was beginning to slow down and it tired her more than she admitted when I came out with the boys when they were one and two and into everything, so there were a couple of years there when even though I was living right in Houston and not an hour's drive away, I'd sometimes go a month without seeing them. Of course there was nothing wrong with Mother and Daddy and they could have come to my house any time they desired to do so, but Daddy has never left home for more than a drive around the county without it becoming a major expedition, and they both acted as if the only reason to come to Houston was if one of them needed to pack a bag and check into the hospital.

And through it all, there was Claire Louise, sweet as could be, out there almost every afternoon checking on them like they were so old and couldn't look after themselves. She'd try to tell the pope how to run his business, she was that way. And she had Mother wrapped around her little finger, no doubt about that. They'd go into Gulfgate for Claire Louise to help Mother get herself a new church dress, and come home with new dresses and shoes for Mother, Claire Louise, and both her kids, all of it charged on Mother's Foley's card I know good and well, because Claire Louise certainly was not making any money on that play-school she was running, and she was not getting a dime from James, because she had been afraid to let him know where she was. Oh, I heard all about that story but it wasn't because Claire Louise ever told a word of it. No, I got my information from an entirely unexpected source.

But I didn't hear about Claire Louise and what she had done to James Wilcox for a while. Certainly I didn't know anything about what she had been up to until just a few years ago. Much as I have never liked my sister, I still cannot believe she has done all the things I have heard her accused of. It does not seem humanly possible that in an individual lifetime of less than forty years anyone could have accomplished all she appears to have done. Which may, come to think of it, explain why my mother has never seen through Claire Louise.

One Mother's Day, Carlton and I and the boys, who were three that April, went out to go to church with my parents. As you might expect, Claire Louise's two girls—Britt, who was almost in junior high, and Maryanne, who was seven and repeating first grade—were there. They spent, as far as I could tell, more time at my parents' than they did their own house. When we got there, Mother and Daddy were just loading up the car with the girls, Claire Louise having gone on ahead for choir practice. This was the first I had heard Claire Louise was in the choir. No one in our family being known for the ability to carry a tune, it did come as something of a shock to me. Mark my words, I said to my husband, there is some man in the choir she is after. Claire Louise never does anything without a reason, and I knew good and well that she was not one to sit around long without a man in her life. Which shows you I was remarkably naive even at that point. It never in a hundred years would have occurred to me that there was a man in her life and that she was keeping it a secret because he was married. I just could not fathom such.

Anyway, I threatened the boys within an inch of their lives if they weren't good in church and promised to stop at the frozen-yogurt store on the way back to Houston if they were, and Carlton and I went over to my grandmother's to pick her up and take her to church with us.

Poor Grandma, she looked a sight. She had on a dress ripped out under the arm and her hair was tied back with a piece of yarn that looked like it had come off a package. "You can't wear that, it's ripped," I told her.

"Oh, don't worry, you'll never know it a hundred years from now." Grandma might have aged some over the last years but she was still herself, which was a comfort to me. She pinned on the corsage I had brought her and gave me a big hug and handed each of the boys a lollipop she'd gotten at the drive-in window of the bank and been saving for them. I could just see her, driving through to get some money and telling them to hand her two of those lollipops for her grandchildren who were coming to visit on Sunday. Used to that would have embarrassed me, my grandmother asking for candy like that, but now I thought it was cute.

After church we all ate over at my mother's, Carlton and me and the boys, my grandmother, and Claire Louise and her two girls, and of course my father who was cooking brisket on the barbecue pit. Then we sat around and talked and both my great-aunts, who were down from Charleston visiting one of their daughters who lived in Houston, drove out. Mary Frances and Ellen, I called them although they were my grandmother's sisters and much older than even my own mother. They, like my grandmother, were in their seventies now and slowing down, which didn't mean they talked any less or any slower. It did seem to me they were louder, though, but maybe it was because I felt like I had heard all they had to say several times before.

I sat in the living room and listened to them, and when the kids wanted to go swimming they both offered to walk back over to my grandmother's and sit with me while I watched them. And my grandmother thought she would take a nap, so my mother thought she could use one too, and Claire Louise thought she had better get on home in case the girls had homework. That more or less brought our little family dinner to an end. I sat out there with my grandmother, who turns out didn't need a nap after all, and Mary Frances and Ellen, and watched the boys swim like little porpoises. We had had them in swimming lessons since they were six months old, and it had surely paid off. They were as at home in the water as they were on land. And the only one took a nap was Carlton, who thought he would lie down for a spell. My grandmother had taken him inside and made him stretch out on the bed in the middle room, even though he said the sofa was good enough, and then she shook out the satin stitch quilt and told him to take a good nap, he looked that tired to her. Carlton told me about it later. He liked the way she mothered him as if he were three years old like the twins. Of course Carlton came from a family of lawyers and more men than women, so he has a good healthy ego and is not threatened by my grandmother treating him like a little child that has to be humored. Something about our family, though, they don't treat men with much respect. The women sort of look after them and fix their plates like they can't do it for themselves, and then try to get them out of the way before they talk about anything of any significance. I had figured this out after years of observing how my mother and my sister and even my own grandmother operated. I must confess, however, that I had not figured it out by myself. I had been seeing a psychologist for over a year now, and I was making right much progress and it was amazing to me just how sick some of the members of our family had come to be.

But at that time, even though I had a significant amount of insight into the dynamics of our family, I still sat out there and gossiped with the women while my husband took a nap inside. And even though I was beginning to be aware how wrong some of that talk was, I was still fascinated by it and wanted to know every scrap of gossip they could dredge up.

10

COMING BACK home after a ten-year absence was not the easiest thing to do, and nothing I would recommend to anyone lightly. Still and all, since my marriage had fallen apart and I had two young children to support entirely on my own with no help whatsoever from my ex-husband, I had little choice but to do as I did. And the years that are critical to good child-rearing, the years when my girls needed me, I was there for them.

As Britt started first grade, I recalled how isolated I had felt living out in the country when all my friends were in town, and I determined that she was not going to have to suffer as I had. I built a house in town, admittedly with some financial help from my parents, as Macy is so quick to mention, but as my parents had not sent me through six years of college I hardly think even a small house set them back nearly to the tune of what Macy's college career cost them. And as soon as I realized there was literally no quality preschool in town, certainly nothing of the caliber of the Montessori program I had previously been associated with, I decided to start a little school of my own. At two, Maryanne needed a developmentally appropriate program, and I have always said if you want something done right, it is best to do it yourself. My little school was such a success, within two months of opening I had a full enrollment and was forced to begin hiring assistant teachers. The school filled a critical need in Molly's Point, and when four years later I decided to resign from my position as director of my school in order to make some career changes that I felt were important to me, I was able to assist Mary Beth Wilder, who had worked for me, in taking over our little school, which is running even to this day. It is a good feeling to know that some of the things I have done have left a lasting and important impression on the town in which I was born, and one of the accomplishments I am proudest of is that I founded that school.

After turning over the managerial reins to Mary Beth, I was free to become more involved in Garland Elementary School, which both of my children were attending, Britt in fifth grade and Maryanne in first grade. I was president of the PTA and was instrumental in setting up the program that raised the money to update and reequip the school library, which was a dismal collection of rummage-sale castoffs when I took it on. Mr. Ben Scales, the principal, who had just arrived in town, was the first to say that he could never have accomplished so much in his first year had it not been for the extraordinary volunteer efforts made by the women of Molly's Point. As the head of the PTA I justly felt some little bit of pride to have been a part of that volunteer effort.

Mr. Scales, or Ben, as he came to be known, was all in all the most exciting thing to happen to Molly's Point, educationally, in some time. Fresh from a master's in education program at Texas A & M, and with over ten years' teaching experience in College Station public schools, he came in with new ideas and programs, which shook some life into our rather stodgy and set-in-its ways school system. My father, who was still on the school board that year, had been instrumental in bringing Ben to town.

His wife, Laura Lee, had been hesitant to move to a small town, having spent all her life in larger cities, and the adjustment was more difficult for her. Because she did not have the best attitude, it made things difficult for Ben and their two children, Casey and Cameron, who were in the third and fifth grades. As Laura Lee and I were the room mothers for fifth grade we spent some amount of time together planning class parties and field trips, and I tried as much as possible to help her feel at home on Molly's Point.

The Scaleses lived down the street from the school, on the same block as I lived on, so we were soon visiting back and forth and cooking meals together. I knew that had Laura Lee been able to get a teaching job at the school she would have been much happier, as she was used to having a first-grade classroom and having so much free time was hard on her. Which is why, when I heard that Minerva Sawyers, who had taught first grade for years in Sinton, was leaving because of her husband's stroke, I insisted that Laura Lee run right over and talk to John Sealy, who was a good friend of my father's and chairman of the school board there. And of course they jumped at the idea of getting an experienced and qualified teacher for their first grade when they had been faced with making do with one of the children's mothers, who had never taken an education course in her life.

Laura Lee came home so excited from that interview, she was like a different person. She rushed into my house where Ben and the four children and I sat around the kitchen table eating hamburgers we had grilled. She was all aglow, she was that happy.

"Sit down and tell us all about it," I told her, standing up to fix her a plate and lay her a place at the table.

"Oh, you don't have to wait on me, Claire Louise."

"Don't be silly, you talk while I get you a plate." And I wouldn't take no for an answer so she talked. On and on about what a great job it was and about how she missed working, and about as good a friend as I had gotten to be she still didn't feel very at home in this town. All of us, Ben and me and the kids, smiled and nodded and couldn't get a word in edgewise for a solid five minutes. But of course she was going to turn the job down, she said.

"Why?" I shrieked, completely taken aback.

"Why?" Ben echoed, as surprised as I was.

She smiled. "Don't be silly. It's over thirty miles away. I'd have to leave here by six-thirty every morning and I couldn't possibly be home much before five. My family needs me. It's not like I'd be here in the same school with all of them."

"Laura Lee, think this over. I'd hate for you to give up a job, the very idea of which has excited you more than you've been excited since I've known you. I'm sure Ben and the kids can help out with meals and such, and I'm right here and more than willing to do whatever needs to be done. Why, any nights you're late, you all can just eat dinner with us like tonight. We enjoy having the company, don't we, girls?"

And all four of the girls chimed in that of course they liked it like this, eating together and getting to play together after school and all.

"But what about when one of the kids gets sick?"

Ben answered that one. "We'll do what we've always done. One of us will stay home."

"Or there's me," I added. "I'm pretty good around a sickbed."

"No, I'm not going to consider it."

"Better think it over a day or two," I advised her. "Out here teaching jobs don't happen very often."

Which is how we left it, and I don't think Laura Lee would have accepted that job at all if I hadn't happened to mention to Mr. Sealy that she was undecided, and he hadn't called and more or less begged her to try it out at least for a month or so before she decided it was too much for her. I think it was him saying that she could leave at any time if it was taking away from her family and they would still be glad for the time she had given them that convinced her.

It went exceptionally well for her, although taking over a classroom in the middle of the year is difficult and she had to work at it late hours some days, but then Ben was all involved with being a school principal for the first year, so their little girls just got in the habit of walking home with my two when school let out and playing till dinnertime when, more nights than not, they all ate over here. Both Ben and Laura Lee didn't know what they would have done without me that year, and I was more than glad to have been of help. I am basically a very giving person and like more than anything to do for others. And as I was cooking for my own two there wasn't any reason not to add several more names to the pot.

Come summer, Laura Lee was again torn. She dearly wanted to go to College Station and work on her own master's degree, which is what she and Ben had agreed on, that he would finish his degree and then she hers. Of course, as she pointed out, they hadn't planned on moving so far away from the university. Since I had already enrolled my own two in Mary Beth's full-day summer program, which she still ran in my garage, which I had converted into a school and now leased to her, I mentioned that if they acted quick they could probably secure places for Casey and Cameron, which would take care of them daytimes for the summer and I was more than willing to be the cook for the six weeks or so she would be gone. Oh, no, we can't keep imposing on you like this, she said, but I did not consider it imposing at all, and in the end desire won out and she left for summer school in College Station, about three hours away.

Summer school being so intense and us having no library beyond the high school one, Laura Lee was not able to get home even most weekends, and with the girls being in school right behind my house, they and their father spent most of their time at my house that summer. And Ben and I were using that opportunity to work on our plans for the coming school year and spent lots of time over at the elementary school working on schedules and fixing up the library and the nurse's office. One of our projects dear to my heart was the idea I had of adding a counselor to our little school. Now I knew as well as anyone that we could never afford to hire a licensed counselor, but I happen to be particularly good at talking with children and I have observed over the years that they are quick to open up to me, so my plan was that I would fix up the little office next to Ben's, which at present was used for nothing more weighty than storing old books, and begin work as the elementary guidance counselor. I envisioned working with each of the six classes several times a week on little lessons and of course talking privately with any child who was having personal or family problems. Ben was so excited about my plan, particularly as I had begun to take a correspondence course from the University of Texas extension service to prepare me for the position.

My year as a guidance counselor was rewarding, if exhausting. Between working full-time and looking after my children and frequently Ben and Laura Lee's two, I had little free time, but I find I don't need a lot of free time. I am a truly high-energy person. And I suppose I still might be happily ensconced in that cozy little office as the guidance counselor, had not small-town gossips with small minds and nothing better to do than create rumors wrecked havoc with my peace of mind.

The first clue I had something was awry was when Laura Lee came in one night upset, and with a face that fairly shrieked she'd been crying. She refused to discuss what had happened, just gathered the girls and Ben up and they all walked on home. Later that night, she called and wanted to know if she could come over and talk. "Sure," I told her, "come over and I'll put the coffee on." Perhaps I was foolish not to think of this myself, but I had become so involved in counseling others that I truly thought she needed my advice on some problem she had encountered. It never for a moment occurred to me she would consider me part of her problem.

"Claire Louise," she began, "I am going to ask you not to talk at all, just listen. I want to say everything before you butt in. Can you agree to that?"

I was taken aback, but nodded. "Of course, I can listen. Remember my job is listening. That is what I do best."

"Then do it," she said. "I want you to know that I have talked all the things I am going to say to you over with Ben and he fully agrees with me and supports my decisions. I want to be fair with you, but in the end I will do what I feel is best for my husband and my two children. Over the past year and a half, you and your children have become like family to me. I have relied on you much more than I should have to look after the girls and cook for all of us. Never having lived in a small town before, I did not realize how people watch one another, how they talk. Now I do. Way over in Sinton, there is gossip about how you are taking over my husband. People are saying you two are having an affair. Now,"—she held up her hand in a stop motion, just as I opened my mouth to indignantly deny any notion of an affair—"now, I have talked to Ben and I am satisfied that there is nothing to that rumor. But I am also satisfied, and Ben agrees with me, that we have taken advantage of you. So I am resigning my job at the end of this year. And until the end of the year, after school each day, the girls will sit in Ben's office and do their homework there until he can come home with them. They are not to come over here for Mary Beth to watch while you and Ben stay after to finish up the day's work. And he or I will cook dinner every night and we'll all eat at our own house from now on. I hope we can stay friends, Claire Louise, but this cozy little group we have here is dissolved as of this moment. If Ben and I are going to stay in this town, we're not going to be the main source of town gossip."

To say I was taken aback is an understatement. I was completely floored by what she was saying. I quite simply had no idea that Ben and I had become the source of town gossip. "Laura Lee," I began, resolving to remain calm and above all else not to cry, "I can't believe what you are saying. Why on earth would people say Ben and I are having an affair? The very idea is ludicrous."

She looked at me very carefully before she said, "You know it and I know it and Ben knows it, but we seem to be the minority holding this particular opinion. A delegation of people came to me this afternoon—for my own good, you understand—to tell me that I had better stay home and keep my eyes open. They seemed to delight in telling me about your rendezvous at the school and at the café in Okaley." The bitterness in her voice was evident.

"How can I argue with rumors? Who told you this, anyway? I demand to know who is spreading these lies about me. Ben and I are professional colleagues, no more. Why, you and I are friends! I can't believe you'll let unfounded rumors cause you to give up a job you enjoy. What will you do with yourself all day?"

"Calm down, Claire Louise. The rumormonger was practically the entire staff at Sinton Elementary. But that doesn't matter. Ben and I have decided to have another baby, and until then I will work as a teacher's aide in the primary program here. He said he had planned to hire someone next year anyway."

"That's the first I heard of us hiring anyone else. And my father is still on the school board."

"Well, if your father won't permit it, then I won't work, I suppose. But I am not going to continue working over in Sinton and jeopardize my marriage."

"But, Laura Lee, why all of a sudden do you think your marriage is in jeopardy? I don't want to tell you how to run your business, but if it were me I would have more pride than to let town gossip make me quit a job."

"Well, you and I are different that way, Claire Louise."

Afterwards things were never the same between us. Try as I would, I felt some ill will toward Laura Lee, and yes, toward Ben, too, for siding with her. Things were strained between our children when Casey and Cameron were no longer allowed to come over in the afternoons, and with Ben's children underfoot after school it wasn't possible to get work done the way we had in the past. By May I had more or less decided to give up my job as a guidance counselor at the school. Somehow Laura Lee's unjust accusations had taken the joy out of it for me. And Ben changed, too, becoming formal and aloof. So in June I called Ben and told him I would not be coming back. He was relieved, I think, which hurt my feelings no end. And as it turned out, that decision was the best one I could have made, because around the middle of July Ben announced he had taken a job in College

Station and they moved back there. I asked my father how on earth he could give a recommendation to someone who left on such short notice, but my father said you couldn't fault a man for moving up in the world, which was what Ben was doing.

It seemed as if that spring and summer were the hottest we had had in years. I was out at my grandmother's every afternoon, letting the children swim just so we could all try to cool off. Macy was out on occasion with her twins as well, but living as they did in Houston it was easier on her just to take them to the West U pool, which was near where she and Carlton lived. I have to admit, although of course I never said a word to her, those boys were a handful. They have settled down now and are turning out well, but when they were toddlers there was nothing those two kids needed so much as to have the law laid down to them. To be honest, we didn't see much of Macy at all. She had a habit of showing up when she wanted something and not before. Certainly she was not like I was, out there every single day looking after my parents and my grandmother. I may have run off when they were younger, but as they aged no one can say I was not there to do for them.

I began to realize that town living was not all it was cracked up to be. With the kids in school I thought about getting a job in Houston but realized that there was nothing I enjoyed so much as the farm, and I began to think about what I meant to do with the rest of my life. While a career was appealing, I realized that my father had no one but me to depend on when it came to his business interests, and I felt it was up to me to give him the security of knowing the farm would be well cared for after he was gone. Gradually I came to be more involved in the day-to-day operations of the farming and ranching business, something my sister has no interest whatsoever in.

When it came time for the cotton picking to start that summer, I realized just how much my father needed some help. I was over at Mother's visiting one afternoon while the children swam at Grandma's when he came in red of face and looking hot and tired. "Damn cotton picker's broke down again, I've got to run over to Sinton and pick up a part."

"Daddy, you look tired. Sit down and let me fix you some iced tea. I'll go get that part for you in a bit. Then you'll have it first thing tomorrow. It's too hot out there to be picking now, anyway."

"Claire Louise, you wouldn't have no more idea what part to get than one of the Hereford bulls would."

"Well, you just write down what you need and then if you want to be double sure, call the man at Folsome Farm Supplies and tell him what to give me. No way I'm going to be able to help you if you don't start telling me now," I added.

"First I heard you wanted to help me," he said.

"Well, you know good and well I'm out here and helping more and more."

"Hum," he said, but he wrote down what he wanted and I was into Sinton and back with his part before five o'clock that afternoon. Afterwards I made it a point to be out there every day helping him to supervise the work and generally familiarizing myself with the business. It turns out it was good I had done so, because not two years later he had his first stroke and more and more of the responsibility of running the family business fell on me.

It was while Daddy was in the hospital recuperating that I began to acquaint myself with the financial end of his business. Heretofore he had been reluctant to accept my help when he was working on accounts, and as I was going through his office I realized full well why he had tried to keep me out of there. The poor man was embarrassed, I am sure, for anyone to know just how abysmal his bookkeeping habits were. Having learned something of bookkeeping from a course I took while I was in Oklahoma, I could see immediately that I could be a big help to my father in the accounting end of his business. In particular some of his accounts needed to be transferred to other banks. He was keeping much more than the federally insured limit in the town bank. Even I, with my limited knowledge at that time, realized the folly of that particular practice. Had I known then that he had over fifty thousand dollars in cash hidden in the back of his closet, I would have just died.

My mother had absolutely no head for business and paperwork, and had no idea where they stood financially. She simply charged what she wanted and listened with one ear when my father complained about the bills. Having been raised with that model before me, it was some time before I realized that it behooved a woman to acquaint herself with financial matters. Particularly in our situation, my family responsibilities were clear. It was up to me to carry on the family business.

After Daddy returned from the hospital, he had a convalescent's temper and was quite short with me when I tried to interest him in the way I had reorganized his office. I also pointed out to him that had he been seriously incapacitated, his family, in particular my mother, would have been in dire circumstances. "She doesn't understand business, Daddy, and has no interest in learning. For her security, I think you need to begin to delegate more responsibility to me." In particular I was concerned that except for my mother no one had access to Daddy's accounts. There he was adamant, however, and went to his grave without ever putting me on the signature cards. That of course was inconvenient, because when he was dying from his last surgery and in the hospital for several months doing so, I had to trouble my mother to sign every single check I wrote on the business and personal accounts. And as you can imagine, there is a tremendous amount of financial paperwork involved in running a farm, and my mother, distraught as she was, would try to get me to explain things to her, which made my life just that much more difficult.

Of course when poor Daddy departed this earth, one of Mother's first acts was to see that my name went on all the signature cards. I am happy to say that my mother was well cared for up until the day she died, no thanks to my sister I might add. And you may rest assured that if Mother spent her last years blissfully unaware of the intricacies of her financial standing, it was no more than she had done for the entire years of her life with my father. Mother didn't know about money matters because she chose not to acquaint herself with them. Her ignorance certainly was not some devious plot of my devising, as my sister took pains to tell anyone who would listen to her. It grieves me to note that as she grew older my poor sister grew as irrational as she accused my mother of being after I left home. Much as I care about Macy Rose, it is difficult to forgive her for some of the things she has said about me. Not that I hold a grudge; that I most emphatically do not. But I would not be human if I failed to notice that never to this day has Macy apologized to me for the things she accused me of. Never. Not once.

I I

W HEN THE BOYS were small and Carlton was working twelve hours a day building up his practice, I had more than I could do just to keep up with my own family. By my own family, I mean Carlton and my two children, not my grandmother and parents and sister and cousins and aunts and uncles living out in Molly's Point. I felt guilty and disloyal that I was not out every weekend looking after Grandma and calling Mother every night, but I was in therapy every week working on that unhealthy dependency, and anyone, Claire Louise in particular, who asserts I blithely washed my hands of the whole lot of them unless they had something I wanted is, to put it bluntly, full of shit. As it was, once she moved back into my parents' house, which she did the year my father had his first heart attack, I had less and less of a desire to go visit because of the way she has of making me feel like I am taking up her personal space just being there. Now, Macy, she would say, sit in here and talk to Mama while I get these peach preserves put up. When I pointed out they still had the preserves in the basement from the past five years, she would say something like, well, it worries Daddy for them to go to waste, so it certainly is not too much trouble for me to go ahead and cook them. This while wiping a hand across her perspiring brow and giving a self-satisfied sigh. And I would tell her she might want to consider the waste of all that sugar, and she would shoot me a drop-dead look that Mother conveniently missed, and sigh again and ask me if it was my time of the month, I was so cranky. Sweet little Claire Louise. Is it any wonder I got to where I hated to go out there? And of course, to hear her talk my kids were always just fixing to break one of the lamps or whatnots, while butter wouldn't melt in her kids' mouths, they were so perfect.

Even her children, innocent as they were of the undercurrents that were all that kept our family together, irritated me. Britt, once she was in high school, was one of those kids who was just so polite to adults you knew she had to be up to something. Sure enough, I heard she had to have an abortion her junior year, and then damned if she wasn't elected senior-class favorite the next year. She took after her mother entirely too much, as far as I could see; didn't matter what she did, she always came up roses. And poor Maryanne, plodding along in Britt's and her mother's wake, not quite bright, getting fatter and fatter, as she sat around and listened to my mother and sister talk year after year about nothing more than the geraniums in the front flower bed. Probably not true, that last comment. From the way Mother turned on me later, it is apparent that they talked about weightier matters than flowers. All the time Claire Louise was out there taking care of my parents, she was taking care that not one dime of their money ended up in my hands. And I was so stupid, it never occurred to me she would do such a thing.

When Mother called me crying early one Sunday morning it took her a good five minutes to quit sobbing and tell me what was wrong. "It's Daddy," she finally said. "I think he's had a heart attack."

"Where is he, Mother? Have you called the doctor?" I fairly shrieked at her.

"Henry and his son came out in the ambulance and took him over to Pine Ridge Hospital. Claire Louise followed him in the car and I'm here at home. She hasn't called me and I can't find my glasses to look up the number of the hospital."

"It wouldn't be in your phone book anyway, Mother. That's a different town." I thought quickly. "Listen, I'm closer to the hospital than you are. I'll go over there and find out how he is and then I'll call you."

"But I can't bear being here alone, Macy. You're going to have to come out and get me."

"All right, I'll do that. Are you dressed?"

"No, I can't find my glasses."

"Well, look for them. It'll take me an hour to get there."

Always, at any crisis in her life, my mother fell apart. Both Claire Louise and I had been raised patting her hand and looking for her glasses. It was second nature to me to run out there and take care of things when she called me. Even if she'd been meaner than a snake to me for days, I still ran when she wailed.

Carlton was awake and listening. "Your father?" he asked when I got off the phone.

"Yes, his heart, Mother thinks. Claire Louise drove in behind the ambulance taking him to Pine Ridge. Mother wants me to come out there; as usual she can't cope." I was sarcastic but I was rushing to comply.

"Do you know how he is?" Carlton asked, adjusting his glasses on his nose and giving me the steady look he gave his clients when he wanted them to stop and think carefully. "Let's don't rush off without thinking," he said.

All I heard was the let's don't part and I was quick to react. "Carlton, this is my father! How can I sit here and deliberate with you like I'm in a therapy session with your partner Abe at a time like this! I have to get over there."

"Right," he answered, and I knew him well enough to know he was thinking there was no reasoning with me now, and that thought made me furious at him.

"Why don't you help me?" I screeched, sounding like my mother, which generally pissed me off. Sometimes I hated all the therapy I had had. I knew just enough to know I was reacting in a crappy way and not enough to do a damn thing about it! "Well," I snarled at him, sounding for all the world like I was throwing down a gauntlet.

"I will. Try to calm down, sweetheart," he said, giving me a hug and saying softly, "we're in this together, you know." I started to cry then, remembering how much I loved him, Carlton I mean, not my father. I think most of the problems Carlton and I had came from when I started acting like he was my father. Or worse, acting like I was my mother.

"I don't want my father to die," I said. "As much as I hate how he was to us, I don't want him to die."

"I know, I know," Carlton said, patting me on the back as he held me. "He'll be okay, one way or the other. Why don't I call the hospital and get a report while you get dressed. Then we'll see where we stand."

"But my mother is stuck out there in the country going hysterical," I said, getting right back into my panic.

"Which she will be whether you get there in one hour or two," he said in the low calm way he has of talking when I'm upset. "Suppose you drive all the way out there and get your mother and rush in to the hospital and your father is not being admitted? Or has been sent downtown to one of the other hospitals? You get dressed while I call."

This was not the first time I realized how lucky I was to have Carlton. How I had ever had enough sense not to drive him away with my shrewish ways, I'll never know, but I thanked God for my good fortune daily. By the time I was out of the shower and dressed, he had a hospital report and had Mrs. Grant from across the street over to stay with the boys so he could go with me.

"Your dad has had a heart attack," he said, "and he's in intensive care. I talked to your sister and she says the doctors are optimistic, but he may need surgery, in which case he will probably be moved down here to Diagnostic Hospital. Since Claire Louise is there with your father, we'll go out and bring your mother in."

"Surgery?" I asked, my voice sounding like a whisper in my own ears.

"Cross one bridge at a time, Macy. Are you ready to go?"

"Yes," I nodded, noticing Mrs. Grant for the first time. "I'm not going to wake up the boys to tell them we're going," I said to her. "They'll be thrilled when they wake up and you're here. Just don't let them con you into cookies before breakfast," I told her. Mrs. Grant was a retired schoolteacher who lived alone across the street from us and she had more or less adopted all of us as her own. She kept the boys for us several days a week and was better at the outdoor games they liked than Carlton and I were. I hadn't known another sixty-year-old woman who could play tennis the way that woman did. The only time she couldn't keep the kids was when she was in one of those tournaments she was always bringing home trophies from, and she already had started taking Travis and Scott over to the court and giving them lessons. Carlton and I were both somewhat in awe of her, and relied on her as much as our kids did.

She hugged me and said, "Now don't worry about a thing here."

"I hope we're not interfering with a tennis match or something," I said, hugging her back and wishing I could stay there with her.

"No, no tennis in this weather," she grinned, nodding at the window, which is the first time I noticed it was raining cats and dogs. "We'll just have to play ball indoors," she said, and I laughed, remembering the first time she had taught the boys to play ball indoors. They weren't quite old enough to hang onto the distinction between Nerf balls and outdoor ones and Carlton and I were replacing lamps right and left there for a solid week.

"We'll call you," Carlton promised as he hustled me out the door. One of my habits he hates is how I rush around like a mad hatter getting ready to go somewhere, and then at departure time start to dawdle and find little unnecessary things to do to keep from actually leaving. So as I leaned over to pick some dead leaves off one of the potted plants in the kitchen window, he took my elbow and propelled me forward. "Let's go," he said, keeping me moving until I was in the front seat and he was backing out the car.

"Wait, I forgot my glasses," I shrieked. "I have to have my glasses in case my contacts bother me and I have to take them out."

"You have them in your purse," he said. "I checked."

He was right, they were there, where I had put them maybe five minutes ago.

Mother was dressed and sitting at the kitchen table drinking coffee when we got there. She had her glasses on, I was glad to note, and she also had on her hat, and her gloves were folded neatly over her pocketbook. Beside the back door was her leather overnight case and there were two dresses, a sweater, a quilt, and her pillow stacked on the little suitcase. Britt and Maryanne sat at the table with my mother, wearing long faces. I was surprised to see them, I kept forgetting they lived with my parents again.

"What about Grandma?" I asked. "Has anyone told her?"

"She's upstairs," Mother said. "The girls are going to look after her."

"Why is she over here?"

"She came over to help me find my glasses. Let's go," Mother said, standing up.

"Carlton, while you get Mother's things in the car, I'll run up and speak to Grandma."

Mother sighed like I was putting her out, but I ignored her and took the stairs two at a time. I found Grandma in Claire Louise's room, pulling the quilt up over the bed. "Are you okay?" I asked her, going over and hugging her. She was flushed and perspiring.

"Fine," she said, pulling away from my embrace. Affectionate as my grandmother was, she, like all the other people in my family, was acutely uncomfortable with actual physical closeness. "I couldn't stand all that moaning and wailing, thought I'd come up here and straighten up these beds, no point in leaving it all for Belle to have to tend to when she comes on Monday. She's got all that laundry to get done. Those two girls must change clothes four times a day." Grandma, on the other hand, only changed about every fourth day. "Then I thought I'd load Britt and Maryanne up and take them on over to my house. I've got my flower beds to tend to and they can swim."

"Britt can drive now," I reminded her. "Do you want her to bring you downtown to the hospital later? Or I'll let Carlton take Mother in and I'll bring you?" I realized I wanted my grandmother with me. "He's your son after all," I said, although I had difficulty thinking of my father as anyone's little boy, particularly my grandmother's, who was much nicer than he was.

"No, Macy, you know I can't stand hospitals and funeral parlors. I'll just wait out here. You call me when you know something."

Poor Grandma, I thought, sneaking in another hug. "I love you," I told her.

"Yes, you do," she said, ducking her head. "Better get on, your mother'll be in a snit."

"I'll call you, Grandma," I said, fighting tears.

I cried a lot that next week.

When we got to Pine Ridge they were just loading my father into the ambulance to take him on to the medical center. Claire Louise took Mother in the car with her, and Carlton and I followed in our car. As soon as we got to Diagnostic Hospital, I hurried to the phone and called Mrs. Grant, who said she and the boys were fine. From the noise in the background it was obvious they had some game in progress, and as I told her where we were and that it looked as if my father would be having open-heart surgery immediately, I could hear Travis and Scott calling to her to come take her turn.

"Everything is under control here, you do what you need to," she told me.

"Thank goodness for Mrs. Grant," I told Carlton. "What would we do without her?" I felt completely superfluous at the hospital. Since my father was going straight to surgery we went to the waiting room on the second floor, where Claire Louise settled Mother in as if it were her private room and conferred with doctors and nurses in as learned tones as if she had several medical degrees herself. Carlton and I just stood around listening.

When we heard the surgery would probably take five or six hours, I suggested that I take Mother on over to our house so she could lie down. "But I want to be here," she wailed, whereupon Claire Louise went and talked to the head nurse and arranged a room on the second floor for mother. "If Daddy lives through this, he'll kill her for running up that expense," I told my husband.

"Let her worry about that when the time comes," Carlton told me. "Whatever you do, don't get into an argument now."

"I have enough sense to know that," I told him, angry because he thought he had to tell me how to behave around my own sister. Since we had a room now, I called Mrs. Grant back to tell her the number but I listened to the phone ring in an apparently empty house. She had probably taken the boys out for ice cream, I told Carlton. Or to play a quick set of tennis, he said, which is when I noticed the rain had stopped and the sun was shining. I was surprised to find that it was after three o'clock in the afternoon. "I'd better call Grandma and tell her where we are and what's happening," I said to the room at large.

Carlton nodded to me. Mother was lying down on the bed, which I'm sure the nurse expected to use for my father when he came out of surgery, and Claire Louise had gone down to the cafeteria to bring her and Mother back something to eat. Since Mother's head was splitting, she had a cold cloth on it and didn't think she would be able to go downstairs. She was able, however, to sit up and eat every bite Claire Louise brought back. After she laid back down, Carlton and I went on down to get something to eat, and then we all just sat and made dispirited conversation until the doctors came in to say surgery had gone fine and my father was in recovery. They expected to keep him in intensive care through the night, so Claire Louise suggested that Carlton and I go on home and she and Mother stay there. She had already requested and had installed a rollaway bed and had arranged her toiletries on the shelf in the bathroom.

By the time I got back down there at ten o'clock the next morning she had them moved down the hall to a room large enough for a hospital bed, a couch that pulled out into a bed, and a double rollaway. She had also been out to the house and had come back with fresh clothes and her toaster oven and little coffeepot and a sack of groceries. Looked like when Daddy did get out of intensive care, she planned to set up housekeeping.

Daddy stayed in the hospital almost two weeks that time, and when he went home it was with Claire Louise in full cry as head nurse. She had his old oak bed pushed up against the wall when she got him home, and in the middle of the room was a hospital bed she had rented. Daddy like to came unglued when he saw that bed. "What in tarnation is this?" he roared, and I could hear him clear as glass down in the basement where I was sorting out clothes for the wash.

I couldn't hear what she and Mother told him, but the man came out within two hours and loaded up that bed and took it back to the store, and Daddy slept in his bed he'd inherited from his grandmother and grandfather the year before he and my mother married. Claire Louise had taken advantage of his absence to clean out his closet and his bureau drawers, and had even taken it upon herself to get into his desk and file cabinet and neaten that up, too, as she told him. I overheard every single word of the conversation when he was letting her have it for messing in his business, because I was right next door in Mother's room folding up the laundry and there's not a wall thick enough to muffle the voices when Daddy's on a tirade.

"Those are my clothes in that closet and in that bureau and you have no call to decide what can be thrown out and what cannot. Now you better get yourself downstairs to wherever you put my clothes and get them right back up here. Do you understand me?"

"Daddy, for heaven's sake, keep your voice down. You're just out of the hospital and you're recuperating from surgery. I'll get your clothes back like you had them if you'll calm down."

"See that you do. Have you been messing in any of my other things?" he asked her.

I held my breath, as nervous for her as if I hadn't been hoping for her to get her comeuppance, ever since I had come out last week and found her in his desk with all his papers spread out all over the dining-room table and floor. When I had asked her what she was doing, she'd told me she was organizing things for him and for me not to go down to that hospital and mention it and get him all worried, with him laid up and not able to tend to his own business. Well, Daddy was home from the hospital and tending to his own business now and from the sound of things Claire Louise should have been regretting she'd been meddling.

"Claire Louise," he said, his voice low and angry, "do you mean to tell me you've been in my desk?"

"Not in your desk, Daddy," she whined, "I just cleaned it up a bit on top so I could see to dust it. I couldn't have you coming home from the hospital to a house all dusty, now could I? Think of the germs."

"Germs, hell, Claire Louise, and quit fluffing up my pillows. I'm telling you for the last time now. You mess with my desk or my papers or my clothes again and you're out! Do you hear me? Out! Kids to raise on your own or not, this is my house and my farm and when I want your advice or your meddling I'll tell you so. Do you hear me?"

"Yes, I hear you. I expect they can hear you in the next county. Now you listen to me, everything I did was for one purpose and one purpose alone, to help you and Mother. You were laid up in the hospital and couldn't take care of your own business, and Mother is helpless, as you well know. So I stepped in and took charge and you were glad enough for me to be looking after things when you were flat on your back, which you will be again, you mark my words, if you don't quit this ranting and raving."

"I may be flat on my back, Claire Louise, but you are going to be flat on your ass out of here if I find you messing in my things one more time."

By now I had given up all pretense of folding clothes and was sitting on Mother's bed in the next room with my mouth hanging open listening to every word they said. My father was as hateful as I'd ever heard him, and I'd have thought Claire Louise would have been dripping tears and wringing her hands to get him to show a little sympathy.

"Claire Louise, get out of my room now." He wasn't talking defiant now, he sounded tired and sick. Surprises never cease—Claire Louise, never one to let anyone else have the last word, left.

After I heard her shut his door and walk down the stairs, I sat on Mother's bed holding my breath. Gradually, I realized the bones in my hands were hurting, I had my fists clenched so tight. My chest felt tight, too, like my heart was filled up with tears busting to get out. But I didn't cry. I felt too scared to cry, I felt as scared as if my life were in danger.

I had to get out of there. I stood up and walked across the hall to my bathroom. Turning on the light, I stared at the room. I felt completely disoriented. Something was wrong but I couldn't think what. I opened the door to my bedroom and stared at the twin beds with their frilly canopies and the posters on the wall when Mother expressly forbids hanging anything up and making holes in her plaster. Ever so slowly, I remembered, this wasn't my room any longer. I wasn't Macy Richards any longer. I was Macy Porter, I told myself, I had a husband and two sons and I did not live here. It seemed hours before the pounding stopped and then my tears started. I felt as tired as if I had been running a race for years. I was so tired I thought if I didn't find a quiet place to rest, I would fall down where I stood. I walked down the stairs hanging on the wall like an old lady. I could hear my mother and Claire Louise in the kitchen, so I turned and went out the front door and walked over to Grandma's. She was out back with her hands in soapy water in the big wash sink she has in the old servant's room next to her garage. I heard her singing off-key as I walked up the driveway. "Grandma," I told her, "I'm tired. I need to take a nap."

She turned and looked at me and came over and put her hand on my forehead. She smelled all damp and sweaty. "Are you sick?" she asked me, and I felt sure we'd done this before. The scene felt like I was watching it from a screen in a movie theater. I'd been here before, I'd seen this one.

"Where's Carlton?" she asked, and I remembered my husband with a start.

"Oh, I guess he's at Mother and Daddy's." I stood and looked at her stupidly waiting for her to rescue me from my confusion.

"Come on inside, you can lay down and I'll call him and tell him where you are."

When I woke up, it was dark outside and I could hear Carlton in the kitchen talking to my grandmother. I pictured them sitting at the round table with the glass top, which had every picture I had ever drawn for Grandma pressed under the top. When the table had gotten crowded she had started overlapping and when she had overlapped all she could, she'd just layered. No telling how many pictures were under there. And not a one from Claire Louise, I thought, wondering where that thought came from. Claire Louise never made pictures for my grandmother. I was the artist, the one who drew little pictures and wrote little books. Not her, just me.

From the sounds of silver hitting china I knew they were eating something and I suddenly felt ravenously hungry. Getting up, I stood shakily for a minute, my head spinning as if I had a fever. What's wrong with me, I wondered, but even as I thought that, my head began to clear. I'm just hungry, I told myself, heading for the kitchen.

12

AFTER I MOVED back out to the farm to look after Mother and Daddy, I realized that I was going to have to make an effort to maintain my friendships with people in town or I would become resentful of my parents for the sacrifices I was making for them. Mother in particular was perfectly happy with me there to take her into town once a day to pick up something at the grocery store or get her hair done or check to see if the variety store had any new piece goods in. Not that I minded doing for her, I didn't mind for a minute. I had joined her Methodist Women's Circle and the UDAC and DAR and had become active in the garden club a good two years before I moved out there. And of course I still helped out at the children's school, although Britt was in high school and Maryanne finishing elementary and there was simply not the same need for parent volunteers there had been in the past when the children were younger. And with my father off the school board, I didn't feel the same degree of responsibility either.

One of the things I vowed was to get out one day a week and go to Houston, shopping or visiting art galleries or seeing a film. I had never taken much time for myself and certainly had had little time for cultural pursuits before now, but I promised myself I would begin taking the time. It was time I started doing for myself.

After I gave up my position as elementary guidance counselor, Mary Beth Wilder and I became close friends. It just so happened that the first year I was not working at the elementary school was the year her own three children were all in public school, and the year she was finally able to hire enough teachers for our preschool so that she did not have to be there all the time. And given time to sit and visit, which we fell into the habit of doing every morning after we got the kids off to school, we discovered we had more in common than we ever would have guessed. We must have had coffee together every morning for the two years before I moved back out to the country.

I suppose the first bond between us was forged simply because we were two of the extremely few women in town raising children without husbands to support us. And we were both proud that we were able to stand on our own two feet without being dependent on any man. Not that either one of us had anything against men, you understand, or would have been upset if Mr. Right were to come along, but it was a source of pride to us that neither of us had stayed in a loveless relationship for the sake of the children.

Mary Beth's husband, Michael Wilder, had been in my class in high school. She was a year younger than I was. Try as we did, I didn't remember very much about her from back in high school, although I did remember Michael. Back then he had been captain of the football team, and since I had been a cheerleader we had been paired off on more than one occasion. We had even dated some the year I was a sophomore, although once I started going out with Ralph I never so much as saw anyone else. Mary Beth was shy in school and never had a date before she went to college. Funny thing, she went away to school for four years and came back home and married the boy she says she had a crush on the whole time she was in junior high and high school. And she says she knew even before the wedding

she was making a mistake, that she didn't want to marry someone whose highest ambition was to have box-seat season tickets
to the Garfield High home games. But when she came home
and he started asking her out, she couldn't say no to him. She'd
spent too many years praying he would notice her. And before
she knew it she was married to him and fixing lunches for him
to carry every day when he went in to work for Houston Light &
Power, like he still does to this day. And by the time they had
three kids she had given up on begging him to take advantage
of the company offer to pay his schooling at U of H so he could
finish his college degree and move ahead. Which is when she
realized it was up to her to get a job and bring in the extra
money they needed every month just to make ends meet. That's
why she jumped at the chance to go to work for me in my preschool and later at the chance to take the business over. By then
she knew that Michael was sleeping with one of the little twits
who had been a cheerleader at the high school not four years ago
and now was running the drive-in window at the bank. So she
told him to get out. He and Lorna Hayes were soon living over
across from the bank in one of the apartments they made out of
Mrs. Lehmann's house, and every other weekend Mary Beth's
three kids took their sleeping bags over there and spent Friday
and Saturday nights sleeping on the hard floors in their living
room. Next thing you heard Lorna was pregnant, and she and
Michael were getting married. "Mark my words," I told Mary
Beth, "that little place they are in is barely big enough for two
people, and if I am any judge of human nature Lorna will be
wanting to give up her job before the ink is dry on her wedding
certificate. Michael may find that young love is not all that it is
cracked up to be."

When I walked in to pick up Mary Beth for our shopping trip
the day after the news was all over town that Lorna and Michael

had taken out a marriage license over at the courthouse, I could tell Mary Beth was upset just by the feel of the air in the house. "What's wrong?" I asked her.

"What makes you think something is wrong?" she snapped at me. Mary Beth has a temper, which I have learned to ignore.

"Oh, just the fact that you're breathing fire was a little clue to me."

"Well, I am madder than shit."

"Why don't you tell me what's wrong, but watch your language, please. You know how I feel about profanity."

"Sorry, but Michael makes me so mad!"

"What did he do this time?"

"You knew Lorna is pregnant? So now she and Michael are getting married Saturday at his mother's, and he wants the children all to bring something nice to wear when I drop them off Friday afternoon. I told him Mikey has outgrown everything he owns except those gunboat-looking sneakers and if he wants anything else on his feet, he will have to buy them himself. And the girls have their Easter dresses and that's it! Lorna had wanted them to wear pink, since they will be standing up with her and Michael! Doesn't that just gag you? Well, their dresses are navy, and if precious Lorna doesn't like that then it is just tough shit as far as I am concerned. Sorry, Claire Louise, it slipped out."

"And have you heard what Lorna thinks of this?"

"Yes, Michael has called back twice already and is now threatening to come over and go through their closets and find something more appropriate to wear to a wedding than navy. I told him if he set foot in my house, I'd call the sheriff and have him arrested for breaking and entering. So then his mother called and asked couldn't she take the children into Houston today after school and buy them something to wear, because all this arguing back and forth was taking all the pleasure out of what is supposed to be a joyous occasion. I informed her as far as I was concerned this was no joyous occasion unless she was calling to tell me Michael and his precious Lorna were moving way the hell out of town. Sorry, Claire Louise, I forgot again."

"So are you going to let them go shopping with Mrs. Wilder?"

"I guess I'll have to. I'm not about to buy them clothes, and if I refuse to let her take them she'll just give the money to Michael and Lorna and they'll go get them something. I trust Michael's mother's taste more than his little slut's."

"Mary Beth, you know how I feel about profanity."

"Oh yeah, sorry."

"Why don't you get the money from Mrs. Wilder and buy the clothes today when we're shopping? That way they'll have something you like, and Lorna doesn't." I grinned at her. Although I was not proud of myself, I was feeling distinctly uncharitable toward Michael Wilder and his cute little fiancée. I had quit going to the drive-in window just to avoid having her tell me to have a nice day.

Mary Beth grinned back at me. Great idea, she said, and that is how Allison and Ashley Wilder came to wear Hawaiian-print sundresses to their father's wedding to Lorna Hayes. It was a big disappointment to me and Mary Beth that we never saw the wedding pictures.

After Michael married Lorna, Mary Beth became obsessed with what they were doing and took to grilling the children every Sunday night when he dropped them off. Mary Beth and I often went into Houston to catch a matinee on Sunday afternoons that summer while my kids swam at Grandma's and hers visited at their father's, and I tried to tell her giving the kids the third degree the minute they walked in the door was not cool. "There are other ways of finding out what you want to know. You watch me when they come in tonight, and whatever you do, don't interrupt. In fact, it would probably be better if you stayed in the kitchen like you were cooking or doing the dishes."

Mikey came in first, carrying his book bag, followed by Allison and Ashley, who were sunburned a bright red. "Oh, my goodness," I said, "don't those sunburns hurt?" That was the wrong thing to say because Mary Beth was in the living room before the words were out of my mouth good.

"Where have you been?" she shrieked. "Look at you! Hasn't that idiot wife of your father's heard of sunscreen?"

You could just see those three kids shut down as she yelled at them, like it was their fault their father had married someone else. "Mary Beth, I know you are busy in the kitchen, now you run on back in there and I will tend to these sunburns." I gave her a meaningful look and she turned and went to the kitchen, leaving the door open behind her.

"Now Mikey, do you know what Noxzema is? You do? Well, run on in the bathroom and bring me the bottle and you girls take off those shirts and let me see how bad it is."

They were only six that year, and both of them had lost their two front teeth, which gave them identical snaggle-toothed grins. Their short brown hair was cut in little Dutch-boy cuts and they were still small for their ages. Right now their big brown eyes were huge, as they watched the kitchen door waiting for Mary Beth to swoop back in and shout some more venom at them. I started talking as I rubbed their shoulders and backs with the white greasy liquid. "Oh, this isn't too bad. It'll probably turn to tan in a day or two. I'll bet you weren't out in the sun that long after all."

"No," Ashley said uncertainly. Mikey interrupted her. "We were in the pool at the house that my daddy and Lorna are going to live in."

"Oh, your daddy and Lorna are moving."

"Hm-mm. They have to get a house because the apartment is too small for a baby bed."

"And you got to see the new house and even swim in the pool?" I probed.

"Yes, because it already belongs to Lorna's aunt, and Grammie is buying it from her for Lorna and my daddy, and the pool is for us, too. And we are going to have our own room there, too."

Now that Mikey had gotten the ball rolling, Ashley and Allison chimed in. "The house is big, much bigger than this one. There is a room for Daddy and Lorna, and a baby room, and a blue room for Mikey, and Lorna is going to paint our room yellow. And we can have bunk beds if we want!"

"That sounds wonderful, but you know I can't imagine such a house in this town, and I thought I knew all the houses in Molly's Point."

"It's a long ways from here, almost to Houston."

"Oh, I wonder why they would want to live away from here."

"Grammie said it was too nice a house to pass up."

"Well, you girls look better now. Mikey, I don't think you even need any lotion. Now you run on into your rooms and unpack your suitcases. I think your mother almost has dinner ready to put on the table. Oh, is your daddy moving right soon?

"I don't know. I think so, because the men were packing the boxes."

"Doesn't that beat all?" Mary Beth muttered to me as she grated cheese for the hot dogs. "The whole time I was married to him his mother never gave us so much as a tea towel, and now she's buying him and that slut a goddamn house with a fucking swimming pool!"

"Mary Beth!" I remonstrated, "I will not stay here and listen to that language!"

"Oh, shit, Claire Louise, I'm sorry. Can't you see how upset I am?"

"Yes, and it's no good crying over spilled milk. You are just going to have to sit down and figure out what to do about it."

"What I'm going to do about it? What on earth could I do?"

"Well, I'm not one to tell a person how to do their own business but if it were me I would see my lawyer."

"What on earth would I see a lawyer for?"

"Well, for starters, I would check into my child support situation. Michael and Lorna are driving around in a new car and now they're getting a big new house with a pool and here you and your three children sit in a little bitty two-bedroom rent house. That doesn't seem quite fair and I'll bet the judge wouldn't consider it fair, either. Michael could be made to provide better for his three kids, it seems to me." I gave her a level look.

"But, Claire Louise, where would he get the money?"

"That shouldn't have to be your concern, but it occurs to me he might get it the same place he's getting the money for his new house. If his mother can afford one house, chances are she can afford two."

13

MACY, THIS was supposed to be the year you were going to have some time for yourself," Carlton said to me as I rushed around jerking pillows into place and hiding dishes in the sink. "As it is, you rush the boys off to school, come home and fly through the house until I'm ready to leave for the office, and then charge out to Molly's Point and spend all day out there. Do you realize this is Thursday and I have had to leave the office every day this week and bring the boys home for Mrs. Grant to look after until you could get here? Last night that wasn't until after six o'clock."

"Carlton, last night was unusual. I'm not going to be that late again. It was just that Grandma wanted me to help her dig up those bulbs and . . ."

"And tonight it will be something else. You have a family right here, Macy, and we're missing you."

"Carlton, don't you do it, too. Don't you make me feel guilty. I can't be in two places at once and I have to be out there. Ever since Daddy got sick, I have this feeling that if I'm not there something terrible is going to happen. Mother doesn't look good, you know. Since Claire Louise moved in, she has lost about forty pounds. And Grandma is getting so feeble, I just want to cry seeing her hobble around. I can't help it, Carlton, I would never forgive myself if something happened to them and I had let them down in their last days."

"Your mother has lost weight because Claire Louise has put her on a diet and is rationing food to her and Maryanne like it's fat camp out there. You know that, you're the one who told me! And your Grandmother is over eighty years old; it's not unexpected she would be slowing down. No matter how many bulbs you help her plant, you're not going to change the fact that she is getting older. But it's not like she's out there in that old house all alone. Belle is there with her now, and she's doing fine. I think you need to look at what's really going on with you."

"What do you mean, going on with me? I'm dealing with a series of stressful situations and I'm doing the best I can." Sometimes I hated the fact I was married to a psychologist. I kept getting therapy whether I wanted it or not. "Carlton, we don't have time to go into this, you're going to be late to work."

"No, I'm not. I've got the morning off and we're going to go sit out on the porch and talk."

"But I can't, I've got a million things to do."

"At your parents'?"

"And my grandmother's!"

"Name one thing you have to do today that is more important than us."

"Carlton, don't be an ass. There isn't anything more important than us, but that's not the issue here."

"Yes, Macy, it is. You and I haven't talked in over two weeks other than to exchange schedules. You haven't been in to have a session with Abe either, not for over a year. Don't look at me like that. Of course I checked with him. You're my wife and I care about you, for God's sake. You're running around in a panic all the time and something has to get resolved. For your sake, first of all, but ultimately for the sake of your relationship with me and Travis and Scott . . ."

"Carlton, I do not want to get into this now. I'm late as it is."

"Well, will you make an appointment and go in and talk to Abe then? Because I am serious, Macy, we can't go on like this. It's been over six months now since your father's heart attack, and you've been out there every single day."

"I'm not going to promise anything, Carlton, and I resent you pushing me like this. I hope you enjoy your morning off. If I had known you were going to take the time, I would have tried to stay home, but as it is, it's too late for me to change my plans."

"What plans?" he asked, startling me when he put both his hands on my arms and jerked me around to face him. "What plans do you have?" he said.

I hadn't seen Carlton this angry and it scared me, the roughness with which he touched me and the anger I saw in his eyes.

"None of your business what I have to do out there!" I didn't mean that, but I just couldn't cope with him too, not then, not with my father looking grayer every day and my mother losing weight faster than was good for her and my grandmother getting so old she leaned on the railing to go up and down the stairs and took a nap every afternoon. Carlton was younger, he was my age. He wasn't old. I couldn't cope with him too, it was just too much to ask.

"Look, Carlton, I promise I'll be in early tonight and we'll have a nice dinner together, I promise, okay? And I'll work out something with my family, but today I have to run."

"Have you forgotten tonight is the night we're supposed to go to Heather's wedding?"

"Oh, my gosh, I did! What time is that thing?" I began frantically digging through the basket on the counter, which held the things I still had to do. "It's not here! Will you leave a message on the machine about when it is? And ask Mrs. Grant to keep the boys? I'll try to be home, by . . ."

"No! No! No!" Carlton exploded. "I will not leave a message or ask Mrs. Grant or go to the damn thing by myself like I did the PTA meeting last week and the dinner for the Stokeses the week before that!"

"I'll be home by five," I said, backing out the door. I didn't slam it, I didn't even shut it.

As I drove out to Mother and Daddy's I kept hearing Carlton yelling no, no, no at me. No, no, no echoed round and round in my head. I couldn't get it out—no, no, no. I didn't cry, I felt frozen up, too cold to cry. I knew I was going to lose somebody, maybe everybody, and I was powerless to stop it. Grandma would die and she wouldn't be there to make it all right anymore. And my father would die and he'd never love me, and my mother would always listen to Claire Louise and take her side of things, and no matter how much I did for her or fixed for her or if I came out there every single day, she would still like Claire Louise better. It was hopeless. And now Carlton was mad at me, too. Carlton, who understood what a rotten childhood I had had and didn't like my parents all that much, he was turning on me and I didn't know what I could do about that, either.

Claire Louise was just backing her car out of the garage when I drove up. "Where are you going?" I asked her, seeing Mother sitting there staring straight ahead at the gate. As I pulled my car into the driveway beside the back door, Claire Louise pulled up beside me. "It's Thursday, beauty shop day."

"I forgot. Do you want me to drive Mother in?"

"No, I've got groceries to pick up and I'm stopping by the feed store for Daddy. He's over in Hillsdale for the auction today and so Mother and I thought we would just lunch at the café." She pointedly didn't ask me to join them, but sat there idling her engine waiting for me to get the hint I wasn't needed and drive away. I'll be damned, I thought.

"Well, I'll just go in and see what needs doing," I said, determined she wasn't going to run me off from my own parents' house.

"Oh, it's locked!"

"I've got a key," I reminded her.

"No, actually you don't. Since Mother thought she heard someone outside last week, I had all the locks changed. For her peace of mind."

"And you didn't give me a key?" I asked, furious with her.

"It must have slipped my mind, and we're late now. Toodles!"

That bitch, I thought, watching her drive away. I waited until she was long out of sight before I started up my car and drove over to Grandma's. I was tempted to get a crowbar and break down that back door, new lock and all, but, as usual, I was too chicken.

Grandma and Belle had pulled all the furniture out from around the pool and on the porch and were hosing it down. "Can you do that to wicker?" I asked.

"Sure, it's good for it," Grandma told me. Her face was beet red but it was good to see her looking perky and up doing. For all she was over eighty, she was in a sight better shape than my mother, who had sat around with her hands folded waiting for someone to do for her as long as I could remember.

"Remember when you used to make me fudge, Grandma?" I asked her. "I'd come in and say I was hungry what do you have to eat, and you'd say we can always make fudge and we'd melt the chocolate chips and marshmallow cream and what all. Do you remember that?"

"Of course I remember!"

"Do you want to make fudge today?" I asked her, feeling like I was going to cry whatever she said.

"Are you hungry? I think we have some M & M's in there, don't we, Belle?"

"Yes, we do, there's a candy jar full in the living room on the mantel."

"I'm not hungry. Can I help you?"

"Pick up that wire brush and scrape the loose paint off that wicker."

After we worked for an hour or so out in the hot sun, we went inside and fixed sandwiches and iced tea for lunch. When Grandma lay down for her nap, I went in the living room and got the jar of candy off the mantel and sat down in front of the television. Belle came in and sat down beside me and we watched soap operas and ate M & M's together in silence.

"You're not yourself today, are you?" she asked me when I picked up the remote control and clicked the show off in the middle of a love scene.

"Belle, what am I going to do?" I asked her. "Carlton thinks I'm spending too much time out here, and yet I worry every minute if I'm not here with them."

"What you worried about?"

"Mostly about Grandma getting old and dying before Mother and Daddy like me as much as Claire Louise, I think."

Belle had been cleaning for my grandmother and my mother for longer than I'd been born, and she probably knew more about our family than any one of us did. She didn't bother to argue with me that my parents liked me as well as Claire Louise. She knew better. "You're not going to make them feel one bit different about you, coming out here every day and hanging around exchanging words with your sister. And your grandma do be getting old, just like the rest of us, every day we be a day older."

"You're not, Belle, you're not getting older. You haven't changed a bit."

"Fact is, I have been changing. Went to the doctor last week and had my heart checked. He told me it's time for me to quit working, go live with my daughter down near Houston and take it easy."

"But I thought you told me her kids would drive you crazy."

"That was ten years ago, Macy. I've got me two great-grandchildren now. It would just be me and Janie and her youngest daughter living there in her house."

"Have you told Grandma?" I asked her. "I don't know how she'll manage without you."

"No, I haven't said anything to her. I wanted to talk to you first. Had me some ideas about what she might do, but I didn't want to mention it to her until I talked to you. It occurred to me she might move in at that home down there where her sister Gertrude lived. Nothing wrong with that place that I can see."

"Grandma hated that place."

"I know. But it wasn't that bad, and she might like it once she moved in. As things stand now, Claire Louise is over here at least once a day poking her nose into things, and your grandma gets right nervous when she's around."

"You didn't tell me she's been coming over here every day." I felt a surge of anger. Even Grandma, who liked me best, she wouldn't leave alone. She had Mother and Daddy. Why did she have to try to take Grandma too? "What does she come over here for?"

"Oh, she's been asking right much questions about what all the bottom land is being used for, now that those men want to drill on it, and your grandma said no thank you. Claire Louise worried her and worried her to let her take care of it. Your grandma had to finally get right short with her and tell her to tend to her own knitting. Then she wanted to take your grandma in to see that lawyer friend of hers, help her get her affairs in order. Your grandma told her your grandfather done left her affairs in order when he died and she hadn't done nothing to upset them, wasn't likely to at this late date."

"I'll kill her, I'll kill that conniving witch. Why can't she leave people alone? You should have told me about this sooner, Belle." I looked in my lap and saw hands that had to be mine clutching and unclutching each other frantically. They were familiar hands, someone's I knew, but I couldn't for the life of me figure out who they belonged to. Quickly I unclutched them and jammed them under my legs to get them out of my sight. "What am I going to do? If you leave, Belle, it will be just her and them. I cannot bear the thought of my grandma out here alone in this house and no one next door to her but my parents and Claire Louise and her two self-centered brats. I can't leave Grandma out here all alone with them, Belle. You know how she used to look after me when I lived here. How can I leave her alone with them?"

With them, with them, with them, it echoed in my head like a metal bucket was stuck on top of my head and someone was drumming those words at me. With them, with them, with them.

"Your grandma ain't all that helpless, Macy. Your sister has been worrying her, but she stands up to her right good. She don't need anyone to look after her."

"But she's over eighty years old, Belle. Claire Louise will wear her down, I know she will." I could tell Belle didn't truly believe my grandmother would be safe out here alone, and her next words convinced me I was right.

"Well, with that new freeway fixed up the way it is nice and smooth and all, you can get out here in next to no time. You been coming out every day as it is. You just keep looking in on her every day and I 'spect she'll be fine."

"But Carlton and I had a fight this morning about me coming out here every day. I can't be in two places at once. You know I can't do that, Belle. I'm going to have to move out here myself if you leave."

"What you 'spect your sister to do to your grandma?"

"Look at Mother, she's walking around looking like a ghost and nodding and whining like a puppet when Claire Louise lets her talk. And she drove Daddy into a heart attack with her lies. The worse she gets, the more they let her get away with it. Well, she's not going to get to Grandma too. Grandma likes me best!" I was crying now and Belle was now, now-ing me like she'd done in the past. "Don't tell anyone you want to move in with your daughter yet, Belle, give me a week or two to work on Carlton. If he'll just go along with it, we can move out here and I can look after Grandma and watch what Claire Louise is up to and be with my own family as well. I don't know why I didn't think of this before!"

Belle didn't answer me. She just raised her eyebrows, the way she does when she doesn't think much of what she's hearing. She was right. Carlton didn't think much of my idea after all.

"Move to Molly's Point! Live with your grandmother! You have got to be out of your mind, Macy! Just this morning I told you I thought you were spending entirely too much time out there, and now you want us all to move in with your grandmother. I don't believe this conversation."

"Carlton, just listen to me. Calm down and listen. I admit the idea is a little startling. It surprised me when I first thought of it myself, but the more I thought the better it seemed. Just give me a chance to explain, please."

"I'll listen, but I'm telling you up front that there is nothing you can say that is going to convince me it is a good idea for all four of us to move in with your grandmother. Do you hear me, Macy?"

"Yes, but listen, Carlton, you're thinking like I was, back before all the changes that have occurred in the past few years. The new road is finished all the way out there and it takes less than thirty minutes to drive from your office to Grandma's. Less than thirty minutes! Think of it. We're way over here on the other side of town so it takes us an hour to get out there, but if we lived at Grandma's you could get into work in the same amount of time it's taking you to drive to the office every day right now. And the school out there is such a good little school. The boys could go to the same school I went to, and we wouldn't have to worry about drugs and crime and all the stuff you hear about in the city schools. You know we have been talking about private schools for that very reason, and think what a savings it would be not to have to pay tuition somewhere for two children for twelve years. And if we sell our house here, after all we've done to it, we'll make a huge profit and we could use that money for the building you and Abe are talking about buying. And living with Grandma our expenses would be cut to nothing."

"Are you through?"

I nodded at him, anxiously watching for the effect all my carefully wrought arguments were having on him.

"First, I didn't realize we were looking to cut our living expenses to next to nothing. Second, Abe and I have already been working on the financing for the new office. I don't believe either of us expects to have to sell our homes to buy an office. Third, the children are only five, we don't have to worry about crime and drugs for a few years yet. And fourth, and most important, as much as I love your grandmother, I do not want to live with her or, for that matter, in that little town you grew up in. I like our house in the city, thank you very much." He had counted his reasons off on his fingers as he'd enumerated them and I just sat there, dumber than a post as Mother would have said. When Carlton talked in paragraphs I felt lectured to, as if I were a child and he an adult. This was so important to me. I felt as if my sole purpose right now was to protect my grandmother, and yet I couldn't think of a single thing to say to convince Carlton to move out there with me.

"I have to, Carlton, I don't know all the reasons why, but I have to move out there." I felt as gray as Daddy looked as we talked, gray and hopeless and overwhelmingly tired. It didn't seem as if I'd ever be able to do another thing. I heard the kids in the den watching "Sesame Street" and I knew I needed to get up and heat up some supper and get dressed for that wedding, but I felt glued to the sofa. It was as if all my stamina had melted, like a can of Crisco accidentally set on a stove burner. Now I'd sprung a leak and oozed out and run into the piece of furniture I sat on. There seemed to be no possibility of moving. I was gone, all run down into nothing but a gray greasy stream. "I have to go," I repeated, but I wasn't sure whether I was talking about to my grandmother's or to the kitchen or to the wedding or where. Then I was crying, hopeless tears, unaware tears, old tears, tears that fell out of my eyes like they were spilling over because there was no room for them anywhere in me anymore. Carlton leaned over and put his arms around me and I melted into him, nuzzling forward looking for my grandmother's soft sweaty smell.

"Macy, we'll work this out. We will. You're not a little girl anymore."

I listened to him and I knew he didn't understand. No one understood but Grandma, and she was over eighty years old and when she was gone there would be no one in the world on my side. Belle was going to her daughter's, and Claire Louise had the rest of them, and all the aunts and cousins in the world didn't make a bit of difference when you were in trouble and they weren't there and you were. I tried to tell Carlton but my words melted into tears before they came out. "I'm tired," I said. "I think I'll take a little nap before dinner." We had been sitting on the couch in our bedroom and I got up and walked unsteadily toward the bed.

"I'll fix some dinner for the children," Carlton said, and I was too tired even to thank him.

I woke in a panic several hours later. "I've got to get up," I said, thinking I was talking to myself until I realized Carlton was on the couch across from me, the small reading light on and a magazine open in his lap.

"It's ten o'clock at night, Macy," he said, watching me peer at the clock on the bedside table. It was as if he could read my mind; I had been trying to figure out if the ten o'clock meant daytime or nighttime.

"We missed the wedding. I'm sorry, Carlton, really I am."

"I know you are, you're always sorry after you've missed something lately. Listen to me, Macy, sorry is well and good, but it isn't enough. We've got to get this situation resolved."

"I know," I sighed, wishing he would move over to the bed and put his arms around me. "I know I've been neglecting you and Scott and Travis. I just don't seem to be able to help it."

"Do you have any idea why you have such a compulsion to be out there every waking hour, particularly as you are not always treated especially well by your sister and your mother?"

Without thinking about it, I got up and walked over and settled next to Carlton on the couch. He put his arm around me and I felt like I was safe again, like for a while I could let myself think about things. "I love you, Carlton, and I know it's crazy to go out there all the time like I've been doing. You are the only person in the world besides my grandmother I've ever felt completely safe with. But you see that's part of it, I keep needing to fix it up with them."

"Do you really believe that Claire Louise is so crafty she can fool your mother all the time, Macy? Think, Macy, your mother is not stupid. She chooses who to love and who to listen to and who to believe. If, as you say, Claire Louise tells lies to your mother about you all the time, then your mother is choosing to ignore all conflicting evidence and believe her. Can you see that?"

"Don't you believe Claire Louise is a liar?" I asked.

"Yes, I do. I've seen her in action a time or two myself, but I hold with my statement that your mother is smart enough to figure that out for herself if she wants to."

"I know you're right. Sometimes I wish I had taken advantage of all those years Claire Louise was gone to turn them against her like she has turned them against me."

"Then you'd be just like her, Macy. Do you want that?"

"No, but I'm tired of always being odd man out. I go out there and it's like I'm in her way!"

"So why do you keep going?"

I sighed. "I don't know, Carlton, truly I don't. Most days I go over and hang around there and do some laundry for Mother or something and then when she sits down to watch her morning shows, Claire Louise starts something she has in mind to do and doesn't need me for, and I go over to Grandma's and stay there. I like it at Grandma's. It's safe there."

"Why is it safe, Macy?" Carlton asked me.

The room was still and cool and the house was quiet, it felt so good to be there, close with Carlton. Why hadn't I known how much I missed this? "I always was safe at Grandma's when I was little. Sometimes when I'd get scared, I'd go over there and stay for several days if Mother and Daddy would let me. Usually they would."

"Do you want to talk about why you were scared?"

"I don't remember, not exactly. I just got scared."

"Were you scared of your sister or your parents?"

"When I was little and Claire Louise was still home, I was scared lots for her. When she got punished, I would turn up the

140

television loud so I couldn't hear. And my mother screamed a lot. Loud noises scared me. I'd run over to Grandma's and she'd tell me not to worry, I was okay, to put it all out of my mind. Then we'd play cards or plant flowers or do a paint-by-number picture."

"Macy, you haven't mentioned your father."

"I don't want to talk about him. He wasn't very involved with us, not ever." I shook my head at Carlton. I didn't want to talk about my family anymore.

"Carlton, it's April coming up summer again. Could we just stay out at Grandma's for the summer, just a little while? One summer. I know you think I'm crazy to want to be out there and I'm not even saying you're wrong, but if I could just have a little time there with her, with Grandma before it's too late."

"Too late for what?" he asked me.

"Too late to thank her." I stopped, puzzled by my own reply. "I don't know what I mean, I just want to be out there with her for a little while. Please, Carlton. You know how the kids love it in the country during the summer, they can swim and ride horses and go to the beach. If we stay out there this summer, then Belle can go to her daughter's like she wants to and that will give us three months to find someone to move in with Grandma."

I felt a surge of hope when Carlton asked, "What about our house here, and our yard, and our friends?"

"They'll be okay for three months and we can come in every week or so and look after things, please, Carlton." I was pleading with him.

"Just for the summer?" he asked. "Macy, look at me, if we do this it is for summer vacation only, and you'll have to agree to that!"

"I will, I will, thank you, thank you." I hugged Carlton and covered his face with kisses.

"I must be nuts to go along with this. You haven't even talked to your grandmother. Louisa may not want us out there all summer long."

"Yes, she will! She'll love it, I know she will. Let's raid the refrigerator! I feel like a banana split!" I said, grabbing his hand and pulling him toward the kitchen.

"I am nuts," Carlton said, "but, Macy, it's times like right now I realize how hard this year has been. I love you, I miss being with you when you're not here, or even when you are here but so caught up in your family out there you might as well not be here. We'll go out there for the summer, but that's it. Do you truly understand what I'm agreeing to? We're going for a summer vacation, not to stay forever."

"I do, I understand! I promise!"

"My god, it's wonderful to see you acting like yourself again. Spontaneous and exuberant. I've missed these times with you, fattening or not," he added, as I scooped ice cream and poured chocolate sauce and sliced bananas and piled it all high in the bowls my grandmother had given me. When he came behind me to hug me, I pretended not to see the tears in his eyes. I didn't want to know I was hurting Carlton, too.

14

LIFE IS FUNNY. It seems as if you can spend most of one lifetime running frantically only to end up in the same place you started. At least that is how mine sometimes seemed to me. After I moved back out to the farm to look after Mother and Daddy, there were horrible days, days when I felt fourteen again and trapped out in the country without a hope of getting away. Truthfully, though, I didn't have many of those days. What I did when I got uneasy, like when I caught myself thinking what on earth am I doing back out here in this house with my parents for heaven's sake, what I did was I would sort of give myself a shake and tell myself to get busy, I had plans to make, things to accomplish. Looking back, that's what I remember most, the sense I had of time running out. I had so much to do, I truly did.

They were getting older, Mother and Daddy were, and Mother's sight was failing although she wouldn't admit it. And Daddy, the only thing he did that was on doctor's orders was to take the prescribed medication. He didn't stay out of the hot sun and he didn't rest every day, he didn't slow down at all. He was still up at the crack of dawn and in and out all day, just like he always had been. Stubborn he'd always been and stubborn he stayed.

One thing did change. Since I moved back home, he wasn't cooking the meals, as he had apparently started doing in the past few years. I did that, or Britt and Maryanne did, for I was teaching them to cook. I also had both Maryanne and Mother on a diet. We all were eating Weight Watchers meals, for that matter, and Mother looked better than I'd ever known her. She was losing weight so fast, though, that she had to get new clothes. There was a point beyond which Mrs. O'Reilly could not take up her old ones. Neither she nor Maryanne liked giving up the cakes and cookies they craved, but I watched them and made sure they stuck to their diets, and they both had to admit when we shopped for new clothes it was worth it to be getting into decent shape again. Fortunately, Britt and I never had any trouble with our weight. Good metabolism, I guess, like Daddy. He has always eaten what he wants.

I had been back in the country so long that sometimes I forgot

I had ever lived anywhere else. I got careless, but then I never truly expected to run into anyone I knew in Houston. It's such a huge city. And how could I have prevented it? It happened in the hall off the parking garage of St. Luke's Hospital. I had driven in to take Mother to get her eyes checked. We were going every three months then, and her glasses were getting changed almost every time. The elevator doors opened and we got into the empty car and on the way up to the eleventh floor the elevator stopped on seven, and Cheryl Wilcox got on with a young girl about Maryanne's age. She stared at me until the doors closed and then she turned her back on us and faced the door. She didn't push a button and I immediately felt afraid she was going to the same floor we were. Sure enough, when the elevator stopped on eleven she stepped aside to let Mother and me get off and then followed us into Dr. Teague's office. She hadn't spoken to me, hadn't even nodded and I began to hope she hadn't recognized me, but I knew that was futile. I'd seen the anger flare in her eyes when she saw me. Cheryl Wilcox, James's sister, knew who I was. The only question I had was what she planned to do about it.

If only I could get Mother out of there. I should have gotten off on the wrong floor. Mother wouldn't have noticed. But I'd been too surprised by Cheryl's appearance to think straight. I didn't want to arouse Mother's suspicions. She had no inkling James Wilcox and his sister had ever existed. I didn't want Cheryl to learn our names. To say I didn't trust Cheryl Wilcox Brooks was an understatement. I knew at the very least she would report back to James and that I did not want at all. The James Wilcox chapter of my life was closed. I wanted it to stay that way. "Sit here, Mother," I told her, settling her in a chair close to the door and the doctor's receptionist. Dr. Teague's outer office is one of those sitting-room arrangements with little clusters of seating separated by potted plants and tables covered with dimly lit lamps and magazines. When we walked in, the waiting room was completely empty, something I had never seen before. "Oh, dear," I said to Mother, wishing I hadn't already slipped up and called her Mother in front of Cheryl, "I wonder if we have our days wrong. I've never seen Dr. Teague's waiting room empty." Cheryl and the child with her were standing over by the door, waiting for us to settle and check in before they chose seats. Very polite is how it would have seemed to an observer, very unnerving it felt to me. I was feeling stalked.

I went over to the frosted window that separated the waiting room from the office area, thinking fast. Perhaps I could get inside the door before I gave any information. I prayed that the person who answered the bell wouldn't call me by name.

"Hi." I spoke quickly, gazing at the expressionless eyes of a nurse I had seen before but who apparently didn't recognize me. "I've brought Mother in for her appointment. Could I just step back into your rest room?" Damn, damn, double damn, I could tell by the way she narrowed her eyes and pursed her lips, pencil poised, she was going to be one of the officious ones. I widened my eyes and gave a fleeting grimace, hoping to convey a sense of urgency.

"There is a rest room out in the hall, second door to your left. What is your mother's name?"

I leaned forward, coughing as I did so. Mother was right there, she'd be saying her name to the girl if I didn't think of something. I coughed again, leaning over the counter as I did so, and pointing helplessly to the box of tissues I saw there. I grabbed at my throat feigning extreme discomfort. The girl followed my eyes and reached for the box of tissues and extended it to me. I was busily reading her appointment book upside down. "Oh, there we are," I said, making my voice sound strained as if speaking were difficult. "There," I repeated putting my finger under Mother's name, "she's Dr. Teague's nine o'clock."

"Oh, Mrs. Richards," said the nurse. As soon as she opened her mouth to respond I realized what was coming, and fell into another coughing fit hoping to keep her words from my ex-sister-in-law. I think I succeeded. She wasn't speaking that loudly, and Cheryl still stood over by the door. Not that it mattered. Cheryl took matters in her own hands to find out what she wanted to know.

"You can bring your mother on back," the receptionist chirped at me. I helped Mother up. Her knees had been bothering her and we had another appointment later that day with an orthopedist. I was wondering what on earth to do about Cheryl now. Even if she hadn't heard Mother's name, there was nothing to stop her from reading the appointment book exactly as I had done. There were only two names down for nine o'clock, Cherry Brooks, whom I would have bet money was Cheryl's daughter, and Mother's, Corabeth Richards. Damn, I was trapped. There was nothing to do but go into the little examination room with Mother.

Once inside I coughed again and said to Mother, "You stay here, I need to go out to the water fountain. I may be a minute, I seem to have a frog in my throat." The water fountain was behind the nurse's station, out of sight of anyone standing at the receptionist's window, but I could clearly hear the conversation being carried on. I stood at the fountain, taking little sips and making soothing motions on my throat to convince anyone who happened out that I was just nursing a sour throat.

"It's us, Elizabeth," Cheryl said. "I've got Cherry here with her scratched eye. It's so kind of you to squeeze us in."

"Oh, Dr. Teague wanted to see her ASAP. Can't have one of his favorite patients in pain. You will have to wait a minute or two, though, his nine o'clock just went in and Dr. Girard is out today, so it's just Dr. Teague seeing patients."

"Oh, we don't mind waiting. You know, the funniest thing, I thought I knew that woman who just went in with her mother. Was that Lana Anderson from Oklahoma?"

"No," the nurse laughed, "that was Claire Louise Richards, who brings her mother in here every three months. They live out near Galveston Island in a little town named Molly's Point. I doubt Mrs. Richards has ever been to Oklahoma. She told me last time she was here just coming into Houston was a big trip for her."

That bitch, I thought, she remembered my name the whole time.

"Small world," Cheryl mused. "I could have sworn that was a woman named Lana Anderson I knew over ten years ago. I don't suppose she could have married and her former name could have been Anderson, could it? I have the strangest feeling that is Lana and if so I don't want to pass up this chance to speak to her. But if she really isn't, well, I would be so embarrassed . . ."

"Let's see," said the nurse, and I could hear papers rustling. That fool was going through Mother's records. I felt like flying out there and jerking them out of her hands. "Mrs. Richards has been coming in to see Dr. Teague for almost fifteen years, but I really couldn't say what her daughter's name might have been. Wouldn't it have changed from Richards, though, if she had married?"

"You're right, I must be imagining things. Maybe Dr. Teague better check my eyes, too!"

"Not today," the nurse laughed.

"Well, let's see if you have any new magazines," Cheryl said, and I went back to Mother's cubicle, seething. The bitch, now she knows where I live.

Cheryl was nowhere in sight when we left Dr. Teague's office, Mother's new prescriptions in hand. We went down to the optician's office to order new glasses and then went over to the coffee shop to eat an early lunch before we saw the second doctor. By the time we were out of his office it was almost two o'clock and Mother was tired and cranky.

"This was too much, Claire Louise, two appointments in one day. Didn't I tell you I thought it would be better to get them on separate days?"

"Yes, you did," I answered her, trying not to grit my teeth. "But I have more to do than run down to Houston every single day with one of your ailments."

"Oh," she sniffed, offended. "Perhaps Macy could have taken me."

"Macy's too busy over at Grandma's," I told her. "I asked her last week if she couldn't run to the drugstore for you and she said she had to help Grandma bake cookies for her bridge club." That was a lie but Mother deserved it.

Let her stay angry, I thought. I have other things to think about. One of the things I had been sure of was that James Wilcox had no idea where I was. Now I was trying to puzzle how what harm it could do if he knew where to find me ten years after I had divorced him. None, I hoped, but I wasn't convinced. James might still want to find me. He might want to see Britt, although I had told him she wasn't his daughter before I left him. Actually, I had told him Britt was Ralph's, but I hadn't mentioned Maryanne. I hadn't even been sure I was pregnant when I left, not absolutely positive anyway, so James didn't know a thing about Maryanne. And to tell the truth, I am reasonably sure that Maryanne is not James's daughter, either. I think she is the child of Tom Smythe, the minister I was in love with years ago. But I can't be sure. From time to time I've looked at her trying to decide, but Maryanne doesn't look like either James or Tom, she looks like my mother. However, I never wanted child support from James, and Texas law has no alimony for ex-wives, so I saw no reason to maintain contact with James.

Of course that was ten years ago, and I had thought when I left Houston for Oklahoma that Tom Smythe and I would be getting married, so there had been obvious reasons not to have James hanging around. After I got my divorce, I even had my name changed back to Richards and Britt's as well. But as I say, that was a long time ago. Did it truly matter if James knew where I was at this late date? My common sense told me no, but still I was uneasy. It turns out that I had every right to be. James stirred up a pile of trouble when he came out to Molly's Point looking for me.

I ran the air conditioner full blast all the way home. Even though it was only late May, the temperature felt like August. Mother was in a snit the entire way, not talking to me, but I ignored her, thinking my own thoughts. The traffic was beastly, in spite of the fact that we left downtown Houston soon after two o'clock. How could I have imagined I would run into Cheryl Wilcox at the eye doctor's? I berated myself. Houston's filling up with over a thousand new people a week and so crowded you can barely get through Foley's department store and I had the colossal bad luck to run into Cheryl Wilcox in a waiting room that was usually standing room only, and us the only two people in the room. I don't know another person in a hundred would have had such bad luck. I am generally unlucky that way, which is why I have to work so hard to get what I want. Unlike some people, good things don't just fall in my lap. I have to work for them. And now I went round and round in my head trying to think what I needed to do next. Or in case. I am a firm believer in figuring out what to do in case. I try to figure out every possible contingency and always have an if-this-then-that plan for any possible eventuality worked out in advance. Which was why I was so angry with myself, I had never even considered the possibility I would run into someone from the Wilcox family in Houston. Not after all this time. I had relaxed my vigilance, something I vowed not to do again.

As we pulled into the driveway, Mother's hand went over to the door handle and she released her seat belt expecting me to stop at the back door and let her out. Instead I drove on into the garage, no reason to stop the car, shut off the engine, help her out and up the steps, and then come back in this heat and put the car away myself. I had had a beastly day, far worse than she knew. "Claire Louise, you are going to have to help me out over here," she whined. "The door is too close to the wall, I can't get it open all the way." That was true, the garage had been built for smaller cars than what we put in it. Still, I was getting out on my side with no help, and I had less room than she did.

"I will be over there as soon as I get out myself," I told her, trying again not to grit my teeth. "But you go ahead and try, Mother, remember, you don't still weigh over two hundred pounds." I laughed to show her I was joking, but she shot me an offended look anyway. Mother does not have a sense of humor.

I'd have known that the girls were home from school even had I not seen Britt's car in the garage. Britt had the stereo in their room blaring and Maryanne was hollering up the stairs at her to turn it down, she couldn't study with all the noise. I reached over and grabbed Maryanne by the arm. "I cannot think with all that noise. You go upstairs and tell your sister I said she is to turn that stereo off right now. Right now. And you get up there in your room and do your homework yourself." Her books were spread all over the kitchen table and there were cookie crumbs over everything. "Maryanne, have you been eating?" I demanded.

"I had two graham crackers, that's all, just two."

"A likely story. Do I have to stay here and watch over you every minute you're awake?" I asked her.

"I only had two and they were stale."

"What are you still hanging around here for? Get upstairs and do what I told you to."

"It's Friday."

"Go!" I shrieked, losing all patience with her, my head was splitting.

After she went upstairs and Britt turned that stereo off, the silence in the kitchen felt like a gift. Thank you, I whispered to whatever unknown god was looking out for me. I fixed two glasses of tea and took four aspirins before I went into the den to placate Mother. I had heard her fall into her recliner with a sigh louder than the stereo.

"Here, Mother, here's some nice iced tea for you. What else can I get you?"

"Oh, I don't need anything," she said in her Poor Pitiful Pearl voice.

"Now don't be silly, drink this and relax. We've both had a full day and you'll feel better after you rest a little."

"But, Claire Louise, I'm so discouraged about my eyes, they keep getting worse and now the doctor isn't optimistic about my knees. I don't want to be a burden to my family." She was weeping now into one of the lace hankies she kept tucked into her belt.

Thinking to myself you've always been a burden to your

family, I said, "Mother, you know you could never be a burden to your family. Now you rest and we'll take care of your eyes and your knees, don't you worry."

I heard my father slam the back door shut, open and close the icebox door, and walk down the hall. "Well, what did the doctor say, you going to live?" he asked Mother.

She sniffed and heaved a deep sigh, giving him the silent treatment now. One good thing about my father, he had a knack for saying something to make her mad, which always helped her over anything she happened to be upset at me about.

"Now, Daddy, don't be crude," I remonstrated with him. "Mother has had a bad day."

"Sorry to hear that. What did the doctor say?"

"She saw two," I reminded him. "And Dr. Teague changed her prescription again. Dr. Alvin doesn't think she is a candidate for knee surgery at this time, so that was disappointing for her. But we're not discouraged, no we're not." I leaned over and patted on Mother like I was cheering up a kid who had lost her candy. "We'll keep working on this ourselves, won't we now? Maybe we'll even get us another opinion. Dr. Teague may not be the expert he's cracked up to be." I myself had no intention of ever showing up in his office again.

"Oh, Claire Louise, I don't know," Mother said, sounding forlorn.

"You're just tired, you lean back and take a little rest in your chair. Daddy and I will see to things in the kitchen." I left the room, pushing her drink over to where she could reach it and motioning Daddy to follow me. "The news wasn't good," I whispered to him in the kitchen. "They can't do a thing to halt the deterioration in her eyes and her knees aren't getting any better either. 'That's arthritis for you,' the doctor said."

"Getting old is tough," my father said, patting his chest to remind me he too had had his bout with ill health. And both of them were only in their late fifties. Unfortunately, the fact that he had had his heart fixed had encouraged Mother to think that no matter what went wrong with her, the doctors could fix it. Some things the doctors can't fix, I would tell her, but she still had hope.

"What you making for supper?" he asked, rooting around in the freezer for some of the low-calorie ice-cream bars I doled out to Mother and Maryanne.

"Don't eat those, they're diet food," I told him.

"What else is there to eat in this house?" he asked me, unwrapping two at one time. "And do I need to remind you this is still my house?"

"No, you don't. Do I need to remind you that it wasn't for me, it would have fallen in around you long ago?"

"I doubt that."

My father and I sparred back and forth like this all the time, neither one of us willingly giving an inch. From time to time Mother reminded him the doctor said for him not to get upset, but I told her no one as mean as Daddy was likely to get upset over anything someone said to him. Even me. "Since it is your house, though, you can cook dinner tonight," I told him. "I'm too tired to do it myself or nag the girls. And don't fix something fried either," I said. "A nice cool salad plate would taste good. Maybe slice up some of that melon in the refrigerator out in the garage."

"I don't cook around here, that's your job," he said with a hateful twist to his mouth.

"No, it is not. It is something I usually choose to do, but it is not my job. And tonight I'm not cooking, you are." We stood and glared at each other. I was unwilling to go upstairs until I had won, and he was capable of standing there and glaring at me for longer than I cared to be glared at. "Have it your way," I said, "but if I cook dinner tonight, then tomorrow I am hiring us a maid. Full-time." Since Belle had moved in with Grandma, we had been making do with a once-a-week ironing lady and the girls and I had been doing all the housework.

"All right, I'll cook supper, no need to get on your high horse."

I figured that would bring him around. The only thing Daddy hates worse than me bossing him around is spending money, and he would have been embarrassed not to pay somebody I hired to work for us. Which, now that I thought about it, was not a bad idea. It was time I had some help around there.

The phone woke me around five o'clock. I knew before I picked it up it was Grandma. If no one from our house had been over that day she called around five and asked were we all still alive. When whoever answered told her yes, she asked to speak to Daddy and they talked about cows or barns or something, and then he asked her to dinner with us and she said no, she and Belle already had something cooking on the stove. Tonight wasn't any different and I was fixing to hang up the phone when I heard her say to Daddy she had been working hard cleaning out the two bedrooms for Macy's crew. That was a surprise to me. What was Macy needing with Grandma's two extra bedrooms? From Daddy's uh-hum answer to her, I realized he knew all about it, and as soon as they hung up I swung my legs over the side of the bed and got up to go downstairs to find out what was going on.

Before I went downstairs, I knocked on the door that connected my room to Macy's old room, which was my girls' room now. One thing about me, I make it a point to respect the privacy of my children. I never enter their room without knocking.

"Homework all done?" I asked. Maryanne nodded yes, but since she was only in fifth grade and had two hours of special math and reading every day, she never seemed to have much anyway. Britt appeared to be a different story. She had papers spread all over the desk. "No, I have a paper due Monday. I wish that teacher had gotten her act together sooner and told us the minimum was ten typewritten pages."

"Maybe she did and you weren't listening," I said. Britt was smart, but she did the least amount of work possible, and I had been told by more than one of her teachers she was sometimes too busy talking to her friends to hear what was being taught.

"She never said a word about the length or the fact that we have to have ten sources," Britt said indignantly. "You can ask anyone in my class."

"I don't need to ask anyone in your class because it doesn't matter when she told you, you still have to get it done."

"I know that," Britt said in the sarcastic tone she knows I hate. "Which is why I am going to the library tonight after dinner and there I will stay till I get this thing written."

"Since when is the school library open at night?" I asked her. If she thought she was driving in to the public library, which was a good twenty miles away at night and a Friday night at that, she had another think coming.

"Since Mrs. Ralston realized that fully half her class wasn't going to have this paper done unless she herself went down there and opened the library for us to work on it. Which proves what I said about her not telling us. You don't think she would open that library for me if I had just been not listening, do you?"

"Maybe not."

"And then I'll type the paper Sunday," she said.

"You'll type it tomorrow," I told her. "You know our rule,

no play on the weekend until your schoolwork is complete." Britt was the world's worst about putting things off until the last minute, and I had finally had to put my foot down and not allow her to do another thing unless her work was done.

"But, Mother, tomorrow is the senior beach party. It's the last time ever I will get to be with some of those kids. I can't miss it," she wailed.

"Most of those kids aren't going anywhere," I told her, "and besides, you aren't a senior, you are only a sophomore. Why should you expect to go to that party?"

"Jason invited me and you said I could go!"

"That was before I knew about this paper you have due."

"Mother, if you don't let me go, I'll hate you forever!"

"We'll see," I told her, remembering I needed to get downstairs and find out what Macy was up to. "Get ready for supper, it's almost five-thirty." Like most country people, my parents ate long before it was dark. It was one thing I had not been able to change. If dinner wasn't ready by the time they wanted to eat, Daddy fixed them both cereal or a sandwich. I had finally given up and gone along with them, for the moment anyway.

"Why is Grandma cleaning out two rooms for Macy?"

"What makes you think she is?"

"Because I heard her on the phone."

"I don't recall her asking to speak to you."

"I picked up the phone and overheard that before I realized the call wasn't for me." He raised his eyebrows at me, thinking he had me at a disadvantage. "What about Macy?" I asked again.

"She and Carlton and the boys are spending the summer with Grandma," he said.

"And why haven't I heard about this before now?" I asked.

"I guess because no one realized they needed your permission," he said.

I glared at him, thinking this new development over. I didn't like it, not one little bit. After dinner I thought I had better walk over and have a little visit with Grandma. I had been neglecting her. And I had better get someone in here to start doing the housework as well. Things were getting away from me.

"Come and get it," Daddy yelled up the stairs, and when I walked into the kitchen he smiled at me. "I hope you're in the mood for chicken-fried steak and rice and gravy," he said. "I even made us some biscuits and thawed out a Mrs. Smith's cream pie I found way back in the freezer."

15

THE MONTH BEFORE we moved out to Grandma's for the summer was heaven. I called her every day, sometimes twice a day, and I called Mother every day, but I didn't go out there over once a week. Carlton and I started feeling like a family again, going to the movies and taking the boys to the zoo on Sunday afternoon. The only thing I hadn't counted on was Mrs. Grant's crestfallen expression when I told her our plans. "All summer?" she said. "My, my." I could tell she was disappointed and I had to stop myself from inviting her to come with us. Grandma didn't have another spare room. Besides, Mrs. Grant wouldn't have come anyway. "You can come out and visit us," I told Mrs. Grant. "And you'll have to come for the big Fourth of July family reunion," I added. She had gone with us last year and had more fun than Carlton and I did. It's easier to like people when you're not related to them, I suppose. At least most of the people in my family.

The day before we left, I had packed all of the boys' clothes and toys and had them loaded in my station wagon. The only thing I still had to do was finish packing for me and Carlton. He was sitting on the couch in the bedroom, which we generally retreated to when he got home, since the boys invariably had the television on to their show when Carlton walked in the door. We didn't allow more than an hour of television a day and I thought that was too much. But it was one time I didn't have to worry what they were up to, which was nice.

"Are you sure you want to do this, Macy, spend all summer out in Molly's Point? I'm afraid it may get tiring for you, being out there all the time, and I know good and well I'm going to get sick of that drive."

"Don't, Carlton," I said. "We've already agreed and the drive isn't any longer from there than it is from here."

"I'm not so sure about that, but just remember, if you get out there and it's not all you expected, you don't have to stay for my sake." He grinned and I could tell he was teasing.

"Did I tell you I love you?" I asked him, smiling and once again applauding my incredible luck in marrying him. Carlton was so nice. Nice is not the word for it, he was good. A genuinely good person. I hadn't known they existed, not genuinely good men. I hoped our boys turned out half as wonderful as their father. Right now they were great but it's hard to tell at five how people are going to be when they are grown. Sometimes I thought of Claire Louise when we had been little, and it was hard to believe she had done some of the nice things I remembered. People grew up and changed. It was scary, how much they changed. It made trusting that much harder, when you never knew for sure, even if they were nice now, how they would be the next day.

The first time I answered the phone at Grandma's it was her friend Miss Mabel, who has played bridge with Grandma every

Wednesday afternoon for the past forty years. "Hello, Claire Louise," she said to me when I answered the telephone.

"This is Macy. Didn't Grandma tell you we were spending the summer with her?" I asked.

"Well, I declare, yes she did, but it slipped my mind. Besides I never could tell you two girls apart on the phone, you sound just alike." People were always saying that, and it infuriated me to hear I sounded just like my sister. Claire Louise talks in this sweet little voice, very affected, and to my ear we sound nothing alike. For the rest of the summer, whenever I answered the telephone I said, Richards residence, Macy speaking. Still I got called Claire Louise from time to time. Some people don't bother to listen to what you tell them.

Every night after dinner, we sat around the pool listening to Grandma's two bug lights from Sears zap the mosquitoes. Sometimes the kids swam, sometimes they had had enough for the day and rode their bicycles up and down the driveway and on the cracked sidewalk that ran all the way around the house. Carlton usually got home about six and was nice enough not to complain about the traffic when he came in. Belle and I always fixed a salad and a bowl of fruit, and we'd nibble on that while we all had a drink and Carlton grilled hamburgers or hot dogs. Every night we had the same thing. The kids thought they were in heaven, and I have to admit I didn't mind either. Some nights, for variety, either Belle or I would stop at the fish market and get some fish to grill or we'd get chicken, or Grandma would thaw out a steak, but we didn't worry overmuch about it. It was wonderful not having to think what to cook. Lunch was leftovers for Belle, Grandma, and me. The boys had peanut butter and jelly sandwiches, and Carlton ate in Houston. Breakfast was bacon and eggs and toast, cereal for the boys. By mid-June, all of us except for Grandma, who never appeared outside unless she was covered from head to toe and had a wide-brimmed hat on her head, and Carlton, who spent too much time in town, were darker than Belle, who wasn't very dark anyway.

Besides swimming, the boys took up wandering, something I remembered with fondness from my own childhood. When you live in the city you forget that country kids can just wander. They were responsible enough not to get out of yelling distance and old enough to entertain themselves for hours catching doodle bugs or digging in the flower bed that from time immemorial had been designated as belonging to the kids. The only difference was now the kids weren't me and my sister or cousins, they were my own two boys and their cousin Maryanne.

This was the first time I had been around Maryanne for longer than an afternoon at a time, and as the summer wore on and she spent more and more time at Grandma's playing with the boys, she began to grow on me. She really was a sweet little girl. Everyone in the family knew she wasn't smart. She'd had to repeat a grade and was always being put in a special class to get help with something, and she looked, well, fat, lumpy kind of, and her expression was always so flat looking. She had little beady eyes like her mother, and my mother too, for that matter, and they'd always been lost in folds of fat that made up her face. But she was ten or eleven that summer and had grown inches taller in the last year and slimmed down.

She would have been attractive if she had ever stood up straight. She had a horrible slump, like she was trying to slink in and out of places as invisible as possible. Her voice was so soft you had to strain to hear her and she never looked you in the eye, two things that drive me crazy. "What do you want to drink, Maryanne?" Belle would ask her, and she would look at the floor and shrug and whisper, "I don't care, whatever they are having." At first it irritated me no end. "They," I would say, "have names, which are Travis and Scott. And you might as well speak up and tell us what you want, you have as much right to an opinion about what you want to put in your mouth as anyone else around here." Then I felt bad because she cringed and looked harder than ever at the floor. She can't help it if she's shy, and for heaven's sake it's not that child's fault she has her mother's eyes, I reminded myself.

The kids loved her. On the days when she wasn't over there by the time they were through with breakfast, they were ready to bicycle over and find her. One thing I didn't allow, though, was them to go over to Mother and Daddy's whenever they felt like it. I know Mother was offended but I felt like it was an imposition for them to wander in and out over there. We had come to spend the summer with Grandma, not my parents and Claire Louise, after all. And I just didn't feel comfortable with the idea they might be over there and me not know it. So they played at home, Grandma's home that is, and Maryanne played with them until it was time for her to go home for meals, which Claire Louise insisted she eat at home with her own family.

Claire Louise had taken to driving over every morning for coffee. Every single morning. She would appear about nine-thirty, motoring over in the way she had of driving, which involved pushing the gas pedal down and then releasing it and letting the car coast, and then accelerating again, and coasting again. It gave her driving a strange pulsing rhythm that made me seasick when I rode with her. You could always tell it was Claire Louise driving up by the um-um-Um-um-umming sound of the car.

"How long has this been going on?" I asked Belle after I had been there a week and she had appeared every morning except Sunday when they were in Sunday school by nine-thirty. It wasn't like we were doing anything other than having coffee. Grandma always sat down at that time and had a snack. She had done that for years, as long as I had known her she had nine-thirty or ten o'clock coffee, as she called it, whether it was coffee or, as was more frequently the case, iced tea. And she always had a little something to tide her over till lunch. But I had never known Claire Louise was there partaking with her.

"Oh, appears to me she started this about a week or so before you came to stay, 'bout when she found out you were coming, I reckon." Belle didn't smile when she said it, but there was a gleam in her eye. Belle didn't miss much, for all she didn't talk much either. Especially since she didn't talk much, people had a tendency to forget she was there. Whenever I wanted to know anything about my family I would go to Belle and if she thought I needed to know she would tell me. She wasn't one to gossip or tell tales, though, Belle wasn't, and if she didn't figure there was any point in her telling someone something, she didn't do it. Even me, she kept lots from. Maybe that was good. Maybe I was better off not knowing all there was to know about my family. It's hard to get the answers, though, when you don't know the questions to ask, and I do think Belle might have saved us all some grief if she had told me earlier what Claire Louise was up to. Always assuming she herself knew. Because she kept a lot she knew to herself, I assumed she knew everything. Maybe she didn't know, maybe not. But back at that time, I thought if it was happening, Belle knew about it. Belle and Grandma were alike that way. If something was just going to cause someone grief, they wouldn't talk about it. You can avoid some problems that way, Carlton says, but there may come a time when you have to pull your head out of the sand.

"Fix a glass for Claire Louise, too," Grandma said as we sat down at the round glass-topped table in her breakfast room. "I hear her car." And there she was, all chatty and friendly, and before she left she would tell us what she had planned for her day and inquire after ours, and she always offered to bring us whatever we wanted from town. She would have liked to bring out the mail, which she had been doing for Grandma for the past year, it turned out, but I told her the boys and I looked forward to the trip every afternoon after naptime and they were taking turns opening the box. She didn't like that, I could tell, but she couldn't think of a reason not to go along with it. I suspected she opened the box every morning and looked through the mail anyway when she picked up her mail in the box next to Grandma's, but maybe I was just being suspicious. Sometimes I was that way around her.

I tried my best to like Claire Louise that summer, truly I did. We were sisters and I wanted to be friends with her, but somehow no matter what we talked about she ended up rubbing me the wrong way. Carlton and I talked about it often, I even tried to talk to Grandma about it, the dissension between Claire Louise and me. But Grandma pooh-poohed me, because she couldn't ever get herself to admit anything any of us were unhappy about was a real live problem. "Oh, well, never know it a hundred years from now," she would say, which I suppose to her meant no reason to talk about it or even think about it. I wonder what she thought about, Grandma did, during those hours and hours she spent on her knees working in her flower beds. Did she worry about things and then tell herself not to, or did she really not bring the subjects up, even in her head with her own self? I think she must have worried, I do, because I cannot imagine that anyone could have lived through the family shenanigans she did and not let them for one minute linger in her mind. I just don't believe it is possible.

We were all looking forward to the Fourth of July celebration. Maryanne and the boys were making party favors and planning games for the children, like they were camp directors and had a month to fill up. And Claire Louise came over every afternoon with more paper goods or soft drinks or recipes for us to cook up and freeze till it was time.

Carlton had even broken down and bought some fireworks of sorts, only sparklers and little things you throw down and they pop, for the kids. That was a first for him, since Carlton does not believe in firearms of any kind, and has always opposed fireworks because they are dangerous. But I must say the day did turn out to be fun.

Claire Louise had one idea that was a good one. She remembered that it was always so hot outside on Grandma's patio and around the pool, which is where most people stayed. Very few people went inside except maybe some of the little babies for naps or the very old folks to cool off. But, she thought, lots of old people in our family right now and some awnings would be nice. So she rented some, huge, wide rectangular-shaped red and gray striped canvas affairs, held up by poles and ropes, spread around the pool on two sides and out in the yard. It was nice. She put tables and chairs under each awning and washtubs with cold drinks. People spread out and visited from tent to tent. She even had the idea of putting different nationalities of hors d'oeuvres in each location so going from place to place would be like moving from country to country and people would mix more. Which it was easy to see they did. My cousin said it reminded her of a lawn party in *The Great Gatsby*, which she had seen not a week ago, so I hoped she didn't notice the awnings were rented from Schroeder's Funeral Home. There were little tags on them but they were small and discreet and I don't think too many people paid any attention to them. For most people, they probably just looked like those tags on pillows, the ones that say not to be removed under pain of death or some such thing.

I hadn't seen my cousin Amanda in years, not since my wedding. She was there and I wouldn't have recognized her if I had seen her anywhere but at a family reunion, walking in next to her sister and her sister's husband. Kara, her sister, lived in Molly's Point, her I saw several times a year. But Amanda had never married and lived in New York, and this was the first time she had been home when I was there. I squealed and hugged her when I saw her; she looked wonderful, I told her over and over. "Doesn't she, Carlton?" I asked, and he said yes, indeed, although he told me later she looked entirely too made up for his taste.

Which is what led me to the conversation I had with Carlton later that night after everyone had left and we had drug all the left-over food inside and packed it away in one of the refrigerators. It was at times like these we appreciated Grandma's fear of running out, for she had four refrigerators and both a chest-type freezer and an upright one. They were all crammed full the month of July.

Grandma and Belle were both in bed exhausted and the boys had fallen asleep in their shorts and stained T-shirts, which I was letting them sleep in. I told Belle we'll just wash the sheets and their clothes and everything tomorrow. Both of them were filthy, but far too tired to tolerate a bath. Carlton had suggested throwing them in the pool, which had become their substitute for bathing most days. It just didn't make sense to see them swimming three or four hours a day and then bathe them again at night, I rationalized.

But I was too keyed up to sleep, so Carlton and I sat in the den back behind the kitchen, the one Grandma added on one summer when her brother, who has been dead over twenty years now, was trying to make a go of it in the construction business. He never did make a success of that business, but Grandma and Grandpa added on three rooms and a bath, a second garage, and a chicken house.

"I had such fun today," I said. "Do you remember how I always hated these things the last few years? But today was fun, I felt like I belonged here for the first time in a long time. I had such a good time. Didn't you think Amanda looked wonderful?" I asked Carlton, which is when he told me he thought she wore too much makeup.

I had to laugh. "You're beginning to sound like some of these country people," I told my city-bred husband. "Too much makeup, indeed. It's country folks that say that about city folks."

"Maybe we both are starting to sound like we live out here. Have you noticed how much you're sounding like your sister?"

His words took the sparkly feeling right out of me. "I do not. There is no way on earth I sound like Claire Louise. She talks baby talk and simpers and I do not sound like that."

"Hey," he said, backing away and making placating noises. "I guess I was wrong," he said, but I was starting to think back to everything I had said.

"What did I say that sounds like her? Tell me one thing," I demanded.

"There isn't one thing, Macy, it's just a feeling I had and I was probably wrong at that." When I kept on scowling at him, he decided he'd better elaborate. "Look, you both were raised by the same people in the same town. It is not unreasonable to expect you would have some of the same expressions and pronunciations. That's all I mean, nothing awful, honey."

I let him hug me and we talked about other things but it kept bothering me, that comment of his. I didn't want to be like my sister in any way. It particularly worried me that I might be like her in some ways I was unaware of. Some ways that I didn't notice but other people did.

The next morning the boys were out with Maryanne picking up anything in the yard that didn't belong there. They were trailing old sacks that looked like the kind people used to use picking cotton. Grandma was right out there with them, pointing like she was playing I Spy. Carlton and Belle and I sat on the porch, not as energetic as them by far. And then Carlton brought up the subject I had been avoiding. "I know Macy doesn't want to think about this, Belle, but weren't you wanting to go to live with your daughter?"

I felt as if someone had dropped a water balloon down my stomach. It sunk clear to the bottom and landed with a thud you should have been able to hear next door. Neither Belle nor I had mentioned one word about her moving or us finding someone else to live with Grandma after the summer was over. Claire Louise had hired a new lady to housekeep for them, Lucy Hopkins, and she was over there doing for them every day. I had wondered about her, but she had her own family to get home to every night, and besides, I didn't want to think about us leaving or the summer ending or Belle having a heart problem or anything else. I was happy and I wanted nothing to change. For once in my life, I had everything I wanted and everyone I loved all together under one roof, safe where I could watch them. Please God, don't let anything change, I would pray every morning, which was the nearest I could come to asking that Carlton be okay all day when he was at work and on the road. And that the boys not get into any trouble when they were out wandering.

And that my grandmother could live forever, right there like she was doing. And that Belle would decide she would rather stay with us than her own daughter. The only person I never worried about was me, it never occurred to me anything bad would happen to me. I don't know why it didn't. Bad things had happened to me in the past.

"I did say that," Belle said. I don't know who she was looking at, because I was watching my grandmother and the children, thinking I should go give them a hand.

Carlton must have read my mind, like he has the uncomfortable habit of doing from time to time. "Don't go, Macy, we need to talk about this."

"Maybe we do, but now is not the time."

"There will never be a good time, but you can't keep ignoring what Belle wants and needs because it doesn't fit in with your plans. That's not fair to her."

I looked at Belle, stricken. Was that what I had been doing?

"Now, that ain't so, Carlton. We haven't talked about it because I don't want to run off and leave Miss Louisa any more than Macy wants me to go. I've been with Miss Louisa off and on since before my own kids were born, since before she had Mr. Stuart. The doctor saying I needed to think about retiring didn't no more make me want to do it than your saying we need to talk about it does."

"Maybe I'm out of line then," Carlton said.

"No, we do need to find her someone else. She needs someone she can count on, not some lady old as she is."

I felt like crying. I didn't want Belle to be old either, but at least she had her daughter, I told myself, who wants her. All Grandma had was my father and mother and Claire Louise, none of whom would take care of her. And me, she had me, who was fixing to let her down because I had a husband with a practice in town, and a house we had restored and loved, and two little boys who liked the country better than the city and were going to have to go back to the city in not much more than a month and start first grade. I remembered my first-grade teacher, Mrs. Hayes, how I had loved her. She was still teaching, I ran into her all the time. She hadn't gotten old that I could see. I was wringing my hands, twisting and pulling them like there was something in them. I looked at Carlton, wanting him to read my mind and tell me we would just stay out here with Grandma.

"Do you know of anyone who would come and live with Grandma?" Carlton asked Belle.

"No, I don't and I have been pondering on it. There's not too many folks who want to live in, not the kind you would want living out here with your grandma. Miss Mabel, your grandma's friend, has her a companion they got from a companion service down in Houston. Nice lady named Elizabeth Perkins. Appears to be real good to Miss Mabel."

I saw Carlton wipe a grin off his face and knew he was picturing the same thing I was, Grandma's little-old-lady friend Mabel with some old geezer she had gotten from one of the escort services that were all over the place now. "I asked her last time she brought Miss Mabel out to play bridge how she come to get that job and she told me all about it. I've got the card with the address and phone number written down inside. Thought you might want to give them a call."

Which we did, and we called every other agency we heard about and asked all around town. I also went over and talked to my Aunt Claire, but she made it clear she wasn't going to be suggesting Grandma move in with her. Not that I wanted that to happen. My Aunt Claire was not the kind of person I would think my grandmother would enjoy spending her last days with. Particularly now since, with her kids grown, she was on the go all the time herself. Once Carlton brought the subject up, it was as if it took on wings, and we told everybody who would listen to us that Belle was retiring and we needed a companion for Grandma.

All this we did over the strenuous objections of Grandma, who said she thought she could manage just fine with a cleaning lady once a month, no more than she cleaned. Which was true. Neither Grandma nor Belle cleaned that much, preferring to be outside digging in the flower beds. But I wanted there to be someone with her, someone for her to talk to and plan what to eat with, someone who liked her and would be there for her if, heaven forbid, she did need help. And we pursued our elusive companion over the objections of Claire Louise, who said she could come over several times a day and look after things, and even my father said it didn't look to him like Grandma was helpless yet, so why throw her money away.

But we kept looking and interviewing people, Belle and Carlton and I did, all of us in agreement that we would feel better if Grandma had a companion. We must have interviewed twenty women that month and one man, who we had no idea was a male until he showed up. There were a couple of people we liked—not the man, of course, because Grandma hooted at the very idea—but there always was a fly in the ointment. Like the lady we thought was perfect and even Grandma liked and she had a real cute little boy, six years old, got along great with my two, and we thought she was as good as hired and was coming out the last week of August to get settled in while we were all still there to get acquainted. Had her little boy signed up for first grade, the bus could pick him up like it used to pick me and Claire Louise up. Grandma was glad to have the little boy, she liked some noise around the place, she said. Good thing, Carlton said, or she'd have had a hell of a summer. Our kids are good kids but not particularly quiet.

Grandma's new companion called two days before we expected her and said she and her ex-husband were getting back together and she was leaving for California. We should have known it. Lots of people come to the coast to get over broken hearts and are gone when they are mended. That's why most people down on the coast don't get chummy with people who are not locals. Most of them are here today and gone tomorrow.

And there we were, us all set to leave and move back to Houston the next week, and Belle's daughter expecting her, and the companion up and quit before she ever started. I was in a panic and even Carlton was upset, much as he tried to hide it. Carlton cared as much about my grandmother as if she had been his own. Belle offered to stay on, but it didn't seem fair to her, now that she was ready to go. She needed to go on and do that. And we needed to get back to our lives, I knew that. Carlton didn't have to keep reminding me. And there really was nothing wrong with Grandma. So we decided we'd just go on and go like we had planned, and Belle's daughter would drive her over three mornings a week and she would help Grandma around the house and I would come out two days, which Carlton agreed was reasonable. And we got a man to come out once a week and do what she wanted done in the yard. And promised the boys we'd come see Grandma every Sunday. We'd pick her up for church and then afterwards go out to eat and they could swim as long as the weather wasn't freezing. So we left, Belle on a Tuesday and Carlton and me and the boys the next Sunday. Belle was crying when she drove off with her daughter. You'd have thought it was a lot farther she was going than about ten miles down the road. And the way I cried when we left, you'd have thought I never expected to see my grandmother alive again. Even the boys started crying, not that they didn't want to go, because they were glad to get back to their friends and looking forward to seeing Mrs. Grant, whom we hadn't seen more than three or four times all summer. They were crying because it was scary for them, seeing their own mother just this side of hysterical. Which is what led me to get control of myself. I didn't want to terrorize my own kids with my fears.

16

LABOR DAY WEEKEND was the last sane time we had around here for months. It was on the Tuesday after Labor Day, the day the kids were to go back to school, that Daddy didn't get up. We didn't know it until Britt and Maryanne had driven off and I had been over to check on Grandma, which I did every morning now that she was all alone and dependent on me. I'd get up, have breakfast with the girls around seven so they could get dressed and get to school by eight. Daddy always fixed his own coffee before six in the morning, long before the rest of us were up. And then he'd go out and work in the barn and do whatever he had to do and come back around nine, and he and Mother would have breakfast together. They had been doing that for years, since before Macy and I were born I imagine. He used to fix pancakes for her every morning, which was probably part of the reason she had a weight problem for so long. Since I'd come back I'd usually fix their breakfast, something more sensible.

I should have figured something was wrong when I came downstairs and there was no coffee brewed, no cup over by the sink waiting to be refilled when he came back at nine. But I just thought to myself, I guess he didn't feel like coffee today, hot as it is. So I fed the kids and went over and looked in on Grandma who was as usual up and outside in her garden. I sat and talked to her awhile like I did every day, and then went on back home.

Since we had hired Lucy I didn't have all the housework to tend to, which was a blessing, but I still had things to do. That was the day I had planned to start on the closets in the girls' room. If there is one thing I cannot stand it is messy closets, closets cluttered with worthless plunder. Which was one of the things like to drove me crazy about Daddy. He never willingly parted with so much as a rusted nail. The basement of our house was so filled with clutter it was literally impossible to walk more than five feet in any direction from the foot of the stairs. I had frequently told him if he ever had a leak down there he was going to regret all that clutter, because everything would be ruined before he could so much as get to a busted pipe. And he told me it was his clutter, for me to leave it alone. Which I did, reluctantly, because I knew it was a health hazard to have that nasty a mess on the floor below where you lived. No telling what kinds of insects and spiders we were breeding. But there was so much accumulation down there I knew I could never make any headway toward changing it as long as Daddy was around to watch everything I touched. So I kept the basement door shut when I wasn't down there putting things in the washer, and once a week, every Monday, I sprayed a whole can of Raid around the door and on the stairs and the floor around the washer.

I knew immediately as I stepped into the kitchen something was wrong. I felt it. I had seen the girls as they left for school. They had driven past Grandma's on their way. Like I told them, she is all alone now and it is not too much trouble for you to stop every morning on your way and tell her good morning and give her a hug. And they knew I expected them to stop every afternoon on their way home as well and park the car and get out and visit a bit. Tell her about their days, ask her about hers, that kind of thing. Like I told them, she isn't that young anymore and won't live forever, so you can take the time to be good to her while she's around. I was thinking about going over and fixing breakfast for her and having the girls and me eat there with her. That way she'd have a little family time too. As it turned out, I never got to implement that plan.

It was almost eight-thirty, Mother should have been stirring around upstairs but I didn't hear her, so I thought I'd better get up there and check on her. I knocked and knocked again, and when she didn't answer I opened the door and walked in. I didn't see her; her bed was empty, though, so I walked over to the door that connected her room to Daddy's. She always went through his room to get to the bathroom. She was there in the little hallway that connected their rooms, her mouth opening and shutting like a guppie's, wringing her hands, trying to say something or walk forward and not a sound coming out of her mouth, not a one. Daddy was on the bed, his head back, his eyes open but empty, still as could be. I thought he was dead, same as Mother did.

"Call Dr. Blynn," I yelled at her, rushing over to put my ear on his chest. "He's not dead, Mother, he's had another heart attack, call the doctor." At that point I truly didn't know if he was dead or not, but I figured if he wasn't he for sure would be if we didn't get him some help soon. Mother hadn't moved, so I rushed into the hall and rang up the operator. It took me a minute to remember to dial O. Up until a few years ago we had had the old ring phones where you ring the handle and a real voice, someone you know like as not, says "Operator here" and gives you what you want. If Ruby Smith had still been the operator she could have told me where the doctor was and what he was doing. But I dialed O and told someone my father was dying, to send an ambulance, and then I had to give directions, which shocked me that there was someone in Molly's Point didn't know where the Richards farm was. And then I called Dr. Blynn myself and told him Daddy was dying or dead and I had an ambulance on the way, and he said he was on his way too.

They got there at the same time, the ambulance and Dr. Blynn and his youngest daughter, Judy, who had been off to nursing school and worked for her daddy, same as her husband did. He wasn't a doctor, Judy's husband, he was a nurse himself. It seemed funny to most of the people in Molly's Point, a man nurse. I myself did not find it strange at all, but then I had been out in the world more than most of these people.

Dr. Blynn listened and quickly helped the ambulance men hook up some tubes to Daddy to help him breathe, and then they got their stretcher up the stairs and took him down and out the front door. It was just like the last time he had a heart attack, except this time the girls were off at school and Judy was there and went in the ambulance with my father.

Again Mother wasn't dressed and couldn't find her glasses, and since the girls had already left for school I knew I would have to help her. It didn't take us ten minutes, though, to be in the car and on our way and that included stopping by Grandma's to give her the bad news. "Call Belle in town and tell her to come out and stay with you," I told Grandma as we drove off. I knew she wouldn't go with us, for all that she is more able to get around by far than Mother. Grandma has never liked hospitals.

Grandma can be a very stubborn, opinionated person, like when she turned eighty she just up and quit driving her car. Nothing wrong with her eyesight or her reflexes for that matter, but she said eighty-year-old women were too old to be out driving cars and she was stopping before someone had to tell her to.

Daddy said that came from years of driving with Grandma's own mother, my great-grandmother, who drove around until she was over ninety and never backed the car out of the garage she didn't hit something. The whole family said it was a miracle that old woman never killed someone. And like as not when her mother hit something, my grandmother was in the car with her telling her to stop, and her mother saying "I've got plenty of room" before she rammed into the pole or car or curb. She even hit a cow once, poor old thing didn't have sense to get out of her way. You know how sometimes they'll just stand in the middle of the road that runs through a pasture. Well, one did that one day and my great-grandmother said "It'll move" and kept going herself and ran right into that old cow. She didn't hit it just a little bit, she hit it bad enough to bust it right open, and one of the men worked for them back then had to come and shoot it and put it out of its misery. They say my great-grandmother just said "It shoulda moved" when she stepped out and saw what she had done.

So Grandma didn't drive anymore, which was inconvenient for her, because when Belle moved in with her after my grandfather passed on, Belle didn't drive either. Didn't matter to Grandma, she had my father take her to town on Mondays, she had her hair done at the beauty parlor and stocked up on groceries and went by the hardware store and that was it for the week. She had, for the most part, quit going to church several years before my grandfather died, said it made her nervous. She watched one of those preacher shows on Sunday morning for her religion.

She even got herself a Sears catalogue a few years back and every day or so she'd order herself something out of there. Back when I was picking up her mail for her, almost every day I'd get a little notice to stop at the window, she had something too big to go in the box. Grandma wasted a lot of her money on junk she ordered out of that catalogue. And that was the only catalogue she ever ordered out of, the Sears one. Anything else came in her mailbox, just throw it away she told Mr. Bains the mailman, Sears Roebuck Company was all the catalogue business she needed. He didn't throw them away, he took them home for his five little girls to cut up. I know because one of them was in Maryanne's class at school and Maryanne once brought home a catalogue with Grandma's name on it that his little girl had brought to school.

It was like we had done this before, only this time we didn't stop in at Pine Ridge Hospital first but went on to Diagnostic down in the medical center. Mother and I went straight to the second floor where they had Daddy in the operating room on second, which is where their cardiac patients go. Mother sat down and I helped her prop her feet up on the needlepoint footstool Aunt Lillie had made. I had carried it in under my arm, knowing she would need it. I also had a blanket to cover her legs with and one of her large-print books in case she didn't want to watch television. She hadn't had breakfast yet, not even coffee, and coffee this late in the morning would make her empty stomach queasy, she said, so I went out to the machines and got a package of doughnuts and some oatmeal cookies for her to eat with her coffee. They had some fresh fruit in there as well, but I knew Mother would say she could never eat fruit out of a machine if I brought that back for her. Truth is she doesn't like fruit nearly half as much as she likes doughnuts and cookies, but I had too much else on my mind to fuss over Mother's diet today.

Judy came out and said good-bye to us, she said she and the boys were going back with the ambulance, now that Daddy was in good hands. She hugged me, and said buck up, and then she was gone. Judy and I had never been friends, but I felt lost there for a minute when she left.

Then I went over to the phone and started making calls. First I called Macy but she didn't answer. I found out later after she packed the boys off for their first day of school, she and Carlton had gone and had breakfast at a hotel and then gone to a museum and shopping over at Galleria, which is why I didn't get hold of her until after three o'clock. I also called Aunt Claire, even though Mother is still barely speaking to her, and told her and my cousin Amanda, whose visit from New York was turning out to be lengthier than anyone had expected. Then I called the high school and spoke to Britt and told her she and Maryanne were to go straight to Grandma's after school and look after her, and I informed her I would call out to Grandma's at four o'clock and if she knew what was good for her she would be there. Which she was not happy about, cheerleading practice being scheduled for after school, but I had been a cheerleader at that school and I knew just how much practicing went on outside the gym, waiting for the football players to get let off from their practice, and I informed her the cheerleaders could just go out to Grandma's with her if they needed to practice all that bad.

And then I called my friend Mary Beth, who was now living in the ranch-style house in town I had built, her ex-mother-in-law having bought it for her as well as the extra lot my school building was on that she had been running anyway. We had planned to get together later that morning and have coffee there at the city café, so I had to tell her where we were and what was happening. She offered to go out and look after things for me or come in or whatever, but I couldn't think of a thing for her to do. I liked Mary Beth, I hadn't seen much of her since I'd moved out here to the farm, but I planned to start getting together with her now that school was in session and Macy was back in Houston so I didn't have to keep my eye on her every minute. "Mary Beth, maybe there is something you can do for me. Run on out to Grandma's and make sure she's doing all right. Tell her I called and asked you to check on her, tell her I'll call her just as soon as the doctors tell us something." I figured I could have called Grandma right then, but the personal touch would let her know how much I was thinking of her.

It was almost two when the doctor came into the waiting room and told us Daddy was stabilized and they were moving him to a room. He had had a heart attack and was in serious but stable condition and they expected him to make it. Mother and I held each other and cried, but I don't believe either of us truly believed he was alive until we went into the room and saw him obviously breathing and with his eyes open and moving from one to the other of us.

Daddy did get better and after several days he was moved back home, but then he had a relapse and had to be rushed back in and he stayed in the hospital over a month that time. I remember it was after Halloween when he came home for the last time. By then we knew it wasn't just his heart, he also had cancer of the liver, a rare kind, but because of his heart there wasn't any question of operating on it or even of chemotherapy. Daddy was going to die, not someday like us all, but someday soon, probably within the next two or three months, the doctor said. He could go home or he could stay in the hospital, but there wasn't a whole lot could be done for him other than make him comfortable.

Macy and I were sitting in the room with him the day the doctor came in with the results of all the tests they had put him through the last week, let's see, the first week of October that would have been. It was after five, and Carlton had come and taken Mother over to their house to rest. Actually we hadn't expected the doctor that day at all so she was going to go over to Macy's and take a bath and eat some soup Mrs. Grant had made and go to bed. We had hired a night nurse for Daddy by then and I was leaving usually about six, before she came on, of course, but after he had eaten and settled down for the night. I'd get home and check on the girls and Grandma. Belle and her daughter had taken to coming every day to stay with her. Then I'd read the note Lucy always left me about what she'd done or what she needed, and go through the mail and try to make heads or tails of the bills and what needed to be done to keep the farm running.

Then the next morning Mother and Macy would get to the hospital about nine after she got her kids to school, but I usually tried to be back up there before seven so I could talk to the nurse and find out what kind of night Daddy had had. I always brought him some breakfast, too, and usually tried to bring in something for his other meals as well. He particularly liked sweets, Daddy did, and he was losing weight so fast, it hurt me to see him.

Mother wasn't doing well, either, up at the hospital all day for weeks on end. Macy and I both tried to convince her she might be better off staying home some days. She could stay over there with Grandma and Belle if she didn't want to be home with Lucy. Lucy was good help but she wasn't good company, not the way Belle was. But Mother was clinging to Daddy, wanting to be there to do for him, like she hadn't done for him when he was home and healthy. Macy and I talked about it some. It was sad to see her trying to make up for all the years she'd lost.

We were sitting on the sofa bed in Daddy's room, the one Mother usually stretched out on when she was there. "I think he's asleep," she whispered to me as the door opened and the doctor stuck his head in. He looked at Daddy there asleep in the bed and motioned to us with his head to come on out in the hall. "Let's go down here," he said, "there's an empty room where we can talk." I knew right there it was not good news. Macy and I looked at each other wide-eyed and actually walked in that room behind the doctor hand in hand. Macy and I hadn't held hands for years, not since she was seven years old and I was eleven I bet.

"He has cancer of the liver metastasized and spread to the lymph glands. We think it is also in his pancreas as well." He gave us more details, which we neither one of us heard.

"What can you do?"

"Keep him comfortable, we can do that. Beyond that, there isn't anything, I don't want to hold out false hope." He sat there and looked at us with kind eyes. "I'll talk to your mother tomorrow."

Macy and I looked at each other. "How long?" I asked what we were both thinking.

"Not long, a matter of months, probably less than six, maybe no more than two or three. He's been losing ground fast the last weeks."

We both nodded, we had seen that ourselves, all of us. "Don't tell Mother, she wouldn't want to know," I said.

"No, she wouldn't," Macy agreed with me. "Mother would rather no one tell her bad news."

"Well, then, I'll speak with your father. I have to tell one of them," he said.

"Then tell Daddy." Sick as he was, he would be better able to stand it, I thought. I don't know if that was the right decision or not, but I think Daddy already knew and I don't think even if we had told Mother she would have believed us. Mother all her life hasn't seen what she doesn't want to see.

The doctor stood up to go. "Stay in here as long as you like, I'll tell the nurses where you are if they need you," he said. He patted us both on the shoulder and left. I watched him walk out of the room with noiseless steps and the door swung slowly and silently shut behind him.

Macy was crying when I looked over at her, her whole body was shaking and she was holding her face in her hands making muffled sobbing noises. I patted her on the shoulder like the doctor had and said, "Life's a bitch, ain't it?" One of Daddy's favorite expressions. I wanted to reach over and hug her, but Macy and I neither one were touchers, none of our family is. Sometimes I ache to touch someone, but when I do it my part that's in contact with theirs feels all cold and exposed and I can't wait to get myself back to myself.

"Why am I crying for him?" she asked me. "All his life he was hateful to me, he never ever said a nice thing to me that I can remember. So why does it hurt to know he's dying?"

Someone, me I guess since there was no one else in the room, said, "Maybe because now you know he won't ever say a nice thing to you."

That produced a torrent of tears from her, so I kept patting. I wasn't crying. Not that I wasn't sorry that Daddy was dying, I was. But I don't cry, not when I'm hurting. I freeze up and feel like a block of ice inside, and it hurts not to cry sometimes but to me the worst thing in the world is for someone to see me cry. And the main person I never ever let see me cry was my father. "Do you want me to call Carlton?" I asked her. "He could come get you."

"No, that would just upset Mother and I'd have to think up something to tell her. Why don't I call and tell Carlton I'm going to be late and then stay here with you." When she reached over and took my hand it was like a shock went through me.

"Do that," I said, standing up and dropping my hand to my side so she would have to let go. I acted like I just wanted to get her to a phone fast, but the truth was I was scared of Macy holding my hand. It reminded me of the little sister I'd had a long time ago, the one I thought I had to protect from anything bad ever happening to her. I hadn't done a good job of protecting her and after I ran off I wasn't even around to try anymore. I almost cried then watching her leave the room, for a minute she wasn't the grown lady I watched like she was up to something all the time, she was the skinny little kid with the pigtails Grandma wadded up in ribbons on top of her ears.

"Call from the pay phone next to the nurses' station," I told her, "and I'll check on Daddy, then we can sit in here." She went and did like I told her. Macy always had.

"I'm glad you're here." That was the first thing she said to me when we walked back into that room. "I wouldn't have wanted Daddy to die and you be gone like you were. Why did you run away, Claire Louise, didn't you know we missed you?"

"To tell the truth, Macy, once I left I was so busy looking out for myself that I never much thought of you. I know that sounds hard but it's the truth."

"But why did you go? You were popular in school and it was

your senior year. Why run away with Ralph? Was it because Daddy didn't like him?"

Now this is truly surprising to me, the conversation Macy and I had that night. It was like for a little space of time there we were sisters. It didn't last. In fact, when I think back to the things we said, I wonder if I didn't imagine the whole conversation. But I didn't imagine our conversation, we truly had it. This is what I remember saying to her: "No," I said, "I didn't run away because Daddy didn't like Ralph, I knew he'd never like anybody I dated, same as he was always sarcastic to all my girlfriends. I'm not sure why I left. I think back and wonder myself sometimes. It's like I was maybe a different person back then. I wanted to hurt them both, Daddy for being such a drunken tyrant and Mother for letting him bully us all the time. It wasn't just that I had to go in the closet with him to let me have it every time Mother and I had a fight, I was used to that more or less. It was the sneers and the way he looked at me when I'd leave on a date. Like he knew just what I was up to. And I was, Macy. Most of the time Ralph and I were out parking and necking in his car near some rice well or another. And I was feeling all breathless when he touched me, and then coming home feeling guiltier than all get out. And sometimes I wanted him, Ralph, to touch me and then when he did and I liked it I would feel the most awful sense of shame and sometimes Daddy's face would get on top of Ralph's and I would forget I was in Ralph's car and think weird stuff like I was in Mother's linen closet and everybody in the world knew what I was doing. It just got to be too much going out with Ralph and my friends and trying to act like a happy little cheerleader and coming home to Daddy and his sneers and Mother there knowing it all and not doing a thing about it. I told myself I could get away in just one more year, but then Ralph started pushing me to run away now. He knew if I went off to college I'd never mess with him anymore. That's what he said, and even when I was denying it and kissing him and telling him I would love him forever, I was afraid that if I went off to college I wouldn't ever want him again. Maybe that's why I left, because I didn't think I could go off to college just like a regular little Susy Coed."

"But you were so smart, you had all A's."

"I know, I never worried about being smart, I just never fit in with the other girls. I felt old and dirty and like I had these secrets they would hate me for if they found out the truth about me."

"I'm sorry, Claire Louise," she said to me. "I hated it when Daddy was angry at you." She paused and then said softly, "You always sassed Mother. I wanted to talk back to them, but I never did. I was scared of them. You know, Claire Louise, I'd have never ever had the nerve to run off like you did. Weren't you scared?"

"Not really," I told her. "I mean I was, I guess, but seems like all my life I'd felt scared. Nothing new in that. And at least I knew I could control Ralph. Ralph I could tell to leave me alone and he'd listen to me. Well, at first he would. Before the drugs. He changed then, Ralph did. Got to where he reminded me more and more of Daddy. And Daddy, although I don't suppose I should speak ill of him, seeing as how he's dying, Daddy was nothing more or less than a drunken pervert who couldn't keep his hands off his own daughter!"

Just then I remembered where I was and who I was. "I'll be sorry I told you this later," I told Macy. "I always hate it later if I talk without being real careful. It's like I'm only safe when no one knows anything about me." It was when Macy reached over to hug me that I knew for sure I'd gone too far. I got that cold chilled feeling I get when I know I'm in danger, that warning roar that threatens to take over and push everything else out of my mind. "Let's talk about something else," I said. "That's all in the past now anyway." It wasn't like me to let go like that, to get angry over ancient history such as it was. It wasn't a bit like me.

I remember her saying to me, "You sounded just like Grandma when you said it's all in the past anyway."

"Well, it is," I told her, "and we've got to figure out what to do about Daddy." We went on and talked and decided to take him home as soon as the doctors said we could, which didn't happen for three weeks, I believe. And we never told Mother he was dying, just that the reason we were having nurses to stay at the house was for his shots, and as soon as he didn't need the shots anymore he wouldn't need the nurses. And that, in a weird sort of way, was the truth.

17

IT WASN'T UNTIL after we walked into our kitchen and dumped armloads of cluttered belongings all over the floor that I realized I hadn't been inside the city limits of Houston for almost three months. Three months since I had gone barefoot in my own house, I marveled to myself as I walked from room to room putting things away, touching pictures, rifling through the sheet music open on the piano. The best thing about coming home was realizing how happy I was to be back there. The second best thing was walking back and forth taking clothes from suitcase to closet. "Just think," I gloated to Carlton, "we've had an almost three-month vacation on an almost island, and the only dirty clothes we brought back are the ones on our backs. Can't beat that, can you?"

He grinned back at me. "Can't beat that," he repeated softly, coming over to hold me close. He kissed me on the top of my head and whispered, "Are you going to be okay, Macy? Is it okay to be home with us and not out there with your grandma?"

I felt such a surge of emotion at the tentative hopefulness in his voice. "Better than okay," I promised. "I feel wonderful to be here in my own house with my own husband's arms around me and my own kitchen floor covered with my own two sons unpacking the doodle bugs they brought back from the country. Oh, Carlton, it's so good to be back home," I said, hugging him back. And then I was kissing him and all I knew was that I was back where I belonged and I wanted nothing more than to get closer and closer to my wonderful patient understanding husband. "The kids are occupied," I whispered. "Let's bar the bedroom door and put up the Do Not Disturb sign." Which we did, emerging from our bedroom a good hour later relaxed and pleased with ourselves and ready to gather up the kids and go out for hamburgers. I'd been wrong, I told myself. The best thing about being home was falling back in bed with Carlton in our very own bedroom. Nothing beats that, I smiled to myself, remembering the past hour.

The next day was Labor Day. Mrs. Grant came over and Carlton grilled steaks and we all sat out on the deck and exchanged notes over our summer vacations. Abe and Roxanne were there as well. We even made homemade ice cream in the electric ice cream freezer Carlton and I had had in the garage still in the box for over a year now. "Hadn't been any point in taking it out to the country," I said. "Grandma would never see the wisdom in using an electric freezer when the old crank kind works fine."

I called her that afternoon while we were waiting for the ice cream to freeze and the kids were jumping in and out of the sprinkler and Roxanne and Mrs. Grant had run over to her house to get a tennis video Mrs. Grant was loaning Abe. I'm just fine, she told me when I asked what was wrong. She'd been in the yard when I called and sounded out of breath when she came to the phone. I asked her what she'd had to eat and she laughed and said I was the third person to call and ask her that question, seemed to her people in our family thought entirely too much about food. So then I asked her about her flowers and she told me they were just fine, about the same as they had been the day before as a matter of fact, and hadn't I better get back to my company? I was glad I called her. It didn't sound a bit like she was pining away for us, I told Carlton.

Tuesday, the day after Labor Day, our kids started first grade. First grade I thought in a panic, they'd be gone from eight o'clock, which was when the bus would pick them up, to almost four, which is when they'd be dropped off at home again. "Our babies are in school," I whispered to Carlton as we walked away from West U Elementary, holding hands, and I, at least, holding back tears. For all Carlton had taken the day off so we could celebrate our newfound freedom, the-kids-are-finally-in-school day we'd christened it, neither of us felt particularly happy to leave them that morning. Travis was placed in room four with Mrs. Butane, Scott across the hall in room eight with Mrs. Brooks. "They're too little for school," I said to Carlton as we walked hand in hand into the restaurant in the Houston Oaks Hotel where we were having brunch, whiling away the time until the shops in Galleria opened.

He looked at me sharply and then let out a hoot of laughter. "They're the biggest kids in their classes," he said, laughing and shaking his head.

I thought back to the rooms my children had just bounded into with little more than a careless "See you later" to us, their apprehensive parents who stood anxiously watching them explore their new world. "You're right," I remembered, "most of those other kids weren't as tall as either of ours. But size isn't everything, you should know that, you're the psychologist," I admonished my husband, determined to worry if I felt like worrying.

"No, it isn't, but our kids are ready for school. It's us, Macy. We're the ones who all of a sudden are not sure we like them growing up this fast."

He was right, Carlton was, they were ready but we weren't. I was discovering something about parenting I hadn't known before. There's more than one way to remember the first day at school, this voice inside me said. Yeah, I guess so, I admitted sheepishly back to myself, wondering for the first time if my mother had cried when I started first grade. Grandma had cried buckets the day I said good-bye to her as I drove off to college, I remembered. But I couldn't recall anyone looking upset when I climbed on that school bus the first day. Maybe my kids don't think I'm upset, either, I thought, recalling the tears I had held back. What do you know? I marveled to myself. And I heard my grandma's voice saying, more than one way to skin a cat, Macy, which relevant or not, I liked hearing.

Despite its teary start, the day after Labor Day turned out to be wonderful for Carlton and me. The nostalgia I felt for my rapidly disappearing babies didn't last much past the first sip of the champagne cocktail with which we started off our brunch. It was a good day, a wonderful day, one I held onto and replayed over and over in my head later when things got so nuts for a while. That's us, that's me and Carlton, I'd remind myself when I was thinking nothing would ever be okay for us again. I'm glad we had that day and all the shimmery summer ones before it, they were the cement that held me together when I didn't know if I'd lost my husband for good. Don't think about this, I'd tell myself, remember the day in the Galleria, or the night we came home from Grandma's. Remember that I'd tell myself, that's you and Carlton. This bad stuff, this isn't you, this is just a little misunderstanding. And then I'd bring out my summer with us and Grandma memories and my Labor Day memories and turn them over and over, remembering the good times to wipe out the bad.

When Carlton and I walked in from our celebratory the-kids-are-finally-in-school day, the phone was ringing and there was Claire Louise on the line telling us Daddy was back in the hospital from another heart attack. All that fall he was more in than out of the hospital. And when he finally went home we knew he was dying. The doctors told him the truth, but he never in any way acknowledged the fact that his death was imminent. At least he never let on to me, perhaps he did to someone else. Mother didn't act like she knew he wasn't ever going to get better, either. She kept talking about when Daddy got back on his feet right up to the end when he was getting morphine shots almost every hour, the pain was so bad.

There was a time, the night Claire Louise and I were there together in the hospital and the doctor told us about Daddy's condition, that I thought we were going to be close again. She talked to me like I was a real person, someone she cared about. She talked about the years before she ran away, about the way my daddy had hurt her and Mother and Grandma and I had ignored what was happening. I believed her then even though for years I had told myself just about every word that came out of my sister's mouth was a lie. I tried to explain our late-night hospital-room conversation to Carlton. She was scared of them, too, I remember telling him. Claire Louise was scared to death of Daddy and Mother, too. It was like she just kept acting worse and worse to cover up she was scared.

Now that I've thought it over and talked about what she said and all the other things I remembered, I do know Claire Louise wasn't totally a liar. At least she wasn't a liar about what happened to her when she was little. My parents were mean to her, and for all I used to think she could have hushed up and not gotten them mad all the time, I was wrong. Claire Louise, before she ran off, wasn't bad. Not really. Not like I thought. She was scared. And they were so hard on her, particularly Daddy. I remember cringing inside when I'd hear her start up, knowing from the first word out of her mouth as soon as she got Mother good and pissed off she was going to be sitting in that closet waiting for my father to come home and take his belt off and let her have it.

That wasn't right. You shouldn't do kids that way, no matter how smartmouth they are, punishing them the way she was punished is wrong. You know, Carlton, I told him, I was lucky. I had asthma and hives, I got hives at the drop of a hat. That's what saved me, that's why she got in trouble and I didn't. I'd start wheezing if Mother so much as looked at me cross-eyed. I remember the doctor telling her time and time again, now don't get this one upset, don't get her overheated, or overtired. She hasn't got the constitution of her sister. I hated it, thinking I was sickly compared to Claire Louise, I wanted to be big and brave just like I thought she was. But, looking back, I can see I was lucky. I got off easy compared to her. Not that what happened to her excuses everything she did afterwards, not at all. But I have to be fair and say Claire Louise did have some reasons to hate my father and my mother, and I guess me, too. After all, I lived there and I didn't stand up to them.

While my father was in the hospital, Mother stayed with Carlton and me most nights. Between looking after her and going back and forth to the hospital and trying to look in on Grandma every day, Carlton and the boys just had to fend for themselves. I regret that, missing the time with them. Basically my kids' first-grade year is a blur to me. But at the time I was so caught up in Daddy and Mother and in all the fighting that came later that nothing else stayed in my mind. My family like to cost me my marriage. That's not true, now that I am in therapy with Abe again I'm working hard to be honest, first of all with myself. To take responsibility for my actions. My family didn't cost me my marriage, I chose to put it second for so long that when I got back to it it wasn't there anymore. I do regret that, deeply. It's hard for me to accept that some things you can't go back and change, no matter how bad you want to.

This time when Daddy went home, Claire Louise had a hospital bed and a machine for oxygen and another little boxlike affair that I never did learn the purpose of all set up in his room. He never said a word about the hospital bed that time. I guess he knew he needed it. She had nurses lined up for around the clock. He did try to argue with her about that, but she said nobody here can give shots to you, and he didn't complain any longer. I guess the pain was already worse than he was letting on back then. Leastways, he didn't want to be without his shots. Between a nurse always upstairs with Daddy, and Mother and Claire Louise and Britt and Maryanne, and Lucy there all day, the house felt crowded. Once again I was in the way. I'd go and help Lucy get meals or run errands or sit with Daddy while Mother napped, but I knew if I didn't show up one day they'd manage just fine without me. That bothered me. I wanted them to need me and they didn't. So once again I was over at my grandma's in order to feel liked. I'd go see her, take her to town, and pick up things for her as well as Lucy. Belle was out there almost every day, too, both of us thinking we had to prop up Grandma, support her when her only son lay dying. But Grandma didn't act like she needed much propping. She kept on tending to her flower beds and playing bridge on Wednesdays, which was always at her house now since she didn't drive anymore, and watching her shows on television and ordering from the Sears Roebuck catalogue. And when I tried to talk to her about what was happening next door, she hushed me like she'd always done. If you can't fix it, don't dwell on it, she'd say.

Once a day, about ten o'clock, she'd walk next door and go up and sit with Daddy for a while. Ellen, the day nurse, would take herself down to the kitchen and have a cup of coffee and something sweet with Lucy when Grandma appeared. She'd pull up the straight chair beside his bed, and look at him careful-like. "Well, Stuart, you're still not feeling up to par," she said, each and every time I was there with her.

"No, Mama, recuperating is slow going," he'd answer.

"Seems to be," she'd say, "seems to be."

And then they would both just sit. Like as not Daddy's eyes would close and Grandma would stare out the window. Then she'd get up, restless with inactivity, and start pinching dead leaves off the plants in his room or turning them to face the sun a different way. Or she'd go to the bathroom and get the bathroom glass and fill it with water and then water the plants that felt dry when she stuck her finger in the soil. Sometimes she'd go back and forth four or five times, filling that little glass with water and his eyes would be open then and he'd follow her back and forth as she went. "You need anything?" she'd ask when she'd done all the plant tending she could do for the time being.

"No," he'd shake his head, "not that I can think of, thank you for asking." They were formal with each other, sounding more like still new acquaintances than mother and son. But they were covering new ground, maybe that accounts for the formality. "You doing okay with the herd?" he'd ask, referring to the cattle, which had been his responsibility since my grandfather died years ago.

"I reckon so, Lester has things in hand," she'd answer. Lester is a sort of cousin, the farmer next to us, who helped out when needed. "He's a godsend," she'd say.

"That he is, that he is," Daddy'd say, and drift off.

"Stuart, I'm going now, let me know if you need me." She'd always stand a minute in the doorway looking at him laying there with his eyes closed before she turned to go. I think she was waiting for him to need her, but he never did, at least he didn't any of the times I was upstairs and within earshot.

"I'll walk home with you, Grandma," I'd say and follow her down the stairs.

"Corabeth, what can I do?" Grandma always asked my mother as we walked through the den on our way out.

"Nothing, thank you for coming," my mother would say, as formal as my father. Claire Louise would fuss over Grandma then and wrap up something she and Lucy had cooked for her to take home, and like as not she'd come over later and take tea with Grandma and chat a bit. She could never let anyone be, Claire Louise couldn't. If she thought you weren't warming up to her, she'd fuss and fuss over you till you did. Almost every day she'd happen to see a new plant in the nursery where she'd happened to stop that Grandma needed. Or a book about her

194

plants. Grandma never read the books, but she always planted the plants. And tended to them, too.

Once I tried to talk to Daddy, only once. I was sitting with him while Ellen his nurse was downstairs and Mother was asleep in the next room. We were the only ones there. Claire Louise was off on an errand and the girls weren't home from school yet. I'd been watching him, old and shrunken and feeble looking, trying to see where the fierce man I'd been so afraid of was gone to. I felt like crying, I felt sorry for him, dying and pitiful looking, and sorry for me, for being about to lose the only father I had ever had.

When his eyes opened he looked at me clear as everything, and his eyes told me he was lucid, something he was less and less of the time now. A voice inside told me if I didn't talk to him now, I might never get the chance again, and I practiced in my head what I should say. I'd get the first sentence planned in my mind and then a scared feeling would spread over me and I couldn't think what could come next. But the voice inside me kept saying, talk to him now, if you don't talk to him now you won't get to.

"Daddy, about the things that happened a long time ago, the bad things, I forgive you. It doesn't bother me anymore what you did." His eyes shifted and I knew he knew what I meant, at least as much as I knew then. He didn't say anything though. "You didn't mean it to be that way, I guess, and you didn't mean to hurt us, I don't believe you did. So if you're in all this pain because you're punishing yourself, then you don't have to do that anymore. It's all over, water under the bridge." I looked at him and felt sorry and relieved that I'd spoken up. I'm not sure where those words came from. When I thought about them later they puzzled me, but at the time they made sense. "One thing I always wondered about, Daddy, sometimes you did nice things for me, I know that, but did you ever love me? I always wanted to know about that." I didn't expect him to answer me. My daddy wasn't the type to talk about love and feelings and such. But he did. He looked up at me and tears ran down his cheeks, tears that might have been from the pain but weren't. "I loved you. I just made a mess of it," he said. I held his hand then and put my face down on both our hands and cried. And when I looked up, his eyes were closed and he appeared to have drifted off.

Later I thought over what he'd said, and I wanted to believe it, I did. But he never said my name and the little voice that tells me when I'm wrong said, maybe he thought you were your mother or your sister, maybe he didn't know it was you, Macy Rose. And my little voice argued back, no, he looked right at you, it was you he meant, you, Macy Rose. And that's what I believe, he knew it was me, he did.

I wish I could have talked it all over with Carlton, nights when I lay in bed over at Grandma's and couldn't sleep I'd miss my husband so much. I'd tell him everything that had happened during the day and I'd imagine what he said back to me and I'd hug a pillow and try to fool myself to thinking it was hugging me back. But the truth was Carlton and I were not getting on too well by then. We'd had one horrible fight when I'd started sleeping at Grandma's instead of coming home nights. "Your children need you, I need you," he said.

"But my father is dying and my grandmother is alone," I'd replied. "Can't you see what I'm going through?"

"Macy, of course I see that, but you're completely cutting yourself off from us. I can understand your need to be out there days, but nights too? Think, Macy."

Looking back, I know he was right, but at the time it wasn't clear to me. I was out there, back home, and wanting to make right what couldn't be made right in the time left, however long that was.

I think maybe Daddy tried to warn me, to apologize even for what happened after he died. Looking back, it was about two weeks before he died that he signed the new will, the one that left everything to Claire Louise. She sent me off to Houston to the rental agency to pick up a wheelchair that he needed. He couldn't stand up anymore, but the doctor thought maybe we could get him up and move him over to the window several times a day if we had a chair. So she sent me to fetch it. I wondered at the time why they couldn't just deliver it, but I didn't think overlong about it. And then there was a list of about four or five other errands to run, spread out all over the place. By the time I got back it was after three, and I'd been gone since eight o'clock in the morning.

Belle suspected something. "Your father had a visitor, big fat man in a suit," she told me. When I asked Claire Louise, she said it was a friend of hers, come to express his sympathy, and I didn't think twice about it. But that night, when I went up to tell Daddy good night like I always did, he was rambling in his talk, like he was most days now. The medicine did that to him, I guess, because right before he had a shot, he was tossing and moaning but he'd make sense then, too. And he hadn't had his nighttime shot yet when he looked at me and said, "Macy, you go on back to Carlton. He's a good man, you should live with him."

"Oh, Daddy, I will," I said. "I'm just out here helping out during the emergency."

"I'm sorry if I messed up your life," he said.

"Hush, Daddy," I said, "my life is not messed up."

"Some things I wish I could undo, shouldn't have . . ." he said, and just then Jeanette, the night nurse, came in with his shot and I told him good night. And although I saw him daily for the next two weeks, he was never again clearheaded enough to talk, and then he died and was gone. And even though it was expected, it came as a shock, and surprised me how sharp a grief I felt.

Carlton came out when Daddy died and stayed with me and Grandma until after the funeral. He left the boys in town with Mrs. Grant, thinking they were too young for all the sorrowing. Maybe that was a mistake, maybe not. I sometimes think if I'd had my kids with me at Daddy's funeral I would have had an easier time remembering what I later learned the hard way. Life is for the living, and fighting over what some person who is dead and gone has left you is nothing more or less than a waste of time and energy. People are important, not things, and love is important, particularly when you are lucky enough to have love freely given to you, the way my husband and children gave it to me all along. But at that time, I didn't think nearly as clearly as I do now. Like I said, some things I learned the hard way.

Carlton begged me to go back with him the day after my daddy's funeral but by then I had seen the new will and nothing could drag me away from my grandmother's house for long. I resolved to fight Claire Louise and Mother, too, if I had to, and I didn't dare leave Grandma unprotected either or she would be next. I knew that as well as I knew I was sitting there.

18

B Y THE TIME Daddy came home from the hospital the last time, I had more or less assumed responsibility for all of the farm and household affairs. It was the only way to keep things going. It took a bit of studying and hours of putting things in place and organizing before I had it all straight in my mind, just how much money he had where and how much land and what have you. I have to admit I was surprised, I knew tight as he'd always been that he'd have saved a tidy sum, but the total amount took my breath away. All in all he was worth in the millions. Most of that in land, but there were savings accounts in almost every bank in the county. It was a relief to know we didn't have to worry about the medical bills, because one thing Daddy had apparently not been in favor of was insurance. There were no policies of any sort. It was in October that I took Mother to town and we opened the safety deposit box. I got her to put my name on all the accounts then too. It was necessary if I was going to have to look after her, she understood that.

When I read their wills that night, it came as a shock to me to see that everything had been left to Macy, everything. Oh, it said whichever one of them went first, the other got whatever they had, but after they were both gone, everything was to go to Macy. And it said in there that I'd been written out because I had run off and I wasn't to be considered in the dispersal thereof, and so forth and so on. When I tell you my blood ran cold, believe me I am understating my reaction by far. I could not believe after the years of my life I had devoted to them, this was how I was being treated. And my children! Also left out in the cold. The next morning, I confronted Mother with it, Daddy being not able to carry on a conversation at that point. I was crying, I was that upset, I don't mind telling you.

"Mother, how could you do this to me?" I asked. "You might as well put a knife in me."

"That was your father's doing," she said. "He was so angry when you left, he went straight to town and wrote out that will. Like as not he never thought about it again."

"But, Mother, if you intend to treat me this way, then I'll be out of here tomorrow. My girls and I will go and that will be the last you ever hear of us. Not that we want to, it breaks my heart to think of leaving you here alone, going blind and Daddy going downhill faster and faster every day, but if you care no more for me than this I have no choice, I have to leave. Likely as not, Lucy will stay with you, but she's not family, not someone you could trust. And Macy would come out once a week or so, but she has her husband who nags her all the time not to spend time with you so I don't know how much you could count on her. It grieves me to think of you out here like that, maybe in want and no one who cares about you like I do and your grandchildren do here with you. But now that I've seen down on paper in black and white what you really think of me, perhaps you don't want me around anyway. Maybe I just thought you loved me, you and Daddy. I guess I was right to run away all those years ago, you don't love me."

"Claire Louise, that isn't true. We do so love you. That will was written years ago. You can read the date and see that."

"But it hasn't been changed, so as far as the world knows it stands," I reminded her.

"I expect Stuart always meant to change it. I'm sure he will soon as he is up and around again."

"No, no," I shrieked, upset as could be. "I'm not going to stay another day, now that I've seen that paper."

She cried and begged me not to leave her, and said she'd get Mr. Shasta, their lawyer, out and see what could be done. But I didn't trust him. He'd written the first will and seen me at least once a week in church for over ten years now and never given me a word of warning. "No," I told her, "I have a friend over in Ruston who's a lawyer. I'll call him. Mr. Shasta is too slow moving."

"But we've always used him," Mother said.

"Not anymore," I told her and I went over to Ruston that day and had Mr. Amso draw up a new will and bring it out and get Daddy to sign it the very next day. The nurses were witnesses and so was Mother, and their signatures are on it and it is as legal as it can be. And the new will was a fair one in view of the circumstances. Contrary to what Macy would like to believe, Mother and Daddy knew exactly what they were signing. Naturally, the homeplace and the farm we lived on went to me. I was, after all, living there and running it, and it was only right that I continue. And the joint accounts were Mother's. She wasn't gone yet, after all. Some of the land went to Macy, some to me. Her contention that I got all the good parcels is ridiculous. She has in total acreage a fair amount, don't let her kid you otherwise. But let's face it, Macy is married and has a husband with a good income, and her life is in Houston. Mine is out here, the farm is mine. She has no interest in it and shouldn't expect to get half of it just because she is also his daughter. I ask you, which one of us has spent the past ten years out here looking after things? Right, I rest my case.

19

DADDY'S FUNERAL was in the morning at ten o'clock and then the ladies of the church had a big meal fixed for the family. There were about thirty or forty of us there to eat. Even though it was up in November it was a warm day, hushed and still, like a storm was coming. The house felt all closed up and stuffy, like a sick person was lying in the bed upstairs instead of having been buried in the ground that very morning.

Out in the sunlight at the cemetery I looked at my mother and saw a feeble lady, held up by her older daughter, who slumped over when she walked forward and peered at people when they spoke to her, as if she were listening hard for clues to tell her who she was talking to. Grandma was on the front row, too, with Carlton on one side of her and Belle on the other. Grandma looked a sight better than Mother. She stood up straight and looked people in the eye and nodded at them and thanked them for coming. Over and over I got hugged and people told me how sorry they were, and I nodded and said thank you for coming, thank you for caring, it's so good to see you, until I felt so tired I couldn't hear what I was saying anymore. Claire Louise and her two girls had on navy linen dresses with big embroidered collars and their blond hair sparkled and glimmered where the sun fell on it. They stood tall and slim, even Maryanne, and all the kissing and hugging and crying didn't smear Claire Louise's makeup. She looked like a television person at a funeral, grieving and stately and beautifully groomed throughout her ordeal. I felt dowdy beside her. My dress was a muddy brown and shorter than this year's style. Carlton had brought it from my closet the day before, when he had come out. And my shoes were run over at the heels. And my haircut from summer was grown out and uneven. I felt guilty there at my own father's funeral, thinking more about how shabby I looked compared to my sister than I did about my poor father, who was now going to have to face the hereafter with whatever sins he had not repented. It occurred to me why church made Grandma more nervous the older she got. The closer you approached your final reward, the more apt you were to wonder whether you would get one. And how you were going to explain certain things.

The ladies put out a big spread of food and then left us to eat our meal in grieving solitude. And after we ate, we sat around for a while and talked quietlike, similar to a family reunion but subdued, and some people told stories about Daddy, nice ones, ones that made you smile to hear. Most of them I had heard before but some of them were new to me. And then one by one they drifted off and Claire Louise said before Aunt Claire and Grandma left she had called Daddy's lawyer to read the will while we were all together. Mother thought it would be best, she added, and I knew right then she was up to something.

When a man walked in, I recalled Belle saying a fat man in a suit came to see your daddy today, and I knew then what was happening. "Mr. Amso?" I asked. "What happened to Mr. Shasta who has been Mother and Daddy's lawyer forever?" Claire Louise had introduced Mr. Amso to us as a highly recommended attorney. "Who highly recommended him I would like to know?" I asked Claire Louise.

Carlton reached over and put his hand on my arm as if to say calm down, but I was too upset at having something put over on me to calm down. Claire Louise said in her curt way, the way she has when she wants to let you know you are not doing what she has in mind for you to do, "Macy, we can talk about Mr. Amso's recommendations later. Right now he's all the way over from Ruston to read us Daddy's last will and testament, and I think we should all settle down and and let him do just that."

Which he did. We all, Aunt Claire and her daughters, Amanda and Kara, and Carlton and me, and Grandma and Belle, and Mother listened in shocked silence. Even Mother appeared surprised to learn she was now a guest in her own home. "Oh," she said when he was through telling us Claire Louise now owned most of everything they had, "oh" in that genteel way she has of saying a whole sentence with one inquiring little surprised sound.

Claire Louise leaned over and patted her on the hand. "Isn't that just the way you and Daddy wanted it?" she prompted Mother. All our heads swiveled to watch for her answer.

"Well, I had thought that, of course, the homeplace would remain in my name as long as I'm around." The nervous little laugh she gave was pitiful to hear.

"Why, Mrs. Richards," Mr. Amso said in an oily voice, "you and your husband and I talked at length about the settlement of your joint property, and I clearly understood you both to wish the bulk of your disbursements to go at this time to avoid the possibility of your heirs having to pay inheritance taxes a second time."

Mother just nodded uncertainly. "I do recall . . ." she said, her voice trailing off as if she was unsure what she was supposed to recall. Her head bobbed like an old lady's.

"When was this will written?" I asked.

"It was signed almost three weeks ago today."

The pieces fell into place. The only day it could have happened was the day Claire Louise had me running on wild-goose chases all over Houston. "So that's when you did it," I told her, looking her straight in the eye and letting her know for once and all I was through trusting her. "You sent me off to run errands for you and then you got your shyster lawyer in here to screw me out of my inheritance and your own mother out of her home." Carlton tried to catch my eye and warn me to stop and think, but I was too angry to feel any compunctions whatsoever about common decency or even simple politeness for that matter.

Mr. Amso drew his oily self up to his full six feet and probably three hundred pounds and attempted to brush some dignity into the baggy stained suit that was hanging to his knees in the back. "I beg your pardon, young lady."

"Don't look at me like that," I told him. "Only a shyster would come out here and write up a will for a man on his deathbed, a man too sick to even know who's in the room with him, much less what he is signing."

"The will was read to your mother and father," he reminded me, "and they both signed it."

"Then how come Mother is so surprised at what the damn thing says?" I asked him. "I demand to see the other will, the one this one supposedly replaces."

He spread his arms out as if to say he had nothing to do with any other wills.

"Where is it, Claire Louise?" I asked her.

"It was thrown away, at Daddy's request," she said to me, looking me straight in the eye as she lied. Her eyes were black holes that day, warning undying enmity to me for the way I was crossing her, but I didn't care. I was mad enough at her then to relish her enmity, to revel in the fact that for once everything was out in the open and people were seeing her for the sneak she was. I looked around the room. Aunt Claire had a pained look on her face and was studying the floor, which is where her daughters' eyes were also planted. Grandma was fidgeting, her hands pulling at each other like they were itching from poison ivy. And Carlton looked more distressed than angry or indignant. "You won't get away with it," I told her. "First thing tomorrow, I am getting a hold of Mr. Shasta; he'll have a copy of that other will and I'll fight this. They plainly didn't know what they were signing." Mother must have felt my eyes on her. She looked away as I sat there waiting for her to speak. "Isn't that so, Mother?" I finally prompted her.

"No," she said, drawing the words out like she was having to think real hard what she would say, "I do believe I signed what Mr. Amso read. I recall that now." Claire Louise's hand had been clamped down tight on Mother's arm reminding her of what she was supposed to say.

Disgusted, I looked away. "Well, you will never convince me Daddy did. Daddy was fair, he would have never left me out like he did."

Carlton spoke for the first time. "Macy, your father didn't exclude you. From the way I just heard it, he left you over two hundred acres of land."

"The dregs!" I exploded. "All I got was what she didn't want. She got three times as much land as I did and all the money and cattle."

"I must intervene here," Mr. Amso said. "All the assets other than land remain under the control of the late Mr. Richards's spouse, Mrs. Corabeth Richards."

"Ha, Claire Louise has her name on every account there is, which is as good as leaving it to her in my opinion."

The meeting ended soon after that. Aunt Claire and her daughters left, no richer than they had been when they arrived. I wondered about that. Much of Daddy's land had been deeded over to him from my grandparents. I wondered if there was other land Aunt Claire had been given. It occurred to me Claire Louise probably knew to a dime how much every relative we had owned, and here I was wondering if they had enough or had been expecting to be left something in that will. Belle and Grandma and Carlton and I walked back across the pasture to Grandma's where Belle's daughter was waiting to drive her back to town. Carlton went inside and came out with both of our suitcases, just as it occurred to me to ask Grandma about her own situation. "What about you?" I asked her. "Does that mean Claire Louise owns your house, too?"

"No," she laughed. "My house and about fifty acres around it is still mine. The rest of it I signed over to your father years ago. It seemed only fair. He was doing all the work running it."

I thought about that for a minute. Was she telling me she agreed with that new will, the one leaving everything to my sister? Finally I asked her. "Well, I know Stuart had planned that the homeplace go to you, Macy, but for the past years it has been Claire Louise out here doing the work. I can see why he might have changed his mind."

"You're going to fall for her scheming too, aren't you?"

"No," she laughed again, "I know Claire Louise and her ways as well as you do. But what's done's done. Water under the bridge. No use worrying over it at this late date."

"But it's not fair, Grandma. All her life she's gotten what she wanted and I've gotten what's left over. I should at least get half!"

"Macy, take my advice, there's only so much land you can stand on at one time. Or money you can spend. You've got things Claire Louise doesn't. A husband, a career if you want it, two fine boys. Take what's yours and forget about what she's got."

I couldn't believe my ears. My grandmother was telling me

to take this slap in the face lying down. And from the look on Carlton's face he was agreeing with her. Angrily I looked from one to the other. Grandma pulled on her gardening gloves and tied her straw hat on her head, preparing to go back to her beloved flower beds. "Let it alone, Macy. Go home and tend to your family and let it alone."

And there stood Carlton waiting, my suitcase and his on the gravel beside his car. Right then I hated him and my grandmother too. They weren't on my side; they as well as everyone else had abandoned me. And then I remembered it was just today we had buried Daddy, Grandma's only son. Of course she was so upset she wasn't thinking straight. "Grandma, it was awful of Claire Louise to get that will read today and Daddy not even cold yet. Of course you don't want to get into that now. I'm sorry." I hugged her, but she pulled back and looked at me straight on. "Macy, I don't want to get into wills and what gets left at any time, and you best leave it lay yourself." But I didn't listen to her. I might have been better off by far if I could have let go of that anger and listened to my grandmother. I should have remembered I trusted her; her and Carlton I trusted. But I was so caught up in my hurt I went and hurt myself worse than my sister ever managed to.

It hadn't occurred to me to go home that night, to leave my grandmother alone on the night her only son had been laid to rest. "I'll stay with you," I told her. "You don't want to be by yourself tonight."

"You go on home," she said. "You've got a family needs you. I've been alone a long time and I'll be just fine." And so I went. When I got home the boys were strange with me, like I was someone they didn't know so well. I hadn't been around them to speak of in over three months and when I tried to talk to them and play with them I felt awkward and inept. "Three months is a long time for six-year-olds," Carlton said. "Give yourself a few days and they'll relearn you." Which was good advice also, but I didn't seem to be into taking good advice back then.

20

MOTHER WAS in the kitchen with Lucy when I got home from shopping. She had a cup of tea in front of her and a plate of cookies, Christmas ones Maryanne and I had decorated the night before. I'd spent all day scouring the stores. With Daddy's illness I had let my shopping pile up later than I ever liked to, but I was making headway in getting caught up on my list, which was a good feeling. "Oh, Mother, you're eating the cookies. How are they?"

"You girls did a good job," she replied, but her voice held the self-pitying note it contained more often than not these days. Sure enough, I looked over and saw her face wrinkling up, she was fixing to cry.

"Now, don't you start," I told her sternly. "Here I've been out all day fighting the crowds so we can have Santa Claus and I come home and you start to tune up. Come on upstairs and let me show you what I've got so we can get these things put away before the girls get home." I managed to jolly her up enough to get her upstairs into the new den, which is what Daddy's room had been turned into. When I remodeled the upstairs, I had bought a La-Z-Boy recliner, one of those that doesn't look like a recliner at all, for her, and I settled her into that before I began pulling out packages and sorting things into piles.

"I bought this rabbit jacket for you to give Maryanne, won't she just love it?" Mother patted the fur and said, "Oh, yes, she'll enjoy this." What I didn't tell her at that time was Santa Claus had also bought three-quarter-length mink jackets for both of us. We had had a hard year and deserved them, I told myself. I had even gone ahead and bought one for Britt, an extravagance for a high school student but it occurred to me that she'd wear it forever, not outgrow it like Maryanne was sure to do the rabbit one. Britt's was actually a bomber-style leather jacket with a mink lining, so when I showed it to Mother I just held it up near her and she didn't realize the lining was mink at all.

I had bags and bags of new clothes for the girls and lots for me and Mother too, and as I pulled them out for her to admire she oohed and aahed and enjoyed herself. Then I started showing her the new ornaments I had bought for the trees.

"Trees?" she asked.

"Yes, I thought we'd have a small one up here, just a family one, and I'm using only the pink and silver ornaments for it. Then for the big tree in the living room I thought we would have these red ornaments and use the plaid bows. And I got the cutest centerpiece for the dining room table, tartan plaid like the tree ribbons and with little Scottie dogs on it."

"Nice," Mother said, fingering it as I held it out in front of her. "But we have boxes and boxes of ornaments in the basement."

"Not anymore," I told her, pleased at the progress I had made in that department. "All that mess was so moldy and nasty. I had James haul off everything that was down there except the washer and dryer."

"What? Claire Louise, there were some valuable things in the basement. And some of those Christmas ornaments were hand-blown."

"Well, maybe they're on someone else's tree this year. I don't have any idea what James did with all that junk, because I told him we had no use for it."

"My mother's wedding dress was in the basement, packed in mothballs."

"It was falling apart, you wouldn't have wanted it, trust me."

"Aunt Myrtle's sewing machine."

"Whatever would I have saved that for? You have a good one Daddy bought you five years ago you've never used."

"What about the old dishes, the ones that belonged to Grandma Richards? Surely you didn't give them away?"

"Yes, I did. You told me yourself you had never cared for dishes with purple flowers and I certainly had no use for them."

"Claire Louise, I distinctly remember you telling me you were straightening up the basement. You never told me you were getting rid of everything down there!"

"Now, Mother, don't get upset. This is precisely why I didn't tell you what I was doing. You have no use for anything down there and if the stairs weren't so steep, I'd take you down and show you just what an improvement cleaning it out has made."

"But you had no right to do that, those things were not yours to give away." Mother's voice sounded as sharp and angry as it had years ago when she had been sending me upstairs to wait for Daddy to come home and punish me. I felt a surge of anger at her in return, all the things I was doing for her and here she was criticizing me for getting rid of some old junk she'd never in a hundred years need.

"It happens to be my basement now," I told her, "and I wanted it clean."

"Your basement? And since when is that your basement?"

"Since Daddy died and left me the house," I reminded her.

"Oh," she said.

I hated to be mean to Mother, but sometimes it was necessary. If nothing else it snapped her out of that self-pitying tone of voice I hated. "Now, Mother, you're tired and cranky, why don't you lean back in your chair and rest a little. I think if I hurry I can get most of these things wrapped up and downstairs before the girls get home."

She was quiet for a long time before she spoke again, and when she did it was as if the previous conversation had never taken place. "I've been counting, Claire Louise, there aren't too many people who will be at our Christmas table."

That got me to thinking. "What about Grandma?"

"She was over this morning and said not to count on her, Macy has asked her to come down there."

"Well, we could ask Claire and her children and their families. Time you two buried the hatchet anyway." I hadn't seen them myself since Daddy's funeral, but it occurred to me they didn't appear to be siding with Macy the way that some of our other relatives had done, and it might be real smart to cement that relationship.

"No, they are all going out to Colorado to be with her husband's family."

"Even Kara and her kids?" Kara had married a local boy, one who as far as I could see had not made particularly good. He worked as a mechanic at the Ford place and always had a headful of greasy hair with an old cap pressed down on top of it. "How can they afford it?" They had three children.

"Claire is paying for the airfare for the entire family, is what Grandma said."

I thought about what Mother had said while I was wrapping packages. Christmas with only the four of us didn't sound bad, it just was not what I had in mind. As I cast my mind over who else there was, I realized there literally were no family members I had any use for right then. The minute Mary Beth's name popped into my mind, I picked up the phone and dialed her number.

"Mary Beth, Claire Louise here. What are your Christmas plans?" And that's when I learned she was dating a widower who had two children just the ages of her kids, someone from Houston she had met when she started attending Parents Without Partners down there. And they were having Christmas at her house with her parents, who were driving up from the valley. Resolving not to take no for an answer, I convinced her, with the company she had coming, the last thing she wanted to do was cook a big dinner Christmas Day. They all needed to come out and spend Christmas with us. Which added nine people to our table, I gleefully told Mother. Then Mother said that made thirteen, which was an unlucky number. Nonsense, I told her, but when I was in town two days later and ran into Hugh Sawyer and he told me his wife was going to be up in Boston with her family over Christmas but he wasn't going to be able to go, I suggested that he join us. And since he was all alone, I insisted he come out Christmas Eve, which is when we open our packages and have a buffet supper, and Christmas morning, which is when we always have my famous sour-cream pancakes I do not make any other time of the year so they will stay special. And when later Hugh told me it was without a doubt the best Christmas of his life, I had to agree with him. I myself had never experienced a holiday more meaningful.

Hugh and I got to be closer and closer friends in the new year. He was such a handsome man, tall with gray hair and clear blue eyes. He owned several western-wear shops in Houston and Dallas and drove a Mercedes and wore handmade boots and expensive Stetson hats. For all he had never lived on a farm, he looked very much the part of a gentleman farmer.

We started going out several nights a week. We'd drive into Houston for dinner and a show, and then sometimes stop for a nightcap on the way home. He had, besides his house in Molly's Point, an apartment in Houston where we sometimes went for coffee and conversation. I felt sorry for him. His wife was a Yankee and hated the gulf coast area. She rarely came down anymore, he said, and with his business he couldn't just take off and go up to Boston at the drop of the hat. I happened to be with him the night she called and said she had bought half interest in a children's bookstore and was going to be working there most days until it got off the ground. He was shocked, and sad, and turned to me with the loneliest look and said, "This is it, Clara Lou (he called me Clara Lou), I've lost her for sure now. I'm all alone."

"No, not all alone," I reminded him. "You have me for your friend, and believe me, I understand what it means to be lonely."

That was the first night we made love, Hugh and I, just two lonely people clinging together in our grief. We didn't know each other well enough to say that we were in love. We were going to take it slow and sure, we told ourselves. We were determined not to get carried away, not to read more into our relationship than was actually there. But the truth was, I had known I was in love with Hugh from the first time he had smiled that slow smile of his and said yes ma'am to me when I asked him if he would like another cup of coffee. He was so gentle, so easygoing. I couldn't understand how his wife could treat him the way she was doing. And I resolved to make it up to him.

About March both Hugh and I started noticing the ads in the paper for cruises. You know how they show up in the winter, and then about February or March you start seeing all the specials advertised. One thing I inherited from my daddy is my love of a bargain, I told Hugh, and he said he had to admit he had noticed that trait in himself. Perfect for a honeymoon, I thought, but as far as I knew Hugh hadn't done anything about a divorce although I knew for sure he had not seen Madeline, his estranged wife, for months. I wish we could go away for a cruise, I told him, but of course I would never take a trip with any man not my husband. Hugh was a true gentleman and knew immediately what I meant.

I don't want to push you into anything, I told him repeatedly, and he assured me that his marriage was over, that it was a mere formality at this point. Then why aren't you divorced? I asked him, curious if nothing more.

Inertia was his answer to me and when the next week he showed me tickets he had bought for a two-week Caribbean cruise for two, I was dumbfounded. "Tickets for Mr. and Mrs. Hugh Sawyer," I read aloud from the cover. "Are you and Madeline—?" I asked, and he stopped me with a kiss.

"No," he told me when I pulled back, "my divorce was final last week."

"I didn't know you had filed," I replied.

"I didn't, she did, and I have the final papers right here. You and I are flying down to San Juan, we'll get married there, and then we'll cruise for two weeks."

My initial reaction was jubilation. I remember thinking I won when he told me he wanted to marry me. But then I had to stop and think a bit. I was not at all used to someone else making plans for me and I wasn't sure I liked it.

"Why didn't you tell me you were getting a divorce?" I asked him, not liking that he had kept that a secret from me.

"Oh, you were so cute hinting and all I decided to wait and surprise you."

"Hinting! Hinting about what? I never for a minute . . ."

"Oh, come on Clara Lou, you remember all those remarks you made about a cruise would be nice if only we could get married. If you said that once, you said it a hundred times."

"I did not, and my name is Claire Louise," I reminded him.

"But you're my little Clara Lou, aren't you?" Sometimes Hugh was just a little too cute, but he meant well and he did have four western-wear outlets and drive the most expensive Mercedes you can buy. Too cute isn't much of a problem stacked up to that.

"Well, I was just thinking out loud maybe. If I did say that a time or two it certainly doesn't mean I was wanting you to divorce your wife and marry me."

"Are you saying you won't?" he asked with a teasing gleam in his eye. I didn't like him to be that sure of me.

"I certainly need to think this over. Come to think of it, I don't believe I have actually heard you propose to me."

"Ah, the lady longs for the formality of a proposal," he joked. "Perhaps on bended knee," he said, sliding off the couch and onto his knees in front of me. "Would you, fair Clara Lou, do me the honor of becoming my wife?" He held both my hands in his and behind the twinkle in his eye I detected a steely glint, and at that moment I recognized that Hugh Sawyer was a determined man, a proud man, and I grasped the fact that if I didn't accept him immediately there was little likelihood I would get a second chance. Hugh, I perceived, was not in the habit of being turned down.

"Oh, Hugh, get up from that floor. Of course, I'd marry you tomorrow if it were possible, you know I'm wild about you. But, much as I want to marry you, as much as I would like to rush off with you right now and disappear into the sunset, I do have other responsibilities I have to keep in mind."

He stood from the floor and sat beside me, still on the couch but now there was six inches between us where before there had been no room at all. I saw immediately my analysis of the situation had been correct. Hugh did not like to have his plans spurned, or even questioned.

He raised an arrogant eyebrow at me, as if daring me to continue. Careful, I cautioned myself. I didn't want to destroy the wonderful relationship we shared. "Oh, Hugh, try to understand. I have two daughters and a mother totally dependent on me. I'm the one who has to take care of every single thing on my farm, not to mention I also look after Grandma. How can I run off and get married without making provisions for them while I'm gone? And what about when we get back? We haven't talked about where we'll live or what we'll do or anything! You're moving too fast, Hugh! I can't keep up with you." The look in his eyes had not softened in the slightest and I felt a flutter of fear in my stomach. Tears rushed to my eyes. "Don't look at me so mean," I said, starting to cry. "I hate it when you look at me like that."

"Now, Clara Lou, I didn't mean to make you cry, it's just that when a man plans a surprise for a woman she's been hinting on and on about, he's a might taken aback when she doesn't act like it meets with her approval."

"Oh, Hugh, of course I approve of your plan, you know how much I love you and want to be with you every minute of the day. But you know surprises can be a little scary too, especially to someone like me who is in the habit of looking out for others and doing all the taking care of and planning. I'm just not used to someone doing for me, not that I wouldn't love to get used to it," I told him, pulling him forward to kiss me. Afterwards we kissed for the longest time until I told him he was going to have to stop, I didn't think my heart could stand all this happiness.

"I had thought you'd move into my house in town," he told me later that night when I got him back to talking about what we would do after the honeymoon.

I frowned at him, thinking this might not be so easy after all. "But I could never live in a house your ex-wife decorated," I told him.

"Then redecorate it to suit yourself," he said.

"But she lived there!"

"Well, you can't expect me to move way out there to the country with all those females. Not a chance."

I hadn't thought much about that. "What about if we build ourselves a new house?" I had the homeplace pretty much in shape now and I thought Mother could stay there. I'd have Lucy help me find someone to live in with her. Maybe even Lucy herself if I approached her right. Truth was, Mother was getting on my nerves lately with her weepy ways. And if Hugh and I built a new modern house on some of my land I could have the fun of building a brand-new house from the ground up. I love to decorate and fix up houses, and I'd never yet gotten to build one without having to worry about suiting other people. There was a hill over on the other side of Grandma's house that would be a perfect spot for a house. I'd thought that often. And the land was mine, too. I told Hugh about it and was surprised when he wasn't right off as excited as I was.

"Seems to me right now our problem is we've got one house more than we need. Doesn't make any sense to build another house."

"But we need a place of our own, one no one else has had

anything to do with. It's important to start off fresh," I told him. "Please, Hugh," I begged him, "I would so love us to have our very own brand-new house. If it's the money you're worried about I could probably help out there, and it's not like we would have to buy the land or anything."

He reacted as if I had insulted him. Hugh hated for someone to imply he couldn't afford something. "Of course it's not the money. I expect you already have in mind what kind of house you would like, don't you?"

"Well, I've always loved colonial houses. The only time I ever got to build me a house all I could afford was a tacky little ranch-style three-bedroom. I'd like to have a big brick house with white columns in front and porches, two- or maybe three-story, big rooms, fireplaces everywhere, maybe even in the master bedroom. Wouldn't that be romantic? And one of those huge big bathtubs two people can get into together and spread out in, wouldn't that be grand?"

He grinned at me and I knew I had won even before he said to me, "Fortunately I know a good builder, I'll call him tomorrow."

21

I MADE A MISTAKE at the will reading, I shouldn't have let on I was upset. All I accomplished was to let Claire Louise know I was on to her. Up till then, I think she must have had herself believing I thought she was little Miss Goody Two Shoes, the way she always pretended to be. After that the gloves were off, so to speak, and she knew I saw her as she was.

In spite of his denials, I firmly believe that somehow or another she got to Mr. Shasta before I did and convinced him not to help me. Or maybe it was what Grandma said to him. Whatever, when I walked into his office four days after Daddy's funeral, I saw on his face he was not happy to see me.

Mr. Shasta looked like the actor who played Scarlett O'Hara's father in *Gone With the Wind*. He was a little portly and had thick white hair and bushy white eyebrows and he nodded in a kindly fashion when he spoke to ladies. I had always liked him. I liked the suits he wore whatever the weather. He had a real fatherly way about him, too, you felt as if you could trust him just looking at him.

"I'll come right to the point," I said. "I want to sue my sister. She has gotten some shyster lawyer from Ruston to write a will my daddy signed when he was not even conscious like as not. And now I have lost everything. I want to sue Claire Louise and get that will thrown out and the right one put back in place."

"You sit down, Macy," Mr. Shasta told me, "and let Mrs. Marshall get us some coffee and then we'll talk about what you have on your mind."

I practically had to pry my hands off the back of the chair they were gripping so I could let go and sit down in the red leather chair over to one side of his office. He waited until Mrs. Marshall served us both coffee and little rolls she had brought from home before he sat down in the wing chair identical to the one I was in. We both sipped our coffee and I concentrated on breathing in and out and relaxing. It was just that every time I thought about what she had done, I got so mad at her.

"Now, I have to be honest with you, I myself was surprised to hear your father had written a new will, but a man has a right to change his mind, nothing illegal about that. You have to be more than unhappy about something to have a reason to sue."

"But I do! That will was written after Daddy came home from the hospital to die. He wasn't lucid even half the time."

"He was lucid some of the time, wasn't he?"

"Yes, but I know good and well he wasn't in his right mind when he signed that document. He wouldn't have done that!"

"Macy, I have no idea what was in your father's mind because I didn't talk to him about the last will, but I think a court would have a hard time believing that he wouldn't have wanted to change his will, given his actions the last years."

"What do you mean?"

"Well, when he wrote the will excluding Claire Louise, she was gone and he had no idea where she was. That will was written over ten years ago, no, my goodness, it must be almost twenty years ago that I drew up that first will for your father. And it has been ten years or so that Claire Louise has been back and living with him. Her children live out there. It does seem reasonable that if he would allow that, he would leave the house to her."

"And is it reasonable that he would leave her four times as much land as he left me? And all the stock and money and every single thing there is? Would that be reasonable?"

"Maybe not, but you forget a person has a right to leave their possessions the way they want to. You can't get a will thrown out because you don't agree with it!"

"But he was so ill, and on medication! Why can't I prove he didn't know what he was doing?"

"How would you prove that?"

"Well, the doctor came every day and the nurses kept all sorts of records. What about that?"

"Macy, I saw your father the week before he died. He knew me, shook my hand, even talked a bit. Other people in town saw him, too. I know how disappointed you are, but I don't think you have anything to sue over."

"You will never convince me Daddy knew what he was signing. Never." Suddenly I knew what had to have happened—

Claire Louise had gotten to him before me. I saw it clear as glass. "She's been here, she's already talked to you, hasn't she?"

"Claire Louise did come in to see me, brought your grandma with her as a matter of fact."

"What did she do that for?" I interrupted him, fairly screaming at him as I did so.

"Calm down, Macy. She wanted to be sure I understood why she had gotten another lawyer. She was concerned about my feelings. As I recall, your grandma was with her because she had just had her hair appointment over at Miss Minnie's."

"And why did she say she had used someone else, pray tell?" I knew I was being sarcastic with him, but it burned me up, another man being taken in by Claire Louise, and the nerve she had taking my grandmother along to watch it happen. Mr. Shasta leaned across toward where I sat, outrage all over his features, but he smiled when he patted my clenched hands. "Let me give you some advice, Macy. I've known you since you were knee-high to a grasshopper, and your family longer than that. Don't let this little disappointment drive a wedge between you and your family. Go on out there and make up with your mother and your sister. No house is worth this."

More advice, none that I wanted to hear. I stood up. "Obviously, you aren't going to help me. There are other lawyers, however, and I intend to fight Claire Louise."

"Now, now," he said, sticking out his hand for me to shake, "I hope we're still friends."

"Of course," I answered stiffly, but I wasn't feeling at all friendly toward him.

Grandma was on the back porch when I walked in the back door. She was bent over with her head down in the bottom of the freezer like she had lost something. "Let me help you," I said, walking over and holding the lid open for her so she could lean farther into the depths of the box. "What are you looking for anyway?"

"I bought some frozen vegetables yesterday when Claire Louise took me to town. I can't think where she could have put them."

I got angry just hearing the name Claire Louise. "Why didn't you wait for me, Grandma? I told you I'd be out today and take you."

"She stopped by and asked me to go with her. You know Monday's usually my day in town, didn't see any reason not to go."

In truth the only reason for her not to go was that I wanted her to feel as angry at my sister as I did. That didn't seem likely to happen. "Carlton called, wants you to call him at his office first thing. Seems like he thought you'd be here earlier. You have car trouble?" She raised up out of the freezer to look at me.

"No, I stopped to see Mr. Shasta. He told me you were there yesterday." Grandma could tell by looking at me my feelings were hurt. I didn't need to say anything to her.

"Now, Macy, there is nothing for you to get upset about. I hoped you were over worrying over your daddy's will."

"But why did you go with her?" I persisted, feeling more slighted than ever. It sounded like she was defending Claire Louise.

"She wanted to stop in, clear up any hard feelings before they got started, there was nothing to it."

"Do you think Daddy did the right thing?"

"What's done's done. Let it go. If it makes you feel any better, I told Claire Louise and Mr. Shasta yesterday I want my will redone. You can have my house and the land I have left. Claire

Louise has got plenty now and your Aunt Claire got hers years ago when we deeded this land over to Stuart. Beats me how you can ever expect to live out here right next to them if you don't start getting along, though. You thought about that?"

I stood there unable to think straight, the thought of this house without my grandmother in it was intolerable to me. Quickly, I erased it. "Don't you go talking about wills, Grandma, you know I want you to stay right here."

"Same's I do, I reckon, but we all have to go sometime and my time will come as well as the next person's. But now I want you to quit this fretting over your mother and father's house. You'll get you one, too, so you go on over there and make up with them."

"I'll try, Grandma, I will, but it isn't right she always gets away with things. I feel like if I don't stand up to her it's going to keep happening."

"Aha, here they are! Why would anyone put vegetables over here with the chicken?"

So you couldn't find them and would have to call her, needing her to rush over and help you, I thought but didn't say aloud. After all these years I knew her little tricks, every one of them.

When I went home that night, Carlton listened to my account of my day and echoed my grandmother's advice. I told him about her will, her changing it to leave her house to me, but again I skated over the implications of what I was saying. I wanted my grandmother to leave everything to me so Claire Louise would feel left out, I wanted that very much. But I didn't want her to have to die to help me one-up my sister.

"You didn't call me back today," he said, which is the first time I remembered his message.

"Oh, I forgot, Grandma told me the minute I came in but I forgot! Was it important?"

"Scott's teacher called. She wants a conference. She's concerned about him."

"Why?" I asked, feeling a wave of anxiety. I was neglecting my children, I knew it, and I could feel Carlton thinking it, even though he was nice enough not to say so.

"No, just that we should come in and talk to her. I made an appointment for ten o'clock tomorrow."

His eyes warned me not to say I couldn't make it, so I bit back the words that rose to the surface, the ones that reminded me I had made an appointment with a lawyer tomorrow to talk about fighting the will Claire Louise had written, which is how I thought of it, Claire Louise's will. Not Daddy's will, not my parents' will, Claire Louise's will. That's what we all did, I thought angrily to myself, we all did Claire Louise's will. Not anymore, I vowed. I can call and change the time of my lawyer's appointment, I told myself, I'll be able to do that in the morning and see the teacher and still run out to Molly's Point and be back by three.

"I'll meet you at West U Elementary at ten o'clock," I told Carlton as he left for work the next morning. "Did she say where we're to meet her?"

"The classroom. The children are going to be at some other activity at that time."

"I'll be there," I promised, starting to tell him if I was a little late to start without me but deciding not to. I'll be there on time, I promised myself.

I was able to change my appointment to nine, which should have given me plenty of time, but I ended up having to wait at the lawyer's and didn't get in to see him until almost nine-thirty and that made it almost ten when I left his office. And in spite of driving fast enough to risk several tickets, when I arrived at the door, breathless from having run all the way from the parking lot, Carlton and Mrs. Brooks, Scott's teacher, were already deep in conversation. It was almost ten-thirty. "I'm sorry I'm late," I panted. "I got caught in the traffic."

From the look I got from my husband, I knew that lame excuse hadn't placated him, but all he said was, "At least you're here now." Unfortunately the class marched back into the room after I had been there less than ten minutes, so we weren't able to talk much. Just long enough for me to find out that Scott had been acting up in class, misbehaving and taking things from other children, and only that Monday he had deliberately hit a classmate and caused his nose to bleed.

Carlton said all the right things, about how we were concerned and glad to be notified, that we had been under stress this year with my father's illness and death, not that that excused Scott's behavior because of course it didn't, but that we would talk with Scott and get back with her, and would she please notify us immediately if there were any additional problems. I nodded, unable to talk, feeling guilty, as if all my child's problems were my doing and knowing they both thought that very same thing. It's his mother's fault, I could hear the teacher thinking. If she were home with him none of this would happen. "This is my fault," I said as we stood in the parking lot after stopping by the office to set up an appointment with Travis's teacher for the coming day.

"Macy, there is nothing to be gained from trying to blame yourself. You've had a tough year. Tonight we'll talk to Scott and Travis, too, find out what's going on. It's not the end of the world," he added as I stood there indecisively wringing my hands. I wanted to rush into the building and grab both of my children and assure them I loved them and I would never ever leave one of them out of my will. Then Carlton really surprised me. He laughed and said, "Most boys get into scrapes from time to time!"

I couldn't believe my ears. "You think it's macho or something your six-year-old son's beating up on kids?"

"Macy, you're overreacting. Let's wait until we talk to Scott tonight, okay? I have to get back to work now."

Which reminded me I needed to get out to Grandma's. I had resolved to be out there every day from now on, even if it was only for an hour or so, that way my sister would know I wasn't going to be caught unaware by any of her tricks.

You didn't go see your mother yesterday, was the first thing my grandmother said to me when I walked in. "I'm thinking about it," I told her, "but I'm still mad at them both."

"It's not a good idea to let it go too long," she warned me. "Time has a way of making apologizing harder rather than easier."

"Why should I apologize to her? She's the one did something wrong."

Grandma sighed and looked at me. "Macy, I love you but you are as stubborn and hardheaded as everyone else in your family, including me. You might learn from my mistakes, though. Carrying a grudge only wears down the carrier."

"I know, I know, just give me a little time."

"What did Scott's teacher want?" she asked me, knowing we had had a conference that day because I had called her the night before. That was another of my resolutions, to call her every single night and check on her.

"He's been fighting," I told her, sighing. "If it's not one thing, it's another. We made an appointment with Travis's teacher for tomorrow, I hope he hasn't been getting into trouble as well. Carlton thought we better check on him while we're at it. So I'll be after noon getting out here," I told her.

"You don't have to drive all the way out here every day, Macy. Once a week would be a gracious plenty."

"But I want to see you," I told her, "and besides it's not that far anyway."

"Well, now you're here, maybe you could clean out the pool for me, that wind last night filled it with leaves and the yard man isn't due back until next Tuesday."

Cleaning the pool took almost an hour and then I had to rush to beat the school bus home. I started to tell Grandma not to tell Carlton I was coming out every day but I knew that would get me another lecture from her so I didn't say anything. I rushed home, against the traffic fortunately, feeling harassed. It didn't seem to matter how much I did, I couldn't get to the point where I felt like things were under control. In fact they were feeling more out of control all the time. And since my father's funeral, I knew Carlton was expecting me to snap back and pay more attention to my own family, something I desperately wanted to do. But somehow or another, no matter how good my intentions, I kept getting caught up in other things. And matters only got worse.

22

HUGH DECIDED not to put his house on the market until we had built the new one, a decision that turned out to be well taken, as it was over a year after we returned from our cruise before we were able to move into our new house. And it did not work out too well for us to live in my house with Mother and my girls. Hugh's statement that men were completely superfluous in that environment was way off the mark. It's just that he was used to his privacy and, to be honest, my children were having some problems adjusting to a new father. Maryanne of course had never known a father, and Britt had long since forgotten what she had known of hers. So Hugh and I lived in his house in town, although of course I was out at my new house every day from when Hugh left for work at least until the workmen quit for the evening. And nights, half the time, Hugh and I would eat with my mother and daughters. As I kept reminding Hugh, his relationship with them would not get any better until he put some time in on it.

It was during the month after we returned from our cruise that I decided to move a trailer out behind the homeplace for Lucy so she could live in, more or less. I needed someone there all the time, someone I could count on, and Lucy and I were as much friends as employer-employee, I told her. But she wanted her own place, one where she could keep her little dog and have some privacy, so I hit on the idea of the trailer. It worked out well. She was able to look after things on the farm for me while I was in town with Hugh. More and more that year I realized how lucky I was to have her. It was Lucy first alerted me to the problems with Britt. Lucy warned me she was up to something the summer after Daddy's death, the summer Britt finished her sophomore year in high school.

I walked over from my house, my old one, to Grandma's where I could see Britt out sunning by the pool. I thought she was alone until just before I got there, then I saw the head sticking up out of the pool. "Hello, Sam," I said to the boy who was hanging onto the edge of the pool, looking at me like he belonged there.

"Hello, Mrs., uh Mrs. Sawyer," he said laughing. "I couldn't quite think of your new name."

"I'm glad to see that it did occur to you. Britt, I would like to talk to you," I told my daughter.

She pointed to a chair next to hers. "So talk," she said rudely, not even bothering to sit up and look at me.

I walked across the pavement stones and jerked the sun visor off her head. "I'll thank you to sit up and look at me when I'm talking to you, young lady!"

She sat up abruptly and glared at me, squinting at the sunlight. "What's wrong with you?"

"I am objecting to your rudeness for starters," I said. Turning to look at Sam, I said nicely and politely, "Sam, Britt and I have some things to get squared away today. It's not a good time for visitors."

"I invited him, Mother," Britt said, clipping her words.

"That's fine," I replied, "but now it's time for him to go home." I glanced at Sam, who was looking from one to the other of us like he was at a Ping-Pong tournament. That made me even madder, the little pip-squeak was waiting to see which one of us won this argument!

"You may go Sam, NOW," I prompted him. He looked at Britt, who shrugged.

"Maybe you'd better. I have no idea what's gotten into my mother."

Britt never came closer to having her face slapped in front of a visitor than she did at that moment. It was all I could do not to haul off and let her have it. I stood there glaring at her, my arms folded across my chest, clenching and unclenching my fists.

After Sam left, I said to Britt, "Get up and come over to the table. We're going to talk and I would like to be out of the sun while we do it."

Slowly, ever so slowly, she stood up and adjusted her bikini, a suit I realized I had not seen before, pulled on a cover-up, and walked over to the table. She sat down, crossing her legs and dangling one thong sandal from the foot she pumped up and down as she sat, sullenly daring me to speak.

"Sit up straight and listen to me," I said to her, working hard to temper my voice so it wouldn't shriek out of control.

She sat up straight, giving me an eyes-wide go-to-hell look only a fool would have missed. I may have been busy lately, I may not have noticed everything my daughter was doing, but I recognized that look she was giving me. Britt was looking at me with total contempt. I have to admit I lost control then, I reached over and slapped her hard across the face. I was sorry the minute it happened but she was asking for it with that nasty look on her face. "I'm sorry I hit you," I told her, "but if you don't get that insolent sneer off your face I can't promise I won't do it again."

Her face cleared as if she had run an eraser across it. The only thing I could see was the red mark my hand had made. She didn't look at me, she didn't look away, she stared at some space over my left shoulder.

"You missed eighteen days of school last spring, and I would like to know where you were. As far as Lucy and I can recall, you never stayed home once. Correct me if I'm wrong."

"My report card must have come."

"That is correct." Actually it had been there for several days before Lucy had opened it and noticed the absences. "Where were you?" I repeated.

"Some days I didn't feel like going so I just hung out," she said.

"Hung out where?"

"Movies, shopping, I don't really remember."

"You drove into Houston?"

"Some days."

"You must not have felt like studying much last spring either, your grades are all C's and D's, except for the F you received in gym. What on earth were you thinking of?"

Britt shrugged. "It just doesn't mean anything to me anymore, school doesn't. I didn't even go out for cheerleader this year."

"What?" I cried, "Naturally I assumed you would have tried out again."

"Mother, you've been so busy with your building projects and your wonderful new husband you haven't had any time for me or the rest of your family either. Maryanne has gotten fat again and Grandmother cries all the time, and you don't even care what's happening to us. Nothing would do but you got our house away from Aunt Macy, and then you spent all that time remodeling and throwing out everything that wasn't nailed down and getting new furniture and drapes and anything else you could think of. Then you started going out with Hugh and that took all your time and now you've got a new house to think about. Face it, you don't care about us, so quit acting like you do."

I was stunned that my daughter could even think such things, much less say them. "That's not true, the things I do are for you.

All of them. I would have stayed in New York years ago if it hadn't been I needed to make a stable home for you and your sister. And look at all I constantly do for your grandmother and great-grandmother," I reminded her.

"Not anymore you don't. All you do is run in and out of Houston, finding wonderful new fixtures for Hugh to pay for and install in your mansion." The sneer in her voice cut me to the core.

"Britt, I married Hugh so you could have a father. And the new house is for all of us."

"No it isn't, don't lie to me. The new house is for you and Hugh. Maryanne and Grandmother and I are going to stay right where we are. That's why you moved Lucy out there, to take care of Grandmother. Now that you've taken Grandmother's house and redone it where she doesn't even feel like she knows where she is anymore, you don't want it, just like you don't want us anymore!"

"But this simply is not true! There are rooms for you girls in the new house. I consulted you both on the color schemes last week."

"No, you didn't. You showed us what you had picked out. And you also moved me into your room at our old house. Why did you do that if we're going with you to the new one? There's plenty of room at Hugh's house in town, if you wanted us so much."

"Britt, is that what this is all about? Why didn't you come and talk to me earlier? You and Maryanne didn't move because I had no idea building our new house would take so much time and I thought it better not to uproot you twice. I gave you your own room at our old house because you and Maryanne had both been arguing about that for years. And although you'll of course live with me when the new house is finished, which the way it is going may take years, I just naturally assumed you would want your own rooms at Grandmother's too. Surely you'll still want to stay some with her. She would be devastated if all of us left her."

"Frankly I would rather stay with Grandmother and Lucy. I think they like me a lot better than your husband does." When Britt said "your husband" her words dripped with contempt.

"Britt, Hugh likes you. Unfortunately he isn't used to children so he isn't at ease with you and Maryanne, but that will change."

"Will it?" she asked skeptically.

"Of course it will," I said, feeling relieved I had gotten to the bottom of this mess. "I am so glad we have had this little mother-daughter talk," I told her. "Now we have got to put our heads together to figure out what can be done about this disastrous showing you made last spring." I waved the report card in front of her, reminding her of the original reason for our talk.

Her shoulders drooped and she slumped down in her chair. "What's done is done," she said, using one of Grandma's favorite expressions.

"No, it isn't," I told her. "I am going to call and enroll you in summer school. You are going to make up both the subjects you got D's in and I will also talk to Joe Poteet, who went to school with me. Perhaps I can even get you back your cheer-leader position," I suggested. "Remember, your grandfather was on the school board for years and years. Why, I even worked as a counselor there, although maybe you were too young to remember."

"I remember, Mother, it wasn't that long ago. And Grand-father is dead, remember? He died last fall, have you forgotten?"

"Britt, that sarcastic tone you are using is extremely offensive to me. I do not want to hear it again. Do you understand me?"

"Yes."

"Yes, what?"

"Yes, ma'am."

"Now I will talk to Joe and you will go to summer school and I will be satisfied with nothing less than A's. Is that clear? We are going to have to work long and hard to bring up these grades so you can get into a decent college. I am not having my daughters facing the world without the security of a college diploma. I have told you that before, have I not?"

"Yes, ma'am."

"Fine, and another thing, I would like to hear a little more enthusiasm from you. I'm working to extricate you from this mess you have gotten yourself into, and I would at the least expect a little gratitude."

"Mother, the truth is I don't like high school anymore, it bores me. And I have absolutely no desire to go to college." She stared at me as if daring me to contradict her, which I was not foolish enough to do.

"Plenty of boring things in this world," I told her, "and to be perfectly honest, I don't care if you are bored or not. I expect you to do well regardless, is that clear? Remember you are my daughter and we have a position to uphold in this town."

She gave a harsh ugly laugh. "What position, the position of providing the town with a daily dose of gossip? People talk about us all the time, Mother."

I glared at her, restraining myself from slapping her again. "Of course they talk about us. Prominent people are always talked about. I hope you have not been listening to gossip, which likely as not does not contain a word of truth."

"Mother, do you ever see anything in any way other than the way you want it to be?" she asked.

235

"You're damned right I do," I told her. "I see things the way they are, and if they don't suit me, then I make it my business to change them. And you ought to thank me for that, I might add. Do you think you'd be sitting here in the lap of luxury if I hadn't fought every day of my life for what we have? Do you?"

Britt sat there and stared at me. She didn't say anything, but I could see she was thinking about what I had said, which suited me just fine. I went right in and called my friend Joe Poteet and signed Britt up for the two courses she needed to retake, and he said we'd talk later about dropping those D's and C's from her record when I reminded him her grandfather had died this year and her mother had remarried and she had been under too much stress to be herself. Not to mention the effect school gossip appeared to be having on her, and I hoped he would take steps to make sure that did not happen in the coming year. About the cheerleading, he said he could do nothing, she had chosen not to try out and the squad was already elected. Try as I did, I couldn't budge him on that point. Well, one more thing, I told him as I was getting ready to ring off, I don't think this Sam Edler is good for her, I hope you can make sure they don't have any classes together next year, which is when I learned that Sam was a seventeen-year-old high school dropout. I was of course forced to forbid Britt to see him when I heard that bit of news. Fortunately her moment of rebellion seemed to be over. She attended summer school regularly, brought home straight A's as I demanded, and I did not have a bit of trouble with her for the rest of the summer. That's the thing about raising children, you just have to be firm in your expectations.

Hugh's friend Mr. Bailey, who was our building contractor, complained it was taking so long to finish our house because I kept changing or adding things, but like I told Hugh, this was my dream house, the one I would live in for the rest of my life, and I wanted everything to be perfect. And it was so sudden, one minute we were friends, the next we were married, so it wasn't like I had all that much time to plan the house before we started work on it. I have heard that building a house together is the single most stressful thing a married couple does, and it occurred to me we were smart to get our stressful time over and done with early on in our marriage. Hugh just laughed when I told him that, he said if the past year is any measure we've got lots more fireworks ahead of us. Hugh's sense of humor was, at times, difficult to fathom.

Thinking back, I realize that from the day Hugh and I married we faced one difficulty after another. If I had that particular decision to make over again, I'd think it over a lot more seriously before I rushed into it. Having one more person to consider sometimes made my life incredibly difficult. Like after I told him about the trouble Britt had had in school, right off he suggested we send her off to boarding school up in Dallas. "Where on earth did you come up with such an idea?" I asked him.

"You want to get her away from this Sam, you'll have to get her out of town. And several of my business associates have sent their daughters up there. They say it's a fine school."

"And leave Maryanne alone?" I asked, incredulous he could even think such a thing, but then Hugh had known my children for only six months, so of course he was not nearly as sensitive to them as I was. "How would that be right? Why, Maryanne would have to go back to riding the school bus."

"Send her too," he said, so cold and callous I wondered if I knew him at all.

"Send my children off? I'd never dream of such a thing."

"I thought you were concerned about their education."

"I am concerned, that's why I have Britt in summer school this very minute."

"Right," he said in the drawling way he has, which I came to realize meant he didn't agree with me but he wasn't going to talk about it any longer. "Mr. Bailey says you have decided to add another room to the house," he said. "Every time I go out there it looks like you've had him pour another slab. The damn house resembles nothing so much as a boxcar train at this point, Clara Lou. That's exactly what it looks like, with one room chained onto another."

"Why, the very idea! It does not! The basic plan is the two-story colonial, four large rooms upstairs and four down. But I added a recreation room and a music room to the back so the house wouldn't feel cramped. All my life I've felt hemmed in by the house I grew up in, I don't want this house to feel that way." I could feel the tears welling up in my eyes, and try as I did to stem their flow, pretty soon they were running down my cheeks. "It sounds like you don't like the house I've put all this work into," I told Hugh.

"Oh, Clara Lou, you're being dramatic. I like it, I just don't see why you can't let the plan alone and quit adding on to it."

"All I added today was a garden room with a Jacuzzi, like the one that's in the *Better Homes and Gardens* that came this week. It's going to be my favorite part of the house, you can't object to that."

"You said the same thing last week about the music room and the week before that about the recreation room and the week before that about all the fancy appliances you had to have for your gourmet kitchen. Now, enough is enough. I have told Mr. Bailey not another single addition. Is that clear? Don't just sit there sniffing at me. Surely there isn't another thing you want to add to this monstrosity!"

"You don't like it! I can tell!"

"Hell yes, I like the damn thing, I'd just like to live in it before I'm seventy years old. If you don't quit changing things that may never happen."

"Well, there really isn't anything else I want to change," I admitted, although my feelings were hurt at his insensitivity.

23

EVERYTHING might have been different if I hadn't run into Scott's teacher that afternoon when I sat waiting for the boys to finish their Suzuki lessons. She was waiting for her little girl, who was a year older than my two. And as we had over thirty minutes to wait, we had plenty of time to talk, and over the course of several weeks of sharing that waiting time, we discovered that we really kind of liked each other, Cheryl and I did. But as we talked, and one thing led to another, pretty soon we were exhanging life stories complete with photos. Which is how I found out she knew my sister Claire Louise, only she knew her as Lana Anderson! And she thought Britt was her brother's child and knew nothing of Maryanne! From looking at her family pictures it was plain to see that if either of the children was the child of James Wilcox, Cheryl Brooks's brother, it had to be Maryanne, who did resemble him, and not Britt, who did not, and, more to the point, was the spitting image of Ralph Anderson who Claire Louise had run off with when she was sixteen.

It was fascinating listening to Cheryl tell stories about my sister, the one I thought had been in New York for ten years, the one who had returned home all upset because she had to leave her drug-addicted husband to protect her children, the one who had come home to look after her poor parents in their old age to the exclusion of any life of her own. That sister of mine had been in Houston for almost half of the time she had been gone. And had been married to a thoroughly nice man whose only fault, to hear his sister talk, was he could not for the life of him see through her conniving ways. And not a word had leaked out in Molly's Point not fifty miles away. When I heard how she had done James, leading him on to marry her and causing all manner of dissension in his family and then running off with a minister of the gospel who was struck down by God not two months after he arrived in Oklahoma, I was amazed. "Struck down by God?" I asked. "What on earth do you mean?"

"The small plane he was in was struck by lightning. That's an act of God if there ever was one," Cheryl said, nodding vigorously to emphasize her words.

"I don't know about that," I replied, having a hard time with this part of her story. "If God was so out to get Claire Louise and Tom Smythe, why was his wife killed with him instead of my sister?" I asked.

"I thought about that and talked it over with Mrs. Landview, who was the church secretary for twenty years until Lana came along. She said from what she could see it looked to her like the Lord called Reverend Smythe and his wife home before they could get in any more trouble. According to Mrs. Landview, there never was a nicer, more gullible man than Tom Smythe before Lana came along and infatuated him. And it was her opinion being left up there high and dry without a man in sight was punishment enough for Lana Wilcox. One thing that does surprise me, I wonder why Mrs. Landview never heard she was pregnant. That does surprise me, must be no one knew a thing about it up in Oklahoma, otherwise she would have heard about that, too." She frowned to herself before she said, "Some good came out of it for my brother, although it was over a year before he quit grieving for Lana and Britt. Now he's married again and couldn't be happier."

I just shook my head, fascinated by the tales she was telling. "But why, if your brother was hurt so bad when she left, didn't he at least come to see Britt after they moved back to Texas?"

"Because she told him Britt wasn't his, and if he so much as showed his face around her she'd tell the child so. And we never even knew where she went when she left Oklahoma. One thing Lana kept a deep dark secret was where she had been raised in Texas! When I think how my mother worried over Britt's other grandmother not knowing about her grandchild! I have to say it, even if she is your sister, Lana Anderson was the most heartless woman I have ever known! Not that James looked for her after we heard she had left Oklahoma. Once she was gone my mother and I were able to convince him to leave well enough alone! Best to let sleeping dogs lie, Annie our housekeeper used to say. It wasn't until I recognized Lana at a doctor's office a year ago that we even knew where she was. I talked to James then, told him what I had discovered. Why, I even got her address from the receptionist. But he didn't want to track her down. Like I told you, he's happily married and has no idea that there is a second child, one who almost certainly is James's daughter."

"And from what you've said about him and his wife, Elizabeth, both of the children would be much better off with him than with my sister. She has the mothering instincts of an alley cat, if you ask me."

"I don't know whether to tell James about Maryanne or not," Cheryl worried. "The one disappointment he and his wife have is that they don't have children of their own, and James would dearly love to have a child. He doted on Britt! I can't tell you how much that child meant to him. He told me over and over after Lana divorced him, it didn't matter if he wasn't Britt's father for real, no man could care more about her than he did. Why, James was the one raised her until she was almost six years old! I have to tell you my mother and I wondered when that child was born. She wasn't a small baby, for all Lana said she was two months premature. But nothing like that worried James, from the moment he brought her home from the hospital she was his child. What good would it do to tell him about Maryanne? Lana, or Claire Louise, as you say her name is, would never let him see her either. It would just cause James more grief to know about her. And as for his wife, Elizabeth, I have no earthly idea what she would think."

"There might be ways," I thought aloud. "I'm going to see my lawyer this afternoon and I'll just ask." I was still pursuing my lawsuit against Claire Louise's version of my father's will, but in truth the battle was not going well. This was the second lawyer I had seen, the second, that is, after Mr. Shasta, who had never even truly listened to my side of the story. Mr. Owen, who I had consulted next, had investigated and done what he called preliminary work that cost me almost six hundred dollars before he advised me I didn't have a case. Mr. Jamison, who I was currently seeing, was more optimistic, but would not take the case without a ten-thousand-dollar down payment, which Carlton was rigid in his refusal to agree to. I had even approached my grandmother about loaning me the money, but she said money spent on lawyers might as well be put right out on the trash heap and put a match to. She has never had any use for the legal profession, my grandmother hasn't. I was tempted to use money from my children's savings accounts. As long as I won the case

Carlton would never need to know. But when I thought that through, I realized he would wonder where I got the money and I didn't want to lie to him. So it was looking more and more like Claire Louise was getting away with highway robbery simply because she had the colossal nerve to cheat her way into practically my father's entire estate. If I'd had the money I would have fought her, I told myself that afternoon, but maybe there were other ways. Maybe there were.

My conversation with Mr. Jamison left me with plenty to think about. As I suspected, there were tests now that could prove paternity. He gave me the telephone numbers of several people I could call.

I could not wait until next Thursday to tell Cheryl. I called her up that night and told her exactly what I had learned, and she was as fascinated as I was. Carlton liked to act like he wasn't interested in what he referred to as my family saga, but as this story about Claire Louise began to unfold he was as entranced as I was, and agreed readily when I invited Cheryl and her husband and their two daughters over for a cookout that Friday night.

Cheryl's husband, Chet Brooks, was a thoroughly nice person, who nodded agreement with his wife when she said they all in their family thought my sister was a little obsessive, and had no regrets when she left James except for the heartache that it did cause him. When Chet said she was hard to be around, Carlton nodded in the way he has, but he didn't volunteer any details on his own. Sometimes it makes me mad when he does that, nods and listens and encourages a person to talk on and on. Likely as not, when he does that I get to talking too much and end up saying more than I want to. But that night the four of us had a genuinely good time, with the conversation ebbing and flowing companionably, and Carlton enjoyed it as much as I did.

After they left we talked about them, the way you will when you've had company and they've left. I'd say did you like the way he such and such and Carlton would say yes I did and I thought it was great we all four seemed to and so forth and so on. The only thing Carlton wasn't particularly keen on was my idea to invite James Wilcox and his wife over. He agreed they were probably nice as could be, but he didn't see any point in it. And that was the way we left it for the time being, although I was curious as everything to see him. But as Carlton told me, it would be too uncomfortable if we sat around with a secret that he might have a child he didn't know about, and on the other hand it certainly was not our place to drop that particular bomb. Cheryl was still up in the air about whether to tell James and Elizabeth, his second wife. She was leaning toward telling him, she said, because if their positions were reversed she would want to know, no matter what hardships it later worked on her emotionally. Like she said, "If I had a daughter out in the world somewhere I'd want to know it so I could fight to see her." Carlton agreed with that, but said we needed to stay way the hell— his words, not mine—out of that decision. He even cautioned me not to egg Cheryl on. This thing has the potential to be a real land mine, he said, and as we learned later, never were truer words spoken.

Cheryl called me one morning to say she had talked to her brother the night before and ended up telling him about where Britt was and all about the existence of his daughter Maryanne!

"Oh, my gosh," I gulped, excited and scared, too. "I hope you did the right thing."

"You and me both," she agreed. "My mother and Chet and I talked and talked, you know it's been over a month now we've known this, and we decided that we didn't go looking for this information, it came to us. You know how you and I have talked about how strange it is your child should get put in my class, and then our kids end up in the same Suzuki class where we sit and talk together two or three afternoons a week, and lo and behold it turns out your sister used to be married to my brother and we none of us knew a thing about it. It's like we were meant to find out, Mother said. And if we were meant to know, the only reason would be so we could tell James. It sounds as if that little girl needs him, Mother said, and so we have got to tell him. And to tell the truth, Mother wants to see her grandchild."

"Go on," I prompted her.

"I have to hurry, my class will be back from P.E. in ten minutes. Anyway, we told Elizabeth first and she agreed, you have to tell James, although heaven knows how this will affect him, she said. So we did. Last night Chet and I went over and told him everything."

"What did he say?"

"He was flabbergasted, unable to speak for a good ten minutes. Then he said some rather profane things about Lana, words I didn't know he used." She giggled. "I'm still nervous," she said. "I hope I haven't made an awful mistake telling him this."

"You haven't," I said, supporting her now the die was cast. "He has a right to know! What is he going to do about it, did he say?"

"I don't think he has any idea at this point. He and Elizabeth would like to meet you and talk with you. I'm hoping you and Carlton and the children can come over tomorrow night. We'll have supper and you can meet James and Elizabeth."

I must admit I felt a surge of elation at that point. Things were working out. Claire Louise was fixing to get her comeuppance. I could feel it. "I'll call Carlton and make sure but I think it's okay. What time?" I asked her.

"Come early. Sixish. And bring some pictures, would you?"

"Sure, see you then." I gulped when I hung up the phone. Later when I talked to Carlton, he agreed to go but worried about what we were getting into. "It's a mess either way we play it," I admitted, "but after all she has done to me I don't have any loyalty to her. And besides, that man has a right to know his own daughter."

Carlton frowned. "Macy, we've only heard Cheryl's side of this story. Don't you think your sister deserves equal time?"

"She'll get her time if she ever quits lying about where she was," I told him, wondering to myself if I was finally going to get Claire Louise in court, where she would be forced under pain of perjury to tell the truth.

James Wilcox was taller than I expected and while he didn't look happy when he talked about Claire Louise, or Lana as he called her, he wasn't the grieving wreck of a man I had expected either. He and his wife, Elizabeth, were obviously a happy couple who sat close to each other on the sofa after supper and conferred quietly together several times like they really were each other's best friends. Seeing them made me go over and sit down next to Carlton and hold his hand, something I had gotten out of the habit of doing of late. I didn't like the way we had been lately, and I realized a lot of the distance between us had come about because I was hiding so many of the things about my family, like that I still tried to go out to my grandmother's every single day. And he didn't even know I had hired a maid, someone to clean for me three days a week. I had been real cagey about that, picking the mornings he had his group sessions at the hospital because he never ever called home during those times. And I had discovered another lady three streets over from us who baked and sold food out of her house. So I picked up casseroles there and froze them to heat up in the microwave the days

I was late. Carlton thought I was turning into a gourmet cook. She also made fudge the kids loved, and they had no idea I had bought that either. I hadn't meant to lie to him. It had just happened that he had complimented something and asked when I made it. I had said oh, it's from the freezer, which he took to mean I was the one who cooked it. And as everyone knows, once you tell the first lie it gets harder and harder to get to the truth of the matter, so it happened that we had been eating more and more of Mrs. Jones's cooking and no one the wiser. I resolved then and there, sitting and talking to James Wilcox and hearing about how my sister and her lies had made such a hash of their lives, to get things straightened out with my husband that very evening. Last thing I want, I told myself, is to end up alone and lonely like I foresee is going to happen to my own sister, a victim of her own deviousness. Why, I prophesied, I'll bet even her own kids turn against her when this comes out, and my mother will be so upset she may never be able to hold her head up in town again. And as for my grandmother, well, she will say right away she knew it all along, Claire Louise was up to no good.

James studied the pictures of Maryanne and Britt for the good part of an hour. I had brought my family album and he sat turning the pages, staring at those images like the intensity of his gaze could bring those children to life right off the page as he looked so hard at them. When he looked up and met my eyes, there were tears running down his face and his wife, Elizabeth, had her arm tight around him. "I want my children," he said, "both of them."

I started shaking my head from side to side. "I don't have any pictures of Ralph Anderson, her first husband," I told him, "but my grandmother has some and I'll try to bring one in for you to look at. Britt is the spitting image of him."

He winced like he was in pain. "I've never stopped missing her," he said, meaning Britt. "Long after I was glad Lana was gone, I ached for wanting to hold my little girl."

"And neither one of them has a father now," Elizabeth added softly. I looked at her and thought, she'll fight with him every step of the way. I knew then it was too late to turn back now. James Wilcox was going to fight my sister Claire Louise for those kids. There was a time when I could have kept my mouth shut, not opened this can of worms, but that time had come and gone. I didn't think it would do any good now if I did go to Claire Louise to apologize to her for accusing her of cheating me out of my inheritance. Even if I wanted to apologize. I didn't want to apologize, I told myself. I was sure of that. But once I got to the point where it was no longer possible, I felt a stab of regret. More than one stab. It's too late for us to ever be friends again, I thought. Once she finds out I am the one who told James about Maryanne, she will never forgive me. "Maybe I could tell James not to tell her how he found out," I told Carlton later that night when we were home.

"No, you can't. You told Cheryl, who told her brother, and you'll have to accept that," Carlton told me.

"But it wasn't planned," I reminded him. "It happened when she was looking at my pictures and recognized Claire Louise. If it hadn't been for that, we would never have known that my sister Claire Louise was her ex-sister-in-law Lana. It's not like I deliberately planned this."

"No, it isn't," Carlton agreed. "All the more reason not to hide your part in it, however."

I knew he was right and I relaxed and fell asleep that night in his arms, feeling safe and at peace with the world for the first time since my father had died. Claire Louise was fixing to be exposed, it didn't matter who got the house anymore as long as Mother knew what a cheat she was. That was the important thing. And because of all that we had to talk about, I completely forgot to tell Carlton about the food and the maid. Not that it mattered, I told myself the next day when it occurred to me as I drove out to my grandmother's, leaving Bitsy Chapman busy cleaning my house, plenty of time to mention it to Carlton. He's certainly not the type to get upset if I hire a little household help.

24

THE FIRST I heard of what Macy had been up to was when I walked into Mother's den one afternoon and found Mother sitting on the sofa staring into space. The television wasn't on and she wasn't asleep or listening to one of the tape-recorded books Lucy got her from the library for the blind, now that she couldn't see well enough to read to herself any longer.

"Macy was here, Claire Louise," she said. The way she said it I thought someone had died. Macy had not been over to see Mother in months, not since she had last threatened to see us in court over Daddy's will.

"What did she want? Is she still looking for a lawyer to help her sue us, throw you out of your own house?"

"No, she didn't mention wills today, she said she came to warn me."

"About me, no doubt," I said.

"She told me a story about a man named James Wilcox married to a woman named Lana Anderson. Seems Lana ran off and left James for a minister of the gospel. Took the kids with her, one he knew about was named Britt, one who wasn't born yet he didn't know existed. He's going to try to get those kids back now that he knows where they are."

I felt nothing so much as shock at her words. I hadn't thought about James Wilcox in months! How on earth had Macy found out about him?

Mother was talking in this awful flat voice and she seemed detached, even withdrawn. I'd seen her more animated when she told me what was happening on one of the soap operas she listened to religiously. "You know anything about those people, Claire Louise?" she asked me. "Seems I remember when you left here you were calling yourself Lana. Were you right there in Houston all those years we didn't hear from you?"

"What else did Macy say?" I was stalling for time and fighting off the panicky trapped feeling that was threatening to engulf me as I tried to think of how to get out of this mess. Of all times, just when I thought I had everything under control.

"Macy said it was an accident, them finding you through her. Seems Scott's teacher this year is a lady named Cheryl Brooks, used to be Lana's sister-in-law. Does that ring any bells? Said she wouldn't for the world have told me, but he's fixing to go to court, demand some kind of test to prove those are his kids, he wants them back, the kids, she said, not the woman. That you, Claire Louise?"

I burst into tears. "All my life you have believed the lies she makes up about me. Why is that, Mother?"

"I'm not believing anything yet, I'm waiting for you to tell me what she said is not true." Mother was looking at me like she could see me, like the veil of blindness was lifted so she could look right at me and watch me squirm. She wants this to be true, I thought. She wants me to be the bad one. She wants it to be all my fault, everything wrong that ever happened she wants it to be because I was bad inside. I could hear her thinking that as clear as anything, just as if she was talking out loud instead of staring at me like she wasn't blind anymore.

"What Macy said is not true, at least not the way she tells it. But of course you will believe her side of the story. You always have."

"That's what she says about you, Claire Louise, that I always believe your lies about her. And now, to hear her tell it, you have done something so terrible I am not going to be able to hold my head up in town when this comes out."

"That bitch. She's going to regret this."

"So it is true. How could you tell us you'd been in New York until you had to leave Ralph because of the drugs he used? How could you lie to your own family like this? I am just thankful your father is not alive to hear what I had to listen to today."

"Mother, the reason I didn't tell you all the details of my life while I was away was because it was over, I didn't see any point in dwelling on it. I have not done one thing I am ashamed of, and Macy's lies don't change that!"

She perked up then and I could tell I was winning her back over. "Well, if you married James Wilcox whatever happened to Ralph Anderson? And who is the father of your children?" she asked, sounding like she was getting interested in the details of this new story.

"James Wilcox is Britt's father. I married him after I came back to Molly's Point and Daddy refused to let me stay!"

"What?"

"That's right, I never wanted you to know this because I knew how it would hurt you, but I came here after I took the bus back to Houston and saw Daddy. He said I was as good as dead to you both and not to ever set foot on his land again. I didn't even get to tell him about how I had to leave Ralph because he was taking drugs day and night. I imagine he's dead now, Ralph is. He was on heroin when I left him and they don't last long once they get on that."

Mother's hands were clutched on her heart, like it was beating so strong she had to work to keep it inside her chest. "No, I cannot believe your father wouldn't have let you come back home. He knew how much I missed you, how I worried so."

"It's true, and it was because of him I married James and stayed in Houston without coming to see you all those years."

"Well, it didn't stop you from coming home after you left James for the minister who was struck down by lightning, did it?" Mother wasn't convinced yet. She was still trying to poke holes in my story.

"No, but Daddy had mellowed by then, although you can probably remember he wasn't real glad to see me at first. And I did not leave James for any minister. I moved to Oklahoma to get away from him because of the way he was. It had nothing to do with Reverend Smythe."

"If it didn't have anything to do with him, how come there is a minister in this story?"

"I worked for him in Houston, when I had to go to work because James and his mother were too tight to even give me enough to buy things for my own child. And since Reverend Smythe knew the horrible way James was treating us, he offered me a job if I went up there. That's all there was to it, Macy's gossip be damned! If she had one semblance of family pride she would never for a minute spread such trash about her own sister. It is more obvious to me than ever that she cares absolutely nothing about you, Mother. Otherwise, she would never hurt you the way she is doing now with these vicious stories about me."

"And who is Maryanne's father?"

"Why Mother, the very idea! Britt's father is James Wilcox, who was my husband when she was born, and Maryanne is James's daughter as well. Of course, I had already divorced him before Maryanne was born!"

"Then why is he suing for tests to prove he's the father? I don't understand that, Claire Louise." Mother was now asking questions like this was a show on television she was trying hard to follow. That didn't bother me, though. It was giving me a good chance to work out what I was going to say to people, the first of whom was going to be the lawyer I was planning to consult as soon as I figured out who to trust.

"Well, Mother, this is just between you and me, right?"

She nodded eagerly, anxious to be the first and perhaps only person to know the inside story. "James Wilcox was a child molester. I found out he was doing some awful things with Britt, it came out right before I left him. I was so hurt, to think I had let that happen to my own child. So before I left I lied to him, I told him he was not her father at all. It seemed best, Mother, I didn't want to drag that poor sweet little child through a court battle, I just wanted to get her away from him. Surely you can understand why I did that, you're a mother yourself! And of course I never ever let on I was pregnant, I had to get us all as far away from him as possible. And I was so scared when I came home even Daddy, hard as he could be, wouldn't turn me away a second time. I told him, I said, 'Daddy, I have had some hard times and I need to be with my mother just like my children need to be with their grandmother.' And he could see I meant business this time, that there was no way I was leaving without seeing you. I finally learned that about Daddy, he was much nicer if you were firm with him."

Mother nodded like she was remembering things the way I

253

was telling them to her. Mother has always been easy that way, tell her a story and pretty soon she's repeating it like she knew it all along in the first place.

"Did Macy say James is going to go to court to try to get my kids?" I asked. It's best to be prepared for things, I told myself.

"Yes, he's going to have a doctor do some tests to prove he's the father, Macy said, and then he'll at least get to see them some if he can't get custody, which is what he's trying for."

It occurred to me then that Mother was looking a tad smug, like she was not at all upset at this turn of events. "If I were you," I warned her, "I wouldn't go spreading these lies of Macy's around town. She's right about one thing, they do not reflect well on the Richards family!"

"The very idea!" Mother said all huffy. "As if I would repeat such awful gossip about anyone, let alone my own flesh and blood."

I knew I needed to get a lawyer myself and I was thinking about who to call. I wanted someone to shut Macy up. I thought about talking to James myself. The last thing I wanted was a case over who was the father of my kids, not right now when I was just barely married to Hugh. I doubted he was the type that would like a scandal about his less-than-year-old marriage. And for all I knew, James might be Maryanne's father or he might not. I'd never myself been sure of that particular fact. What if I can get to him, shut him up, maybe let him see them and tell folks some uncle story or something. Would that work?

I had my answer the next day. There was no way James was going to be satisfied with anything less than custody of Maryanne and unlimited visitation with Britt. Which meant that I had to get me some expert advice and fast. Although I didn't want to, I went to Hugh. He had plenty of money and lots of contacts and I was desperate. I had plenty of money myself now, of course, but the only lawyer I knew was the one who had written Daddy's last will and testament and I didn't think he was as slick as whoever James was seeing that was recommending tests and all.

Hugh reacted exactly as I expected. First he sneered, like he had something on me, and he asked for all sorts of sordid little details, and only then did he agree to call his lawyer for me. Mr. Simpson was exactly what I needed. He didn't waste time with you did whats and so on, he got right down to here's the problem, now let's fix it. It occurred to me, not for the first time, I would have made a good lawyer myself. I have a way of getting to the heart of the matter. I would have preferred not to have Hugh along with me, but since this was his lawyer I hadn't been able to figure out how to see Mr. Simpson without him.

"Now, Mrs. Sawyer, let me see if I have these facts straight. You have two children, one Britt Nicole Richards and the other Maryanne Richards. Those are the names on the children's birth certificates, I assume?"

"Well, no, not exactly. When I got my divorce from James I changed my name back to Richards but the paper did not actually change Britt's as well. I should have attended to that," I told him.

"So Britt was born during your marriage to James Wilcox and he thought her his natural daughter for the five years you lived together as husband and wife? Is that essentially correct?"

"Yes, but the moment I found out he was abusing her, I took her and left. I went to Nevada and got a divorce and didn't ask for a dime of child support, I wanted her to have no further contact with that nasty man. Why he didn't bathe more than once a week, and his teeth were black from decay!"

"So Britt's birth certificate reads Britt Nicole Wilcox?"

"God, this man is persistent!" I turned to Hugh as I spoke. "No, the birth certificate doesn't read anything! I lost it years ago!"

"Calm down, Clara Lou," Hugh said. "Joseph can't help you out of this mess you're in if he doesn't have the facts."

"I know, I'm just so upset. After all these years I thought I had put those horrible times behind me. What scares me more than anything is the thought of my children having to sit in court and listen to all the lies Cheryl and her brother and my own sister are apt to tell about me. I can't bear it, Hugh, you have to do something." I was sobbing on his chest and he patted me several times on the back before Mr. Simpson stood up and walked over to the couch on the other side of the room.

"Why don't you two move over here?" he asked, pointing to the love seat that faced his couch. "Let's see if we can't get all the facts sorted out before lunch. I have to be in court this afternoon and the sooner I know exactly what we're dealing with the sooner I can advise you.

"So the legal father of record is James Wilcox, and that is the name that appears on Britt's birth certificate? Correct?" he asked.

I nodded.

"And Maryanne's birth certificate, whose name appears on it?"

"Well, actually, I put Ralph Anderson's name on hers because I was back here and I was just trying to erase that James had ever existed. It wasn't that I was ashamed of him, I just didn't want Britt to ever have to remember the things that man did to her."

"And if the children were subjected to medical tests, who would their fathers be?"

"That's just what I'm here for! You must never let that happen! My children cannot be subjected to such an indignity!"

"I understand you, Mrs. Sawyer, and I am in no way saying I would recommend that you permit such a procedure, but for my information, I need to know what such tests would reveal."

"James is their father."

"Both of them?"

"Yes, both of them." I was in a tough spot, sitting there talking to Joseph Simpson, with Hugh listening to every word I said. I had no intention of admitting anyone other than my ex-husband of record had been the father of my children. In fact my entire plan consisted of admitting James was the children's father but contending that because of the abuse he had inflicted on them I had felt I had to keep him from knowing their whereabouts. It appeared to me that if I admitted straight out that I was not questioning his biological fatherhood I could avoid the embarrassment that would ensue if he forced me to have them tested and it turned out neither of my children had been born in wedlock, so to speak.

"So there is no question in your mind that James Wilcox is actually the father of both of the children?" he repeated.

"None whatsoever," I told him, looking him straight in the eye.

"And in the ten years since you divorced him, during all that time, you have never contacted him, the children have not seen him? Is that correct?"

"Yes, it is."

"And to the best of your knowledge, he has not attempted to contact you, or to see the children?"

"That's it exactly! We haven't seen hide nor hair of him for all these years! So what right does he have coming in now and wanting to see my children? They don't even know he exists!"

"And the reason you removed them from his sphere of influence was that he was abusing your oldest daughter?"

"Yes, that's right."

"How did you learn of the abuse?"

"I came home from work one day and found Britt crying and she told me what her daddy had done to her to punish her. I can't repeat what that poor child told me, it is too awful. I told her then, 'Britt, Mommy promises you that will never happen again. No one is going to hurt my little girl. Your mommy will protect you.' And we left for Nevada that same week."

"Are there any other witnesses to this abuse?"

"You'll never convince me James's mother didn't know what was going on, not that she would ever admit it. But that woman knew, I'm sure of it."

"And Britt was five years old when this happened?"

"She was five when we left, I don't know how old she was when it started."

"Did you ever ask her?"

"I tried to, she would cry and tell me she didn't know, she couldn't remember. She'd shake her little head back and forth—'No, no, no,' she would say. 'I can't remember. I can't.' It was too pitiful. When we left, I said, 'Britt, that bad man is all gone now, you just put it out of your mind. Forget it like it never happened.' And I never ever said his name to her again, nor did she mention him to me.

"You know," I continued, thinking out loud, "I think you should adopt the girls, Hugh. That would take care of all this nonsense from James once and for all don't you think, Mr. Simpson?"

"Not necessarily. I believe we had best get this matter settled before we even think of adoption," Mr. Simpson said.

It hurt me to notice that Hugh did not rush to say of course he wanted to adopt my poor fatherless children. It hurt me a lot. But I didn't say a word at the time. There truly wasn't anything to say, I realized. If a man doesn't love children, he doesn't. That's all there is to it. And Hugh didn't appear to love my children, at least not enough to adopt them.

25

Y OU DID WHAT?" Carlton asked me, looking at me like I had lost my mind.

"I told Mother about Claire Louise, I thought she ought to know before it gets all over town. I don't know what you are so upset about, you sound like Grandma."

"So your grandmother also told you to keep your mouth shut."

"No, my grandmother did not tell me to keep my mouth shut. My grandmother would never say such a thing to me. She said Corabeth would never believe any ill of Claire Louise, so I might as well have saved my breath."

"What did your mother say when you told her?"

"Actually, she didn't say much of anything. Just that she couldn't believe it."

"She didn't thank you for telling her, did she?"

"No, but I didn't expect her to."

"What did you expect, Macy?"

"I expected her to see what a liar Claire Louise is, that's what I expected!" I hated it when Carlton acted like he knew more about why I did things than I myself did. And it was particularly galling when he acted like he was now, all disapproving and superior. He was my husband. The least you would expect would be that he could show some support for me.

"And did it work, what you did, I mean? Did she say, 'Oh, now, I see, Claire Louise is a liar!'?"

"You know she didn't. Why are you badgering me like this?"

"Because I want you to look at what you are doing, that's why! As far as I can see, going out to tell your mother all about how awful your sister has been accomplished absolutely nothing except that Claire Louise is probably madder than a hornet at you now. Are you pleased with the outcome of your actions?"

"I don't care if she is mad, Carlton, you know how angry I am at her. So what if she's mad? That certainly doesn't bother me!"

"Macy, you say you miss the family closeness and you want to see your mother more, but the way you're acting, all you're doing is creating more problems than ever for yourself with both her and your sister. Your mother is not in good health, she is practically blind. She feels extremely dependent on your sister and is not at all likely to change the way she sees Claire Louise at this late date. Why can't you just leave them alone, see them from time to time, but quit trying to turn them into something neither your sister or mother will ever be?"

"Is that how you think I'm acting?"

"Yes, it is, and you're getting as obsessive about this latest incident as you were about your father's will a year ago. Can't you let it go?"

"I don't want to talk about it anymore. It's obvious we cannot agree on this particular topic."

"All right, let's talk about something else." The sigh he heaved sounded like he was giving up on me. That bothered me, I didn't want Carlton to give up on me. I knew that sometimes I didn't act with a lot of common sense when it came to Claire Louise and my mother, but what Carlton couldn't see was how important it was to me that they see the truth the way I did. Over and over that's what it came down to in my mind, they had to see the truth and quit the lying. "Abe mentioned today there is an antique auction Saturday," Carlton said. "Would you like to go with them?"

"I had thought I'd take the kids swimming out at Grandma's if it's nice weather, but . . ." I hated to turn Carlton down. He was right when he hinted we hadn't been getting along too well lately, and I knew I needed to spend more time with him. "What about if I get up early and run Scott and Travis out there to spend the day with her? Then you and I could go back out after the auction and take her to dinner."

"Why drive all the way out to Molly's Point twice? Let's get Mrs. Grant to baby-sit and then we'll take her with us after the auction and go get your grandmother and we'll all eat at San Jacinto Inn. Your grandmother would like that. Abe and Roxanne might even want to join us."

"Great idea," I agreed. Later I was so thankful we had gone out to Molly's Point and taken Grandma out to San Jacinto Inn, which had for years been her favorite place to eat. That was the last time she ate out anywhere, that trip with us was. She fell the next week and broke her hip and was in the hospital for over a month. She came home from the hospital in November, one year almost to the day from when my father had died. She could get up from bed and get in a wheelchair only if someone was there to lift her. And it broke my heart to see how thin she was and how much it pained her to move at all. My grandmother, who had been able to sit cross-legged on the floor and play old maid with my children just last summer, was now virtually bed-ridden. And what was even harder to see, she didn't have any of her old spark for living. She just lay there and nodded when we talked to her, but she wasn't pushing to get up and regain her mobility. It was like she was being as still as she could so nothing would hurt.

Belle had agreed to come out and stay, but it was apparent Grandma needed someone stronger to help her move around at all and we started looking for a lady to move in. Since Grandma had come home from the hospital, I had been out there by 7:00 A.M. every single day. It had been almost six weeks now, but I was determined not to leave my grandmother to Claire Louise like had happened to my father. And you may believe me when I say she was trying to move in and take over. She had even had a wheelchair ramp installed in her new house and was talking about moving Grandma over there.

"I'll see her in a nursing home before she's living in that monstrosity you just built!"

"Macy, you are so jealous of me that you can't think straight! Grandma is all alone and you know as well as I do how she has always hated nursing homes. All I am doing is proposing to move her over to my house until she gets on her feet again. I haven't heard you offering to take her in yourself."

That was a real sore point with me, because I had wanted to move her in with us and Carlton had pointed out how hard it would be. Our house is tiny, only two bedrooms and the boys' toys all over the house. But what we were doing to look out for Grandma for the moment was causing a real strain on me as well as Belle. I was staying with Grandma from seven in the morning until seven at night and then Belle was coming over and spending the night with her. But we couldn't keep it up forever. It was hard on Belle, who was almost eighty herself, and I was back to never seeing my own family, which wasn't good. I knew that, but when I thought of staying home I imagined Claire Louise coming in and preying on Grandma, acting all sweet around her and like as not bringing her fat lawyer friend out to change Grandma's will for her, and I saw red, I truly did. That's why I didn't trust the nurses Claire Louise found either. Grandma didn't need them, I said. Belle and I could do for her.

"Carlton, let's move out there, at least until she's better. Her

262

house is plenty big enough, the kids can ride in with you in the morning and stay with Mrs. Grant after school until you're ready to drive back out. That way I'll see you and the boys and can look after Grandma too."

"No."

"But it's going to be our house someday, Carlton."

"Macy, even if you got along with your mother and sister I would be extremely reluctant to move out there right in the middle of them. I like Houston, and I do not care for family compounds, particularly ones where no one is civil to anyone else. The answer is no, I will not move out there with you and the children. I think you should hire someone to stay with your grandmother or move her to a nursing home. There are some excellent ones right here in Houston."

But still I dithered back and forth. Belle and I talked, and I tried to talk to Grandma. "What about if I drive you to South Park Retirement Community, Grandma, just so you can see it? It's real nice, Carlton has been there. And I could see you all day, you could even come over to my house when you're a little better."

Grandma had been home over a month and she wasn't any better. She was if anything worse. "I'm doing fine right here in my own home. You know I don't care for nursing homes. Mr. Shasta's mother died in one. I never did think they looked after her good in there."

"But that was twenty years ago. They're better now and I would be there every single day to make sure you were okay."

"Do what you think best, then. I know I'm just a bother to you. I hate that I got old. But, Macy, I think it is best if people die in their own homes. I've always thought that. It's more natural that way."

263

I cried then and said, "Don't talk about dying, Grandma, don't. You're going to get better, your hip will heal and next spring you'll be out in your garden with your flowers."

"No, I won't. My bones are too old. I'm not getting better. You need to face that, Macy."

"I will not. Tomorrow I'm going to call and get you a physical therapist, that's what you need. Someone to help with your exercises."

We had a sheet of exercises that she was supposed to do, but every time Belle or I started her on them she'd cry and say it hurt her bad, and we didn't have the heart to push her. Grandma had never been a complainer or a quitter either, and so when she said it hurt we both knew it must really be hurting her. But I could now see how our coddling her was encouraging her to get weaker and weaker, and what a mistake that was. The next day I had Kathleen Miro out, a physical therapist we got from the nurse's registry. After that first day, she didn't want to come back. Grandma wasn't up to it, she said, and though I convinced her to give it a week's try at the end of the week Belle and I had to agree with her. What she was doing wasn't helping. If anything Grandma was weaker than ever.

The first of December Belle came down with a bad cold, the kind where you cough and cough until you have to hold on to something not to fall over. It was the weekend of our first norther of the year, and it was cold and wet. Her daughter called me Friday about five and said, "Macy, Belle is in bed with this cough and she has a fever. She can't come out and stay with your grandma tonight." I had been expecting the call all day. Belle and I had both been afraid she was coming down with something the night before. She had tried not to get too close to Grandma then. The last thing we needed was for Grandma to

264

get sick on top of the broken hip. Claire Louise was there when I hung up the phone, and she had obviously understood every word of the conversation.

"I've fixed some chicken and dumplings for Grandma's supper," she'd said when she walked in. "Grandma, you know how you've always loved chicken and dumplings." Grandma nodded and didn't open her eyes.

"She's trying to rest, Claire Louise," I said, "and she had chicken Belle's daughter fixed her last night. I doubt she wants any more chicken tonight. I was going to heat her up a little beef stew in the microwave. She has about ten freezer bags of it she fixed herself. That'll stick to her ribs better than any thin chicken broth will."

"My chicken and dumplings is not thin, the gravy is just as thick as anything and the dumplings will be good for her. You just leave that stew in the freezer, this is already made up."

We sat there glaring at each other, which is how all our conversations ended these days. She had not forgiven me for telling Mother about James Wilcox, not that what she thought about me gave me a minute's pause. To tell the truth, it was easier to be around her, now that I didn't have to act like I trusted her. She knew I didn't and I knew she knew it, and as far as I was concerned things could stay that way indefinitely.

"And don't you worry about Grandma, either." She moved over to the bed and began patting Grandma's thin hand and then started adjusting the covers. Grandma moaned a little, like she did when the bed moved even the least little bit and she wasn't wide enough awake to stifle back the sound.

"Leave the bed alone, Claire Louise, can't you see all that patting is hurting her?"

"I'll stay with her tonight since Belle can't come," she said, continuing to smooth the covers and giving me a go-to-hell look.

I didn't say a word to her, just picked up the telephone and called Carlton. "Belle is sick, I'm going to have to stay with Grandma tonight. Why don't you and the kids come out here?"

"The kids have a soccer game tomorrow," Carlton said. "What's wrong with Belle?"

"She's got a bad cold, has a cough that sounds awful. I could hear her in the background when I was talking to her daughter," I said.

"I'm sorry to hear that. How is your grandmother today?"

I made my voice purposely cheerful and said, "A little stronger, I think. I'm fixing to get her up to watch the news with me before supper. She's having some of her own beef stew, she's been looking forward to it. And I'm going to peel a navel orange for her, you know how good they are."

"You're in the room with her, I take it?" Carlton said.

"Yes."

"Is your sister there?"

"Yes."

"Oh, Lord, do you need me to come out, Macy?"

"That would be nice."

"All right, we're on our way."

"Can you bring me some clothes and my bathroom stuff?"

"Sure, we'll be there in an hour or so."

"Thanks, Carlton."

I hung up the phone and flashed my sister a look that was supposed to let her know once and for all she was not going to be able to intimidate me with her bullying. "Carlton and the kids are on the way out. I'll stay with Grandma."

She ignored me and turned back to Grandma, whose eyes were open now, although I'm not sure how much of our conversation she was following. Grandma had gotten vague lately. She always knew us and answered questions we asked her right enough, but she seemed to spend a lot of time drifting off somewhere else. It scared me, her going away in her mind like that, and I kept trying to get her interested in playing cards with me or watching television, but she just didn't seem to care. I had bought one of those bird feeders with suction cups and tried to get her to watch for the different ones that came right up to her window now, but I might not have bothered, for all the interest she took in them. Like I told Carlton later that night, my main hope was to get her a little active by spring where I could wheel her outside to the garden. I thought once the flowers started coming in again she would perk up, even if she couldn't get down on the ground and grub around like she always had.

"Grandma," Claire Louise said, ignoring me, "Mother said to tell you she was sorry she didn't get over to see you this morning. Once that norther blew in she didn't feel up to getting out in it."

"That's all right. Tell her to stay in, no point in getting out in messy weather."

"Well, you know how she is, she worries if she doesn't get to see you every day."

"Tell her not to worry."

"What can I get you, now that I'm here?"

"Not a thing, I don't need a thing."

"Would you like me to adjust this light for you, get you a book to read? Here's that one I brought over yesterday."

"I haven't felt like reading today."

"Well, what about the tape-recorded books? Mother sent you one she just loved."

"Maybe tomorrow."

"I'm going out in the kitchen now and fix you a nice dinner."

267

"That will be fine."

I followed Claire Louise to the kitchen, thinking I was going to dump that whole pot of chicken and dumplings on her if she said one more word about it. "You better get on over to your monstrosity," I told her. "Hugh's probably wondering where you are." I had been as amazed as everyone else when she married that man, who was at least thirty years older than she was and was undoubtedly the most sarcastic person I had ever heard. It served her right, I thought, listening to him put her down every time she opened her mouth. Even Carlton agreed with me when I wondered why they had married. Hugh didn't even pretend to like her.

"And what about your children? Surely with two houses full of people you have to take care of, you have something more to do than hang around here where you are not needed."

"The girls are visiting their father in Houston," Claire Louise said, smirking at me.

She said it to see my reaction and I was so surprised that my jaw dropped. "Their father?" I echoed, unable to think what else to say.

"Yes, their father. We have resolved our differences and they are going to be spending time with him now."

"I should think you would be ashamed of hiding them from him all these years," I said. "How did you explain that away to Mother?"

"None of your business why I did things, but I do want you to know your meddling in my affairs didn't turn out at all the way you hoped it would."

"I never meddled in your affairs, Claire Louise. Cheryl and I just by accident figured out who you were and she decided to tell her brother. I had absolutely nothing to do with that!"

"And you never told Mother a thing either, did you?"

"Yes, I told her, and I'll do it again if I uncover any more of your lies."

"I never lied. I was protecting my children, which you could have found out if you had bothered to come to me for the truth instead of running around spreading vicious gossip."

"That's crap and you know it. If you were protecting your children so much, how come they're with their father now? Answer me that."

"Because I met with him and his wife after my lawyer told him what was what, and I am now convinced that he has changed and it would be good for the girls to see him from time to time."

"And get them out of your hair? You've never given those kids the attention they deserve! I suppose the change you're referring to in James is the fact that he is now vice-president of that aviation company and has plenty of money. I'm sure that's what you're after. You ought to be ashamed of yourself. I'm ashamed of you."

"Macy, you are so suspicious and so willing to think ill of anyone, I won't even dignify your comments with an answer. But let me remind you, the next time you even think about meddling in my life, you better think again. I'll sue you for slander next time."

"Slander's only a crime if a person lies, Claire Louise. I've never said a thing about you that isn't the truth."

The back door opened then and Carlton and the boys came in bringing a swirl of icy cold air with them, which was probably all to the good. My sister and I might have come to blows right there in the kitchen if someone hadn't interrupted us at that point.

26

THE FIRST CHRISTMAS after Hugh and I married was, in a way, our anniversary, and he bought tickets for a second cruise for us without consulting me. The first thing I thought when I saw those tickets was I never should have let him get away with surprising me last year. It had, if nothing else, established a precedent that I had no intention of continuing.

"Oh, Hugh, whatever have you done?" I asked him when I saw those tickets. "How on earth could we go away over Christmas? That's family time and you know how important my family is to me."

"I'm your family now, Clara Lou, I'm your husband and December twenty-fifth is the anniversary of our first date. I want to celebrate with you."

"This is so sweet of you, Hugh, and of course I want to celebrate with you too. As a matter of fact, I had thought of all sorts of special things we could do right here."

"Well, I've decided we need to get out of town, away from this damn house, which is taking forever to get built, away from your sister with whom you are forever feuding, away from your kids and your mother and Lucy and her dog. We need another honeymoon, Clara Lou."

"Oh, I agree, it sounds like heaven to get away, but I would so much rather we wait and go again in the spring, Hugh. Now come on, admit it, doesn't that sound better to you?"

"No. I've got these tickets and we're leaving here December nineteenth. And if you're not on that boat, I'm sure I can find someone else to use your ticket."

I was so shocked I sat and stared. Hugh didn't sound for a minute like a man in love with his wife, one who wanted to make her happy. It was obvious to me that not even tears would wipe that scowl off his face. "I am distressed you would say such a thing to me, Hugh," I said, looking at him with a stern yet hurt expression. "You know I want to be with you, but what about my responsibilities?"

"You told me last week the girls are going to stay with their father for two weeks at Christmas, and Lucy is here with your mother, and your sister is in residence next door with your grandmother. I expect you to be where you belong, with your husband."

"I've got to think," I said, feeling manipulated by Hugh, definitely not a good feeling. I needed to think, to figure out how he was doing this to me. He and his lawyer, I was beginning to realize, had not done the best they could for me regarding this situation with James. It was on their recommendations that I had agreed to the liberal visitation schedule Britt and Maryanne now had with James. Essentially they were with him all of the time school was not in session, and in the space of a few months I could see that I was losing much of my influence over them. I wasn't happy with that at all, but every time I mentioned going to court, Hugh reminded me that his lawyer thought it likely I would lose, since I was the one who had left James and because Britt absolutely denied any memory of him, good or bad. So there I was, as Hugh and his lawyer almost gleefully pointed out, with a story no one alive could back up against a man deprived of his children for ten years.

"Don't dare go to court," Hugh and Joseph Simpson said, and consequently I had been more or less trapped into letting my kids spend all kinds of time down there in Houston with those people who I knew full well had nothing good to say about me. I didn't like it, of course I didn't like it, no woman would, I tried to tell Hugh. "You should have thought of that before you hid out," he would tell me, and the surge of anger I felt when he talked to me like that was as intense as any I had ever felt at my father.

More and more I missed Daddy. He had cared about me, I realized as the days passed. Sure he hadn't been a perfect father, who was? But he hadn't been all that bad either. Mother and I had found some old photographs in the bottom of her hope chest. She'd forgotten they were there years ago. And this year for Christmas I had gotten silver frames and everyone was getting a picture of Daddy and Mother for Christmas. I thought it was a nice idea. We didn't have enough family mementos around, it seemed to me.

Maybe marrying Hugh had not been the best idea I ever had. In some ways I had been better off with Daddy alive. He had more or less gotten to where he let me do whatever I wanted. With Hugh everything, every single thing, was a battle.

And, because I was living in town with Hugh, there was Lucy living with Mother, or as good as. When Britt and Maryanne were at home, Lucy slept at her trailer. The rest of the time she was with Mother, who truly could not be by herself now. So between having to keep my eye on things at Mother's, as I still thought of the house although of course it was mine now, and with Hugh's house in town to oversee, his housekeeper having departed in a huff not a month after our honeymoon, I was very busy. And to tell the truth, caring for Hugh's house was a particularly thankless chore. I did not see a penny of money for everything I did there for him and for his house. Why, we had been married for almost a year, and do you think we had so much as a joint account? Let me tell you, we did not. Hugh deposited a pittance in a household account for me every month to use on his house, and the way he went over those statements each month you would think he was two steps away from welfare himself. If there is one thing that I truly cannot abide it is a niggardly man. That I truly cannot live with, I cannot. Why, Hugh had some of the most primitive notions. He was the only man alive that did not have a single charge account, not one. Pay cash or don't get it, he would tell me when I asked. I take that back. I just remembered another person I knew who did not hold with credit. It was my daddy. Fancy me forgetting that. They were of an age, Hugh and Daddy, come to think of it. Perhaps Hugh had some bad memories of the Depression, perhaps that was it. That was the reason Daddy had always been so tight. He had grown up doing without. Could Hugh also have grown up doing without?

Even so, I told myself, even if that is the reason, it doesn't help me now. Thinking how he might have gotten that way didn't give me a clue as to how to change him, to change his ways. And more and more I realized I was going to have to change him in order to stay with him. As I have said, I cannot abide a niggardly man. Hugh wasn't that way before we married, at least as far as I could tell he was not. Not for the first time, I thought to myself there is something to be said for long court-ships. There truly is. Here I was on my second, some would say third husband, and once again, as I got to know my husband some serious flaws were being revealed. It was enough to put a person off marriage for life.

I heard a really nasty rumor about Hugh and Mr. Simpson. I heard it over in Ruston one day where I had gone to pick up some supplies for the house. The clerk had turned to the owner of the store and said, "Order here for Hugh Sawyer. Bet he wants it yesterday." The way he sneered I knew he didn't think much of Hugh so I thought I would see if I could fish a little.

"Is he usually in a hurry for his supplies?"

"Sure is, the ones he gets legal anyway."

"I don't know what you mean," I said, looking at him like he was the most interesting man I had talked to in a long time.

He got cautious for a minute. "You ought to know Hugh Sawyer. You're picking up his order, aren't you?"

"Well, the truth is, I don't know him well. I've just gone to work for him and it would be such a help to me if you could tell me about him. Kind of help me do well in my new job, you know." I looked at him with my eyes wide like my whole future depended on his help.

He and the other man I took to be the owner exchanged a long look. Finally, the other man said, "What the hell, you just do what he says and keep your mouth shut, you'll be okay. And whatever you do, don't ask him how he made that fortune! He likes to act like he was to the manner born, but I hear tell he and old Joe Simpson made a tidy sum selling black-market oil and tires during the war."

They both laughed then, and I went on outside to drive the pickup back to the loading dock to have them load up the lumber I had ordered. On the way home, I thought to myself, I'm not surprised. Hugh is a hard man, I can see that. The question is, do I stay with him or not? He was building a gorgeous house on my land and he was old, almost seventy, and he didn't have anybody but me, but still, it was hard to stay with him. He didn't act seventy and like he needed me. He acted like a tyrant. And I didn't care for that at all. But I thought to myself, oh, well, I'll get by until this house is built. I can manage that at least. And Hugh, true to his word, was paying for every nail that went into the house. He was doing that, although I had to keep an almost constant eye on the workmen building the house. For all Mr. Bailey was such a wonderful foreman, I never went over there I didn't discover some example of sloppy work that had to be corrected.

One thing I did do, the next time I went over for supplies I made sure to go in my new Suburban, the one I had gotten Hugh to buy me since I was on the road so much picking up things for our building project, and I wore my full-length mink coat, the one Hugh had gotten me for my birthday at the big after-the-season sale at Sakowitz when we came home from our honeymoon last year. And I walked into Mier's Building Supplies and presented those two men with my list and stood glancing at my solid-gold Rolex watch from time to time as they filled my order. And then when they presented me with an invoice, I wrote a check signing it Mrs. Hugh Sawyer with a flourish. And as I was leaving I looked pointedly at the owner, who was the one behind the counter at that moment, and said, "Some people who want to do well in business better watch how they treat their customers. Gossiping isn't always in a small company's best interests." By that time I knew Hugh was a big customer of his, had been for years, and I wanted him to sweat a little and wonder what I had told my husband. On the way home, I laughed and laughed. How those little men had squirmed. It did me good to give them their comeuppance, served them right for gossiping, I said to myself, I bet they think twice before they spread rumors. The truth was I hadn't said a word to Hugh, didn't intend to. But I thought to myself, never know when that bit of information will come in handy. You just never know.

To top off my troubles, there was this situation with James.

What was I going to do about him? I absolutely would not lose my children's loyalty to him, I would not. But I could not for the life of me see how to get them out of his sphere of influence. Maryanne was always talking about "my daddy" in this adoring little voice that grated on me like fingernails on a chalkboard, and with Britt, James could do no wrong either. The truth of it was, he was undermining me. Why, he had bought Britt a new computer without even consulting me, and last weekend when Maryanne came home, she slipped and told me Cheryl had taken her to some fancy doctor for testing! "What kind of testing?" I asked, trying hard not to show I was livid. I could tell they had warned her not to tell me, the way she clapped her hand over her mouth the minute the words were out, so I was careful to act only curious and interested, not upset at all.

"Oh, it was games like blocks and mazes and lots of questions and then I read for the doctor and answered some math questions. She said I was real smart and worked real hard," Maryanne bragged, clearly pleased with the attention she had gotten.

Damn, I thought, realizing he was having her tested for learning problems, something I knew full well she had, it having been diagnosed years ago. I listened to her talk on, thinking about what I would say to him on the phone the next time he called, when all of a sudden this little voice inside me said, hey, wait a minute, Claire Louise, give James enough rope and perhaps he will hang himself. What he had done was not legal. In order to test a child the custodial parent has to give permission, something I had not even been asked to do. Let him keep this up and I would have something to go to court about. He was subjecting my daughter to the stress of tests without my permission. What else would he do, I wondered? Or even worse, what had he and that bitch Cheryl, who had never from the moment she laid eyes on me liked me, already done? I resolved to listen to Britt and Maryanne very carefully in the future, no telling what I could discover. But it took time, all of this took time, and I seemed to meet myself coming and going these days, and now here was Hugh insisting I take off for two weeks and go on a cruise with him!

"Hugh, what about Grandma, if you would go over more often to see her, you'd know how bad she is. How can we get on a ship and be away for two weeks? You know how she counts on me to be there most of every day."

"Macy'll take care of your grandma, she's as good as moved in over there."

I could have sworn he smirked at me when he said that. I looked closely though and his face was straight, his eyes almost flat looking, so maybe I was wrong. One thing about Hugh that puzzled me was how he felt about my sister Macy. When we were over there, he was nice as could be to her, that was plain to see. Only once had I tried to talk to him about it. "Hugh, you don't realize what a snake in the grass Macy can be," I told him. "Of course she is my sister and I love her, but if I told you some of the things she has done, you'd find it hard to believe I'm sure."

"Nothing people do surprises me much," he said.

"Well, that may be so, but I doubt you have known anyone like Macy. Have you ever heard of a sister would tell her own mother tales about how her sister ran off with a minister? Why, she like to gave poor Mother a coronary with her lurid lies!"

"No," Hugh said, "but then I never knew a sister who ran off and hid her kids from their father for ten years, either."

That really ticked me off when he said that, it truly did. "Are you implying I didn't leave James for some very good reasons?" I asked him, ready to do battle if he answered no, I don't think you had good reasons.

"Oh, I'm sure you had reasons, I'm just not sure we all would agree about what they were, that's all."

"And what does that mean?"

"It means I've lived long enough to know every story has more than one side, Clara Lou, even yours."

"Well, I'd like to know what is the good of having a husband if he doesn't take your side in an argument?" I asked him.

"No good at all," he said, and he laughed like one of us had said something funny. I did not understand Hugh when he said things like that, it made me wonder was he a little, well, you know, kind of touched. He was, after all, older than Mother, and I thought maybe his mind was wandering. Hugh drank more than he needed to and he was never without a cigarette. He probably had at the very least hardening of the arteries. Which explained some of his more bizarre utterances. But it didn't, in my mind, explain how come he was always so chatty with Macy like he had become since we came back from our Christmas cruise, which I had only with extreme reluctance agreed to. And I had only agreed after Hugh had promised he would never again purchase a ticket on a plane, boat, or so much as a bus without first consulting me.

Take the second week in February, for example. I had gone over to Grandma's and was cleaning out one of her kitchen cabinets as I was cooking a big pot of stew. I had called Lucy, told her to bring Mother and Maryanne over, we were having a family dinner with Grandma. Britt was on a date, a study date, she assured me. I felt reasonably sure she was telling me the truth. Her grades had been fine for the last year and she was applying to colleges. It looked like she at least was over her little rebellion. Although even there it appeared James was doing his best to undermine me. Last week, without so much as a never-you-mind to me, James and his wonderful wife, Elizabeth—who also can do no wrong, according to Maryanne—James and Elizabeth drove up to Dallas and spent the weekend showing my daughters colleges! Britt came home with brochures from TCU and SMU and even Baylor University, where they stopped in Waco on the way back! I called James the minute they got home and told him what I thought about him taking my children out of town without telling me. "I am sure that is illegal," I said, "and if you plan to pull something like this again, you can forget all about seeing them. I will go to court!"

He was apologetic as all get out then, which proves my point that you have to be firm with people else they will run all over you. "I'm sorry you are upset," he said. "You are absolutely right, I should have asked you."

"Yes, you should have," I told him.

When it came to colleges Britt would have no trouble, I told myself, glad she had her rebelling behind her. With Maryanne, I confess I still had to worry. She just didn't have the brains her sister did. The best that poor child could do was C's. It was a shame she tried so hard and only got average grades, whereas her sister did little or nothing for her A's. But then life isn't fair, I told my kids, which is why you had best be prepared to fight for whatever you get.

As you might imagine, Macy was not pleased when I showed up with the supplies for dinner, but as usual I ignored her scowls and went about my business. I had of course asked Grandma did she want me to fix her a little of my stew and she had answered me do what you want, which sad to say was the most she said these days. So, as I said, I ignored Macy's dirty looks and went on about my rat killing, as Grandma used to say. After all, Macy wasn't the only grandchild Grandma had, as much as she would have liked to pretend she was. Hugh was there. He had no real choice if he wanted dinner. We had finally moved into our new house, but nothing was unpacked and the kitchen was in such a mess it was hard even to get a cup of coffee in the mornings. The way it looked, it would be weeks before I cooked in there, which suited me just fine. I thought it was high time I did for Grandma, I told Hugh.

"It seems to me you might consult your sister before you plan meals over at your grandmother's," Hugh said to me. It was remarks like that that made me wonder just whose side my husband was on.

"I asked Grandma," I told him. "It is, after all, her house."

"Your sister Macy has moved in there, apparently endangering her marriage to do so. So it might behoove you to respect the fact of her residence."

"Hugh, when you talk like that, I honestly do not know whose side you are on!"

"Does everything boil down to taking sides, Clara Lou?"

"I do wish you would call me Claire Louise."

"Or Lana, how about that? I hear you once liked that name."

"That was a long time ago. Why don't you go in the den and catch the news. I'd like to hear the weather for tomorrow." As you can see, Hugh's mind wandered. I was noticing it more and more.

That was the night when Lucy's daughter called, said she was leaving her husband and wanted to come stay with her mother. And I said, "Lucy, why don't you let Lucinda move in with me, I need someone to help out in my new house."

Lucinda, if she was for sure finished with her husband, was a find. She was almost forty, Lord help me so was I for that matter, and had no kids to distract her, and she had cleaned for folks for years according to her mother. I did tell Lucy, though, you tell Lucinda if she is just running away from her husband for a while, I don't want her. I have no time to train someone how I like things just to have them up and leave me and go on back to their husband. As it turned out there was no call to worry about Lucinda going back to her husband, he was arrested for drunk driving that very weekend, and she, being a religiously motivated teetotaler, would not so much as talk to him on the phone after that. As I said, Lucinda was a find, she could work rings around her mother. She could even put me to shame when she got going, which was saying something as I am quite efficient myself.

By the time Lucinda had been with me less than a month we had the house looking like it had been lived in for years. I was that pleased, the children loved their new rooms, particularly Maryanne, who told anyone who would listen to her about how she had three rooms now, one at her grandma's, one at her mother's, and one at her father's. I was glad she was happy, poor child. I did worry about her. She had put on weight again and her face was starting to break out. I told myself she was going through an awkward stage, that was all, but I was afraid Maryanne was going to go through life as one of those dowdy, heavy, peasant-looking women. Although she had nice hands and feet, I reminded myself, so maybe she would shoot up and lose that baby fat, and it is a fact that lots of teenage girls get acne. It was impossible for me to watch her diet, though, with her out from under my roof every weekend and all summer.

One thing I didn't want for my daughter, I didn't want her to have to go through high school fat and ugly. Life is no fun for fat ugly women, but for high school girls who are fat it is pure hell. There was a girl in high school when I was there that people joked about all the time. Oh, if you can't get a date, ask Alexis, they would say, and laugh. Nobody was so bad off they had to ask Alexis. And sometimes I feared Maryanne was looking like Alexis. Her breasts had gotten so big she was into a C-cup bra and if she didn't stand up straight, which she rarely did, they hung down to her waist. And her hair was thin and straw colored, no other way to describe it. Her eyes were gray, plain dull gray. Maryanne took after James's side for sure, I'd never heard of anyone on our side of the family looked like her. Even Mother, when she used to be fat, was never ever sloppy. She kept herself up always. She took pride in her appearance, Mother did. And Grandma, who to tell the truth was awful sloppy at times, was, until her decline, such a handsome woman she could get away with it.

One thing about the women in the Richards family, and the Scotts too, which is what Mother was, the women are good-looking. Smart too, but no one flaunts that. Maryanne wasn't either smart or good-looking, though. I confess, Maryanne was a concern to me.

27

AFTER BELLE GOT SICK, I had to move in to look after Grandma. There simply wasn't any option. I soon gave up asking Carlton to move out there, too. He was adamant he wasn't going to do that. But he did come out every weekend and I tried to spend some time with him and some with my kids. It broke my heart that I was missing so much time with them, but it seemed like any time I tried to leave my grandma's house, I saw my sister walking in with the fat lawyer behind her. It's just like Daddy all over again, a voice would say in my mind, it's just like Daddy all over again. And so I would have to stay there right by Grandma. She needed me to protect her. Carlton and I gave up talking about it. He couldn't get through to me, he would say, and I'd tell him that was precisely the way I felt trying to tell him anything. We weren't fighting, though, that was one thing. We just weren't talking much at all.

I felt tired all the time now. It seemed I never fell asleep that I didn't wake up to check on Grandma every few minutes, and I never felt rested any more. Belle found a girl in town who was about half my age and wanted to work. Laura, her name was. Belle's daughter would drive Laura out every morning for me, and Laura would help with the cleaning and cooking. Keeping up with the laundry was one of the worst things. We were changing Grandma's bed several times a day. She forgot to ask us to get her up. Poor thing, it was so pitiful.

"Macy, I wet myself," she'd say, and she'd cry, she was so ashamed. She hated it, being old and hurting and not knowing when she needed to go to the bathroom. "Don't you worry," I'd tell her, "accidents happen. Laura and I will get you all cleaned up." And we'd be real careful moving her, but still she would cry like it was hurting real bad. My stomach clutched up in knots every time I had to do that to her. I hated to hurt her so.

She ate almost nothing. We were fixing her food and mashing it up like we were feeding a baby. And most of the time, Laura or I would feed her, to try to get her to eat as much as possible. But she went downhill faster and faster. I had the doctor out nearly every day. "Do something," I would tell him.

"All I can do is give her more of the same medicine, Macy," old Doctor Blynn said. "She is failing, that's the only word for it. You need to get out more, though. You're looking peaked yourself. It won't help your grandma for you to get down."

But I couldn't. No one understood that. Claire Louise was over at Grandma's every day as it was. If I so much as left I knew she'd be in there in a minute trying to take her over like she had everyone else. Not my grandma, I promised myself. Grandma doesn't like you, Claire Louise, I would think to myself every time she came in acting like Little Miss Merry Sunshine. Grandma never liked you.

"Grandma, I've brought your mail, here are some Christmas cards, I bet. Let me help you open them." And she would pull up her chair and sit right by the bed, opening cards and reading messages and talking in her little-girl voice. God, I hated her voice worst of anything.

"Do what you want to," Grandma said.

I had tried to get our mail delivered, and I got Belle's daughter to bring me things I needed from the store. I didn't want Claire Louise running around doing for us and talking all over town about how good she was to do it. But she'd gone behind my back and told the postman she'd bring our mail out, he didn't have to bother, and I let it go because I didn't want to cause a public stink. That's the way she was. She got what she wanted because the rest of the family didn't want to cause a public stink by fighting her. But I let the mail go. Grandma more than anyone hated public scandals, I reminded myself. When she is gone, though, I surprised myself thinking one day, when Grandma is gone Claire Louise is going to get the biggest public stink of her life.

As soon as I thought that, I tried to stop the thought. No,

she won't be gone, I told myself. Grandma will get better come spring, when the flowers are out. She'll get better. But I couldn't believe it anymore, as much as I tried to make myself. I couldn't truly believe come spring she'll be better. The best I could do was this, I didn't let myself think about spring coming anymore. One day at a time, one day, I'd remind myself when I started to get scared. Don't borrow trouble, Grandma would tell me. A funny thing happened. Grandma had stopped talking to me, she'd more or less stopped talking to anyone by this time. Yet, even so, she was still there sounding just like herself, loud and clear in my head. I'd say to her in the morning, "Grandma, I've gotten you some of this apple cinnamon oatmeal you like," and she would just lay there, I knew that. But in my head, I could hear her say, "Oh, that will taste good, Macy." And she always thanked me, I heard her even if she couldn't say it out loud right then.

I set the card table up beside Grandma's bed, and when we weren't using it to feed her, I started playing canasta with her again, a card game she had taught me to play when I was barely old enough to know what the cards meant. Used to, when I was a child, I'd walk into Grandma's house and it didn't matter what she was doing, she would drop it and do something with me. One of the things I loved was to play cards with her. "Let's play cards," I'd say, and she'd get out the card table and set up the chairs. Grandma's bedroom was the size of two bedrooms because that is what it had been, two bedrooms. She'd had the wall between the rooms knocked out so she had room in her bedroom for a four-poster double bed and three big chests and a couch and two big wing chairs. That's where I slept, on that couch, which always had been exceptionally comfortable.

But back to when I was little. Back then we'd set up the card table in front of the couch and unfold the chairs and Grandma would get the cigar box where she kept her canasta cards and take two big handfuls, one for each side of the card shuffler. And I would turn the handle, listening to those cards whirring down. It didn't matter to Grandma how many times I wanted to shuffle, she'd just wait and let me shuffle until I had them like I wanted them. And then she'd deal out the cards and we would play. It came as a surprise to me to learn when I was older that some people played with a certain number of decks and paid attention to whether the cards were all there. We didn't, not my grandmother and me. We just scooped up the cards and played with what we had.

But now I put the cards on the card table, which I pushed right up next to her bed, and I sat on the other side of the table, across from her. "The card shuffler can still shuffle the cards down, Grandma," I said to her. "Do you want me to deal for you?"

"Do what you want to," she'd say. I'd swear I could hear her although she never said it out loud, just in her mind where I could hear her words loud and clear in my own mind. Grandma and I always could read each other, that's what made us so special together. Always, when I was little and too upset to talk, she'd know what was wrong and fix it without me having to say a word. That's all that was happening now. I was reading her mind, that's all in the world it was. Claire Louise liked to rant and rave, trying to stir up trouble. She was saying I had lost my mind, sitting there talking with a woman who was practically in a coma. I knew what she was saying; she even said it to me once. But it didn't matter what Claire Louise thought. She was jealous, always had been. I could see that. She was that way, Claire Louise was, always wanting what someone else had. Didn't matter to her she had Mother and Daddy, oh, no, that didn't matter to her. She wanted to come first with Grandma, too. Well, I was ready to tell her there was at least one thing in this world she could not have. Grandma was mine, no matter how many lies Claire Louise told about me. Grandma was mine. Not that Claire Louise mattered to me any longer. The only thing I had to do was look out for Grandma. That was what I had to do. And as long as I stayed right there by her whenever Claire Louise walked in like she owned the place, I knew I could do that. One thing I could do, I could protect my grandmother from my sister. And anyone else, for that matter.

Grandma and I had these plastic boxlike things that held your cards for you. I had gotten away from a hand holder after my hands had gotten bigger but now it was hard for Grandma to hold her cards so I got the card holders out for us to use again. I'd arrange her hand first, then mine, and since I dealt now she always got to go first.

"You have a right good hand, Grandma, look at it."

"Not bad, not real good, but right good," she agreed. "I don't need that four, you discard it."

So I discarded that four for her and then drew for myself. "Oh, darn, Grandma, I wasn't paying attention, I could have used that four. Too late now, I'll just let this four of diamonds go."

"You have to watch what you're doing in canasta," Grandma reminded me. "Keep your eyes on the cards." She drew a joker, fifty points right there, and decided to go down after only her third draw. Sometimes I like to hold all my cards and go down and out at the same time. Grandma knows that trick of mine, so lots of times she will go down fast, to keep me honest, she'd say. And once she was down, she could draw two cards to my one, something I couldn't let continue long. Why even if I went out fast, she didn't hold anything in her hand to count against her.

"You're tricky today," I told her, when she put down three

nines beside her joker and two jacks. "How am I going to compete with that?"

Since she had already put down nines I went ahead and started a dirty book of them. I don't generally like to go down with dirty books but I doubted I would get seven with her already having three on the board, and I for sure didn't want to slip up and discard them with her having a clean book started right there in front of me.

I drew two cards and put them in her tray for her. "Play the nines," she said. "I'm lucky today."

"You sure are," I told her, as I put another four and an ace in my hand. "Neither of these two cards goes with a thing in my hand. I'll still be looking for three of anything and you'll have your two books and be out on me."

"Some days are like that, you just have to watch your cards, Macy," Grandma laughed. One thing about my grandmother, she loves to play cards.

"Once you get over this sick spell, Grandma," I told her, "we are going to have to take us a trip to Las Vegas. Lucky as you are at cards, we could clean up."

"Macy, you know I don't gamble!"

"I know, Grandma, I was just teasing you."

"We have to have . . ."

Claire Louise walked in then and interrupted what Grandma was fixing to tell me we needed. "Mail call," she chirped, after she walked in without so much as knocking.

"We're playing cards," I told her.

"Well, I've got a fistful of mail for Grandma."

"She'll look at it later."

"This looks important, I think we'd better take care of it now." And she opened the envelope right there, without so much as asking Grandma did she want to open her own mail.

"It's from the bank," Claire Louise said, "you have a CD coming due, Grandma. I think I better take care of it for you."

"Let me see that," I said, taking it out of her hand. I looked at the paper and then put it down beside Grandma. "Isn't this the one Mr. Shasta is taking care of, like the others?" I asked her. She didn't say anything. She nodded a little, though.

"You know how money gets her tired out, Claire Louise," I whispered at my sister. "Mr. Shasta takes care of everything for her, just like he has ever since Grandpa died. You have no consideration, bringing those things in and getting her worried. That's why I wanted the mail delivered. When things come that are going to have to go somewhere else, I can just hand them right back."

"I'll take it back," she said, reaching for the paper.

"No, you won't. Now that it is here, I'll deal with it." It was later, when I went to put that paper in the drawer, that I remembered I had a drawerful of papers I had put there for Mr. Shasta. I kept thinking I would take off one morning and drive to town and give him all that paper, but then every morning there seemed to be some reason that kept me from going. Like today, Grandma had felt like playing cards and I didn't want to go off and leave her. I'll go tomorrow, I told myself, forgetting tomorrow would be Saturday.

When Carlton walked in I was so surprised to see him that it didn't occur to me it could be the weekend already. "Is something wrong?" I asked.

"Macy, it's Saturday," he said.

"It can't be, I was going to wash my hair before you came."

He hugged me then, but I couldn't let him do that for long. Whenever Carlton hugged me I could feel something weak inside me trying to let go and melt down, and I knew if I let that happen, he would have to use all his strength just to hold me up. I felt afraid I would fade away, so I couldn't even stand by myself, if I released the feelings inside me when Carlton put his arms around me and drew me close to him. It was hard, though, not to stand there and let him hold me and hold me. Pulling back kept getting harder and harder. I wanted to put my head down on his chest and cry and cry, but when I felt the tears coming up, instead of Carlton I saw my daddy's face the way he used to sneer when I cried and he said, "Tuning up, Macy?" and I pushed myself away and tried with my hands to make my hair look like I had at least combed it.

"Are the kids outside?" I asked, looking around for them.

"No, they had a Cub Scout thing today. Roxanne is taking them for me, and they'll stay at Mrs. Grant's tonight. I thought maybe you and I could talk some this weekend. Did you realize Christmas is a week away, Macy?"

I looked over to the calendar, the cloth one that hung on the kitchen door, the calendar that would be a dish towel after this month. I looked at it carefully, but I knew I must have lost track of time. "Did we have Thanksgiving?" I asked Carlton, knowing the minute I saw the look on his face I had said the wrong thing. "I'm being silly," I said, acting like I had been joking, but it worried me that I couldn't remember Thanksgiving. What had we done? I thought to myself. But Grandma will remember, I told myself. I can ask her later.

Carlton walked back into the bedroom and looked at Grandma a minute, then he took her hand and held it and leaned over and kissed her on her forehead. I was glad to see I had brushed her hair back and put one of the yarn ribbons in it she liked to hold it back with, I'd even put lipstick on for her. I didn't remember doing that. "Take care, Louisa," he whispered, softlike, being careful not to wake her up.

"Has the doctor been here today?" he asked me when we walked back into the kitchen. Carlton had his arm around me, it felt nice, his arm did. Kind of warm and solid, something I could count on.

"Yes," I said.

"No, ma'am, he ain't been today, that was yestiddy," Laura reminded me.

"Oh, so it was, the days all run together."

"Macy, you look exhausted. When was the last time you had a full night's sleep?"

"Every night I sleep," I said.

"Well, I want you to do something, I want you to go in and take a nice warm bath and let me fix you a cup of tea. Then I want you to lay down there in the back bedroom and sleep as long as you can. Will you do that for me, Macy, if I promise to sit right here in the living room and watch your grandmother?"

"Well, she is sleeping now, but when she wakes up she'll want to finish that game we started. You know how she loves cards."

"If she wakes up, and wants to play cards, I'll play with her."

"Oh, Carlton, you hate to play cards!"

"I'll play anyway or I'll read to her. You've got three or four books in there. I'll ask her which one she wants to hear and read to her."

"That's a good idea, I like that."

"Then go on in and run your tub. I'm fixing you some tea."

I woke up hours later, so late it was dark outside. I sat up in bed, not knowing for a minute where I was, I felt loggy, like I had been drugged. Then I remembered, Grandma! What if she had needed me? I jumped up and stumbled getting out of the unfamiliar high bed. The bed I was in had been my great-grandmother's. I always had wondered why they made beds so

291

tall back then, you needed a step to get up to this one. I slipped on the step and turned my foot under when I fell, but I sort of rolled over onto the carpet and didn't hurt myself. I made a noise, though, as I rocked against the dressing table and knocked the old milk-glass lamp off. It did break, the lamp did. That's what made all the noise, the glass shattering.

The overhead light came on and Carlton rushed over to me, telling me to sit still so he could take care of the glass and I wouldn't cut myself.

"But what about Grandma? Who is with her?"

"No one, but she's okay. There, I've got it all, I think. Lucky it broke into big pieces."

"That's an old lamp. I think it was Mammy's too." Mammy was the name we had for my grandmother's mother. I barely remembered her. I had only been about six or seven when she died. She had lived here with my grandparents, Mammy had. In this room. The room I was sleeping in had been Mammy's. On the chest by the door were framed pictures completely covering the top, all of Grandma's side of the family. There was a picture of Mammy holding me. I'd had on the long hand-embroidered christening dress every baby in our family wore, and beside the wicker chair Mammy sat in holding me was Claire Louise, hanging on the arm of the chair. The picture was in black and white so you couldn't tell color, but I remembered the dress Claire Louise had on. It was white batiste, with rows and rows of red smocking. Grandma had made it for her so she could have a special dress for the christening, too. That dress was in the cedar chest at the foot of Grandma's bed. I thought I better go get it out and see if it needed laundering. Sometimes cotton will yellow if you don't look after it. I didn't want that dress to yellow.

The baby christening dress I had at my house, I'd had it laundered and then framed in a shadow box and it was hanging on the wall at my house. "Is my dress still on the wall at home?" I asked Carlton.

He looked at me like he had to think if he had seen it lately.

"You know, the christening dress?" I asked him, starting to feel anxious. What if something had happened to that dress? It was a family heirloom. How would I tell Grandma what I had done if I lost that dress?

"Oh. Yes, it's there. Are you okay?" Carlton asked me, leaning down to massage my ankle.

"Yeah, it's just that high bed, I forgot I had to get on the step to get down. Can you fix Mammy's lamp? I hate to tell Grandma I broke it."

"I'll fix it. There's some food in the kitchen."

"Well, I have to check on Grandma first." He followed me into the room where she was sleeping, looking all nice and peaceful and rested. I noticed the cards were right where I left them and so were the books. "You didn't finish the canasta game?" I asked.

"No. She didn't wake up enough to play cards. Or to listen to a book." He saw me look at the books and answered my question before I asked it.

"Did the doctor come?"

"Yes."

"And I'm sure my sister was here."

"She and your mother and Maryanne were here this afternoon."

"They didn't touch anything, did they? Or get Grandma to sign any papers? Did you watch them? I should have reminded you, you have to watch Claire Louise like a hawk. The other two are okay, but Claire Louise you can't trust."

"Nobody did anything, Macy. Your mother sat in there while Laura tried to feed Grandma, and Claire Louise and Maryanne looked through old pictures."

"Which old pictures?" I asked.

"The ones in the album on the coffee table."

"I guess everything is all right, then."

"You look better, Macy, not so drained. How do you feel?"

"Better. Thank you for watching out for Grandma, Carlton. I appreciate it. Not too many people I can trust to look after her, you know."

"Dr. Blynn and I talked. He's sending out a nurse to be with her, Macy, also a hospital bed. First thing tomorrow."

"Why do we need a nurse? Between Laura and me we're doing fine."

"You are doing a great job, Macy. No one could look after Grandma better. But the nurse will help at night, so you can get some rest."

"I don't know, Carlton, a nurse might not be able to hold up to Claire Louise. You know how she can be. Call Dr. Blynn and thank him but tell him I think better not on the nurse. And no hospital bed either. Grandma would hate it."

"The nurse is from seven to seven at night. You do need her. Grandma needs medication in injection form and she's going to need IVs for nourishment soon. Then we'll need round-the-clock nurses."

"Did the doctor say so?"

"Yes."

"And the hospital bed too?"

"Yes."

"Was Claire Louise here when you talked to the doctor?"

"No, he came this morning."

"Well, I guess it's okay, but I wish you had waked me."

"You needed your rest."

"I better see about the news. Grandma always likes me to watch the weather and news, it lets her know about what to expect."

"Macy, it's almost eleven o'clock. The weather is over."

"Oh, I slept over twelve hours. Imagine that, I don't think I ever slept that long before." I laughed at myself when I realized I was yawning just talking about sleeping.

"I think you need to go back to bed now. Let me watch Grandma for you."

"Funniest thing, I don't even feel like arguing with you," I said as I let him tuck me in.

28

HUGH HAD A SPELL the week before Christmas. If it hadn't been for me, he would have died. He'd been having one of his poker parties, the parties he and his cronies had been holding for years. This one, like most of them, was in our den. Hugh knew I hated those things. The men sat around and drank like fish and ate junk food that he picked up on his way home from town, potato chips and dips in little white plastic packages, tortilla chips and jars of picante sauce, nuts. He even set out bowls of M & M's. It was far and away the tackiest thing I had ever seen.

And the smoke was so thick you could cut it with a knife. No matter what I did I could not get the odor out of that room after one of his parties. I had finally been forced to take down the drapes, the ones I had had made special to go with the couch, a nice forest green hunt-pattern fabric. I had taken those down and had them cleaned and had not even bothered to have them put back up. I called and had a man come out and install mini-blinds for me. The look was not nearly as cozy, not at all what I had in mind originally, but I could wipe those blinds down with lemon-scent ammonia the day after one of those parties and get the cigar smoke out. The couch and chairs were another matter; I had not been able to find anything short of a thorough upholstery cleaning that worked on them.

And as if the parties weren't bad enough, Hugh had this Old English sheepdog that sat all over the furniture and shed so much you would think he'd have gone bald. I had insisted from the day we moved in our new house that the dog belonged in the yard. I'd had the builder build us a nice dog lot, shady on one end, sunny on the other, plenty of room to run, a nice dog-house. It was exactly where a dog belonged. As it turned out, on the rare occasions when Felix, Hugh's dog, so much as set foot in that lot, it was accidental at best. The day we moved into our lovely new house, Hugh took the dog bed he had for that animal, an old, faded, ripped-out bag-looking thing he said he had gotten at L. L. Bean, and put it right down in the corner of the den. "Felix, old boy, this looks like your room."

"But I've built him a whole house," I said. "Surely you noticed the dog lot."

"I noticed it, so did Felix. Figured you must have in mind to get you a dog. Mine lives in the same house I do."

Which of course is exactly what happened. Hugh could be so hardheaded about that animal. I had to keep baby gates up on the door from the den to the rest of the house. If I didn't that dog would get in our bedroom and lift his leg right on my side of the bed. I know good and well he did. I caught him at it more than once.

Contrary to what my husband maintained, I am an animal lover myself, always have been. I have a horse now I ride from time to time, I have several calico cats out in the barn, and up until a few years ago I had a poodle. Actually, it was one I bought for Britt, but it latched on to me and went everywhere with me. That dog even slept with me. That should have told Hugh that I am an animal lover. People who don't love animals don't let them sleep right in their own personal bed, for goodness sake. Poor Whitney, she died just a few months after Hugh and I married. She just up and took sick and died. I think it probably was out of fear, poor thing. Hugh wasn't all that careful of her. He was all the time stepping on her, and she was scared to death of Felix, who was so clumsy he'd trip over her just walking to his food bowl. After Whitney died, I didn't even try to get a new dog. I felt as long as Hugh insisted on having that huge dog of his, it wasn't fair to bring another dog in to fend for itself.

It was almost midnight when Hugh had his attack. I was sitting in the music room, over on the love seat in front of the bay window, reading and watching the rain fall outside. I love to sit inside on a winter night, when it is cold and rainy outside, and turn on my outside security lights and watch the lights highlight the rain streaks. It was coming down hard out there. Another ten or twenty degrees and I'd be watching snow, I remember thinking to myself. Not that it was likely to snow. Molly's Point has had snow, but not in my lifetime. I had a can of Stanley's air freshener, the vanilla scent I believe, beside me, and every so often I walked through the room, over to the side closest to the den and sprayed it around. Not that it did much good, but it held back the smoke a bit, I liked to think.

I heard them laughing in there, one of the men must have said something dirty, that's all they laughed at as far as I could tell, when suddenly something crashed to the floor and broke.

The floor in the room is Mexican tile, something I am eternally grateful for when I mop up muddy paw prints every morning after Felix has been outside and tracked back inside the house. It gave me the chills to think I might have chosen that expensive beige Berber carpet I had been so taken with. But the drawback is when you drop something on Mexican tile it is broken, no question about it.

Turns out it was Hugh dropped his glass, full of whiskey, all over the floor and then he sat there with his mouth open looking dazed.

"What happened?" I asked from the music room. No point in rushing in; I needed to know whether I needed a broom or a mop.

I could hear them talking to each other but no one said anything to me, so I went on into the den. The men were grouped around Hugh asking him what was the matter and he was shaking his head. His hair flopped around like Felix's. "Nothing," he said, "I just felt a little funny."

I noticed he looked funny, white and pasty, and he had little beads of sweat on his face. "You've had too much to drink," I said, "or is it something else?"

"No," he said, shaking his head again and taking one of the linen napkins he must have gotten out of the sideboard to wipe his face. "Felt all hot and then got the sweats for a minute, must have been something I ate. Don't believe I'll mix the clam dip and the hot sauce anymore tonight."

"Better call the doctor," one of his friends said, and then they laughed and someone said that was a hell of a way for Hugh to try to get out of a losing hand. They called it a night and by the time I had cleaned up the glass—naturally he had been using one of the heavy crystal ones I pay twenty dollars apiece for at

Sakowitz—and mopped up all the liquor, Hugh had gone and fallen in bed without so much as brushing his teeth. One thing I have never liked about Hugh is how he'll fall into bed in his underwear. No matter how dirty he is or how clean my sheets are, he'll fall right in that bed all sweaty and stinky. Sure enough when I got in there, he was flat on his back in bed snoring. And that damn dog was piled up on the floor beside him. When I took Felix by the collar and tried to move him out of my bedroom, he refused to budge, he even growled at me low in his throat. Hugh rolled over then and I said, "Wake up and get this hound out of here, I'm not sleeping in a room with a dog smells like he does. You're bad enough yourself, Hugh, you smell like a brewery." I know that sounds mean but it was the truth.

"Sleep somewhere else then," Hugh said, rolling back over and pounding on his pillow.

"Damn you," I said, grabbing my pillow and a quilt. Tomorrow, I told myself, first thing tomorrow, I am turning the yellow room into my own personal bedroom, I've had enough of sharing a room with these animals.

When Hugh staggered out of bed the next morning, he was walking stooped like he had pulled a muscle, which is what he decided must have happened. He hurt in his chest, he said.

"That's enough for me," I said, picking up the telephone and calling Dr. Blynn then and there. He was leaving to go check on Grandma, he told me, just walking out the door. He'd stop over at my house and check on Hugh on his way.

He took one look at Hugh, listened to his chest, and said, "You need to get yourself to a hospital. You've got a problem."

Hugh was sitting in his recliner in the den, and the cards and ashtrays running over and the dirty glasses were still all over the room. "You can see how he got to be this way," I told Dr. Blynn.

"Look what he was up to last night. He played poker past midnight, smoking and drinking all the time."

Dr. Blynn looked over at Hugh and winked, I swear he did, and they both laughed at something Hugh said that I didn't catch. But I had the last laugh. Hugh was admitted to the hospital and didn't get out for a week, and when he came home he was under strict doctor's orders—no smoking, no drinking—and a cookbook, *Diet for a Healthy Heart*, came home with him as well. The worst thing about having Hugh home was having to let Felix back into the house. However, by then I had moved myself to the yellow room. I didn't think it was right to sleep with a man who was just out of the hospital. He needed his rest, and I can be a restless sleeper myself.

With Hugh home from the hospital and on his special diet, I had all I could do to keep my eye on him. Lucinda was no help at all there. In fact she more than once threatened to quit because of his smoking and drinking. He didn't change a whit, Hugh didn't, as the result of his brush with death. He still drank and smoked like there was no tomorrow and I soon gave up cooking for his condition. If I didn't have the salted peanuts or the sugared food he wanted in the house, he was in his truck and driving to town after them. So, in spite of strict doctor's orders, Hugh went on his merry way, digging his grave with his own teeth. He wouldn't even keep up with his medicine. I was always after him to see he had it on time, and unless I watched him take it, like as not he would ignore that too.

And then there was Mother, sitting over across from Grandma's in the house I had fixed up so nice for her, doing nothing every livelong day except watch television and feel sorry for herself. And in between us all lay Grandma dying, with my sister Macy hovering over her day and night like she could keep it from happening. I was frazzled, running from one to the other, placating Lucinda when Hugh drank all afternoon and cussed at her, trying to cheer up Mother with little trips, going over to check on Grandma, looking after my own children. Always, if it wasn't one thing it was another. I am exceptionally good in a crisis, but more than once I said to myself, when things settle down here, I'm taking a nice long vacation. I don't know how I expected them to settle down, but I knew for sure they would sooner or later. That's a fact. Things change if you give them time. All you have to do is work for what you want and wait for it to happen. I knew I couldn't go on like I was. I fully expected circumstances to change, but even I was amazed at how fast all the changes happened.

The first to go was, surprisingly, Mother. I hadn't expected that. Except for her eyesight she was, as far as any of us—including, I might add, both Dr. Blynns—knew, in perfect health. So it was a big surprise when she woke up one day, complained of being dizzy, and the next thing I knew she was lying in a heap at the bottom of the stairs. Lucy and I were there in an instant, we had heard her fall, and we both knew right away she was dead. Her legs were twisted under her and her body was at a funny angle and she wasn't breathing. Dr. Blynn came out and sure enough, she was gone. We hadn't moved her, thinking maybe we would break something, but as it turned out she was already broken something awful, both legs and her neck, they said. Dr. Blynn did an autopsy and said as close as he could tell, she died of heart failure. Probably before she fell she was dead. That was a comfort to us to hear. We couldn't have prevented the heart attack, but both Lucy and I had said more than once, if only we had gone up there to help her down the stairs.

Macy's husband, Carlton, was at the funeral and so was Hugh, and my girls were there, but Macy refused to leave Grandma to come, in spite of the fact that Grandma had a nurse with her as well as Laura now. In addition to us, the immediate family so to speak, most of the townspeople attended the funeral. She did have a nice turnout, Mother did. The ladies from our church had a meal for us all laid out back at the house when we arrived there after the funeral. Lucinda was in the kitchen looking aggrieved when we got back from the funeral, and as we sat down to eat, the kitchen door opened and Macy walked in wild-eyed, her hair looking like she hadn't combed it in days. She had on an old housedress that I swear had been Grandma's, and in spite of the fact it was the dead of winter, three days before Christmas and rainy and cold, she had on some of the those earth mother–looking sandals hippies wear. Carlton went over to her and tried to get her to sit down in his place at the table but she refused to sit, just stood there and looked around the room.

"Of course there's no place set for me. Why should there be?" she asked like she was carrying on a conversation with someone that she had been talking to before she came in the room. "Isn't that right, Claire Louise? You wouldn't have a place set for me because you don't want me here. This is your house, yours you stole from me and Mother, too. You stole it from her as well. That's why she died, she didn't so much as have her own house anymore. Everything you wanted you took, the rest you threw out, isn't that so?"

She walked around the room, looking at things, picking them up and putting them down like she was in a shop looking for price tags. "It's all yours, isn't it? Every little thing. Mother used to write people's names on things, on the bottoms with masking tape, so when she was gone everyone would get what she wanted them to have. Like this bowl," she said, "this is the cut-glass bowl Aunt Emmie gave Mother and Daddy for a wedding present. This used to have my name on it." She turned the bowl upside down, not paying a bit of attention to the fact that the plastic fruit in it spilled all over the table. "Just as I expected, my name's gone. You took it off, you took my name off every single thing, I wouldn't have expected any different. It would have surprised me to find my name on so much as a flowerpot in this house. That's why Mother died not speaking to me. It was all your doing. How do you think it feels to have your own mother not speaking to you up till she's dead and gone? Did you ever think of that, did you?"

Carlton was standing beside her the whole time she was talking, trying to get her to go, to sit down, anything. But she kept on and on, talking like she was talking to me, but not once looking straight at me. Finally he put his arm around her and she slumped against him, run down like a windup toy that has come to the end of its steam. She just sputtered a little and quit talking. "Let me take you on home, Macy," Carlton said, looking softlike at her with a tender, protective expression. She didn't know how lucky she was, Macy didn't. Part of the reason I had had to fight so hard all my life was I had never had a man look at me like that, not once. Never.

"Yes, no point in waiting for a will here, I know what comes next. Besides, I have to get back to Grandma," Macy said.

I felt a surge of something then when I heard her. Maybe it was glee, more likely relief. Right after Daddy died, Mother and I had gone down to her new lawyer and videotaped her new will. There would be no contesting this one, I thought. I had it on tape. Whatever Mother had was mine.

After they left, there was a silence around the room I didn't like. I looked around at my family. Maryanne was shoveling in the food like someone was fixing to take it away from her. Britt was looking at me with a glittering expression in her eyes, like she had plenty to say but was holding it back. Hugh had a glass of whiskey in his hand. I was supposed to think it was iced tea. And Lucy turned her back and stuck her hands in the dishwater. As wakes go, this wasn't much of one. To top it off, Lucinda had been bitten by Felix that morning and was presently laid up on the couch in the sun room, flatly refusing to come back into my house as long as that dog was there.

"Mother would have liked this chicken casserole," I said, trying to lighten them up.

"Did you do that, Mother, did you? Did you cut Aunt Macy out of every single thing? Is that true?"

"I don't care for your tone, young lady," I said to Britt. "Watch what you're saying."

"It's true, isn't it? She doesn't get anything."

"Your grandmother wrote her own will, she left her things the way she wanted them to go. Not that it's any of your business."

"You make me sick, Mother," Britt said then and left the table. I stood up to follow her but something stopped me. I looked around the table and not a person there would meet my eye. Maryanne kept on eating, Lucy wiped her lips, Hugh stood and fixed himself another drink.

"She's upset, everyone's upset," I said, and I went into the sun room. It didn't occur to me until I stood in there looking around that I had come looking for Mother. I had come in that room to talk to her, to tell her how bad my own family was treating me. It didn't help to find the room empty except for Lucinda, who glared at me like I was the one had bit her. I felt doubly alone then. My mother was gone and my father was gone, and my husband I couldn't count on, and my own daughter was rebelling against me. I kept thinking of how Carlton had looked at Macy. Even when she looked like hell and was busy making the world's biggest ass of herself, he was standing there with his arm around her, looking down at her like he was going to take care of her come hell or high water. I left the house then, just walked out of the front door without so much as a farewell to anyone and walked across the pasture over to Grandma's. I saw the lights on in the house but I didn't go in. I stood there beside the shrubs outside Grandma's bedroom window and looked in. She was on the bed, hooked up to tubes, the nurse was in the chair beside her, and over on the couch Macy was curled up asleep, her head on Carlton's shoulder. Every so often he would lean over and smooth back her hair and kiss her on the top of her head. I looked at them until it started to rain, and then when I was so cold my feet felt like blocks of ice I walked on back to my own house, my new one. The only greeting I got was from Felix; he growled at me when I kicked him in the ribs to get out of my way and when I kicked him again, he showed me his teeth. I could tell Hugh was in his room. I could smell the smoke from his cigarettes and I could hear the television going, but I didn't go in to say anything to him. It hit me, he'd been home for a while, and it obviously had not occurred to him to wonder what had happened to me. For all he knew or cared, I could have been out in the pasture helpless. It was an awful feeling to realize that I could have died out there and it might have been days before he would have sent someone to look for me. It was then my feelings for Hugh began to change. I hate to say this, but if he hadn't died when he did I would have divorced him. I swear I would have. I just couldn't bear to look at him after that night. Not that I had to much longer.

29

THE YEAR MY grandmother and my mother died was a year without holidays. Thanksgiving came and went, then Christmas, even my own children's birthdays, and each day was so much like the one before and after it. I could no more tell one from the other than I could make my grandmother open her eyes and talk to me again. Something happened after Mother died. It was like she took a part of Grandma with her. No more would she talk to me in my head, Grandma wouldn't. I tried and tried to get through to her, but the voice was gone and nothing I did brought it back. At first I thought it was the reaction she was having to my mother's death, which Claire Louise had insisted on telling her about in spite of my objections. Then it occurred to me maybe it was the nurse and the tubes. Maybe that was why I couldn't hear her anymore. I sent the nurse out of the room and unhooked the tubes and held her. That was Christmas Day. Carlton and the boys had come out early to show me what Santa Claus had brought and they had stayed until almost dark and then he had left, taking the kids home to bed. They were tired, worn out from all the excitement. They'd been so keyed up all day and then so tired when they left that for once they didn't ask if I was going with them. That was nice, not having to turn them down. I hated to say, no, Mama can't go, she has to look after Grandma, to them over and over. Even though it was true, they were too little to understand. You'll understand someday, I said to the empty room when they were gone. Someday when your whole past is dying on you, you'll understand what this feels like.

So I unhooked Grandma and held her and talked to her.

"Grandma," I said, "it's okay, I'm here, I'm here with you. No one else is in the room, no one but you and me. I know you're sad my mother died, I am too, but it isn't like she liked me, or you either, for that matter. She didn't like me, not ever, she didn't. You though, I don't know, maybe she used to like you before I came along and you took my side. Is that what happened, she liked you at first and then she didn't anymore? She was that way, Mother was. She liked a lot of people at first, but then after a while it was like they did something wrong just by being themselves. She was off them like all of a sudden they had started to smell bad. She liked babies, though, and she liked people she only knew a little, but she didn't care for anyone who was around her too much. So maybe she didn't like you even before I came along. Maybe that was it. Tell me, won't you, Grandma? Please tell me, it's important. I need to know why they didn't like me. Neither one of my parents ever liked me. Why was that?"

I listened and held her, and heard nothing. She didn't talk to me. She hadn't said a word for three days, not since I had come back from Mother's funeral. Maybe that was it, Grandma knew I hadn't gone to the funeral, just over to the house. "Is that it? You're upset I didn't go to her funeral? But you didn't want to go either. You hate funerals. We talked about it, remember? You said I ought to go but funerals were so depressing you didn't think you were up to it. So I didn't go either. But Carlton went, and Aunt Claire and lots of other people. It isn't like no one was there, there were plenty of people to send her off." Again I listened, but she was silent. And then the nurse came in, all upset I had unhooked her, and I had to let her put the tubes back in. I hated the way Grandma looked with those tubes, one in her arm and the other in her nose. Grandma never cared much about her looks but she didn't like those tubes interfering, I was sure of that. Besides, tubes scare me. Once people get tubes, they rarely get better in my experience. Tubes that last longer than a day are usually fatal. I hated myself when I thought things like that, I truly did. Morbid thoughts don't do anyone any good, Macy, I told myself. It was something Grandma might have said, but she didn't. I didn't kid myself. Grandma wasn't speaking to me; that was me talking to myself.

She died on New Year's Day, Grandma did. She went almost without saying another word to me. Right up until the end she was silent. Then, in the middle of the night, about one o'clock in the morning, I woke up on the couch where I slept. We had a night nurse there, the doctors insisted, and Carlton backed them up, but the nurse was sitting over by the bed reading. She had one of those little battery-operated lights that hooks over your book so you can see. I woke up and I knew my grandmother wanted to talk to me alone. I could feel it. "Go make you some coffee and take a break," I told the nurse, "I'll watch her and I'll call you if the IV backs up." They had had trouble with it earlier in the day, but it had been working fine since she put a new bottle of fluid on.

"Are you sure?" she asked, and I could tell she wanted to go.

"Yes, I'll call you if she needs anything."

She left then, and I took her seat and pulled it up as close to the bed as I could get it. "I'm here, Grandma," I said.

"Macy, it's a new year, starting now."

That surprised me. I hadn't guessed she was keeping up with the dates and the days. The last weeks, when I'd told her the weather every night, she had ignored me.

"I can't hang on any longer, Macy, even for you. You're going to have to let me go."

"No! You can get well, I know you can. We have to get rid of these tubes, they're sapping your strength."

"It isn't the tubes, Macy Rose, listen to me! Have I ever lied to you?"

I had to stop and think. As far as I knew Grandma had never lied to me. Often she would tell me to forget something or not to think about it, but she never out and out lied. "No, you always told the truth," I admitted, scared of what was coming.

"Listen then, this is the truth. I'm tired, tired of this body dragging me down. I'm going on, I'll see you again, but not soon. Later in the hereafter. You have to do something for me. You have to get out of here."

Her words were coming fast like she was in a hurry to say them before I interrupted her or maybe before she ran out of time. "I'm going on and I want you to get out of here, leave and go on home, go on back to your home, back to your family."

"I can't leave you," I protested.

"Macy, I'm dying, I don't need you. Your family needs you, but I don't."

I cried when she said that, because I knew it didn't matter if Grandma needed me or not, I needed her. "I need you, don't leave me," I said, putting my head on her chest and crying. "Don't go. I'll be alone with them."

"You're not a little girl anymore, you have a husband, children. Go on now."

Those were almost the last words she spoke to me, the last things I ever heard her say. I lay there with my head on her chest, crying and begging her not to go until I couldn't pretend any longer she was there. And then the nurse came in and pretty soon Doctor Blynn was there and Carlton came and he sat beside me. I had Grandma in my arms now, the tubes were gone finally, and I rocked her like she was the scared little girl and I was the grown-up who could keep her safe. "Don't worry, don't worry," I told her over and over. "I'm here, nothing bad is going to happen to you." Then they came in with a stretcher to take her away and I screamed then. I couldn't save her, I couldn't. Carlton had to hold me back while they took her away. I'd held on to her so long that even though I knew she was dead it was more than I could stand to let them take her out of my sight. She needs me, she needs me, I kept telling myself, long after she was gone. And then I cried when I heard another voice, hers again, say, no, I don't need you, I'm okay. But I'm not, I thought, and she said one last thing, she said, you can be if you will. I didn't believe it then, but I do now. That's a good feeling, to know that never, ever, not even at the end when she left me, not ever did my grandmother tell me a lie. Not many people can say that, that there is a person who always told them the truth. She did, though, Grandma did. If she couldn't tell the truth, she didn't say a thing.

Carlton and I went to Grandma's funeral three days later, and then we went back to her house which, true to her word, Grandma had left to me. Claire Louise was there, with Hugh and her kids, and Aunt Claire and my cousins and their kids, and there were other people around but I can't quite remember who. After we ate, I said to them, "Grandma said everyone is to take something to remember her by so before you go take something with you."

Nobody spoke until Carlton said, "Maybe today isn't the time for that. Perhaps people would rather wait until later, Macy."

I looked at them all, one after another. "No, you'd better get something today, it may not be here tomorrow."

Claire Louise pursed her lips at that. I knew it was galling her that for once I was in charge. I was the one who could say what was what. Funny, all my life I had wanted to one-up her, and now here was my chance. Not a person in that room didn't know I had been left every single thing by my grandmother and her nothing, and even in my moment of triumph I didn't feel a thing. Not glad, not happy, nothing. I felt nothing. I could tell she was thinking to herself that hell would freeze over before she would ask for anything. That wasn't her way. Not to ask right out, honestlike, in front of everyone. Claire Louise liked to get what she wanted deviously, where no one quite knew how it had happened.

What I said next surprised me, I hadn't thought it at all, but when I heard the words out in the air the same as everyone else, for the first time so to speak, I knew they were true. I knew what I was saying was what I was going to do. "I'm going to close her house, take everything out of it and move it to my house in Houston. So if you want something you had better take it today."

Maryanne spoke up then, her eyes red from crying, or maybe that was the way she looked nowadays. She had gotten fatter than ever, I was surprised to see, and she had a furtive way of looking at people, like she didn't want her eyes to stay too long on theirs. "Can I have the little ring with the blue stones, the one her mother gave her?"

I knew which one she meant, it had tiny sapphires in it, all over the top and little diamonds. Mammy had given that ring to my grandmother when she was sixteen, and Grandma always wore it on the little finger of her left hand. Without a word, I went in and got it from the cedar chest where Grandma kept her jewelry box and handed it to Maryanne. I started to say "Be careful with it," but I knew that would hurt her feelings so instead I said, "She would like for you to have it." I felt good inside, like I had thought of something nice for the first time in a long time. Maybe I can find me again, something inside me thought, but then Claire Louise stood up and began to look speculatively around the room, and I felt the hate and anger fill me up again and all I could think of was I would never leave this house as long as she was here to snoop in it the minute I was gone.

After Maryanne broke the ice, everyone except Claire Louise remembered something they wanted and they left, one by one, taking a little piece of my grandmother along with them. When Claire Louise left, she went out with a curt nod, not taking a thing with her. I'll be back, I could feel her thinking, but maybe I imagined it.

The next days passed in a blur. I was home in my own house, which felt like a stranger's house. I slept during the days on the couch. At night I'd get into bed with Carlton but pretty soon I'd be up wandering around the rooms touching things, trying to feel if they were mine or not. Mostly I felt out of place, like I had something to do, something waiting on me, but I was in the wrong place for it to happen. The day after Grandma's funeral, Carlton had arranged to have every single lock on her house changed and I had shut all the shutters and locked them. I had emptied out the refrigerator and the freezer. I gave every bit of food in the house to Laura and I took all Grandma's houseplants home with me to take care of. As for the rest of the house, it was all still there, just like she left it. Pretty soon I'll go back and finish it, I told myself. Pretty soon I'll finish it. Those words were in my mind day and night, go finish it, go finish it.

On the weekend we went out there, Carlton and the boys and me, and we wandered around looking in rooms and cupboards. Everything looked older than I remembered, and most of Grandma's things were shabby, I saw for the first time. It surprised me how old and dirty Grandma's things had become. I looked at her old couch, the one in the bedroom I'd slept on for the past months, and saw for the first time that under the throw cover she'd ordered from Sears was a floral-print sofa with the arms worn out and the maple trim scuffed and tacky looking.

"Macy," Carlton said, "why don't you make a list of the things you want to keep and we'll move them. The rest of these things you might want to consider giving to Belle and her daughter."

Belle, I had forgotten Belle. "Was she here the day of the funeral?"

"She was at the funeral, but she didn't come back to the house."

"I thought maybe you and I could live here," I said to Carlton as we sat at my grandmother's breakfast-room table watching the boys run in circles out in the driveway, caught up in some childhood game only they knew the rules to. Travis would run as hard as he could after Scott, harder and harder, always close to catching up but never quite making it. And suddenly, for no reason I could ever see, their roles would reverse. Suddenly Scott was running, running, trying to catch Travis and again never quite making it. They could run like that for hours until they collapsed in exhausted giggles, pleased that once again they had played out their game without a break in stride. The trick was never to completely stop, never to slow down until you collapsed. And never, no matter how hard you tried, never ever to catch up, never ever to touch.

"It's cold out there on that ground," I said to Carlton. "Maybe you should call them in."

"They're okay. To answer your question, Macy, I could not live out here, not in this house, not in this town. I'm sorry if that's what you want, I just cannot do it."

I wasn't surprised to hear him say it. I'd known for a long time that Carlton didn't share my feelings for my grandmother and her house. I'm going to have to put up a fence, I thought. A big fence all the way around. A fence with a gate only I could open. It's either that or tear it down, tear down Grandma's house, and I knew I couldn't do that. I can't live here, not if Carlton won't, and I can't tear it down. And no one else can live in my grandma's house, that wouldn't be right. Grandma wouldn't want strangers in her own house. So I'll build a big fence, one with electric wire on top. Better yet, I thought, I'll build a brick wall that will keep undesirable elements out. A brick wall with electricity on top.

The next day, without telling Carlton, I called a fence company to go out and get started. But the man called me back later the same day saying he would need a deposit to get started on that big a job. I'd never priced brick walls before. I had no idea how much one could cost. Nobody puts one around fifty acres, the man told me. Except maybe the Chinese, he said, laughing. Did I plan on building the Great Wall of China? he wanted to know. I hung up on him. Carlton was still home and was looking at me funny, and I didn't want to have to explain. That left barbed wire, I thought, which would never keep her out.

Finish it, my voice inside me said, finish it, but I didn't know how. I knew the answer was out there, out there in the country where I had grown up on the same piece of land as my daddy before me. Out there was the answer to finishing it. Grandma was gone now, but so was my daddy. There wasn't any reason for me to go out there. Even Mother, ineffectual as she had always been, even Mother was gone. Finish it, the voice said, so I went back to do it although I had no idea what it was.

I started going to Grandma's again every day. Every morning after the kids and Carlton left I would dress and drive out to Grandma's house. I went through all the things in her bedroom first, one by one, touching everything, shaking the clothes out and folding them again and putting everything back exactly like she had it. And I went through my grandfather's things too. It looked like they were just the way they had been the day he died, my grandfather's clothes were. They were there in his closet looking as if he might still even now come back and need them. It surprised me some, my grandfather had been gone so long I barely remembered him. I wondered why Grandma had never cleaned out his clothes. Just never got around to it, I could hear her voice telling me, just never did get around to it.

I looked at all the dishes and the silver, I counted every single thing and started a list of what was there. And then I remembered the attic. I hadn't been up there since I was a child. I spent days in the attic looking at all the old bits and pieces of her life she had stored there. My father's old schoolbooks, Aunt Claire's faded ribbons from her corsages back when she was a high school belle, my father's football uniform, boxes of letters and wrinkled old pictures. One day after I had been through most of the attic and was thinking maybe I should start on the other bedrooms, I looked out the window and saw it wasn't winter any longer. The grass was green and the trees were budded out and it was time to get out in the yard.

I found Grandma's hat and her gardening tools and started on the flower bed over under her front bedroom windows. I slowly loosened all the earth and turned the soil carefully, not knowing what she might have left under there to come up in the spring. I didn't want to disturb anything resting there, waiting for the sun and warm weather. I remembered her compost pile, out back behind what used to be the chicken house but had been her garden shed for years now, and went and filled a wheelbarrow with the rich black soil from the bottom of the pile. I soon lost track of how many trips I made for more mulch, but I realized I had stayed too long when I noticed it had gotten dark. I went inside to turn on the outside lights and to fetch Grandma's oldest outdoor coat, the one so stained it didn't matter any longer, and came back out to finish the flower bed. I had to get it ready for spring. I knew I was running late anyway. Tomorrow, I'll get Belle, I thought, she'll help me with the flowers.

It surprised me when I came around the corner of the house for another load of dirt and saw Carlton there beside his car. "I thought you might be here," he said.

"I can't leave yet. I have to get this one flower bed done."

"The children were worried when they came home from school and you weren't there."

"I forgot," I said, knowing it wasn't enough to say I forgot, but not knowing what else there was to explain it. "I forgot. After I finish this I'll go home and apologize."

"Macy, this isn't the time or the place, but I am going to say it anyway. I can't take it any longer. I can't put the kids through this type of existence any longer. Either you come home with me now and get yourself straightened out, or I'm leaving you."

At first I thought the cold I felt was from the night grown chillier. This coat isn't working, I thought, I'm still cold. My hands were like ice in spite of the gloves I wore. I looked at Carlton. His eyes were hard, almost like my sister's, hard and glittery. It was when I looked at his eyes I realized the cold I felt wasn't from the night air.

"I said I was sorry, I won't be late again. Just let me finish this flower bed and I'll be home right after. I promise."

He put his hands on me then, one on each shoulder, and he looked at me like he had something important to ask. "Why are you doing this? Why are you fixing the flower bed?"

I realized when he asked me that, he wasn't thinking straight.

Carlton didn't know Grandma as well as I did, but he knew her well enough to understand how important her flower beds were to her. "Carlton, you know how much Grandma's flower beds mean to her. You can't expect me to let them go just because she isn't able to tend to them."

He looked at me for the longest time. I don't think he much heard what I said, because when he turned to go he didn't say a word. It was later than I realized, I saw when I went into the kitchen after Carlton drove off, but since he had already left I thought I might as well spend the night out here, just this once. That way I could get an early start in the morning. Just this once, I said to Carlton when I called him to tell him not to worry. "Stay as long as you need to," he said, "but don't expect us to be here waiting for you when you finally get back to us. The kids and I are going on with our lives. You've made your choice, I hope you're satisfied. Macy, one more thing. If you grow flowers out there, it's for you, no one but you. Your grandmother is dead."

I hung up the phone then, sorry I had called. I was right, I thought, Carlton isn't thinking straight. That's it, he just isn't thinking straight at all.

As for me, I was doing what I had to do. There was no other way to describe it. Just like when Grandma got down, when she couldn't fend off the family any longer, I was the one to be there for her. I never had any choice at all, you know, I had to do for her. People who grow up in the city, they don't understand what it's like out there in the country. You have to be able to count on your family, that's all you've got. It's not like you can run next door to the neighbors. In the country, there's no police to call, no lady across the street to run to. You've got you and your family and that's it. God help you if you can't count on your family, that's all I've got to say.

30

SOME FOLKS said it was history repeating itself when Britt ran away from home the end of her junior year, but it was nothing like I had done, nothing whatsoever. In the first place, Britt had no reason for leaving, none at all. And in the second place, she didn't disappear. She went straight down to her father's house, and I knew exactly where she was. I tried to talk her into coming home, but she was adamant. She was staying in Houston with her father. I talked to my lawyer. There were things I could have done, steps I could have taken, but it didn't seem worth the effort. She'll come home when she's ready, I told myself, just like I did. She'll be back. Maryanne continued to go down there every weekend, and when James enrolled her in a special school and said he was keeping her too, I didn't fight that either. Let them go, I thought, it's not the end of the world.

With the children gone, and Mother and Grandma dead, it was just me in Mother and Daddy's old house, and Hugh living over in our new one, and Macy in Grandma's, and she was out working in the yard day in and day out. She'd put up a barbed-wire fence all around her fifty acres, so I couldn't walk across any longer but had to drive out to the public road and go down a piece and drive in to my new house. As the days passed, I went less and less. Hugh was holed up there. He had some of his cronies over all the time smoking and drinking, and I couldn't bear to look at what was happening to my bright new house. It was like watching someone desecrate your dreams to see scuff marks appear on the floors and chips on the dishes and the carpets getting filled with cigarette smoke and ashes. Lucy went over every day and did for him, and Lucinda had taken to looking after me and Mother's house. True to her word she hadn't been back to the new house since Felix bit her. It was Lucy told me Felix died. I went over the minute she called to offer Hugh my condolences. He was walking in from the pasture with his shovel when I got there. "I'm sorry about your dog," I told him, trying to give him a hug, which he shrugged off.

"I'll bet you are," he said walking past me.

"I am sorry," I said. I followed him into the house wanting to say something, something to heal the rift between us. I couldn't think how we had come to drift so far apart. I remembered back to the Christmas we met. How had this happened to us? I wondered. "Hugh," I said, taking his hand, "let's talk." I would have said more, but he jerked his hand away like mine was poison. "Be that way then," I said and left, thinking to myself I would outlive him as well as the rest of them.

And that is what happened. Late in June, I stopped by over there to pick up Lucy's list before I left for town to do the grocery shopping. Lucy was out back, hanging out the sheets on the line and she hollered at me her list was on the kitchen counter so I walked in and saw Hugh there at the table, slumped over, his hand clutching and clutching at the table. His face was red, like it was on fire, and his eyes were bulged out like he was choking on a piece of meat or something went down the wrong way. He saw me and I could tell in his eyes he knew it was me and I thought he was trying to ask me a question, but even though his mouth opened and shut no words came out. "What is it you want, Hugh?" I asked him, staying way away on the other side of the room. I remembered all too well how he had rejected me the last time I had tried to touch him, and I didn't intend to put myself in that position again.

His mouth opened and his eyes bulged even wider, and I

319

thought he was reaching out to me, but I had my pride. I wanted to hear him say I'm sorry, I want you back. So we were caught there frozen in time, him trying to ask but no words coming out and me waiting to hear him ask. I don't know how long we stared across space at each other like that before Lucy came rushing in, thinking I was unable to find her list. "Mr. Hugh, my God, Mr. Hugh!" she shrieked, pushing me against the door frame in her haste to get to him. Lucy was a servant, she was used to being treated like an object. She didn't have to wait for him to be nice to her.

"His pills!" she yelled. "Get his pills!"

I saw then what she meant. There were pills all over the floor. Obviously he had felt an attack coming on and spilled them before he could get one in his mouth. She picked a pill up off the floor and tried to shut his mouth on it, but he wasn't helping. He wouldn't swallow, it seemed. "Call the doctor, we have to have help," Lucy screamed, and so for what felt like one time too many, I went to the phone and called the operator and told her we had someone dying, to send an ambulance. Dr. Blynn, either one, young or old, would do, I remember telling her.

It wasn't long before all the people that come around when someone dies were there, the doctors, the ambulance driver, another man in a white suit, a man I have never understood what his job is, they were all there, but by the time they got out to the house there was nothing to be done other than load him up and take him to the funeral home. No church funeral for Hugh, I told the driver. Hugh didn't believe in them. I called the funeral-home director and told him the same thing, just a simple nonreligious ceremony, Hugh is a nonbeliever, I said. It bothered me some to think I wouldn't be seeing him in the hereafter, but to tell the truth, not all that much. Truth was, Hugh and I had never truly hit it off.

It surprised me, the number of people who came to Hugh's funeral. I hadn't realized he had that many friends. Macy came, too, which I hadn't expected. I thought she was so out of touch with what was happening she wouldn't have known Hugh was dead. But she was there without her husband, who I had called to tell about Hugh the night of his death. Carlton had said he was sorry but he hadn't stayed long on the phone, like he was only being polite to a barely noticeable acquaintance, I thought at the time, not talking at all like this is his sister-in-law who has just lost her husband. I had once thought we could be friends, Carlton and I, but it was obvious Macy had poisoned his mind against me.

Macy didn't seem to be doing so well herself these days. She had left Carlton and her kids to come out and live in my grandma's house, which she rarely emerged from except to go to the grocery store for supplies or the nursery for bedding plants. I had even seen Belle and her daughter over there of late, helping work in that garden. No telling how she had talked Belle into that. I myself had been forced to hire a yard service for both of my lawns, neither Lucy nor her daughter Lucinda having the remotest interest in gardening. It didn't matter to me, though, I would much rather a crew of men come in once a week, take care of what needed to be done, and then be gone. Much better that way, it seemed to me, than forever having to be after it.

I called my lawyer the day after Hugh's funeral, I needed to know the contents of the will, something Hugh had not found fit to share with me. Mr. Simpson suggested I come in, he didn't like to relay information of this sort over the phone.

"Why don't you come out here?" I said.

"Well," he said, and I could hear him rustling through papers as he talked, "today and tomorrow are out of the question. If you're in a hurry to know, then I suggest you stop by here about two-thirty."

"All right, I'll be there," I said, hanging up without another word. He had his nerve, after all the business I had given him.

At two-thirty I was in Mr. Simpson's office, dressed in a Laura Ashley sundress, my hair freshly done, and wearing pearls. I didn't exactly look like a grieving widow, but the dress had a black background, which was the best I could manage. I wasn't there ten minutes, either. Hugh's will was remarkably short and to the point. He left me his interest in our house, along with a tacky comment about how with it being built on my land he didn't think he could do much else. All of his money, the land he owned around the county, every single thing he left to the city of Molly's Point, to endow, of all things, a park for the people. There was a single other bequest—$200,000—that he left to the city also, this sum designated to go toward the building of an animal shelter. I was flabbergasted. It had never occurred to me Hugh would write such a ridiculous document. Here he was from the grave, still thumbing his nose at me and making a fool of me in the eyes of everyone in town.

"If this gets out, I'll sue you for libel," I told the complacent fool of a lawyer, sitting there trying not to smirk at me.

"Libel?" he bleated. "How on earth can the release of information in what is in fact a public document constitute libel?"

"Just you make sure you keep it to yourself, if you value your professional standing in this town," I said, leaving before my anger got away from me and I said more than I wanted to. Damn Hugh, I thought, driving home, I should have divorced him, I would have come out a lot better. All I had to show for those years I had stayed with him was a measly house I had owned from the day it was finished. Damn, damn, double damn, I would never trust another man, I vowed. This was it, this was the last time I let a man make a fool of me.

I knew I had to put the best face on things. After all, I was Claire Louise Richards and I had my place in town to uphold. After I left the lawyer's office I drove around town looking and thinking. It had been so long since I had had absolutely nothing to do, nowhere to go. I didn't like the feeling. I told myself, Claire Louise, it's time you get yourself involved in some civic service. Those are exactly the words I used. I'd done for Mother, and done for Grandma, and done for Hugh, and now they were all gone and I was left. It was time I did for myself. Whatever I wanted I could do now. When I got back to the driveway leading up to my house, it was a puzzle deciding which one to go to. I had two houses now, both mine, and both empty. It bothered me I couldn't go to one and walk to the other any longer without getting out on the public road.

That's what I needed to do. I needed to make it up with my sister. We were all we had left, her husband and kids were as gone as mine were, I realized. Macy and I needed to be together, we needed to bury the hatchet. I took the middle driveway, the one leading to Grandma's house, and drove up in front. I parked my car under one of the big oak trees and when I didn't see anyone out in the yard, I sounded the horn, so if they were outside I wouldn't surprise anyone.

Macy must have heard the car because just as I took my hand off the horn, the front door opened and she stepped out, a shotgun in her arms, its barrel pointed right at me.

"Macy, it's me, put that gun away."

She pointed it down at the ground then as she walked toward me, not asking me to come inside the fence. When she was directly across the fence from me, she said, "What do you want?"

"We need to talk. We're sisters, we need to bury the hatchet. We're all alone, Macy, it's just you and me now. Our parents are gone, Grandma is gone, even our kids have left us." I was surprised to hear my voice catch when I said that. "It's just us now, Macy. You and I are all the family we have left."

"No."

"Macy, don't be a fool. You're alone, I'm alone. We're kin, all we have left. We've got to make up."

"No. You've killed them all, every one of them. Don't expect me to keep you company now that you're afraid to be alone." She stared at me for what seemed like forever. Then she added, "I'm not like you. My kids didn't leave me."

"Well, you left them, same difference in the long run."

Macy stood there, shaking her head back and forth. "No," she said, and turned and went back toward the house. Like as not, she forgot I was even there. Mark my words, I said to myself, she'll be the next to go. Macy does not look well, that she does not. But I followed her into the house. I knew she wasn't going to shoot anyone. We needed to talk, even a fool could see that.

31

I GUESS if Claire Louise hadn't come over that day, driven right up and tried to make friends with me again, I might still have been living at Grandma's trying to make that place a home for me, for the scared-little-girl part of me that somehow or another thought of Grandma's house as the only safe place in the world. But Claire Louise did come, and I suppose that means I have my sister to thank for what happened after that, all of it, the most part of which was me coming to my senses while I still had time to. I looked down at me that day and what I saw was a wild-eyed stranger. A stranger in Grandma's housedress, one of the stained ones she wore for yard work, a stranger wearing one of the old straw hats that hung on the hall tree by the back door, a fearfully strange person holding a gun and looking like she had escaped from a bad movie. That's me, a voice inside me said, as I stared, startled and more than a little confused at the reflection that gazed back at me from the plate-glass window in the front of the house.

"Macy, I didn't kill anyone. They died. Mother and Hugh and Grandma all died, you know that."

I didn't answer her at first, even though my mind registered the words she was saying. I was too busy trying to ask the person in the plate-glass window how she had gotten there.

"It's almost the Fourth of July," Claire Louise said. "We have to organize the reunion."

"No," I told her, "there's no one left."

"There are fifty to a hundred people who come every year. Just because Mother and Grandma died doesn't mean we don't have a family anymore." I could see Claire Louise start her planning then, just like she was doing it all right out loud in front of me. She was going to start up the reunion. She would be the one doing the newsletter next year, and she'd go on back to the UDAC and the DAR and the church choir. Claire Louise was planning out what she was going to do next. I felt it, I saw it coming. Funny thing, I could see her planning out her future just like a newsreel on television. She'd make up with Aunt Claire and she and Kara could exchange visits and—. I stopped seeing her future as abruptly as the pictures had started reeling themselves through my head. It didn't matter to me, I realized.

"Well, come in," I told my sister Claire Louise, who I seemed to have stopped hating with a passion, "come in if you want to, but I've got things to do."

She followed me in the house, looking around like she was inventorying as she went. Even that didn't bother me. I felt like one of those funny pictures you see sometimes. You think it's a horse and you look and look and then all of a sudden you see the hidden picture in the horse and now all you can see is the flowers. No matter how hard you look, the horse is gone for good and the flowers are there to stay. That's the way I felt about Claire Louise. No matter how much I remembered I didn't trust her, didn't like her, had to be cautious around her, all I saw now was a sister who had been my best friend when I was smaller and now was someone I didn't have all that much in common with anymore. I don't want what she wants, I surprised myself thinking. I don't want to be important in this little town. I don't want a big house and to be the one to hold the Christmas party for the DAR. I want to be myself, with my own husband and my own kids in my own house in Houston. Please God, it's not too late, I prayed. Don't let it be too late. Carlton had called me every night for a while and then less frequently, and I had made it a habit to talk to the kids every afternoon after school and just last weekend they had come out. Carlton had driven them out to swim and play. It's not too late, I thought, it's not. But I felt a flash of pure panic when I realized that I couldn't remember the last time my husband had put his arm around me, or touched me, or even talked to me about anything he was doing. What if there's someone else? I wondered, and scared myself so bad I had to stand up and start pacing.

I walked over to put the gun in the closet, out of sight. It wasn't loaded, none of the guns that had belonged to my grandfather were ever loaded. Still, to be safe, I checked it again before I put it away.

Maybe it was putting the gun in the closet, maybe it was hearing the faraway-sounding voice of my sister saying, "Remember the night Daddy put his gun up and somehow or other it went off, you remember that, Macy Rose? That's what I thought of when you came out the door carrying that gun right now. I thought to myself I hope to high heaven that gun doesn't go off like it did the time Daddy was putting it up, not with it pointing at me!" I heard her nervous little laugh. I even realized, from somewhere far off where I had gone while I was standing there in the dining room of my Grandma's house talking to my sister, that Claire Louise had been scared of me. She hadn't been all that sure I didn't aim to shoot her, accidentally or otherwise. But I couldn't think of Claire Louise then. I couldn't even see her for the roar in my head and the blackness that was swirling all around me. It got blacker and blacker, the blackness that was clouds of vapor swirling, like those in a sauna, only dark not white, but thick you know so thick they're like cotton candy, a movable tangible miasma, that's what it was. Only the air around me wasn't sweet and sticky like cotton candy, just dark and swirly, and so seductive, so seductive that the fear I felt from the roaring in my ears only added to the bizarre excitement I was feeling. I couldn't for the life of me have stopped looking around in there. I was drawn in, pulled in by the power of the blackness. Don't go, part of me warned, but I was fascinated by the danger.

Something bad was happening to me. The noise in my head was as loud as it had been the night the gun did go off. And then it stopped, the noise did, and all I could hear was the echo of the gun, the fading echoes of the reverberations it had made the night it had gone off and the bullet had gone clear through the linen closet and ricocheted off the bathroom tile gouging out big chunks before it finally fell harmless at last to the bathroom floor.

I was ten years old again, ten years old and scared of guns and loud noises, and most of all scared of my daddy when he was angry. He'd been angry when he'd come up the stairs to put his gun away. I could always tell when he was mad by the way his feet sounded on the floors. When he was feeling okay he slid his feet, dragging the heels as he went, but if he was upset at something his feet sounded like soldiers marching across a stage, sometimes brisk, sometimes taking heavy serious steps that sounded like a bass drum being pounded out. The madder he got, the more staccato he walked. Then he sounded like a snare drum. That's how I heard him that night. The night the gun went off his steps were snare-drum steps.

He'd marched up the stairs and jerked the door to the gun cabinet open. It happened as he lifted the gun from the floor where he'd laid it when he reached up on top of the cabinet to get the key. Once he had the door open, he'd leaned over and picked up the gun and suddenly there was a loud booming noise, and he and I were there looking at each other, me scared, him angry as the rifle bullet ran around the upstairs of our house. I watched him as he surveyed the damage done to the closet door and wall. "Lucky we weren't in there," he laughed. I nodded at him. I always agreed with him, that was what I did. And then I felt the fear growing in my stomach, the terror that came when I looked in that closet. You weren't there this time, I reminded myself, you weren't in there when the bullet went through. Not this time, not this time, not this time echoed through my head, for all the world like the bullet bouncing around in the bathroom.

And then, still lost in the past, I ran, as fast as I could, over to Grandma's and she was holding me and I was crying and telling her Daddy shot the gun off and it went through the closet and into the bathroom, and she was saying there, there, at least no one was hurt and I said he hurts me Grandma, he does.

No, I thought, no, no, no . . .

"Mind if I put some coffee on?" Claire Louise said, looking at me funny as her voice chased the noes out of my head.

"Suit yourself," I said, not really listening to her. Suddenly, I knew what I was going to do. The plan was all there in my head as clear as if I had been thinking it out for days. Without thinking it over at all, I was on the phone, calling Mr. Shasta, making an appointment with him for later in the day. I knew exactly what I was going to do. I was going to get out of here. I was going to get out of Grandma's empty house and go home and . . . that's as far as I could go right then, I'll think about the rest of it when I get home, I told myself, I will, I promised. I'll think about it all when I'm out of here.

"What month is it?" I asked Claire Louise.

"Almost July," she told me, looking at me funny as if to say, how can you not know the month for heaven's sake.

"I have to go home. I can't believe I've stayed out here this long." I shook my head. It seemed weird, that was the only word for it, weird. Why had I stayed out here? Grandma was gone, Mother and Daddy were gone, and my own husband and children were in Houston. Why was I here?

I called Carlton then, but his secretary said he was busy. I told her to tell him I was coming home, I'd be in before too late. "And tell him I'm sorry," I added. I wanted to say more but I felt strange, giving a message like that over the phone.

Claire Louise was watching me like I'd grown two heads. "Are you sure he wants you back?" she asked.

"No, but I've got to try, I miss him, I miss my kids. I must have had brain damage to stay out here."

She looked at me sharply, I could feel her wondering if I was trying to make a joke. The truth was it hadn't occurred to me to say it to be funny, that bit about brain damage, but when I heard it I remembered that she and I used to say that. Any time one of us did something we couldn't account for, we'd say, "Oh, I must have had brain damage," and laugh together. Without willing it, I laughed, and she laughed too, and then we hugged each other, and even cried a little.

"I'm sorry, sorry I wasted all those years hating you. I don't hate you anymore, I don't think I hate anyone. I feel like I'm getting over a sickness, a sickness I didn't know I had until I saw myself out there in the front yard holding a gun and acting like a wild woman."

"Let's don't talk about the past," Claire Louise said, "let's just forget it." I smiled to myself then. That was always her way, forget the past, don't explain it, don't dwell on it either. Maybe she's right, I thought, only I don't think I can let go of things that easily. Claire Louise is like Grandma that way, I thought, and I knew something was different about me when I realized that even the thought that Claire Louise and Grandma had something in common didn't bother me.

"I'm going home, to my husband and children if they'll have me back. I suggest you get your kids back, too," I told her.

"Oh, they're not gone, they're just living with their father so they can take advantage of the West U schools. You know how much better those schools are than the ones out here."

So that's how you're rationalizing it, I thought to myself, feeling sorry for her for the first time in a long time. Poor Claire Louise, I thought, but I didn't say a word. Claire Louise wouldn't want pity. That would be the last thing she'd want from me. "Take anything of Grandma's you want," I told her. "I'm taking her cedar chest and the cast-iron toys but that's all. The rest of the things here I'm leaving for Belle and her daughter."

"You're giving Belle and her daughter all of Grandma's things?" Claire Louise shrieked, as shocked as if I'd said I was putting a torch to them, something that had, sad to say, occurred to me earlier.

"I'm giving Belle the land and house and every single thing in it. She loved Grandma and she and her daughter are living in a house that barely has a floor in it. I don't know why it didn't occur to me before. I don't need this house, and neither do you, but Belle does. I have an idea Grandma would have left it to her in the first place if I hadn't been so adamant that I should get it because you had Mother and Daddy's."

"But you can't give Belle this house, it's been in the family for years and Belle is . . ."

"Black?" I finished for her.

"Well, Macy, it's not that I'm prejudiced or anything, but black people don't live in houses like this."

"Claire Louise, Belle is the one took care of everything out here, you know that. This is more her place than any of ours. I'm seeing Mr. Shasta this afternoon and I'm giving it to her. Grandma wants me to."

"Oh, my gosh, I thought you were better, but if you're hearing Grandma talk to you again, then I'm not so sure."

It sounds mean to write it down, what she said, but the way she said it, it wasn't mean at all. It was like she really cared that I might be crazy again, hearing voices like they all thought I was doing before. But it isn't true, that I heard voices that weren't there. I did hear voices, but they were real, sometimes voices in my own self that told me things, like intuition some people call it, or talking to themselves. And some of the time Grandma did talk to me, not out loud, but from inside her head to inside my head, so no one else heard, but that didn't make it any less real.

And the truth is, she talks to me still, Grandma does. This voice I recognize as hers comes to me and tells me things from time to time. I know there are those that think that makes me crazy, but they're wrong. I'm not crazy to think the part of my grandmother that kept me going for all those years is still there, loving me and helping me. There's a lot we don't know about the hereafter, and no one can tell me angels don't hang around to help those of us still walking around here on earth plugging away trying to get it right. And that's where she is, my grandmother, she's off being an angel and not too busy from time to time to give me a little push in the right direction. To tell the truth, I think there are angels there for all of us, we just have to listen to them. Like the day she passed over, Grandma said to me, you can be happy if you will. I heard her voice again as I sat in her kitchen, talking to my sister for the first time since Grandma died. Go on, go back to your family, you can be happy if you will. I heard her then, I swear it.

I wished Claire Louise would leave. Not that I was mad at her, I wasn't. But suddenly I had so much to do. I felt all this energy in me pushing me to get going, to do what I needed to. "I'll bet we can get the cedar chest in the back of my station wagon," I said to my sister. Which we did. We had to unload every single thing in there and push and pull to get it out the door, but then it was easy as anything to lift up into the back of my car. And after I put the linens and old clothes from the cedar chest back inside it, I put the toys in all around the clothes. And that was it. I was ready to go. But I still had almost an hour before I was to meet with Mr. Shasta, so I went back inside with my sister and called Abe, Carlton's partner. Although I hadn't seen him for therapy in years, it suddenly seemed important that I go talk to him again. He gave me an appointment for the next day and didn't even act surprised to hear from me. Next I found the lists I had made, pages and pages listing every single thing my grandparents had owned.

"What are you doing?" Claire Louise asked as I searched the pages.

"I have to cross off the things I'm taking, I'm giving this list to Mr. Shasta so it'll be clear what Grandma is giving Belle." Then I remembered I had told Claire Louise to take what she wanted. "You'd better tell me if you're taking anything. I'll cross it off, too," I told her.

She stood up then and we walked through the house slowly, room by room, both of us aware it was for the last time. After we left, this house wouldn't be Grandma's, it would be Belle's, and no matter how often we visited Belle, we'd be coming to see her, not Grandma. Not ever again would we come to see Grandma.

"Remember the rockers," Claire Louise said, pointing to the two children's rockers that sat on either side of the fireplace. One was wicker, the other mahogany. "The wicker one was mine, the wooden one yours."

"Yeah," I said, smiling at the memories. "I wonder which one was Aunt Claire's when she was little?" I said, surprised it hadn't occurred to me before that those chairs had belonged to someone else before my sister and me, just as much as they had ever belonged to us.

"I wonder, too," Claire Louise answered me, "and I wonder which of Belle's grandchildren will claim them next."

We smiled at each other then, letting go of the children we had been, the ones with the overwhelming needs to know exactly what belonged to which one of us.

She picked up a crystal goblet, one of many on the sideboard, all different colors and patterns. Grandma had collected them for years. Claire Louise looked at them and turned them over to read whatever she could from the bottom of the stems. "These are valuable," she said.

"I know, Grandma loved them. So did Belle."

"Right," she said. "I'm taking the painting of Grandma and her two children, nothing else." She lifted it off the wall then, leaving a bare place on the paper where it had been. There was Grandma, younger than I was now, with a chubby-cheeked little girl who grew up to be Aunt Claire in her lap, and the boy who had become my father leaning on the back of her chair. He had been almost eight then, but his hair was still in long blond curls. Most people looking at that picture would think he was a girl.

For the first time in a long time, I said to my sister, "Why did she leave his hair long like that until he was almost ten years old? His hair was in ringlets!"

And Claire Louise said back to me the words Grandma had always answered when I had asked that question in the past. "He had the prettiest hair she had ever seen, she couldn't bear to cut it off."

Then I said to her what I had always said to my grandmother, "But didn't he hate it, that he looked like a girl?"

This was the part where she was supposed to say, "Why,

no, it never occurred to him to worry over it." That was what Grandma had said next, every single time I had asked. But Claire Louise changed the words. "Yes, he did. He hated every damn blond curl." And for the first time ever, the words satisfied me. I nodded. He did. That's right, he hated every damn curl.

I arrived home before Carlton did but the kids were there, so happy to see me I had to fight myself to keep from scooping them up and sitting down on the floor with them both clutched to me as I squalled about what a fool I had been. Actually, I'd been afraid they had gotten along so well without me they'd have become indifferent to me, or worse yet, acted like I was some distant relative they barely knew. But instead they jumped on me with an exuberance that almost knocked me over and took my hands and led me to their room so I could see every single project they had made in vacation bible school that week. "The project we made for you is in your room," Travis said, and Scott took my hand to pull me across the hall. I did cry then at the thought of my two kids waiting patiently for me to come to my senses, making little plaster-of-paris hands for me to sit on my dresser, and never once saying you were gone too long, Mom. Mrs. Grant was there in the doorway, watching us with careful eyes. After the boys went back outside to finish the game my appearance had interrupted, she picked up her purse and said, "Well, if you're home for now, I'll be going."

I could feel her wondering what was going on, and how long I would stay this time. Suddenly it was important to me that I explain things to her. I thought irrationally that if I could make Mrs. Grant understand, then everything would be all right with Carlton.

"I had to take care of my grandmother, Mrs. Grant, and it took me a long time to let go of her. But I'm home now, and I want you to know how much I appreciate that you've been here all these months when I've been neglecting my family."

She didn't unbend a bit, although I could see by the way she gave a little nod to herself that she agreed I'd been neglecting my kids. And I knew for sure that it was going to take more than just walking back in for me to be a part of their lives again when Scott ran in and asked her if he could have a cookie. "Not before supper," she started to say, and then looked over at me. "Maybe you'd better ask your mother," she said, looking across at me. He stared at me, as did Travis, all three of them wondering heaven knows what. I felt scared then, out of touch. I didn't know when supper was, or what it was for that matter either.

Quickly, I improvised. "It's almost six. Let's wait till Daddy gets home. We can go out for a pizza." As soon as I said it, they leaped for joy and ran outside again, their feet barely touching the floor. I felt like I had taken a cheap shot, and I wondered what Mrs. Grant was thinking. "I'll go now," she said. "Call me if you need me."

It was hard to think we had been friends. She had just treated me more like an adversary, I realized, wondering if she would ever like me again.

"You're here," Carlton said when he walked in the door. Not "you're home," I noticed, he said "you're here." I wondered if he made that distinction on purpose.

"I'm home," I said watching him carefully. "Is it too late?"

He didn't answer me, but turned and walked to the refrigerator and pulled out a beer. "Would you like something?" he asked.

"I want to talk to you. I want to try to explain." Before I could go on, he opened the sliding-glass door and called to the boys to come inside and wash for supper.

"I told them we'd get a pizza," I said.

"That's fine," he replied, still without looking at me.

As the evening progressed I felt sicker and sicker inside. Carlton talked over and around me, but plainly felt he had nothing to say to me. After we got home and the children watched a show on television and were bathed and put to bed, we sat in the living room in chairs at opposite sides of the room looking for all the world like two strangers forced to share a space together.

"How long do you plan to stay?" he asked me, making it plain that if I got up to leave that very moment it wouldn't bother him.

"I'm home for good."

"What about your grandmother's flowers?" he asked, sounding more tired than sarcastic.

"They're Belle's now. I saw Mr. Shasta today—I'm giving the house to her."

That surprised him. His eyes widened, but he looked away, not asking for any more information. He appeared determined not to care, not to get involved in the least little way in what I was doing.

"Carlton, I know this has been hard for you, I think I know anyway. And I'm sorry. I can't explain those months I was so caught up in my grief and self-pity that I stayed away from the three people who mean more to me than anything else in the world. What I want is for you to give me another chance, not that I deserve it, but I love you and I want us to get back to where we were before."

He looked at me then and I could see the Carlton I loved in his eyes, looking at me with warmth and compassion, but as if from a distance, as if there was an invisible wall there that words couldn't erase. "I love you, Macy, but I don't want to go through what I've gone through for the last year again. I've learned to get along without you. It hasn't been easy, it's been damn hard at times. And I don't want to jeopardize the progress I've made just to have you up and leave again whenever the mood strikes you."

At least he was talking to me, I thought. As long as he'll talk to me there is hope.

"But I won't do it again, I'm over that, whatever it was. I'm not even mad at my sister any longer."

I told him then about what had happened that day when I had gone out to greet Claire Louise with the shotgun, and how I had caught sight of myself in the reflection from the glass and thought I didn't recognize that crazy lady. It's like all of a sudden everything turned around for me. It looked different and I couldn't for the life of me understand why I had been so obsessed with my grandmother's house in the first place. Without thinking, I walked over and sat on the floor beside him, I reached up and took his hands and held them in mine. "You still wear your wedding ring," I told him. "Please say you still love me."

"I love you, Macy," he said, with a sigh that sounded like it had come from deep within him, "but I don't trust you, I don't trust us. And trust is even harder than love to get back."

"Will you try?" I asked. "Just try, please. I'm begging you, mainly for my sake, but for the kids too and for you. We were so good together." I was crying then, and so was Carlton, although he didn't appear aware of the tears slowing welling up in his eyes and falling down his cheeks.

"Let me think about it. I need to think," he said, and he disengaged my hands from his, like touching me was too much for him any longer. "You can sleep in the bedroom," he said, "I'll sleep out here."

"But what will the kids think?" I asked, and the flash of anger I saw in his eyes warned me I'd said too much.

"Maybe you should have thought of that for the last eight months," he said, glaring at me.

"You're right. I'm sorry I didn't," I said, softly. "I have an appointment with Abe tomorrow. Did he tell you?"

"No, we don't discuss every patient we see," he said curtly. Then he felt bad, his words had come out so surly. "I'm glad you're doing that, Macy. I know this has been hard on you, too."

He left the room then and went in the kitchen. I waited a minute before I went to bed, but it occurred to me he wasn't coming back until I'd left the room, so I quickly went into the bathroom to brush my teeth and wash my face and was in my own bed for the first time in months before I heard any sounds at all from the living room. I heard him turn on the television set and I wished more than anything his arms were around me. I sat up once and thought to go in the children's room, just to look at them and maybe kiss them softly, but I was afraid Carlton would think I was being dramatic, so I settled back down to toss and turn for hours before I fell asleep.

32

W E DID HOLD the Richards and Scott combined family reunion that year, same as always except for the first time in my memory it was not held at my grandmother's house. We held it instead at my house, the old one. I didn't think I could ever again set foot in my new house. At least I knew that I wouldn't be able to go back there until I had completely redecorated the entire place. Right now it held only grim memories for me. So the family party was held at my house, the one I guess will always be Mother and Daddy's in my mind. Britt and Maryanne drove out for it, and Aunt Claire's entire family came. There were relatives from Waco and Lubbock who showed up. I've forgotten the exact number, but I remember we had well over seventy people there. The oldest one wasn't Grandma this year, though.

It was eerie, how the reunion was the same and not the same in any way whatsoever. First of all Mother was gone, and Daddy too, of course, but the main people I missed were my grandmother and my sister. Macy didn't come, I talked to her on the phone and she said she would try, but the day before the party she called and said it was just too soon for her to come back. Maybe next year, I remember I said to her, and she said, maybe, but maybe not. Maybe never, she said before she hung up. Don't say that, I told her after she wasn't on the line any longer, never is too long a time for family. After all, I told myself, I ran away for ten years and look at me, I'm back and more here than most of the people who never left. She'll come back, I told myself. Just like Maryanne will, and Britt, too. Something about the Richards place, the Richards name, it was important, you couldn't turn your back on it. We had a past, a heritage, something we couldn't leave behind. They would understand that some day, they would, every single one of them.

Off and on all afternoon, I heard squeals, and I'd look over and wonder who was that swimming in Grandma's pool. I'd look careful-like, wondering for a minute before I remembered, that was Belle lived there, Belle and her daughter, and must be some of her grandchildren were out for the holiday with her. It was like looking at a negative to look over there and see only black people where you expected white faces and arms and legs. It felt funny, I can't deny it.

Belle had come to see me the day after Mr. Shasta had called her and told her the house was hers, she could move in whenever she wanted, Macy had told him to tell her. She'd tried to call Macy, she said, but Macy hadn't returned her calls. She had a letter from Macy Mr. Shasta had given her, she didn't tell me what it said, but I could tell from the way she held it and smoothed it over and over with her hand that it meant a lot to her. "It don't feel right, me living in your grandmother's house, Miss Claire Louise," she said, looking at me with worry in her eyes. "I told Mr. Shasta, 'If Miss Macy can't live there, then that's not to say some of their family don't want to.'" I could tell by the way she was looking at me she was asking for my permission to live there, to take the gift my sister had given her. It crossed my mind to say, it isn't right, Belle, don't do it, but I saw her hands smoothing and unsmoothing that letter, and for all they were black and mine were white, her hands looked like my own mother's to me. Just for a minute there, she wasn't Belle, the lady who had worked for my grandmother and my mother all her life, she was my mother who had looked after me and was going to come back and live right with me and love me this time and never ever let anyone hurt me. I can't account for it but that's exactly how I felt.

"Belle, I talked to Macy the day she went to see Mr. Shasta. That's your house. Nobody but you and your kin can live in it. And I'm glad," I said, surprised at myself.

"But all your grandmother's things," she said, still worried and unsure.

"She left them to you, Grandma did. That's what Macy says, and she was there with her, right to the end."

"Not going to bother you then, living next door to black folks?" she asked me.

"Maybe sometimes, about as much as you get upset at living next door to white folks," I said, and grinned to let her know I was kidding. "You've lived there longer than Macy or I ever did, Belle."

"I thank you kindly then," she said. "I never expected no fine house like this to end my days in," she said and left. It occurred to me as she walked down the steps that Belle had perfect posture. Eighty years old and she was still ramrod straight. That was something not many people could say. Later, when I thought back over that conversation, it surprised me some, the things I had said to her. I realized I wanted Belle to think well of me. There weren't many people I truly cared what they thought of me, but for some unfathomable reason it was important that Belle think I was okay. Better than okay, I wanted Belle to think I was a good person.

The next day I looked over and saw a U-Haul truck next door. Belle and her daughter were moving in. I didn't feel the same as I had at first. I felt, well, mixed feelings. I thought a long time about what to do about Belle. I truly did. On the one hand, I wanted to be neighborly, I wanted her good opinion as well as that of any other person in town. But on the other hand, nothing was going to change the fact that Belle and her daughter and her grandchildren and all the rest of her family were black. I felt trapped. I couldn't just go over with a home-baked welcome-to-the-neighborhood plate of cookies, but I couldn't ignore her either. Only, if I went over there, then she might think I expected her to visit me back and that wouldn't do either. After all, Lucy and Lucinda, my own hired help, were black themselves. How would it look, them working in my kitchen and Belle coming to call on me, expecting to sit in the living room and talk like we were friendly acquaintances? So what I did was, I had Lucy bake up some fresh blueberry muffins and put them in a basket with a bright ribbon and then one morning on my way to town, I drove over and presented the basket to Belle who was there with two of her grandchildren, both of whom were running around in bathing suits waiting for her to take them out to the pool.

"Lucy made some muffins, I thought you would like some," I said, handing her the basket. Belle did like black people always did when white people drove up to their houses, she walked outside to the fence to talk to them like it wasn't expected they'd get out of their cars and come up to the door. I hadn't honked my horn or anything rude like that, I just drove up slowlike and she came walking down the steps to where I sat in my car. "Marcus, you come here," she called to one of the children. When the little boy, who looked to be about eight or nine ran over, she said to him, "Take this basket in the kitchen and put these muffins on a plate so Miss Claire Louise can have her basket back."

"The basket is for you," I said.

"Oh, well, that's right nice of you." She smiled at me, but the smile only went as far as her mouth, it didn't touch her eyes a bit. I sat there wondering what I should do if she asked me in, like as not she was standing there remembering it was my grandma's house and wondering should she ask me in.

"You settled and all?" I asked.

"Yes'm, thank you."

I noticed Belle talked different from time to time, I wondered if it had always been that way. When she had said it was right nice of me she had sounded like my grandma talking, but when she said "yes'm" it sounded like she was talking black. I wondered if she did that on purpose, changed how she sounded from one conversation to the next.

"Are your grandchildren having a good time, swimming and all?" I asked, leading up to saying I'd better go so she could let them swim.

"Somewhat, they haven't rightly learned to swim yet, so I have to watch them."

"Erin Caldwell, in town, gives lessons," I said without thinking it through. Erin Caldwell was white. Doubtless all her students were white, too. Doubtless Belle was thinking the same thing I was.

This was uncomfortable, no other way to describe it. I hate to feel uncomfortable, I truly do. Belle stood there waiting on whatever I had left to say. She didn't appear in a hurry for me to leave, and neither did she ask me to get out and sit a spell. In a flash, I said the first thing came into my mind. "I have to go on into town, garden-club business, I'll see you later," I said, putting my car into gear. It was then I noticed I hadn't even cut the engine off. No wonder she didn't ask me in. And then I thought, again, oh, damn, Grandma was always big in the garden club. Do you think Belle expects I'll ask her to join? But no, she wouldn't expect that. She never expected it when Grandma was alive, but then it was Grandma had the garden, now it was Belle. Race relations are a sticky business, I thought to myself. "I have to get a move on," I said out loud. I wanted to go by Front Street where Harrison Jason had his law office. Just go, I told myself, tell Belle good day and leave. Doesn't pay to think too much about some things.

"Thank you for the muffins and the basket," Belle said again as I said my good-byes.

"You're welcome."

It'll get less strange as time goes on, I told myself, driving to town. Harrison Jason was a member of an old Molly's Point family. Actually he was a year or two younger than me and had lived in California for years. In fact, he had just moved back to town during the last year. His wife had died, leaving him with two children, both under five, and he'd moved back here to be near family. It was such a sad story. His mother had been diagnosed with terminal cancer not a month after he'd come back. She was in the hospital now, barely hanging on, not expected to live. I had always been so fond of Mrs. Jason. I made a point to visit her every day. Today I had some of my muffins in the car. I thought I'd stop by and leave them for Harrison before I went by to see his mother.

Problems do have a way of working out if you just are careful to go after what you want. Like the situation with Belle, the one I thought would never work out. Turns out things got better by the very next week. We evolved our friendship into an entirely respectable one of amicable if distant interactions. Actually, one thing did occur that might have developed into a problem but didn't. As it happened, Maryanne came out to spend the month of August with me. Britt was in some summer program at Rice University and was too busy to do more than visit occasionally, but Maryanne came out and settled into her old room like she had never told me she was living with her Daddy forever and I could give her room away for all she cared. The first morning she was home, she came down in her bathing suit, ready to go for a swim.

"It's not our pool," I said, "it's Belle's pool now."

Without so much as a word to me, she picked up the phone and called Belle and invited herself over for a swim. When she came home that afternoon after staying over there all morning, eating lunch with them and then swimming for several more hours in the afternoon, she informed me she was giving Marcus and Dorothy swimming lessons and helping Belle with her flower beds the next day as well. And that formed the basis of all her days that month. She had come out to see me, but as had been the case for years, she spent most of her time next door. Had I not come to be so busy with my church and civic activities I might have regretted the little time we had together, but in truth it was enough just to have her around. Lucy and

Lucinda both fussed over her, fixing her favorite foods and going next door with her, ostensibly to watch the children swim, but primarily to socialize with Belle, it occurred to me. And, as I said, it wouldn't have made any sense for them to ask me over. After all, we were different races, and, for all that I am a firm advocate of integration, I do not feel that integration necessarily applies to a person's own home and hearth. Besides which, there was never so much as a day that I didn't have important things I needed to get done.

I wondered some if I should worry. After all, that was my daughter who was spending most of her waking hours with black people. But it didn't matter, not yet that is. She was just a child, Maryanne was, although by the time she got older I knew I would have to put a stop to that friendship. I'm as liberal as the next person, but still and all, I knew how things were, how the cow ate the cabbage so to speak. And white people who spent overly much time with black people were looked down on, no two ways about it. I wasn't going to worry this summer, I told myself, but by next year I'll have to have my own pool. Then Maryanne won't have any reason to hang around over there. Macy of course had every right to give that house to Belle, I told myself, and I admired her charitable impulses, I did indeed. It was the type of thing I myself would have done. But it was making a difficult, somewhat touchy situation for me. Not many white people who lived as well as we Richardses did had to contend with black people living right next door to them. I told myself, this is breaking new ground, Claire Louise, and no one is as well equipped as you to rise to such a challenge. And I did, if I do say so myself, an excellent job of carving out a suitable relationship with my neighbors. I was friendly, polite, but not familiar. And they respected that, they surely did, Belle and her family.

Looking back, it seems as if the summer I spent contending with the fact that fifty acres of my family farm, the Richards family farm, was now owned by blacks, is what led me into the political work I did more and more of in the coming year. One of the accomplishments I can point to with the most pride is the fact that I, Claire Louise Richards, was instrumental in starting up the Republican party in Galvez County, and this in a county that had never had a vote cast it did not go to a Democratic candidate. My growing interest in politics led me to spend more and more time with Harrison, who also turned out to be a firm believer in the two-party system.

By September Harrison and I were involved in setting up his office. With his children and his concerns about his mother, he needed someone he could count on to run the office, and as he said, I fit the bill admirably, knowing the town the way I did. He talked about hiring me but I wouldn't hear of it. After all, what are friends for, I asked him? And it wasn't like I needed the money. As the fall went on, Harrison and I became closer and closer. It was almost as if the more his mother deteriorated, the more he depended on me. It was understandable; he had been through so much, the death of his wife, his mother's illness. We had that in common, our recent bereavements. I was careful not to allow him to read more into our friendship than actually existed. As I told him time and again, we were friends, nothing more. I had had one bad marriage, one very bad disappointing relationship with the father of my children, and I had made a second mistake marrying Hugh. I never could have known how a drinking problem would change a person before I lived all those months with Hugh.

Therefore, as much as I admired and respected Harrison, I repeatedly told him I will not get serious about you. No more relationships, I said. We will be friends and that is all. Harrison

347

intimated from time to time that he would like to see me in a more serious light, perhaps even contemplate a more permanent relationship, but I was adamant. No more men except as friends, and Harrison, who was if nothing else a perfect gentleman and one who held me in the highest esteem, resigned himself to accept my declaration.

33

THE SUMMER AFTER my grandmother died, Mrs. Grant and I reconstructed our old relationship in a sort of pasted-together kind of way. We never, not a single time, alluded to where I'd been, or whatever her thoughts might have been on what amounted to my virtual abandonment of my husband and children. She and I just tiptoed around each other for the first few days I was back, talking at each other nice and polite, and then without much fuss we were all chatty and companionable again. Not that I truly felt all that comfortable. I have to admit I felt self-conscious when I was around her, or any of our other friends for that matter, for some time, on into the summer for sure. But Mrs. Grant was too nice a person to be openly critical of me, and I was too confused by my own behavior to risk bringing it up with her. In my mind I was sure she thought I was a bad person, but I resolved to be so good in the future that she would grow to respect me again. I don't know what got into me, I told myself daily, but I will be very very careful it never happens again. Over and over I promised myself, I'm going to be good now, I truly am.

Mrs. Grant was over almost every day visiting me and doing something with the boys, and then like as not we'd all four get in the station wagon and run out for a Whataburger for lunch. In the afternoons she and the boys would play tennis and I'd sit on a quilt under a tree, ostensibly to watch them while I read a magazine. Generally they woke me up from the doze I fell into as I sat in the shade on those hot humid afternoons. On the days they didn't play tennis after lunch, I'd take the kids to the pool in the afternoons and we'd rush to get home by five-thirty so they could buy something from the snow-cone man. Travis and Scott dearly loved the snow-cone man, I realized anew every time I watched them run outside clutching their quarters in grimy little hands. "Wait," they'd screech, "wait, wait," they'd call in high-pitched voices, frantic that he'd turn the corner and that day's summer magic potion would vanish around the corner with him. I knew inside of a week we'd become such regulars that if he did miss us on his initial pass, he'd for sure come back by a second time. I tried to explain that to Scott and Travis, but they didn't ever seem to hear me. "He's coming, he's coming, Mommy. Hurry up! Hurry up!" they'd cry, dancing impatiently from foot to foot, all the while eyeing the street anxiously.

We finally decided to go to the bank and get a whole roll of quarters, which we emptied into a basket that sat inside the garage on the shelf behind the box where we kept the basket-balls. The boys could reach that shelf easily now, so instead of the ritual frantic search for Mommy's pocketbook, which I never seemed to leave in the same place, one of the boys would run for the garage and the basket of quarters while the other ran to the end of the driveway to flag down the man whose face we came to know as well as that of the man who directed traffic at the corner of their school, but whose name we also never did learn.

Scott and Travis were so cute licking the frozen ice crystals frantically while the sticky purple syrup and melting ice ran out the sides and bottom and caused the paper cones to disintegrate as the boys clutched them tighter and tighter in a futile race against the temperature and the flimsy containers. Seeing how they enjoyed those icy treats, I bought them a little machine to make snow cones at K mart, thinking they'd have fun making their own. Which they did, for about two hours. Then the syrup was all gone, mostly spilled or sampled, and once again the snow-cone man drove slowly down the street announcing his arrival with organ-grinder music and there the boys were, frantically jumping up and down wanting quarters so they could buy some real snow cones. The play ones weren't right, they said. Only play. It was true. The play ones were only pretend, a game. Running to meet the snow-cone man was real. We sold that snow-cone machine, barely used and only slightly sticky, in our August garage sale.

I didn't feel guilty when I was with my kids. My days with them were too distinct and too busy, and while from time to time I had sharp pangs of regret when they referred to something in their lives I'd missed, there was such an intensity to our days that, with them, I reveled in the moment. Now was enough, too satisfying and rewarding in and of itself to allow me to dwell overlong on my regrets about the past year. I guess I'd been home about a week when I realized we were really and truly okay, my kids and I were back together emotionally in a way I hadn't known I'd lost until I looked for it and it wasn't there anymore.

It was a Friday morning and the weather was rainy and cool in a manner totally uncharacteristic of a June morning. Mrs. Grant and I were sitting in the kitchen drinking iced tea and talking about going to Foley's for the summer white sale advertised in the *Houston Chronicle*. "But if this rain clears up, I've got a tennis date," she was saying, when we all of a sudden heard an ear-splitting shriek that occurred almost simultaneously with the slamming of the screen door. Before I could do more than fumble for my shoes and start to stand up, Scott was there, flinging himself into my arms, crying and holding one hand in the other. His brother was wrapped around my legs, crying as well, yelling, "The door caught his hand, the door caught his hand." Mrs. Grant was at the refrigerator in two bounding steps and as quickly back with ice wrapped in a towel for the hand, which fortunately was not severely injured, while I sat there crooning over and over, "It'll be okay, it'll be okay, Mommy's here, Mommy's here." Tears came to my eyes then, tears of relief that Scott was okay and tears of gratitude that I'd been there for him, and most of all, tears of thankfulness that he had run to me and not Mrs. Grant. I could feel one of the big icy scared spots inside me melting away right there as I sat holding him and surreptitiously wiping my eyes on the back of his Houston Astros T-shirt, which had been clean and fresh from the dryer not thirty minutes before and now looked like it could have been the rag I used to wipe up spills from the floor. "Let's go to Foley's," I said, standing up, "but first you have to change that shirt. Both of you need clean ones," I smiled, happy and optimistic for the first time since I had driven back into Houston over a week ago. Maybe, just maybe it'll be okay with Carlton, too, I told myself, crossing my fingers in a silent prayer.

Truth was, my relationship with my husband was still difficult, the only problem that didn't seem to solve itself that summer. With the boys and Mrs. Grant, I'd regained my place, my role as Mommy and friend, back from a trip, one that sure enough had been a long one, but after the first few days my newness wore off and our old careless camaraderie returned. I felt like, with the three of them, I was back to my real life. Carlton continued to be, well, distant is the only word comes to mind. He was polite and spoke to me about affairs that concerned the kids or the house or the neighborhood, but there was no personal level, no depth of feeling to our relationship. Mainly what we had was a depth of distance. And he steadfastly continued to sleep on the couch in the living room. After a while I gave up asking him to move back to the bedroom. It was embarrassing and demeaning to be told time after time not to worry, he was more comfortable where he was. I wasn't, I told him over and over, I wasn't comfortable sleeping apart from my husband. I'm sorry, he'd tell me, polite, but from the tone of voice he used it was apparent he was indifferent. If I cried he handed me a tissue and said, "Now, Macy, crying isn't going to change things," before he left the room.

If it hadn't been for the kids I might have left him, I might have moved out from sheer misery at being treated like I was a relative he was forced to put up with but would rather not. And I knew, when I wasn't too scared to think about it, if it hadn't been for the kids Carlton would have left me long before the summer. He scared me, Carlton did. He was so distant, so far from the man I had loved and counted on. Over and over I blamed myself for taking him for granted, for abandoning him to care for my grandmother. Over and over I asked myself, how could I have done that, just left him, left the children? How did I do that? It was like I'd had some disease, some compulsion. It didn't make sense to me, the Macy I had been for the past year. Sometimes I caught glimpses of myself in a mirror and was surprised at who looked back at me. It was like I had never seen myself before. Strange is the only word for it. So how could I blame my husband for not trusting me? I didn't trust myself, when I thought back to the things I had done. I knew I needed to know why, what went wrong with me, so I could make sure it didn't happen again.

But, to be honest, I also didn't want to know why. I didn't want to know any more about the past than I already did. I know if Carlton had been content to let me back into our old life without a fuss, I'd have been relieved to let the past go, you know, sort of creep on forward walking real quietlike at first so the dust behind me could settle, and then march on forward like nothing bad had ever happened. But Carlton wasn't forgetting the past year. He went right on acting like I was some stranger he'd somehow or another gotten stuck spending a life with. And part of me, the optimistic part, knew good and well the only hope in the world I had of putting my marriage back together was getting enough of a handle on what had made me act so nutty for the past year so I could for sure say to my husband, that's not about to happen again. I'll figure this out, I'd tell myself, and I'll explain everything and Carlton will come back to me. Sometimes another part of me would answer, but, Macy Rose, you yourself know there's no one left to die, so how on earth could this happen again? But even then, even if it was just Carlton being stubborn, I still had to convince him, didn't I?

Nights were the worst time, the times when everyone in the world was asleep but me, and I'd lay there in bed, all by myself, and search though I would, the hopeful part of me was nowhere to be found. It was during the nighttimes I'd remember my mother and the time she had to be hospitalized. Mother had shock treatments, I'd remind myself, and probably whatever was wrong with her was something in the blood that was now cropping up in me. They used to say that. My mother would say to my father when someone in town did something she considered low-class or scandalous, I'm not surprised, not a bit, she'd say. As you well know, blood will tell. So there I was, my mother dead and gone, but I'd think, if she was right, if blood does tell, then here it is telling in me. And when I was feeling real down, I'd think, well, Carlton is probably going to leave me. He's waiting to tell me, give me time to adjust before he asks me for a divorce. Like as not he's going to want to get custody of the kids, and then when I'd think that, I'd get to feeling so scared it was hard to breathe without it hurting. Because the way I'd been acting, I knew any judge in his right mind, if he had to give the kids to one of us, would choose Carlton. Even I, bad as I felt about myself those nights, agreed with our mythical judge. No doubt about it, Carlton was the better parent, but how on earth would I live if I lost my kids as well as my husband? I'd ask myself. By then I'd be crying, and I'd count the days until my next appointment with Abe and I'd tell myself it isn't going to happen, somehow or another this won't end up in court, I'll figure out what went wrong and fix it and . . .

I talked with Abe over and over about the things I had done and how they seemed to have destroyed my relationship with my husband. Give it time, was all he could say, not very good advice from a psychologist, it seemed to me. Somehow I expected more. I expected him to come up with something to get Carlton and me back together again, happy like we were before my family affairs had caused us such trouble. But Abe just said work on yourself, your own conflicts, and your relationship with your husband will work itself out. If you don't care about yourself, you can't expect people to care about you. Good advice, I can see that now, but at the time, I mainly felt angry at Abe as well as Carlton. They were partners and friends. It seemed as if the longer Carlton held me at arm's length, the more I blamed

Abe as well. But no matter how I railed at Abe to do something ("He's your partner"), no matter how angry I got at him, I was always there in the office twice a week, sitting with my hands folded in my lap waiting for my appointment.

Abe and I talked about my family and me until I was sick to death of the whole subject. Over and over I'd tell him about the things my parents had done or left undone, how I had perceived their inability to love me, their preference for my sister. We even got into my grandmother, and for the first time ever I said out loud she wasn't perfect either, that a lot of the things I had thought about my grandmother were things I had made up to make myself feel special. At first it felt like a betrayal, to see her as less than perfect, but then one day, sitting there talking to Abe, I remembered her telling me to go on, be happy, and I knew my grandmother had felt as guilty as I did over things she could control and things she couldn't. Seemed as if most of the people in my family had been more or less guilt-ridden.

"Understanding all this old family stuff is impossible, and to be honest I don't think it is all that useful. What I am really worried about is my husband," I said to Abe.

"Hm-hum," he said, a word that formed most of his therapeutic vocabulary, I thought to myself on the days I was angry at him. I got so tired of going over and over the same old litany of complaints that gradually I began to dredge up new ones. "There are other parts to my childhood, things I half remember and both believe and don't believe," I heard myself saying one day.

"Mm-mm," Abe replied, but a light in his eyes and a tensing of his shoulders in the way he leaned ever so slightly forward told me he was interested in what I was saying. Rebelliously, I clamped my lips shut, thinking to myself, he can just ask if he wants to know. He's the doctor. Let him ask the questions, and maybe I'll tell him and maybe I won't. When I thought things like that I always felt like, well, kind of like a bratty kid. Stubborn and rebellious and determined to plant my feet and not be dragged anywhere I didn't choose to go of my own free will. I won't say another word, I thought, and then heard myself talking at the same time I was resolving to make him ask.

I heard myself telling Abe about Claire Louise's diaries, the ones I had read years ago, telling him things I'd never in my life allowed myself to think about, much less say aloud to another person outside the family. "Do you think that's true? Could my father have punished Claire Louise, that way, I mean? She hated him, she hated both of them."

"What do you think?"

I had been seeing Abe again for weeks now, long enough so I knew that hell could freeze over before he would answer a question. In many ways it's a rip-off. Psychologists go to school for years and years to learn how to do nothing more than sit in their offices listening to folks talk and work out every single one of their own answers to whatever questions they've come into therapy to find out about. Doesn't seem like it would take over a couple of months to get good at saying "Hm-mm" and "What do you think?" no matter what the provocation. I had elaborated on this point with Abe on more than one occasion, and he had yet to say more than "Hmm" in reply, although when I got really upset he might venture an "Is there a reason you are aware of that you're feeling so hostile right now?" That in my opinion was an extremely hostile remark in and of itself.

But on that day I barely noticed when he answered my question with a question, perhaps by then I was getting more accustomed to answering my questions for myself. "I don't know, I don't think so," I replied, and I clamped my lips shut, thinking it didn't make a bit of sense in the world to keep going round and round the same old barn door. "Remember, I've told you time after time, my sister Claire Louise was and is a liar. She's my sister and of course I care about her," I added, anxious to propitiate whatever gods there are that say you absolutely must not hate your sister, "but it doesn't make any sense whatsoever to keep talking about the things Claire Louise said."

Abe didn't remind me I was the one who had brought up my sister in the first place. He glanced at his watch and noticed we were out of time, and stood up, telling me he'd see me at two o'clock on Friday.

We talked that night, Carlton and I did. One good thing about me being in therapy was at least on Tuesday and Friday nights Carlton and I had something to talk about other than what the kids had done that day. And I wouldn't be honest if I didn't admit that I had noticed when I talked about my therapy Carlton was all ears. He listened and asked questions and sometimes he would lean over and pat my arm or give me a quick supportive hug as I talked. Which I did, I talked on and on about whatever I'd covered with Abe that day. And then, to make what were the best times I was having with my husband those days last longer, I'd talk about stuff we'd already covered, or speculate on upcoming topics, or ask his opinion on something or another. And it was on Tuesday and Friday nights that I'd feel the hopeful part of me growing. Hang in there, I'd tell myself, Carlton still loves you, I know he does, he just is too stubborn to admit it. And scared, too, even then I knew that. Carlton was scared to get hurt again. It truly is not a good feeling to know that the person you love and trust more than anyone in the world is scared you'll hurt him again. Again. Again means you hurt him before, bad, bad enough so he remembers it. I'd give anything in the world not to have Carlton feel that way about me, I told myself. Over and over I told myself that. Regrets don't make it go away, though. It takes more than being sorry I was learning.

"The closet?"

"Upstairs in our house, the house I grew up in, there is this big closet, huge, with shelves on three sides, deep shelves that can hold stacks and stacks of sheets and blankets. And still the closet is so big it's almost like a little room, it is . . . or was." I looked at Carlton and he nodded at me. Go on, I remember, his nod said. It was Friday again and I was telling Carlton about my session that afternoon. "I found myself telling Abe about the upstairs linen closet in my parents' house," I continued, smiling a silly-me smile at my husband.

"What did you tell him about the closet?" Carlton asked, not treating it like a silly-me topic at all.

"Not much," I admitted. "I told Abe that even though he was giving me a discount because of you, that it wasn't worth the little bit of money I was paying him to sit there and talk about a closet that had been gone no telling how many years now. And, as it was, by the time the closet came up, my forty-five-minute hour was over anyway." I shrugged and started to say, You may rest assured that when I go back on Tuesday I'll have something more important than closets to talk about, but Carlton asked me just then what I remembered about the closet. Now, to be honest, I was sick to death of the closet and I didn't really want to talk about it, but Carlton was acting so supportive and interested and we were sitting together and having margaritas and eating hot Mexican peanuts someone had brought us from Nuevo Laredo and I didn't want to spoil it, so I sort of took a deep breath and relaxed and thought, well, if he wants to hear this then I guess he might as well. Funny, how important things sneak up on a person that way.

"Well, my mother always sent my sister up to the closet to wait for my daddy. Go upstairs to the closet, she would say, and when your father gets home you're going to get it. If Mother was real mad, which she generally was, she'd grab Claire Louise and jerk her around and point her toward the stairs. Mother's hands felt like claws when she was angry."

I took another deep breath and kept talking. "The first thing Claire Louise did after Daddy died, the day after his funeral, she had men out there and they ripped that closet right out of the wall, I mean it was gone before he was cold in the ground. Carlton," I interrupted myself, "you know this, I know I've mentioned it before."

"Macy, the thing with the closet. My god, do you realize how awful that was? You've always said your sister was sent to the closet. Are you sure they didn't send you there as well?"

When Carlton asked me that question, he was leaning toward me and I felt myself sort of reaching for him. I was trying hard to think of the answer to his question but it felt like such a hard question. It made it easier to keep looking for the answer when he put his arm around me and sort of pulled me over to him until my head was resting on the top part of his arm. "I never thought it was me, but sometimes when I think about the closet, I get the cold shivers, like it *was* me in there waiting for my daddy, not Claire Louise. I always worried about her. I can remember that."

"But your mother never sent you to be punished?"

"No, never, I'm sure of that," I replied, but my voice didn't even sound to me like I really and truly meant no. Carlton looked at me so serious, his eyes the warm brown color I loved. I could tell he wasn't buying it either.

Carlton and I sat there, close together, closer than we'd been since I returned, and the couch we were sitting on was the same one he'd slept on every single night since I'd returned. We sat on the couch and listened to that NO as it hung around in the air. It was as if it gathered itself up and got stronger and began echoing around me like the punch line to a terrible joke, something grotesquely funny that kept beaming itself back at me. "No one ever forgets they were punished, do they?" As I asked that question, the roaring in my ears started up, telling me be careful, careful now, Macy, it cautioned. My voice sounded like a little kid's, I remember noticing that, but it didn't sound like any little kid I knew.

"Sometimes they do," Carlton answered.

"What happens then?" I pushed the roaring back. I wanted to know, I wanted to finish this.

"Sometimes they remember later, sometimes they don't."

"Claire Louise wrote about me in her diaries, but I thought it was lies." I guess I was whispering now, the words felt like I had to push them out, but out was the only direction they'd go in.

"What did she write?"

"That it was bad enough what he did to her, but now he was after me, too. In her diary she said they made her sick, both my parents did, and she said she hated them, over and over she said that." I didn't say anything for a long time and then I heard myself say to Carlton, "I hated them, too."

It scared me, saying that. You weren't supposed to hate your parents. If you did, it meant something was wrong with you. I believed that, I believed that if it was really and truly so that I hated my own parents, then for sure something was bad wrong with me. And then I felt the overwhelming guilt and the raging fear and I knew that I had better be very very careful and very very good, or something awful was going to happen. Careful,

careful, I cautioned myself, but it was getting harder and harder to push those awful scared feelings back. They came more and more, no matter how careful I was, I'd say or do something, and then I'd sit there all panicky and frozen feeling knowing for sure people were going to find out all about how bad I was.

"Something's bad wrong with me," I told Carlton. I heard myself telling him the truth, I knew I was telling him the truth but at the same time it was as if I had never heard these words before now. "Bad wrong. I realized today while I was talking to Abe I hated my parents, really and truly hated them." I sat there, holding my breath, watching him as carefully as if he were a poisonous spider.

He's going to leave me now for sure, I told myself.

"So did I, Macy Rose, so did I. I hated them for what they did to you."

He said it so soft and gentle I didn't believe the words I was hearing at first. I sat there with my mouth hanging open looking at him and thinking to myself, well, it is true I am hearing voices again. But then he went on and I knew it really was Carlton talking. "They weren't very nice people, Macy. I'm sorry to say this but it's true. Your mother and father weren't very nice people. Makes perfect sense for you to hate them. For God's sake, you had to live in that hellhole they created." His voice got louder as he talked and he sounded hard and angry, and although I was relieved to know it was in fact my own husband talking to me I couldn't for the life of me think what to think about the words I heard him saying.

Then I got scared, real scared. I felt the fear growing in me until that's all there was, the roaring screaming scary stuff that filled me up.

It was the anger I'd heard in Carlton's voice that did it, the anger that scared me so bad. All my life I'd hear people sound angry, and I'd get real still and careful inside. Just for a minute there it wasn't my husband I heard talking all angry about my parents. It was my father talking and he was angry. He was growling and snarling at me and I knew I was in trouble again, that in spite of my resolutions I hadn't been good enough and I was in trouble again. My stomach clutched in on itself and I got up and ran to the bathroom, knowing with absolute certainty I was fixing to vomit up every single thing I had eaten for lunch that day. I barely made it to the bathroom in time to fling myself onto the floor in front of the toilet and proceed to throw up every last thing that was in my stomach. Afterwards, I lay there on the cool tile floor, feeling empty and floaty like. I could hear Carlton outside the door, trying the handle, which even in my panic I had locked because I never ever went into a bathroom I didn't lock the bathroom door, and I heard Carlton quietly telling me to open the door, to let him in. He was there, I could hear him, but barely, like he was way far off, like maybe he was a person in another lifetime calling to me from across a divide I hadn't crossed yet. "Open the door, Macy, open the door," he whispered.

"If the closet door had a lock, I'd be safe," some little-kid voice in my head said.

"Open the goddamn door, Macy," Carlton said, still in a quiet voice, but he sounded so angry, so determined he was going to get in there with me.

And that is when the dam broke, the wall behind which I had hidden all those scared-little-kid memories crumbled to pieces, right there in my own head, I heard the dam I'd constructed over twenty years ago fall apart with a sharp ripping sound. And with the dam gone, the flood of tears it had held back rushed forward, free at last to wail their anguish, my anguish, I realized. I sobbed loudly, surprising myself with the vehemence of the sound, and then I put my head down in my hands and cried and cried until I couldn't cry any longer, I cried until I'd cried out all the tears in me. I cried for the little kids who had been Claire Louise and Macy Rose and had pretended to the whole world that nothing was wrong at their house because they were afraid to bring the whole house down on everyone's heads. I cried because the person I'd trusted most hadn't saved me. One by one the memories floated in, I saw myself back in that house, my mother angry at me, sending me upstairs to wait for my father, and then turning her face from me when I came back downstairs later. She knew, I told myself, she knew he was abusing us, she just pretended not to. Even Grandma knew, I told her and she believed me, she was just scared of them too, scared of what they'd say, scared maybe they'd say she couldn't see her own grandkids, I think that was it, we were all so ashamed of what people would say to or about us.

One by one the shameful secrets of my childhood floated out of the dark closet of my mind where I had buried them. It wasn't lies, every word Claire Louise said had been true. And not just for her, for me too. I'd been there in that closet time after time. I'd been there.

I don't know how long I lay on the floor before it came to me that Carlton was still outside the bathroom door. I heard his voice saying quietly, so as not to scare the boys, "Macy Rose, open the door. If you don't, I'm going to take it off the hinges, do you hear me? Can you hear me? Macy!" I got up off the floor then, although to tell the truth I felt almost too drained to move. I unlocked the door and stood looking bleakly into the mirror at the pale faded-looking person who was me. Carlton didn't say a word at first, he just walked over and held me, he put his arms around me and held me and listened as I told him what I'd remembered. There in that vomit-smelling room, he put his arms around me and kissed me, and said, "There, there, it's all over now, it's all over."

"But it was so awful, so awful," I whimpered, wishing I could think of a word that was bigger, a word that would convey all the pain and shame the memories carried.

"It was," he said, "it was worse than awful, but it's over now, Macy, and you survived it. Thank God for that." Carlton got a damp washcloth and tenderly washed my face. He took a brush and brushed my hair back out of my eyes. Through all his min-istrations I stood talking in a weak voice, telling him about one memory after another. Although I felt too drained to stand even, too tired to move my mouth to say another word, the words kept slipping out of me. One by one the words came, like they weren't connected to me anymore. It was as if my words were all the water left in a hose that had been cut off and disconnected. There wasn't any force in them any longer but still and all they were going to roll out of that hose, one after another, until the hose was all coiled up again and they were out, every last drop of them was going to come on out.

For a while there, now that they didn't feel connected to me any longer, those memories fascinated me. I turned them over and over, talking about what I remembered, adding detail upon detail. And then gradually, their bright newness began to fade. The colors of the pictures faded until the memories I held were no more than tired old black and white photographs. Old memories. People I used to know. Someone I wasn't any longer, somewhere I wouldn't be going back to. "It's over, isn't it? It is,

I guess it's over now." I nodded to myself, gradually becoming aware that I was safe in my own bathroom with my husband's arms around me.

"It's over, Macy," Carlton confirmed. "The closet is gone."

Later, much later that night, Carlton reached over and hugged me, just because, he said, like he always used to do and hadn't done in a long, long time. And I cried again. Even though I thought all the tears I had within me were gone, more came up, but these tears were different, these were happy tears. I needed that hug. Carlton's hug right then told me more than words ever could. His hug told me I wasn't a dirty nasty person, I was who I'd been trying to be, Macy Porter, a nice person, a good person even though some bad things had happened to her. I like you, his hug said. Even if bad things happened to you, you're not bad. All that and more my husband said to me with one hug.

The next morning when we woke up it was Saturday, the sun was shining, and the first thing the kids asked was, "Can we go swimming?"

"Do you think Belle knew?" I asked Carlton, still not able to think of much beyond the revelations of the past evening.

"I couldn't say, she didn't live with your family, but she was out there so much of the time, maybe she did, maybe she didn't. Does it matter?"

"I guess not. Let's call her and see if we can stop by this afternoon and swim," I suggested impulsively.

"We could go antiquing in the country first," Carlton agreed, suggesting a pastime we had loved since before the children were born. On Saturdays we'd pack a picnic and drive aimlessly around on little country roads. Over time we had learned where there were antique stores open on the weekends, places where we could poke around for hours if we liked. Occasionally we even bought something.

"I guess maybe I won't need any more therapy," I told Carlton.

"Don't rush into any decisions right now, Macy," he cautioned me. "You've been through a lot. Could be seeing Abe will be helpful to you. And, as you so pointedly told him," he added, grinning at me, "it's not like it's costing us all that much."

"Yeah," I agreed, smiling back at Carlton, feeling happy once again to be the recipient of his cheerful teasing. Several times that afternoon a wave of pure happiness washed over me, the feelings so strong they took my breath away. "There's a song I remember, but I'm not sure what the name was or even who sang it," I said. " 'You don't know what you've got till it's gone.' Do you remember?" I asked.

"You haven't lost anything," Carlton told me, kissing me and pushing my hair back from my face at the same time. He never did tell me if he knew which song it was I was talking about.

I was driving when we pulled up at Belle's house. I don't know what was different about it. I couldn't truthfully point to a single thing that had been changed, but as I drove up it looked unfamiliar to me, strange, new, I don't know, just different.

The children were out of the car and heading toward the pool, which was sparkling and shimmering in the heat of the day. I could see there were several kids in the water, but I didn't see Belle out there so I hurried up the steps, opened the back door, and walked in yelling, "Belle, it's me," just like I used to do when I was a little girl coming next door to see my grandmother. I stopped and looked around, the rooms were smaller, all of them. I wasn't imagining it. Carlton was right behind me, and then Belle was there, stepping out of the kitchen with her hands covered with flour. It was a relief to see her. Belle, at least, hadn't shrunk.

"I'm making biscuits," she said, "and I've got chicken to fry. You going to stay to supper now, you hear?"

And the next thing I knew I was sobbing in her arms and she was patting me and saying, "There, there, Macy, no point in crying over spilt milk."

I started to giggle then and asked her what milk did she think I had spilt, and she said you know, that's just a way of talking, and I said yes I guess I did, and Carlton said did she have any chocolate cake made and she said she reckoned she did if those kids hadn't been in it, and Carlton said he'd just look in the cupboard and see, one piece wouldn't hurt his supper, and I sat down at the table to watch Belle as she cooked and Carlton as he devoured a piece of cake bigger than Dallas, which he washed down with a glass of milk, and I thought to myself it's nice to have a family to come home to.